FROZEN IN TIME

FROZEN IN TIME
Twenty Stories

JOSEPH EPSTEIN

Guilford, Connecticut

An imprint of Globe Pequot

Distributed by NATIONAL BOOK NETWORK

British Library Cataloguing-in-Publication Information Available

Library of Congress Cataloging-in-Publication Data Available

ISBN 978-1-63076-193-6 (hardcover)
ISBN 978-1-4930-3628-8 (paperback)
ISBN 978-1-63076-194-3 (e-book)

♾™ The paper used in this publication meets the minimum requirements of American National Standard for Information Sciences—Permanence of Paper for Printed Library Materials, ANSI/NISO Z39.48-1992.

Printed in the United States of America

*For Harvey Pool and Loren Singer,
friends from the Old Country*

Contents

Sandy in Her Tub 1

Arnheim & Sons 15

Oh, Billy, Where Are You? 27

Dad's Gay 43

Out of Action 55

Wild About Harry 73

Widow's Pique 85

Second Family 97

Remittance Man 109

My Five Husbands 121

Irwin Isaac Meiselman 139

Adultery? 153

Onto a Good Thing 163

Race Relations 175

The Casanova of LaSalle Street 193

Kizerman and Feigenbaum 205

The Man on Whom Everything Was Lost 221

The Bernie Klepner Show 233

The Viagra Triangle 247

JDate 257

About the Author 273

Sandy in Her Tub

SANDY REUBEN IS HAVING A GOOD SOAK BEFORE GOING OUT THAT EVENING for dinner at her parents', when Jeffrey, her husband, knocks, enters, and sits on the edge of the tub. Sandy looks up from her copy of *Vogue*.

"No need to wear a necktie tonight," she says. "They'll be just the four of us for dinner."

"I wasn't planning to," Jeffrey replies. "In fact, I'm not planning to go at all."

Sandy drops the magazine outside the tub.

"We accepted this invitation two weeks ago."

"I've been unhappy in this marriage for a long time," Jeffrey says. "I'm out of here."

Sandy sits up in the tub, her breasts above the bubble bath.

"Out of here?"

Now Sandy is standing, in her full nakedness, water dripping off her, looking as if she had just discovered an eel.

"Are you fucking crazy?" she says, yells actually. "And why are you telling me this here, now, in the bathroom?"

Stepping out, she nearly slips on the bubbly wet mess on the floor, and yanks a thick white towel off the nearby towel rack with which she covers herself. "Are you nuts, or what?" she says. She thinks about slapping him, but is afraid if she does so she will lose her hold on the towel.

Jeffrey gets up from the edge of the tub and leaves the bathroom, slamming the door on his way out. Sandy reaches for her baby-blue terry-cloth robe. Slipping it on, she glimpses herself in the mirror. She has a small potbelly on which there is a caesarean scar from the birth of her third child, blue veins on her legs above her knees, breasts that have begun to sag. She leans in closer, over the double sinks, to the wall-wide mirror to inspect the wrinkles gathered around her eyes.

Sandra Reuben is fifty-two. She has three children. Jonathan and Jacob are both at New Trier High School; her daughter, Ardis, is thirteen, recently diagnosed as having ADHD and put on Ritalin and just beginning what looks to be a difficult adolescence. A little diva of temperament, she is already showing lots of moodiness, tears, and tantrums. Raising these kids has pretty much been left to Sandy, even though for the past seven years she has been working full-time as a lawyer, specializing in domestic law, for the firm of Ganser & Maher in the Loop.

Jeffrey has never been a fully engaged father. He went to soccer and little-league games when the boys were younger, but Sandy always felt he was just going through the motions. Jeffrey is a dentist, a periodontist, a successful one. Six or seven years ago, though, he began complaining that his work gave him no satisfaction. He started seeing a therapist, a woman named Lindsay Leibowitz, who has an office in the Old Orchard Professional Building in Skokie, two floors above Jeffrey's. At brunch at Benny and Max's one Sunday, they ran into her. Jeffrey introduced them. Dr. Leibowitz looked to be in her late thirties, slender, dark hair, well dressed. They seemed pleased to see each other. Do you suppose, Sandy thought at the time, he's banging her? Not possible, she concluded, not my schmuckleheimer husband. Now, with Jeffrey's announcement that he wanted out of their marriage, she had to rethink this earlier judgment.

"Banging her," "schmuckleheimer"—Sandy learned such talk from her father, who always spoke around her as if she were the son he never had. She also used such language at Ganser & Maher, where she is the only woman partner. Her father, Max Lansky, is a cardiac surgeon, on the staff at Rush-Presbyterian. No one has fewer pretensions than her father; no one was more critical or more openly, almost proudly cynical. "I assume the worst about people," he told Sandy when she was in her teens, "and I'm not often disappointed."

Sandy once asked her father why he was so judgmental.

"Judgmental?" Max said. "Judgmental? Wherever did my beautiful daughter find such a stupid goddamn word? If by judgmental you mean that I make lots of judgments, you're right. At work I judge whether and where to cut a vein or clean out and reconnect an artery. I'm always making judgments. And why restrict my doing so to veins and arteries? Isn't it as important to make careful judgments about people, about their weaknesses, strengths, overall quality? Always be judgmental, sweetheart, there's no other way to live."

Max—he always insisted Sandy, his only child, call him by his first name—did not have a high opinion of Jeffrey Reuben.

"Why anyone would want to be a dentist beats me," he said when Sandy first mentioned she was going out with Jeffrey. "To stand there all day with your hands in other people's mouths, I don't get it." That Max had his own hands, with their short thick fingers, in other people's chests, Sandy chose not to point out.

If Sandy's father hadn't much regard for Jeffrey's profession, he was even more dubious about his future son-in-law's personality. "What's he, a depressive?" he asked Sandy the first time she brought Jeffrey home. Max even criticized his posture. Jeffrey was tall, thin, slouched in the way tall young men—he was 6'3"—who were never good athletes sometimes are.

"Is the kid nervous around me," Max asked, "or is he just missing a personality?"

Jeffrey was daunted by Max Lansky. Who wouldn't have been? Sandy and Jeffrey were the same age, and he was going into his last year of dental school when he proposed. Max asked Sandy why she wanted to marry him.

"Because he's solid, he's steady, and he loves me—he really loves me," she said. She didn't tell Max that he could also make her laugh. Quiet and reserved though he seemed, when courting her, Jeffrey would do goofy madcap, whimsical things. Once at Gio's Restaurant in Evanston, out with their friends the Ehrlichs, when the waiter took their drink orders before dinner, he neglected to ask Sandy what she wanted. When she said that she would like a margarita, the waiter said he was sorry but her friend (nodding here at Jeffrey) had instructed him, when she was in the ladies' room before they were seated, that she had problems with alcohol and was not on any account to be served a drink. Another time, when they were at a dinner party with people she hadn't met before, she noticed everyone speaking slowly to her, enunciating carefully. Only when the woman sitting on her left apologized for not being able to sign did she begin to understand, as Jeffrey confessed later, that he had told the other people at the party that she was deaf but an excellent lip reader. But not long after they were married, this kind of thing stopped; Jeffrey, for some reason, had lost his whimsy, his sweet silliness.

Jeffrey's parents had run a dry cleaners, on Devon, west of California, before they sold out to a Korean syndicate and moved to Delray Beach. Max paid for the wedding, a "pretty goddamn gaudy affair, if I do say so myself," or so he described it, at the Gold Room at the Drake Hotel. He lent his new son-in-law the money to buy into the practice of a man in his sixties named Jerome Werner. (The money has long since been repaid.) He also helped the kids, as Marsha Lansky still referred to Sandy and Jeffrey, with the down payment on their first house in Morton Grove. With the spread of bypass heart surgery, of which he did a lot, Max Lansky had become a rich man.

Sandy had never seen her father actually operate on anyone, but she had seen him at Rush-Presbyterian, his stomping ground. She met him one day before lunch in the surgical waiting room while she was still in high school.

"Here comes Dr. Lansky now," the receptionist told her. Sandy looked down the hall and saw her father approach, in his white coat, his name in blue thread sewn in cursive over the left breast pocket, his heels clicking against the marble floors as if he were wearing boots. (They were Bruno Magli loafers.) He might have had a white silk scarf tossed over his shoulder, which he didn't, like a test or fighter pilot, so authoritatively heroic did he seem. Nurses, patients, families of patients, everyone looked upon Dr. Max Lansky with uncomplicated reverence. Sandy reflected that her father may have held in his hands the hearts of many of the people in this room. At that moment she wished she didn't have to call him Max but instead could call him Daddy. Max Lansky was 5'4", 5'5", tops, stocky, dark, with a thick head of still black hair. He gave off fumes of strength, physical as well as mental. His eyes, like his hair, were black, and his hairline low. He had been a superior athlete as a boy—a gymnast and a swimmer at Senn High School, a champion at both. He must have radiated confidence his entire life, or so his daughter thought.

Max had had more to do with raising Sandy than did her mother. By the time she was seven or eight, Sandy realized that her mother, Marsha, was steady enough but not inspiring in the way Max was. Max was his wife's protector, he was also the family's social playmaker, and Marsha felt no need to struggle against his domination. Marsha had been pretty as a girl, small, bosomy, dark, on the model of Elizabeth Taylor, but without much force. "You've got your mother's good looks and my brains, kiddo," Max once told Sandy, "and those aren't bad cards to have drawn in life. A man's mind and a woman's body can make for an interesting hand. I'll be eager to see how you play it."

Sandy has long thought that her father must be disappointed in her. He had sent her east to school, to Wellesley, where she did well, but where she also decided against going to medical school. Max never said anything about this decision, but it couldn't have been to his liking. Max insisted that Sandy at least enroll in law school, so that she have serious work to do in life. In his rough way, Max was a bit of a feminist. So at her father's expense she went to the University of Chicago.

When Sandy told her father that Jeffrey Reuben had asked her to marry him, Max said, "You know, kid, Rocky Marciano's mother is supposed to have been glad that her son gave up his baseball career to become a boxer: 'I didn't raise the boy to become a catcher,' she's supposed to have said. I didn't raise my daughter to marry a dentist, kiddo. But I also didn't raise her to let me stand in her way. I hope it works out." Not exactly a fatherly blessing, but there it was.

Jonathan was born the third year of Sandy and Jeffrey's marriage, and Jacob arrived two years later. Max soon took the boys in hand. He had regular-season Bears tickets, on the forty-yard line, and when they reached the ages of nine and seven, the boys went with him to games. He bought them baseball mitts, paid to have a glass backboard erected just off the Reubens' driveway, spent more time with the boys than most grandfathers would. They adored him.

If Jeffrey felt rivalrous about Max's relationship with his sons, he never made an issue of it. Max picked up the boys on a Saturday or Sunday, almost as if he were Sandy's first husband with weekend visitation rights. Jeffrey tended to view it as giving him more time to indulge his own interests: trading stocks on his computer, fiddling with a 1962 vintage Jaguar E-Type that he kept in the garage, jogging. Max never expressed his feelings about his son-in-law in front of him, but he had a way of ignoring him that was perhaps worse than direct insult.

At four o'clock on Friday afternoons, Jeffrey had his regular session with Dr. Leibowitz. When Sandy asked Jeffrey what he talked about during these sessions, he tended to be vague. His relationship with his parents, he would say, or his perhaps too great need to succeed in the world. She wanted to ask him if he discussed their sex life during his sessions with Dr. Leibowitz but held back.

If Sandy were the one in therapy and sex came up, she probably would have said that of course their sex wasn't what it was when they were much younger. What with three kids to raise, and her husband running a lucrative dental practice—he had four dental technicians, prepping patients, taking X-rays, assisting him in gum surgeries—and her working full-time handling domestic cases in the Loop, sex was much reduced in their priorities. Sandy was OK with that, she could live with it. Whether Jeffrey could was a question she never bothered to ask.

When Sandy told her father that Jeffrey had begun to undergo psychotherapy, Max's only reaction was to tell her he wasn't surprised to hear it. "I hope he doesn't get hooked on it. For lots of people it's the goddamn highlight of their week, their fifty minutes with their shrink, pay please on your way out. I hope your husband doesn't turn out to be one of those sad schmucks."

In fact, Jeffrey was going on his seventh year in therapy without having a very clear set of complaints, at least so far as Sandy was able to discern. When her father asked her why her husband was in therapy, the best she could offer was that Jeffrey was unhappy. "Really," said Max. "Unhappy? Too bad. But then, I hear, so is Africa."

Her robe tied, a towel round her still wet hair, Sandy walks into the large dressing room she shares with Jeffrey. A small suitcase is missing, as are a number of his shirts, a suit, and pairs of trousers. In his dresser, she discovers that he had also taken underwear, socks, and handkerchiefs. She calls out his name—the kids are out of the house—and receives no answer. She has no idea where Jeffrey might have gone. Maybe to his new lady friend. "On second thought," she says to herself, adapting a formula her father once told her were W.C. Fields's deathbed words, "fuck 'im." She decides to go to dinner without Jeffrey.

What Sandy hasn't decided is whether or not she will tell Max and Marsha about Jeffrey's departure. But when her mother opens the door, with her father standing right behind her, and asks where Jeffrey is, Sandra blurts out, "He's gone. I guess we're getting a divorce."

Her mother looks properly shocked, is speechless, in fact.

"So you've finally decided to get rid of him," Max says.

"Not quite accurate," says Sandy. "Jeffrey is leaving me. For another woman, I suspect."

"No kidding," says Max. His right eyebrow shoots up, as Sandy imagined it might do when examining the heart and arteries of a patient beyond saving. "I wouldn't have thought the kid had it in him."

At dinner—Marsha has made veal scallopini, asparagus, a salad; Max opens a bottle of Pinot Noir—they discuss what is to be done.

"Any notion who the dentist's lucky lady might be?" Max asks Sandy.

"I don't know for sure if there is another lady," Sandy says. "But if there is, my best guess is his therapist. But then it could be one of his patients, or even one of the girls who work for him."

"He does know that he's divorcing a divorce lawyer, does he not?" Max puts in. "May I say that I fully expect you to take him for everything he's got, including his own fillings?"

"Right now I don't think that's the question, Max," says Sandy.

"What is?" her father asks.

"The question is to find out what's really going on. Why he's found life with me no longer tolerable? And also what room in his new life does he plan to allot his children?"

"How about you, baby?" Sandy's mother asks. "How're you holding up?"

"This came as a surprise, Marsha, I have to tell you."

"Get over the shock, kid," Max says. "View it as strictly an opportunity, a chance to get your life back. You're still an attractive woman, and with brains."

Sandy recalls the view of herself in the mirror an hour or so ago. Had Max seen it, he might have revised his estimate. As for her brains, her father always seemed to think more of them than did she.

"He sounds confused," Marsha says. "I mean the way he told you he was leaving, then running out of the house. That's not rational. Like he's undergoing a midlife crisis."

"Midlife crisis? Surely you don't believe in such horseshit, do you, dear?" says Max, spearing a long, slender asparagus.

"For all I know," Sandy added, "that may be Jeffrey's explanation to himself."

"I hope you nail his ass to the barn door," says Max, and asks Sandy to pass the platter with the veal.

Sandy waits three days before calling Jeffrey at his office. When he calls back, she asks him where, precisely, things stand at the moment.

"How are the kids?" he asks, avoiding the question.

"They're fine," Sandy says. "I told them that you were in Honolulu at a dental convention. I wanted to give you time in case you decided to change your mind about all this."

"That's not going to happen," Jeffrey says, "at least not as long as things stand the way they do."

"What's that supposed to mean?" she asks.

"Look," Jeffrey says, "maybe we would do better to talk about this face-to-face."

That night, at six o'clock, Sandy and Jeffrey meet at McCormick & Schmick's, a seafood restaurant in Old Orchard, the shopping mall in whose professional building Jeffrey has his dental practice. They take a booth toward the back, where it is quiet.

Jeffrey, wearing a black polo shirt and chino pants, looks tired. When the waitress asks them what they want to drink, he orders a martini—unusual for him, who is not much of a drinker. Sandy orders a glass of Reisling.

"I assume that you have been living with Dr. Leibowitz," she says, deciding not to waste time on small talk.

"Why would you assume that?" Jeffrey asks.

"A suspicion," she says.

"Lindsay Leibowitz is a lesbian, Sandy. I've met her partner, Stacy, on more than one occasion. The fact is that the last two nights I slept on the couch in my reception room. Tomorrow night I'm moving into the Doubletree."

"Who is it, then, that you're leaving me for? Someone working in the office? A patient? I'm entitled to know."

"Another woman has nothing to do with it."

"Then what's it all about?"

"Your father," he says.

"Max?"

"I've had enough of his contempt," Jeffrey says.

"Not this again," she says.

"He's treated me as if I were the black sheep of the family from the get-go," Jeffrey says. "I thought maybe over time it would ease up, but it hasn't. I've told you this time and again."

"Look, my father may have a touch of snobbery, I've always given you that."

"Why against me? I made more than seven hundred grand last year. I save people's teeth. I reduce their pain. What's so terrible about that?"

Once again, as at other times in her marriage, Sandy can't bring herself to tell him that he is of course right, that her father does look down on him, always did, and probably always would.

"What do you want me to do, Jeff? I can't control my father."

"Maybe not. But I don't think you ought to stand by and let him treat your husband as if he's just come up out of steerage, which is what over the years you've consistently done. In the Bible somewhere it says a man shall leave his father and mother and cleave to his wife. Shouldn't the same be true of a wife leaving her mother and father and cleaving to her husband? You're not so hot at cleaving, Sandy."

"I love Max," she says angrily.

"As I understand cleaving, it means that in any conflict between your family and me, you're supposed to side with me. I've never felt that you have—not ever."

"OK, I love you and I love Max. What am I supposed to do?"

"Lindsay Leibowitz thinks maybe your father loves you too much. A reversal of the Elektra Complex, she calls it."

"What a perfectly stupid, utterly predictable thing for a shrink to say! What're you doing in therapy anyhow? You've never really told me."

"Did you ask?" he said. "Your old man drove me to it. I thought I was doing all right in the world until I met him. He's spent a fair amount of energy over the years letting me know I don't measure up. The son of a bitch shot my confidence." Sandy notes Jeffrey's eyes begin to water. She's glad her father isn't here to see it.

"My father has a high standard. I'm not sure that I measure up to it myself."

"Forgive me, Sandy, but you do measure up. In your father's book you will always measure up. Just as I never will."

"I know he's not an easy man, my father, but I also happen to think he is a pretty extraordinary one, too."

"What does he really have against me?" he says.

"I suppose he feels you don't come up to his standard."

"Who the hell does?"

Sandy could think of only two people who did: Michael DeBakey, the Houston heart surgeon, and Walter Payton, the Chicago Bears running back. She mentions neither of them.

"What do you want me to do?" she says.

"I want you to find a way to get your father off my back. Have him show me at least minimal respect. And, if he's feeling magnanimous, I wouldn't mind his tossing in an apology while he's at it." Jeffrey pays the check. She goes home. He returns to the couch in his office.

Sandy is back in her tub, soaking. The kids are asleep. Diana Krall is singing, softly, on a CD player on the bathroom counter. She has decided that she does indeed want Jeffrey back. She realizes, too, that she has been wrong in not attempting to curb her father's treatment of her husband. Jeffrey is right; it is of course contempt, not snobbery, that Max had confronted him with from the very beginning. She feels more than a little guilty about trying to pass it off all these years, even to herself, as Max's oddity. It's been a failure of imagination on her part, and she feels terrible about it.

On the CD player she keeps in her bathroom, Diana Krall is singing "The Night We Called It a Day." What is it about songs, Sandy wonders? The appropriate sappy ones have a way of turning up just when they shouldn't. She wasn't raised to be sentimental. Clear thinking is called for. "There was nothing left to say," Diana Krall moans, "the night we called it a day." Bullshit, Sandy thinks. There's a lot left to say. Jeffrey may be no Michael DeBakey or Walter Payton, but then neither is Max Lansky. Jeffrey is in many ways the perfect husband for her. He lets her work long hours at her firm when required. Allows her, so to speak, a controlling interest in raising their children, which was the way she wanted it. Gives her the freedom she needs without the least jealousy or resentment. Truth is, though it was important that Jeffrey loved her, she wasn't raised to be a woman smothered by a husband's love.

Max has to be told to knock off the way he talked about, thought about, and acted in front of Jeffrey. He is her husband. He loves her, and she loves him. Cleaving; she has to learn to cleave, damnit. She decides to set up a meeting with Max tomorrow, and get this straightened out, or at least she hopes she can get it straightened out. Diana Krall, thank God, had gone on to sing "Dancing in the Dark."

Sandy is sitting in the cafeteria at Rush-Presbyterian. She has arrived ten minutes early for a morning coffee meeting with her father. Max never arrives anywhere early but always precisely on time. She has a cup of coffee before her and is studying the passing physicians, in their white or gray coats, trying to make out the names over their left upper breast pockets: Dr. Roger Lowenstein, Dr. Jennifer Kirkpatrick, Dr. Paul Krickstein, Dr. Burton Ginsburg, Dr. Carol Blumenthal, Dr. Sandeep Gupta, Dr. Kelly Isner . . .

"I see you are watching my fellow physicians, the *goniffim* on parade," says Max, coming up from behind. "I brought you a blueberry muffin, just to remind you to be glad that when you were a kid I never called you Muffy."

Max seats himself across from Sandy. He puts three Splendas in his coffee, no cream.

"Now what's the reason for this meeting, kid? I've got twenty minutes." Sandy notices that Max's Bruno Magli loafers are covered with plastic booties. For all she knows, he may be in the middle of a heart surgery and took a break to deal with his daughter.

"I met with Jeffrey last night and he told me, in effect, that he is not so much divorcing me as divorcing you."

"Meaning?"

"Meaning he's been suffering under your lack of respect for him and can't take it any longer."

"A joke, right?" Max asks.

"'Fraid not, Max," she says. "He means it."

"Sorry." Max says, "I call 'em as I see 'em."

"You've got to learn to call 'em different—for my sake, and for the sake of your grandchildren. Turns out, whatever your view of Jeffrey, I love him. He's my husband. And with three kids I'm not so re-marriageable as you might think."

Max doesn't answer directly. Strangely for him, he looks slightly perplexed.

"What exactly am I supposed to do?" he says.

"You might call Jeffrey and tell him that you regret you have not respected him the way you should, and that you will be careful not to let it happen in the future."

"In other words," says Max, "an apology. How about something less equivocal, like, 'I'm sorry if I seem to have underrated you, now go fuck yourself'?"

"Max, I need you to save my marriage."

"I have to think about this," Max says.

"Don't think too long, Daddy, please." Sandy realizes that she has called him Daddy. The word slipped out. If Max notices—and he doesn't miss much—he pretends not to have.

Max looks at his watch. He reminds Sandy that the Bears are playing the Packers at home, it's a Monday night game, and so he probably won't have the boys home until past midnight. Sandy asks how Marsha is.

"Look, kid, I better return to work. I'll get back to you in a day or two about this Jeffrey business." He gets up, comes around the table, kisses her on the top of the head, grips her hand in his, squeezes it gently, and walks off.

That night, 11:23 p.m. on the digital clock in the bathroom, Sandy is in her tub, her nightly soak. Brooding over her meeting earlier in the day with Max at the hospital, she has decided that there is no chance he is going to apologize. She must have been nuts even to ask him. Still, she had to try. A big decision awaits: whether to give up her husband or her father—a lose-lose deal.

A knock at the door. Ardis should be asleep by now. She is in no mood for one of her daughter's weepy sessions.

"Who's there?" she asks, a touch of petulance in her voice.

No answer, but the door opens and it is Jeffrey. He is wearing a dark gray suit and red-and-blue rep tie.

"I've some news for you," he says. "I had a call late this afternoon."

"From my father?"

"The great Max Lansky himself."

"Wanting?"

"Wanting to know if I care to go to the Packers game with him and the boys Monday night. He has an extra ticket."

"Really," says Sandy, sitting up in the tub.

"There's more," Jeffrey says. "He tells me that he has been suffering some sensitivity in his gums on the upper right portion of his mouth, and he'd like to make an appointment to have me look at it."

"Did he make one?"

"He did, for two weeks from today. But your father, being your father, couldn't hang up without saying, 'I assume you know what you're doing.'"

"What did you say?"

"I said what I do may not be rocket science, but then neither is cardiac surgery."

"And he answered?"

"He answered, 'Touché. Pick you and the kids up at 5:30 Monday.' And hung up."

"Well," says Sandy, "it's not exactly an apology, but it isn't too bad for a start."

Then Jeffrey kicks off his shoes, removes his jacket, and gets in the tub with Sandy, all slouchy 6'3" of him, socks, shirt, trousers, necktie, wristwatch, and who knows what he has in his pockets.

"What're you doing, you moron?" she says, leaning over to touch his cheek.

"I'm back," he says, "back for good," loosening his tie, the old goofy smile on his face.

Arnheim & Sons

ARNHEIM & SONS OPTICAL, INC., IS IN ITS FOURTH GENERATION. THE FRATER-
nal twins Eugene and Paul Arnheim took the business over from their
father, Chaim, who had learned the craft of lens-making from his father
and grandfather in Amsterdam. Having fled the Nazis, Chaim reopened
the firm in Chicago in 1938, and it now operates in two floors of a building on North Avenue just west of Damen. His sons greatly expanded the
business and eventually came to supply many of the lenses for such large
firms as For Eyes and Lenscrafters.

Spinoza was a lens grinder, Chaim told his sons, emphasizing the historical tradition and honorableness of the work. He kept a large portrait in
oil of the philosopher in his office. After their father's death, Eugene and
Paul commissioned a portrait of Chaim Arnheim, which they hung next
to that of Spinoza in the same office, which they came to share. They occupied, between them, a large antique partners desk acquired from an antique dealer on Wells Street and at which they worked, facing each other.

For as far back as either could remember, the twins were never in the
least rivalrous. They felt themselves lucky to have each other's full-time
company and support. Their talents and temperaments were different.
Eugene was an exceptional athlete during his high-school years and somewhat introverted; Paul was more attractive to women and more outgoing
generally. Knowing they were destined for their father's business, neither
took education all that seriously.

The world seemed to contrive to keep them close. They married
pledge sisters from Alpha Epsilon Phi at the University of Illinois; the
girls were good friends and grew even closer after marriage. At Arnheim
& Sons, Eugene was the inside man, running the day-to-day operations,

while Paul hustled up new business and kept current accounts satisfied. Arnheim & Sons prospered under their control, and it made the brothers wealthy men.

The trouble began when Eugene's son Charlie was brought into the business.

Eugene and his wife Susan had had difficulty conceiving. They put themselves through the nightmare of a fertility clinic without result and were about to adopt when Susan, miraculously, or so it seemed, at last became pregnant and stayed pregnant in their twelfth year of marriage.

Paul remembered Charlie as an attractive child, affectionate, nice-looking. He was a little wild as an adolescent, true, once having been suspended for a week from Highland Park High School for kicking in a locker and then telling off a teacher. Paul never said anything to his brother at the time, but he thought that Eugene was maybe a little too easy on Charlie. The kid seemed to keep pretty much his own hours through high school; there were rumors that he was a heavy pot smoker. Eugene bought him a small BMW to drive in from Glencoe, the suburb where his family lived, to the Chicago campus of the University of Illinois west of the Loop. He didn't insist the kid work summers as Paul's daughters did without having to be asked. But, then, Paul recognized that he was fortunate in his girls, both of whom were good students and disciplined self-starters—Miriam had gone to Radcliffe, Rachael to the Rhode Island School of Design. They were a decade older than Charlie, and it seemed to Paul that kids, boys especially, had grown more irresponsible, more childish, during those ten years. Why should Charlie have been any different?

Upon his graduation, Charlie made some noises about hoping to make it on his own. His first year out of college he entered an executive training program at Marshall Field's, but things didn't work out. Retailing didn't interest him all that much, he said. Eugene and Susan offered him a summer-long trip to Europe to explore new possibilities. But he lasted less than a month, remarking that Europe no longer felt like where the action was; America had the ball now, he said, and America was the place to be. He also said that he had reconsidered the prospect of working for Arnheim & Sons and would like to give it a shot. "My best shot," he added.

Charlie seemed to work hard at learning the business, at least for seven months or so. He did monthly shifts with his father and then with his uncle, so that he could learn the business inside and out. He worked with his father in the shop, as Eugene called their small factory, among their thirty-eight employees. He applied himself to understanding payrolls, budgets, accounting worksheets. When Paul took him out with him to introduce himself to customers, Charlie made himself genial, which wasn't the least difficult for him, for he had more than his share of natural charm: tall, slender, wore clothes well, had a nice smile. Paul never put it in words to any of these customers, but it was clear that he was introducing his clients to the heir apparent, the last male Arnheim.

And then one morning, across their partners desk, Eugene announced that Charlie was leaving. He had a girlfriend, an Argentine, who had gone to medical school at the University of Chicago, and he was following her home to Buenos Aires. When Paul asked if Charlie was planning to marry this young woman, Eugene said he didn't know for certain; he wasn't sure if things had gone quite so far, but he assumed that this must be what his son had in mind.

"I see," said Paul, who really didn't see at all. His first reaction was annoyance at all those months wasted teaching his nephew the business. But he was not about to criticize Charlie, lest it seem in some way a criticism of Eugene.

"It's a generation thing," Paul's wife Marilyn said. "Nowadays kids don't get serious until thirty, sometimes later. I'm always hearing stories of some kid deciding at forty-two that he or she wants to go to law or even medical school. Maybe they're all planning to live to a hundred, when they will die while out jogging. Go figure."

Paul couldn't, quite. He wasn't sure, either, whether he was pleased or disappointed when, three months later, Charlie came home from Argentina, his relationship over, and decided he wanted to return to Arnheim & Sons.

"According to Charlie," Eugene told Paul, "the girl's family are what passes for upper-class in Argentina, and he didn't, as he put it, 'make the social-class cut' with them. Argentine daughters, unlike American ones, apparently still obey their parents, if you can imagine that."

"Did Charlie want to marry the girl?"

"He didn't say. Truth is, he doesn't seem much shaken up."

Paul asked no more questions. Eugene said no more about it. And Charlie came back to Arnheim & Sons as if he had been away on an extended vacation. The brothers tried to give Charlie more responsibility and that meant he spent more time with his uncle than his father. His talent was more akin to Paul's than Eugene's; he was good working with customers, but impatient with details. Paul decided to send him on the road, in the hope of opening up accounts on the West Coast. He had some success, too. His father and uncle began to feel that Arnheim & Sons might be safe for another generation. Who knew, when Charlie had children, maybe beyond that.

Then, eight months or so after Charlie's return, on a Friday afternoon just before closing, Eugene telephoned Paul, who was out calling on customers, on his cell phone to suggest that they meet for a drink at the Standard Club in an hour. Paul was anxious; was something up with his brother's health?

"I've got some news," Eugene told his brother.

"Bad?" Paul asked.

"Elena Olchek is leaving," Eugene said. Paul was flooded with relief for a moment, and then became worried. Elena had been with Arnheim & Sons for twenty-five years crafting lenses for people with difficult vision problems, a job that would be hard to find someone else to fill—and one so specialized that it would not be so easy for her to find work elsewhere.

"Elena sick?"

"More complicated than that," Eugene said.

"What's the problem? We pay her well. You've always treated her with great regard. She asked us to hire her daughter, we hired her daughter. What's her name?"

"That's the complication," said Eugene. "Charlie. Charlie knocked up the daughter."

"Her name is Marlus, right?" was all Paul could think to say.

"Some of this is ancient history," Eugene said. "I first heard about it three months ago. No way Charlie was going to marry the girl. Nor was Marlus about to have an abortion. Serious Catholics, the Olcheks."

"It is Marlus," Paul said, because he had nothing else to say.

"We lucked out, I suppose," Eugene said. "The girl had a miscarriage yesterday. But Elena wants nothing further to do with the Arnheim family. I offered her $25,000 to help with expenses before Marlus lost the child, and that was apparently a big mistake."

This could have been the moment to hash out the problem Charlie had caused, to talk about Charlie problems in general, but Paul loved his brother too much to say anything that might cause a rift between them, and so they spent the rest of their time discussing how to replace Elena Olchek.

Paul never brought up Marlus with Charlie. He continued to bring him along in the business. He even turned over a few smaller accounts to him, giving him sole responsibility for managing them. And this Charlie seemed to do well enough, until one Monday morning, opening his mail, Paul discovered that a small firm in the Southwestern suburbs called What Do Eye Care, a company now handled by Charlie, had cancelled all further business with Arnheim & Sons. The letter gave no reason.

Alma, the secretary he and Eugene shared, told Paul that Charlie had taken a long weekend to go skiing in Vail. Paul decided to call Jim Williams, the head of What Do Eye Care—he was the firm's founder and Paul had opened the account himself sixteen years ago, so he learned from his files.

"He called me an anti-Semite," Williams said.

"What?"

"Your nephew took me to a good lunch," Williams said. "We had agreeable chit-chat, some of it about business, some about sports. Then before dessert and coffee arrived, he went off to the washroom, and when he returned he seemed suddenly changed."

"How changed?" Paul asked.

"I'm not sure, but he seemed different. Next thing I know, out of the blue, he says it."

"I'm so sorry, but can I ask if there's anything you can think you might have said that could have created the impression?"

Williams was silent. "My wife is Jewish," he said finally. "My kids are being brought up as Jews."

Paul apologized for his nephew's behavior and asked if it were possible to win his business back. Williams said he had already gone over to a competitor.

When Charlie returned from Vail, Paul called him into his office, showed him Jim Williams's letter.

"Charlie," Paul said, "Williams says you called him an anti-Semite."

"I did?" Charlie answered, genuinely surprised. "He said that?"

"Not something I would make up, kid," Paul said.

"Is it too late to apologize? I'll call him. There's some goddamn misunderstanding here. Why would I do that?"

"Don't know," Paul said, "especially when his wife is Jewish. Anyhow he's taken his business elsewhere."

After this awkward exchange, Paul began to think his nephew was on drugs. He decided not to say anything about it to Eugene. When he and Eugene talked about What Do Eye Care having left Arnheim & Sons, Paul lied; Jim Williams had had a counter-offer from another optical firm so low that he couldn't refuse it, Paul told him.

Another six months or so went by. Then Sylvia Kleiderman, the bookkeeper who had originally been hired by his father, brought Paul three requests for expense reimbursements Charlie had put in for trips to the Northwest, presumably to scare up new business, but for which he claimed to have no receipts, the airline having lost the suitcase in which he had kept them. The expenses came to $7,386.

Charlie had never been told to scout up business in the Northwest. He was, Paul surmised, trying to cheat his own family business. He had been given a decent salary, and anything expensive that he might have wanted—a new car, a down payment on an apartment—Paul was fairly certain Eugene would have helped him acquire. The reason for his stealing seemed obvious.

That evening Paul stayed late, and after everyone was gone for the day, he went into Charlie's small office. In the left-hand lowest drawer of Charlie's desk, he found the only book in his office, a copy of a school text on macroeconomics. Paul opened it, and found it had a hollowed-out center that contained a razor blade and two plastic straws, each cut in half, and three small plastic packets of white powder.

"Sylvia tells me that you put in receipts for trips I have no knowledge you ever took," Paul said to Charlie the next day after going into his nephew's office and closing the door.

"Oh," Charlie answered, very coolly, Paul thought. "I was in northern California and figured I would check out possibilities in Portland and Seattle. I thought it worth a look-see."

"Was it?" Paul asked.

"I think it was," Charlie answered. "There's a firm in Tacoma, name of Corrigan and Wieboldt, that's supplying most of the optical firms in both cities. And my sense, from talking to retailers, is that we can beat them, both price-wise and on delivery time."

"Really?" said Paul. "Sounds interesting. You should write up a report on that."

"I had planned to," said Charlie. "I'll get to it straightaway."

Paul felt a passing wave of admiration for his nephew's gall. He also felt a stab of pity for the kid, lashed to a drug problem that had locked him into stealing and lying.

"Charlie," Paul asked, "are you in any kind of trouble? Do you have any problems that maybe I can help you with?"

"What kind of trouble would I be in?" he answered. "No, I'm good. Really. I'm cool."

Paul had no idea how to bring up the book in Charlie's desk to Eugene. Yet he knew they couldn't let Charlie continue working for Arnheim & Sons, at least not in his present condition. If they did, they could only expect the firm to lose more customers and Charlie to do more stealing.

Paul waited more than a week before bringing up the subject with his brother. He arranged for a table in the far corner of the dining room at Lake Shore, their country club, which was mostly empty at 4:30 on a Sunday afternoon. He had arrived ten or so minutes early to collect himself, to go over what he intended to say.

Eugene entered in chino pants, a blue button-down collar shirt, and a maroon cashmere sweater. He retained the confident walk of the successful boy athlete. Even though they were not identical, Paul always studied his brother's face for signs of aging, assuming that his own growing older was proceeding at roughly the same pace. Eight or nine years earlier, Paul had seen on television a 1940s movie called *The Corsican Brothers* in which Douglas Fairbanks Jr. played both parts of Siamese twins separated at birth, each of whom directly felt the pain undergone by the other. If one brother was flogged in the provinces, the other felt the lashes in Paris; if one brother was wounded in a duel in Paris, the other felt the stab in his flesh in the provinces. The movie, as they say, spoke to Paul. He sometimes thought that he felt more deeply about Eugene than he did about his own wife and daughters.

"How goes it?" Paul asked, when his brother sat down at his table.

"All calm on the western front," Eugene said. "About the eastern front, I'm afraid to look." Of the two brothers, Eugene was the habitual worrier, with Paul assigned the role of optimist. Eugene was financially frugal, Paul looser, more the sport, with money. He sometimes thought that, taken together, he and Eugene comprised one complete, and rather superior, human being.

They began by talking about family matters: Paul's young grandchildren, Eugene's plan to spend a few weeks on a golf holiday in Arizona with Susan, the prospect of their going in together on a condominium in Sarasota, which they had talked about in a vague way for some while now. After they had ordered coffee, Paul felt he couldn't hold back any longer.

"Gene," he said, "it's Charlie."

"What about Charlie?" Eugene asked.

"We have a serious problem with Charlie. He's on drugs. I'm sorry. Cocaine. I'm so sorry."

"How do you know?"

"I was suspicious, and I didn't tell you. He blew off our client in Oak Lawn, What Do Eye Care, by telling him off. He recently put in fake expense claims for more than seven grand. Going back a bit, there was the defection to Argentina, the incident with Elena Olchek's daughter. It doesn't add up to a happy result."

"How do you jump from that . . ."

"Because the other night, after Charlie had left for the day, I went into his office and found the stuff in a book in his office."

"You went through my son's things in his office?" Eugene said. "Jesus, Paul, even I wouldn't do that."

"I felt it was necessary, Genie, or believe me I wouldn't have."

Eugene shook his head. "You should have come to me before rifling through my kid's things. What you did is out of bounds."

"I didn't *rifle* anything. I opened a few drawers. I found a book. The main point's Charlie's in trouble, and so are we."

"You should have come to me first," Eugene said again.

"I apologize if I've done anything wrong," Paul said. "But what are we going to do? Charlie is a danger to himself and to the firm."

"I'll talk to him," Eugene said. "I'll find out what's going on. You leave it to me from here on out." He called for the check, and they sat in awkward silence. After Eugene signed for the check, they rose and left the dining room. Eugene said nothing as he got into his Lexus. Paul watched him pull away as his own Porsche was brought around.

Monday morning, in their office, Eugene got up to close the door and returned to his chair behind the partners desk. "I talked to Charlie," Eugene said, "and he denies the drug thing absolutely."

"You didn't tell him I found evidence in his desk?"

"Of course not," Eugene said. "What I said was that you thought his behavior suggested he might have a drug problem."

"And he replied?"

"'Uncle Paul is full of shit.' His words. When I asked him why he thought you would tell me this, he said that he thought you might be envious of him."

"Envious of what?"

"Of his success with customers. Some of them, he claims, feel you're getting older and now you've made your pile you're losing interest in them. That's what they've told him."

Paul was astonished. He waited a moment to reply, "You can't really believe that crap, Gene."

"He's my son," Eugene said.

"I know," Paul said.

"Did you actually see the drugs in his desk? Are you 100 percent certain it was cocaine?"

"I didn't kitchen test it. I didn't taste it, I didn't blow it up my nose, but I saw it. It was there in small clear plastic packets. In a hollowed-out book. Why would I make any of this up? I want my nephew to succeed. I want Arnheim & Sons to go on and on and on."

"You're asking me to believe my boy is a liar, a drug addict, and a thief. That's a lot to ask, Paul."

"It's the drugs making him steal and lie. You have to help him. We have to help him. The kid's in trouble."

"He tells me there's no problem. He says the problem's you."

"You believe him. You believe him over me?"

"This is a terrible subject," Eugene said. "We better get off it."

"No, we better stay on it," Paul said, and suddenly he was yelling. "It's everything to the future of this business."

"You're out of control," Eugene said. "Maybe you're the one on drugs."

And then Paul found himself on his feet, and, with no intention of doing so, he slapped his brother. It was an inept, even a slightly effeminate slap; and as soon as it was loose more than anything in the world he wanted it back. He grazed his brother's cheek with a ragged nail. A thin trickle of blood appeared high on Eugene's cheekbone. Eugene got to his feet, his fists clenched. Paul stood there. He imagined them tumbling across the partners desk, papers and arms flying, and it seemed ludicrous, melodramatic, comic even.

Instead Eugene, with a terrifying calm, said, "Leave."

Only when he was behind the wheel of his car did Paul notice that his hands were shaking.

Eugene, usually in the office by 8:30, failed to come in the following day. At 9:30, he called from home.

"Paul," he said.

Before he could say another word, Paul said, "I apologize. I was way out of line. I handled everything all wrong. Please forgive me. Please, Genie."

"I'm out of here," Eugene said. "It's over. I can't work with you. Not after last Friday."

"One argument, Genie, our only argument."

"It was on the worst possible subject," Eugene said, "the very worst. I've nothing more to say." And he hung up.

Paul received a call an hour later from Lou Freifeld, the firm's attorney since their father's time, to say that Eugene wanted Paul to buy him out and that Freifeld would negotiate on Eugene's behalf. The terms were reached in a day; documents were Fedexed back and forth; the sale was completed in a week.

The Arnheim twins never spoke again.

Paul tried to run the firm alone, but after three years found himself exhausted and, his physician found, during his most recent yearly physical, he had incipient ulcers. One man alone could not run Arnheim & Sons. Paul arranged to sell the company to a large firm in Atlanta called Omni Optical. As part of the sale, Paul agreed to stay on for a year. And so Arnheim & Sons died in its ninety-seventh year. When he departed the premises, Paul took with him only the paintings of Spinoza and his father Chaim. He left the partners desk behind.

Eugene retired to Sarasota soon after the split. Later, Paul and Marilyn settled in Palm Springs, where, almost daily, he thought about picking up the phone and calling his brother. Once, a few years after their breakup, he did call and, to his relief, got his brother's voice mail: "Gene," he said, "it's Paul. Call me when you get a chance: 760-492-3884." Eugene never did.

Charlie left Arnheim & Sons with his father, of course. Two years later, he tearfully confessed to his parents that he did in fact have a cocaine problem and needed help. Eugene thought of calling Paul and telling him he was right, but decided it was too late for that. What was done was done. At considerable expense, he sent Charlie to Hazelden. There, alongside rock musicians, movie starlets, and wealthy young hedge-fund operators and their wives, he conquered his addiction. Not long after he got out of Hazelden, with his father's financial help, Charlie enrolled at John Kent Law School, attending classes at night.

Charles W. Arnheim is today one of Chicago's most successful personal-injury lawyers.

Oh, Billy, Where Are You?

WHEN I TOLD MY MOTHER I WAS GETTING MARRIED, SHE REPLIED: "SO, LOUIS, darling boy, you waited until forty-eight to marry a woman your own age who can't give you any children and who has already failed three times at marriage? And this is my son who's supposed to be so intelligent?" Common sense, not tact, has always been what my mother has prided herself upon.

"Please don't make a judgment until you meet Lynne," I said. "She's an extraordinary woman, you'll see. Besides, be fair, one of her husbands died of a stroke."

"Let's hope she didn't give it to him," my mother said. "I don't care what you say, three husbands means something's wrong. Three previous husbands speaks to a serious flaw."

The fact was, I considered myself lucky that Lynne Ross had agreed to marry me. She is a great beauty, dresses with unfailing style, and brought no children for me to have to help raise. A dermatologist with a successful private practice on Michigan Avenue and on the staff at Northwestern Medical Center, she was, by my or anyone else's reckoning, a good catch, a better one than most people would say I was for her. A professional matchmaker might have said I was going up-market, Lynne headed down.

As for me, one of the most complicated questions you can ask is what do I do for a living. I went to law school, at DePaul, but found law practice too constricting, too boring, really. I suppose I'm an operator, a hustler, a scrambler, all words I happen to consider honorifics, whatever the rest of the world thinks. I put together real-estate deals, I arrange meetings between the right people, I sometimes briefly take over small businesses, patch them up, and then turn them over to new owners. I keep a one-room office in the 30 N. Michigan Building; if you walked into the joint you'd think it was a set from a black-and-white Sam Spade movie. I'm not there much. Mostly I work, as the old-timers used to say, out of my car. "Always keep a low overhead," my father used to tell me.

When I was a teenager and shlepping his sample cases, my father gave me a great deal of advice, a lot of it irrelevant, but the one thing that stuck in my mind was his iron rule: "Always work for yourself. Only a schmuck works for somebody else!" With the exception of those few years I worked for my father, I'm pleased to say that I haven't worked a day in my life for anyone but myself.

In my time in the field, as I like to think of my two decades and more chasing (and occasionally being chased by) women, I believe I've developed a reasonably good eye for quality. Beyond the age of thirty, most women are, like me, whether they know it or not, in business for themselves, operators, hustlers, scramblers, out to grab what pleasure is available and make the best possible deal they can. Most men, too, let me add, in case you jump to the mistaken conclusion that I'm down on women, which I'm not. I happen to like a lot more about women than rolling around in the sack with them. I often find I can be less on guard, more myself, around women than around men, where the competitive thing has a way of edging in.

I first met Lynne as her patient. I had developed something called winter's eczema, which gave me a terrific rash on both my shins. She had sandy-colored hair, wonderful skin, great legs, and—here was a new twist for me—impressively upright posture, which I somehow found very sexy. She instantly recognized my condition, daubed my rash with an ointment, wrote me a prescription, told me to make an appointment to see her again in two weeks. She was very formal, business-like; charged me $150 for ten minutes of her time.

For two weeks I thought about that posture, the way it did good things for her short haircut, made her neck seem longer, her small breasts more upright, allowed her to carry her head in an attractive way. That she was a physician wearing a well-fitting grayish coat with "Dr. Lynne Ross, M.D." sewn in cursive in blue thread above the left pocket no doubt added to her allure.

At my second appointment, Dr. Ross asked me to lift up my trousers so that she could see my legs.

"I'll bet you ask that of all the boys," I said. "Or have you heard that one before?"

"I haven't," she answered. "But I've heard better. Your legs, by the way, are fantastic. I don't mean that the way it sounds. I mean that your rash has healed completely. You see, you've flustered me."

"Good," I said. "I mean good that I flustered you. So now that I have you flustered and off guard, is there any chance I might one night take you to dinner? I'd like that a lot."

"Sorry, but I have a policy never to see patients outside the office."

"But I'm healed, completely cured. After I leave this office I'll no longer be your patient. And, if the rash returns, I promise to see another doctor. Maybe you can recommend someone now."

"You're very determined," she said. "Did you ever sell vacuum cleaners?"

"Almost everything else but. How are you on Italian food?"

"You're indefatigable," she said.

"I'm not sure what that means," I said, "but I certainly hope so."

We had dinner at a restaurant called Francesca, on Bryn Mawr, off Sheridan Road. The place was much noisier than I remembered. When did restaurants get so noisy? A friend in the business tells me that the young like the feeling of tumult; they don't want to be overheard whispering at the next table; they prefer to shout intimacies at each other.

Lynne ordered linguini with seafood; she manipulated her noodles, with the help of a large spoon, very adroitly, I thought. I ordered a veal dish, a little nervous about making a mess of myself with tomato sauce. Destroying shirts and ties with the stuff has been a little specialty of mine.

"How come you decided to practice dermatology?" I asked her.

"No night calls," she said. "In dermatology, patients don't call you at night. I was married to my first husband while I was finishing medical school. He wasn't that keen about my practicing medicine. Actually, as I was soon to learn, he wasn't that keen about my practicing breathing, either."

When I told her I had never been married, she asked me how I had avoided it. "Nobody wanted me that badly," I replied, "despite my obvious charms."

She smiled, twirling a forkful of linguini in her spoon. I was pleased to see that she had a sense of humor. Most of the really beautiful women I've known tend to come up a little short in this department.

Lynne's first husband, Irwin, was a lawyer. The marriage lasted less than three years. Her second husband, Richard, was a cardiac surgeon. He was also a player; never met a nurse under thirty, she said, who didn't require, as she put it, "breaking in." She thought she had at last come into safe harbor with her third husband, who was neither doctor nor lawyer but instead made a serious fortune as a commodities trader. She was his third wife also, and he'd had kids with the first two, so owing to the prenup she'd agreed to sign, when he went down with his stroke, she didn't come away with a great deal of money. But that was all right, she said; at least Harry (she referred to each of her former husbands by his first name) had left her with a notion about what a good husband is like. As soon as she said it, I wondered if I myself knew what a good husband is like. I decided, looking at her, I wouldn't mind trying to find out.

Lots of women are able to attract men, but a far smaller number are closers. Lynne, with four marriages (mine being the fourth), was obviously a closer. Where or from what did this power in her derive? I still can't say for sure; all I can tell you is that there was something in her that made me want to protect her, and the idea of my being able to do so was as powerful in its appeal as her good looks and elegant manner. Did her three previous husbands, I wondered, feel the same impulse?

I won't bore you with the details of our courtship. It lasted something like eighteen months. I sensed it would be best not to employ a full-court press but instead pick her up around half-court, giving her plenty of room to bring the ball up. We went to plays and movies, lots of chichi restaurants, very expensive. She was interested in cooking and had me over for meals on weekends. We did all right—maybe a little more than all right—in the sex department. We bought each other extravagant gifts. I let her slowly make small alterations in the way I dressed. We each kept our apartments and didn't finally move in together until our wedding.

We married at City Hall, on a Tuesday morning, a court clerk our sole witness, after which we both went back to our offices to work for the remainder of the day. We had a one-week honeymoon trip to Hawaii, and when we returned I gave up my small apartment on Richie Court and moved into her larger one at 3800 N. Lake Shore Drive.

I don't think anyone would spend a lot of time puzzling over what attracted me to Lynne: she was beautiful, accomplished, intelligent. Some, like my dear mother, might question my judgment in marrying a woman who had been married so often before. But in fact Lynne passed my own personal test by being unfailingly kind to my mother, which isn't always easy. As for my mother, after she became partially reconciled to my new wife, I became for her something like the heterosexual equivalent of the son in the old Jewish joke who brought his mother sadness and joy: the sadness was that the son was homosexual, the joy was that at least he was going with a doctor.

But the more interesting question, I suppose, is what did Lynne see in me? I've stowed away a fair amount of money, but she did well enough on her own not to need mine. If I prefer to think myself more savvy about the world than she is, she, no argument here, is much more cultured than I am. All I can think to say on my own behalf is that she may have sensed how protective I felt about her, and responded to that. I've also heard about women who love men because they realize how much more the men love them. The origin of the universe may be easier to explain than the reasons people marry.

Lynne's ninth-floor apartment was light and bright, with a view of the Waveland Park clock tower and the Belmont Harbor out her front windows and of Wrigley Field, five blocks or so away, out the back. She had redone the kitchen, put in new floors. Of the four bedrooms in the place, she used one as a den in which she had her television set and stereo; another she used as an at-home office, the third was her bedroom, and the fourth, which was once a maid's room and which she kept locked, she told me was filled with things she still hadn't straightened out since she had moved in three years earlier.

After our marriage, when I moved into the apartment, I suggested that perhaps this unused room would be a good place for me to keep my clothes, possibly my computer, and a few other items. I sensed her hesitance and so didn't push it. When I brought it up again a few weeks later, I felt her tense up before she agreed to show me the room.

Far from being the mess I expected, this small room contained, in the most careful arrangement, shelves with athletic trophies on them and photographs of a young man in basketball and baseball uniforms and in tennis clothes. A blue-and-gold University of Michigan basketball jersey, number 19, was mounted and framed and hung on a wall. A glass case, with a light on the wall above it and a photograph of this same young man in a Marine officer's blues, contained medals: a Silver Star and a Purple Heart. In other photographs of him scattered around the walls, he was gracefully muscular and very handsome: he might have been my wife's twin, except his hair was dark, curly, and close cropped, his face, in the posed athletic and Marine photos, serious, even slightly stern, suggesting great powers of concentration.

On a table in the center of the room were three thick photo albums, containing photos of two children on horseback, swimming, deep-sea fishing. The young man was Lynne's brother, Billy Ross, and the small room we were now standing in, which had heavy maroon drapes pulled closed, was her shrine to him. I figured that this was not the time to tell my wife that, my senior year at Sullivan High School, I was the eighth man on a basketball team that finished the year with six wins and thirteen losses.

I had known that Lynne had had a brother, five years older, who had died flying a helicopter in Vietnam. She had looked down when she gave me these few bits of information. I mumbled that I was sorry and said nothing further, and the subject hadn't come up again until this moment.

"I didn't know your brother was so serious an athlete," I said, noting all the trophies.

"He was all-state basketball at Lane Tech. He started for Michigan. He also played baseball for Michigan. He was a natural athlete." When we left the room, she locked the door.

Once Lynne had shown me the room she created for her brother, she felt freer to talk about him. But her information came out in dribs and drabs. She said that as a kid she had lived in the glow of his fame. In West Rogers Park, everyone knew Billy Ross. Along with being an all-state basketball player, the White Sox had offered him a signing bonus of a hundred thousand dollars, a big number in those days, but he turned it down to go to college. He planned to go to medical school, to become a surgeon.

Once, when we were watching a *60 Minutes* segment on Vietnam, Lynne said: "My brother could have got out of Vietnam, but he didn't want to. Our father fought in World War II, and Billy idolized him. He told me Vietnam was going to be the adventure of his generation, and he didn't want to miss out on it."

Lynne kept her maiden name after our marriage, which she had done during her previous two. We went off to our separate labors together most mornings. Running a full-time medical practice didn't leave much time for cooking, so we usually met for dinner at a downtown or near-north-side restaurant. Sometimes we'd bring in food from Chinatown. She dragged me along to Steppenwolf for plays, many of which I didn't understand and those I did I found I didn't much like. I did better going to the symphony with her, where I could at least let my mind drift off to the business deals then on my plate or nap off. I kept my Bulls and Bears season tickets, but used them less and less.

At one Bulls–Trail Blazers game I did go to, at halftime, my friend Mel Rosen introduced me to Irwin Harris, Lynne's first husband, the lawyer. Irwin was in his middle fifties, with a lawyerly look of slightly oily prosperity about him, beginning to run to stoutness. No man, I'm sure, likes to be in the company of another man who has slept with his wife, but, for some reason I didn't find this guy as irritating as I thought I would.

"She's a great girl," he said. "Smart, too. And still a beauty, I'll bet. I haven't seen Lynne in ten years."

"She is all those things," I said.

"Did you get to meet her parents before they died?" I shook my head no. "Remarkable people, Sid and Essie Ross. He was in scrap iron. Went to work in a Hickey Freeman suit and changed into coveralls and worked in the yard with the blacks and the Polish guys. A very tough guy. Aggressive. Used to play softball at Loyola every Sunday and in his fifties could still beat out slow grounders to third. Loved his kids, but especially Billy. Billy was everything to him. When Billy died in Vietnam, the lights, I'm told, went out in Sid's eyes."

"Did you know Billy?" I asked.

"Never met him," he said.

"She hasn't spoken all that much about her brother to me," I said.

"But," he continued as if he hadn't heard me, "if I were to name a correspondent in my divorce with Lynne, it would have been one William Ross. The main problem with our marriage was that I couldn't come anywhere near the standard set by her brother. I hope you get closer. Have you been given access to the Billysaleum yet?"

Before I had a chance to answer, the buzzer for the second half sounded, and it was time to get back to our seats.

I'm not sure why, but I decided not to say anything to Lynne about my meeting her first husband. What, really, would be the point?

"You know," Lynne said to me one evening after an early dinner at home of omelets and salad, "I often wonder what Billy would be doing now if he were still alive."

"He would be how old?"

"Today's his birthday," she said. "January 9. He would have been fifty-four. He'd been accepted to Yale Medical School. But he was worried that Vietnam would all be over by the time he got out. He was planning to do surgical research after medical school. He would have been marvelous at it."

"He had to have been an extraordinary guy" was all I could think to add.

"Billy wasn't like anyone else. I think I knew that even when we were little kids. He was always advanced for his age, far ahead of everybody."

"Were you ever envious of him? Did you ever sense that maybe he set the bar too high for you?"

"I might have felt some of that if I'd been his younger brother. But as a sister I felt nothing of the kind. I just remember being proud of him all the time, of his brains, of his athletic prowess, of the way he carried himself. Everything he wore looked perfect on him. All my girlfriends had crushes on him. He was always very kind to them, kind to everybody, really." Her eyes began to tear up.

On Lynne's 49th birthday, I took her to a restaurant in Evanston called Trio, where not only did I not recognize a single item on the menu but the waiter, a young guy with a very ambitious hairdo, gave us very careful instructions on how to eat each dish. I had bought a Bulgari watch for my wife, which I was planning to give her before dessert arrived.

"Billy always made a terrific fuss over my birthdays," she said. "He would come up with sweet goofy gifts, surprise me with tickets to musicals and things for me and my friends to do. Once he actually got Mel Tormé to call just before I was to blow out the candles on my cake for my sixteenth birthday party and sing 'Happy Birthday' to me over the phone. I have no idea how my brother managed it, but it was really Mel Tormé. After Billy died, for years I felt I never wanted to have another birthday."

Lynne and I didn't have our first argument until we were married a year and a half or so, which may be a world record, though I haven't checked this in the *Guinness Book*. We didn't have money problems to argue about; being childless, disputes about child-raising caused no conflict. What we finally argued about—what I, to name the goddamn culprit, really argued about—was Lynne's showing up an hour and a quarter late for dinner one Friday night at a restaurant on Halsted Street called Vinci. I'd had a rough day. I'd also had two martinis—not a usual thing for me—and was working on a third. I made the mistake of taking our table, reserved for 6:30, instead of waiting for Lynne at the bar. She was usually punctual. I tried to call her office, but no one answered. My irritation turned to anger and crested up around rage when, at ten of eight, she walked in.

"Where the hell were you?" I said.

"It's a complicated story," she said. "I'll explain."

"I hope it's also a good one," I said, though I knew I wasn't going to let her tell it. I was, I now realize, the booze working its ugly magic, a lot happier at that moment being angry. I began dressing her down, in a loud voice, right there in the middle of the small and crowded restaurant. Dumb. Really stupid. She fled. When after a minute or two I went out in the street to find her, she was gone.

By the time I got back to the apartment—having driven slowly, hoping the effect of the martinis would wear off—Lynne had long before arrived, pulled blankets and pillows off our bed, and taken up residence for the night in the room she kept for her brother, the Billysaleum, as

Irwin Harris had called it and as I, too, now started to think of it. She had locked the door from the inside. When I knocked, apologizing, she refused to answer.

She was gone when I woke Saturday morning. When she returned later in the day, I apologized again, told her how stupid I felt, it was the martinis doing the talking, that it would never happen again.

"I'd rather not talk about it," she said.

And we didn't ever again. But I always felt that that night was the first time I had failed her, shown my coarseness. She didn't ever say so, but I always thought she was thinking that her brother Billy would never have done such a thing, not in a million years. Had he been alive, he might even have come around to straighten me out for talking that way to his little sister.

Every so often, at a concert, or at High Holiday services at Temple Sholom, we'd run into someone who had gone to high school with Billy. When they would mention him to Lynne, she seemed to glow in a way that never resulted from my conversation nor anything else I did.

A plumber came in one day to fix our back bathroom toilet, which had gone on the fritz, and he turned out to be a guy named Jack Mruk, who had played with Billy at Lane Tech. He was a big guy, maybe 6'4", dark, with a receding hairline, who looked as if he might have to shave three or four times a day.

When Lynne remembered who he was, you could feel her excitement.

"I'd heard your brother got killed in Nam," he said. "Lousy luck! I never had to go because of my bum knees. Bad knees are my biggest gift from all of those years of basketball I guess."

"Weren't you a year ahead of Billy?"

"Yeah, but two years older. I'd had rheumatic fever as a kid and had to stay home from grade school for a year. Billy was the best I ever played with. Completely unselfish guy. He was always feeding me the ball. He made me look good."

Mruk told a story about the time Billy had dribbled out the clock with more than two minutes to go against a Chicago Vocational team. He told her about the time the two of them, he and Billy, each scored more than 30 points in a game against Von Steuben, the first time in the city any team had two players score in the 30s in the same game. Jack Mruk had Lynne's absolutely full attention. As she listened to him talk about Billy, I ceased to exist.

That night I had a dream in which I was playing a half-court basketball game with Billy Ross and Jack Mruk against me. We were all naked. I stood by helplessly as they scored basket after basket. My heart sank at my inadequacy.

I might have had a chance against a living brother, but against a brother dead for decades, none whatsoever. I assume Billy Ross had had weaknesses, excesses, like the rest of us; or at least that, given enough knocks in life, some would eventually have shown up. Maybe he would have turned out to be a drinking man, or a gambler, or an impatient father, or a skirt chaser—something besides the perfect brother permanently fixed in his sister's mind and memory.

Around this time we went to a wedding of a younger cousin of Lynne's at the Gold Room at the Drake. Until then I had never danced with my wife. I did my slow-dance box step, pleased that I had managed not to step on Lynne's toes.

"Hey, Lynne," her Uncle Maury said when we got back to our table, "remember how you and Billy used to get up at deals like this and everyone would clear the floor to watch the two of you dance?

"When they were kids they did everything from jitterbug to tango together," Uncle Maury continued, turning to me. "You'd have loved it, Lou. They were a knockout." I looked over at Lynne, who was looking off more than twenty years in the distance.

I wished I'd meet someone who would tell me something really terrible about Billy: that he cheated at poker, or had a child-porno collection, or wore funny shoes. I started thinking so much about my wife's relation with her dead brother that I did something I had earlier told myself I would never have to do as long as I lived. I saw a shrink.

A little fellow, Dr. Levitas had no couch in his office, but two plush chairs, in which we sat facing each other. He wore a gold bracelet on his right wrist, and expensive shoes that rode up over his ankles. Odd touches of vanity, I thought, for a man of science. "Sometimes, you know, the Electra complex in young women is misplaced, attaching itself not to the father, as is normal and healthy, but to male siblings or uncles or even older cousins."

"What, exactly, is the Electra complex?" I asked.

"Like the Oedipus complex, but played out in the psychodrama of young girls."

Even I knew about the Oedipus complex. "Instead of wanting to sleep with her father," I said, "my wife has never got over wanting to sleep with her dead brother? Is this what you're telling me?"

"To say this in an authoritative way, I would need to talk with your wife, which I should be pleased to do. But the question is, how do you feel about all this?"

"I feel like a schmuck," I said.

"For entering into a marriage so fraught?"

"No," I said, "for paying you $175 to listen to this horseshit." At which point, I got up from my chair and walked out of the office.

The reasons for my resisting Levitas's interpretation of my wife's behavior aren't very complicated. In business as in my life, I don't like investigations of motives that go underwater beyond a certain level—so deep that you can't deal with them. Because Lynne missed wanting to crawl into the sack with her old man she now wants to do so with her dead brother was about fifty fathoms deeper than I was prepared to go.

Besides, it was difficult enough dealing with my marriage on the surface, which was that Lynne had had a brilliant and immensely attractive older brother, and because of him she had set her ideal of what a man ought to be inhumanly high. Two earlier husbands couldn't make it; a third had had the good fortune to peg out before he disqualified himself; and I looked to be the next guy who wasn't going to make it, either.

We were dining at home on a Sunday night, after which we were going to watch a movie on television. I hadn't planned to do so, but just before we were about to take our dishes into the kitchen, I found myself saying, "Babe, forgive me, but I have to tell you that I'm worried about us. I worry that I'm going to lose you because you don't think I'm the man your brother was."

"Nobody could be," she said. "I've long ago known that no one could replace Billy. But Billy was my brother. You are my husband. Big difference there, you know."

"But do you also know how tough on a husband it is knowing that your happiest memories are about a boy who has been dead for more than twenty-five years? The other night when Maury Grolnik was talking about you and your brother as a kid dance team, I felt you'd left the room on me, and for a much better place than my company could ever provide. Whenever Billy's name comes up, I feel wiped out."

"I'm sorry," she said. "I don't mean for that to happen. You must believe me."

"It does happen, though, and it hurts. It hurts a lot."

"Oh, Lou, I wish you had known my brother. Everything about him seemed golden. He never said anything stupid. He was beautiful and kind, Lou, and so generous, you could feel his goodness."

"But he's dead, babe, and he isn't coming back. I know you know that better than anyone, but forgive me if I say it doesn't always seem as if you act on that knowledge."

"I try, Lou, you have to believe that I really do. And now that I know how you feel, I'll try harder. I promise."

We took a pass on the movie, went to bed early, and made love tenderly and lengthily. Lynne fell off to sleep before me, and as I held her in my arms I looked down at her intelligent and tranquil face; she seemed even more beautiful in her sleep. Later in the night she turned over and, in an agonized voice in her sleep, called out, "Oh, Billy, Billy, where are you?"

I woke the next morning defeated, hopeless. Much as I loved my wife, I felt I couldn't go any further with things as they were. Lynne had gone to the university hospital early for grand rounds.

I phoned the janitor, a sly Romanian who called himself Stefano, to ask his help in unlocking the door to the Billysaleum. After he had done so, I went inside and emptied out its contents: pictures, photo albums, medals, trophies, the works. It was a wild thing to do, but I figured, screw it. I piled everything neatly in the foyer to our apartment, six or so feet from our front door, and on top of it all left the following note:

Lynne,

I've decided to close up my office and work at home. I needed the room in which you've kept your brother's things for my computer and a few file cabinets. We can put your brother's stuff in our basement locker. Hope this doesn't inconvenience you too much. I'll be at the Bulls-Clippers game and probably won't be back much before 11.

Love, Lou

Not very subtle, agreed, but I felt the time for subtlety had passed. Lynne usually got home by 6:00 p.m. I decided it would be best not to call but to wait for her to call me. The day dragged on and seemed longer than two bad fiscal quarters. I couldn't concentrate. I drove around the city, had lunch alone in Chinatown, dropped into the East Bank for a sauna and soak in the Jacuzzi, grabbed a sandwich, and drove off to the game. I couldn't concentrate on it, either. Watching these multimillionaire kids run up and down the floor, all I could think was that one ball wasn't enough for these guys; they needed six or seven balls on the court to cover everyone's selfishness.

I struggled to stay for the full game, a blow-out, Bulls 109, Clippers 86. To delay my return, I stopped at the Bagel on Broadway and had a plate of scrambled eggs, toast, and a pot of tea. It was well past midnight when I turned the key in the door. The pile of Billy's stuff had been removed from the foyer. I turned down the hall to the Billysaleum to see if it had all been put back and found that the door was locked. Lynne was nowhere in the apartment.

In our bathroom, I found a light blue envelope taped to the mirror. I put down the top of the commode, sat down, withdrew three sheets of notepaper within written in Lynne's good-student girlish hand, and read:

Dear Lou,

When I came home earlier this evening to find my brother's things on the floor in the hallway, I felt first dazed, then angry, then enraged. Why would you do such a thing? I asked myself, but of course I knew. You are not the first man I've been married to who has complained about my brother's being his rival—an unbeatable rival, they claimed. But I had thought of you as different, more independent, less likely to worry about false rivals, beyond all that. I guess I was wrong.

I loved my brother and love the memory of him even now, so long after his death. I can't help it. I had hoped that you would have understood this and been able to live with it, and not feel in some sort of empty competition with a dead man. I took you for a larger man than you apparently are. My mistake again.

I have moved into the Seneca Hotel and plan to stay there for the next three days. That should give you plenty of time to clear your own things from the apartment. Please don't try to get in touch. There really isn't anything that we have to say to each other. I regret that things haven't worked out. I regret it more than you can possibly know.

Lynne

I read it twice, brushed my teeth, put on my pajamas, and slipped into the bed that had Lynne's clean, vaguely perfumed, understatedly sexy scent, which I would never smell again. Eventually I drifted off into a dream in which I was playing basketball, this time one-on-one against my dead brother-in-law. We were in a large empty gym in which the bounce of the ball echoed loudly. I was in gray, rumpled sweat clothes, needing a shave, toting a middle-aged man's potbelly, wearing black wing tips and silky black socks with clocks on them. Billy was in his sleek blue-and-gold University of Michigan uniform. I had the ball. I feinted to my right, he lunged, and I dribbled behind my back and through my legs, and slipped easily around him to the left. At the free-throw line, I leapt and soared, in slow motion, and slammed the ball authoritatively in the hoop. I looked back to see what Billy thought of my move, but he, along with all the hopes of my marriage, had vanished.

Dad's Gay

My kid sister Ellie calls infrequently, and never at my office, so when my secretary told me she was on the line, I became immediately apprehensive. She's a bit of a hippie, Ellie, with no good habits but a kind and trusting heart. She's in her late thirties, and never married, though, I gather, with lots of men in her past. She's stayed in Chicago and keeps an eye—an unsteady and inconstant one, I've always assumed—out for our father since our mother died three years ago. Straight out of law school, I moved to New York, where I live today.

"Ellie," I said. "Everything all right?"

"I'm calling about Dad," she said.

"What about Dad?"

"You sitting down, Steven?" she asked. "I have something amazing to tell you."

"What? What is it?"

"Dad's gay," she said.

"A joke, right?" I said.

"No joke," she said. "When I visited him earlier today I discovered that he has a roommate, a guy in his late twenties or early thirties named Randy. I didn't quite get his last name. But I was there long enough to recognize that Dad and Randy are more than friends."

I don't recall the rest of our conversation before I hung up the phone. Ellie's phrase "Dad's gay" refused, as they used to say when I was a kid, to compute; the two words, Dad and gay, felt like opposed magnets, each fiercely repelling the other. I won't say that my father is the last man I should have expected to be secretly homosexual, but he was pretty low on the list. Besides, he's sixty-seven years old.

He was not without his charm, our father, though he didn't waste much of it on Ellie and me when we were growing up. Until his retirement four years ago, he was the vice-president for community relations at the University of Chicago, which meant that he often represented the university at public functions, both intra and extramural. He dresses with care, is well-spoken, tactful.

He never said so outright, but I don't think he cared much for his job. The problem was the University of Chicago. If you weren't a great scholar or scientist, you were viewed there as little more than a servant. And my father, who is more than a bit of a snob, couldn't bear thinking of himself as anyone's servant.

As a younger man, in his mid-thirties, working for the *Chicago Sun-Times*, my father won a Pulitzer Prize for a series of articles on racial segregation in Chicago real estate. He used to say that journalism was a young man's game, which was why he got out of it in his early forties to take the University of Chicago job. Whenever anyone ever mentioned his Pulitzer, my father would almost invariably answer, "Pulitzer Prizes go to two kinds of people: those who don't need them and those who don't deserve them." No one, at least in my presence, ever asked him into which category he fell.

My mother idolized him. She was a good soul, my mother, but, as became evident to my sister and me before we reached the age of ten, a bit of a ditz. She wasn't much of a cook, often burning things or forgetting to include essential ingredients in complex dishes she probably shouldn't have attempted in the first place. She was wildly disorganized and forgetful, so that often, when we expected her to pick us up after piano lessons or little-league games, she would show up an hour or more late.

She also labored under the misapprehension that she was an amusing raconteur. She could take a full fifteen minutes to tell one of her supposedly riotous stories—about, say, a large toothbrush attached to the key to the ladies' room that her dentist gave his patients, or the confusions of a bookseller on Michigan Avenue who gave her a hard time—whose punchline never failed to fizzle. Ellie and I were both embarrassed for her when she set off on one of those stories before company. But our father, usually so tough on bores and boors alike, at least when recounting their behavior to us at our dinner table, showed infinite tolerance for our mother's lengthy and ill-told stories.

I cannot say that I loved my father. I suppose I never really connected with him. There was something a bit distant about him, something a little cold; it was as if he had something very important on his mind that my sister and I weren't worthy of being let in on.

Someone once said that the reason master bedrooms in American homes and apartments do not have locks on their doors is so that children can enter their parents' bedroom, catch them making love, and later in life have something to tell their psychiatrists. I never caught my parents in the act of lovemaking, nor can I easily imagine it now. My father was always kind, even courtly, to my mother. I cannot recall them ever arguing in any serious way, at least in front of Ellie and me. But I don't have many memories of them kissing or embracing, either. The element of intimacy, at least physical intimacy, between them didn't seem to be there. Still, credit where credit is due, my father stood by my mother through the four-year torture of her Parkinson's disease, nights and weekends performing all the functions of a practical nurse, and doing so in the most affectionately solicitous way, right up until her death.

Not one of those full-court-press dads, my father never attended my little-league games, never took me to sports events or concerts or spent much time alone with me generally. Somehow I didn't mind. Strange though it may seem to say, I didn't miss his attention. I worried mainly about his disapproval. I didn't fear my father, exactly, but I did worry about being the target of his contempt, which I knew, from hearing him talk about faculty at the university, could be withering.

Every family has room for only one non-conformist, and in our family that place was reserved for my sister, who through her adolescence and college years—Ellie dropped out of five different colleges and ended up without a degree—drove our parents, but especially my father, crazy. I was the good kid: excellent at school, no trouble at home, the very model of a bright and obedient Jewish boy. I could do without my father's approval, I suppose, because I received all I needed in the classroom.

Because school was easy for me and I had expressed an interest in becoming a lawyer—I'm not sure I can tell you why—my father decided that he wanted to see me go to Harvard Law School, which eventually I did. "You must understand, Steven," he once told me, "the world is stupid, always judging a man not by his true quality, but by his family connections or wealth or where he went to school. Go to Harvard Law School, which is probably no better than any place else—God knows, some of the worst people in the country seem to have graduated from it—and I promise all sorts of doors will open up for you."

So I gave up playing on the baseball and track teams in high school and concentrated on my studies with sufficient intensity to get into Harvard. Entry into Harvard Law, after my undergraduate years, when I also devoted myself to my studies, proved no difficulty.

If my father was pleased by my accomplishments, he failed to mention it. He was right, though, about Harvard Law School opening doors. I was on the *Review* there, graduated in the top tenth of my class, and was offered a job at the firm Sullivan & Cromwell, where I have remained all these years, specializing in estate planning; eight years ago, at the age of thirty-six, I was made a partner.

My main point is that I always viewed my father as a bit—maybe more than a bit—of a cold fish. So the news that he was gay, which suggested that all the years of his marriage he was smoldering with a secret passion underneath his cool exterior, raised a good bit the voltage of my shock at Ellie's announcement.

I have no strong opinions about homosexuality. Although I knew a fair number of gay guys and a few lesbians at Harvard, I have never had a friend who was gay, nor even a gay acquaintance I saw with any regularity. I'm reasonably sure that no one at Sullivan & Cromwell is homosexual, partners or associates, male or female, at least as far as I can determine. But then, let's face it, I have no reason to be impressed with the efficiency of my gaydar, when I never had the least clue that my own father is gay.

When I called Ellie that evening from home, hoping she could fill me in on more details about her discovery of our father's homosexuality, she didn't have all that much to add. She reminded me that our father, after our mother's death three years ago, moved out of Hyde Park, the university neighborhood, and bought a three-bedroom apartment on Sheridan Road off Glenlake overlooking Lake Michigan. He installed his "catamite," as Ellie called the man living with him, in one of the bedrooms, kept the master bedroom for himself, and used the third bedroom for his study. He was writing a book on the history of the American press, a project he had long talked about but never had much time for when working at the University of Chicago.

"He seems happy," Ellie reported. "When I left his apartment, he even hugged me—me, his wretched troublemaking daughter, the wicked witch of the West—if you can visualize that. But why don't you come see for yourself?"

I decided I would, and booked a flight for the following Friday, planning to return on Sunday. I called my father, telling him that I had some business in Chicago and would like it if we could meet for lunch or dinner on Saturday. The truth was, I hadn't seen all that much of him since our mother died, and I didn't want him to think I was coming in as a result of what he would likely suspect was Ellie's news about his being gay. He told me to come ahead, suggesting that lunch on Saturday was best. He said that he had someone he wanted me to meet. He didn't invite me to stay over at his place while I was in Chicago.

I suppose I could have stayed at Ellie's apartment. So far as I knew, at the moment she was living alone. But the prospect of the chaos of my sister's life, which figured to be reflected in her living arrangements, put me off, so I booked a room at The Drake.

Ellie picked me up at O'Hare in her eleven-year-old Honda. As I threw my bag into her trunk, I noted her several bumper stickers: for the past two Democrat party candidates for president, others that read, If Animals Could Talk, We'd All Be Vegetarians; Yoga Ain't for Yuppies; If You're Pro-Choice, Follow Me to The Polls; Save the Earth, We'll Destroy the Other Planets Later, and a combined white cross, Jewish star and Islamic crescent on a blue background used to spell out the word Co-Exist. I noticed that she also had a peace sign tattooed on the inner wrist of her left hand.

Having had a brief fling as a modern dancer, Ellie was working part-time as a Pilates instructor, filling in her income with work as an office temp. Five years younger than me, she was approaching forty, and, as far as I could see, utterly unsettled in life, though she did not seem particularly concerned about it. Last year I made a shade under three-quarters of a million dollars. I mention this because a few years ago I asked Ellie if I could possibly help her out with a few grand a month. She thanked me but said she was doing fine as it is in a way that made it clear that the subject of accepting money from her older brother wasn't really open for discussion.

I loved my sister without being especially close to her, if you can understand that. My two kids, Sarah and Aaron, especially loved their Aunt Ellie. Every Jewish kid needs a crazy aunt, and for them Ellie filled the bill nicely. Ellie and I had our own Aunt Sally, my mother's younger, also unmarried, sister who danced the hora more wildly than anyone else at Jewish weddings and bar-mitzvah parties, and fed us popcorn and Jell-O for dinner when she stayed with us during those times when our parents went out of town by themselves. Our kids didn't see all that much of their Aunt Ellie, but they didn't seem to need to see much of her to love her.

Ellie and I stopped on the way to The Drake for an early dinner at a restaurant on Halsted Street called Vinci. We had pasta dishes, and I ordered a bottle of Cabernet Sauvignon. Awaiting our food, we settled into discussing Topic Number One.

"So Steven," Ellie said, "what's your take on our old man's hot new sex life?"

"Truth is," I said, "I can't get my mind around it. If you'd called and said Dad had knocked up a woman forty years younger than him, or was running for the United States Senate, this I could have taken in. But our father being gay, that's something else again."

"Pretty wild," Ellie said. "On the other hand, why not? I mean who knows what secret desires people carry around. Most people take these buried desires to their graves, where they get buried for good. Not our father. Give him credit for that."

"I'm not sure that credit is what is at stake," I said.

"You didn't expect him to ask our permission to be gay, did you?" she said. "You're not thinking of disowning him, I hope."

Leave it to Ellie to think outside of the box. But, then, in her entire life she had never really been inside the box.

"What kind of homosexual is he, by the way?" I asked. "Flamin'? Swish? Leather? Milquetoasty? I can't imagine him as any of these basic types. There was never anything the least effeminate about our father. Or did I miss something? Was I asleep at the wheel all the years we grew up with him? Did you ever sense he was gay?"

"I didn't have a notion. As for the kind of homosexual Dad is, he defies all categories by being absolutely his old self," Ellie said. "He looks and acts and is the old Dad, except now, in his late sixties, he happens to be sleeping with a man thirty or so years younger than himself."

"What do you suppose they do?"

"I've long ago ceased much to care what people do in bed," Ellie said, "unless it's my bed. Still, it's amusing to think of our dignified papa as amorous, let alone with a man."

"Why doesn't it amuse me?"

"Maybe," Ellie said, "that is a question you need to ask yourself."

"What I can't get over is his having lived almost his entire life with so deep a secret at the center of his existence. That can't have been easy. Who knows, it may also have made him the refrigerator of a father that he was."

"I find it hard to imagine him any other way, a father with a built-in ice-cube maker."

"And yet you find it easy to imagine him gay?"

"I guess I don't find it a problem," Ellie said.

"If I ever figure out why I do, I'll let you know," I replied.

I was to pick my father up for lunch at his new—to me at least, who hadn't seen him for nearly a year—apartment at 6101 N. Sheridan Road. When I rang from the desk in the lobby, a voice other than my father's answered and said that I was expected and to come on up, apartment 38A.

I was met at the door by a slender man in, I estimated, his early thirties, tanned, with coppery-colored hair and almost periwinkle blue eyes. He was wearing chino trousers, a blue button-down shirt under a red V-neck sweater, white tennis shoes. He looked to me like nothing so much as a recently and happily retired surfer.

"Hi. Your dad'll be out in a minute," he said. "I'm Randy Thernstrum," and he put out his hand for me to shake.

As I was shaking his hand, I thought, perversely, my father couldn't at least find a Jewish gay man, of which I gathered there was no shortage? "This apartment has spectacular views," I said.

"Doesn't it, though," Randy said. "It practically sits out over the lake. Your dad told me that he always wanted to live looking out at Lake Michigan, the only point of topographical interest in our fair but extremely flat city."

The east portion of the apartment was all glass, with its southernmost portion opening on to a small balcony on which my father had installed a gas grill and a small ironwork table and two chairs and from which there was a clear view of the skyscrapers in downtown Chicago. Light flooded in; the rich azure of the lake provided, in effect, the eastern wall of the apartment. My father had bought all new furniture for the place; at least I recognized none of the things from our Hyde Park apartment on Kimbark Avenue. Everything was modern, glass and black leather, elegant but a touch severe, nothing like the slightly overstuffed, chintz-covered comfy furniture our mother favored in our old apartment.

"Your dad tells me that you're a very successful New York lawyer," Randy said. "Pretty awesome."

"Not as successful as some," I said. "But tell me, what do you do?"

"I'm an administrator at a charter school on the west side, in the Austin neighborhood."

"Done that long?"

"Two years. Before that I taught American history at St. Scholastica High School in Rogers Park."

"Have you known my dad for long?" I asked, wanting to discover if my father had been seeing him when my mother was still alive.

"Less than a year," he said, "but we hit it off immediately."

Just then my father walked into the room, looking very much like, well, as Ellie said, like himself. I'm not sure what I expected him to look like. I assumed a loosened collar maybe, a pair of gym shoes, possibly jeans. But, no, he was in his standard get-up: gray trousers, white shirt, black knit tie, brown tweed jacket, tasseled oxblood loafers, closely shaved, as always. He kept himself slender, his black hair now streaked with gray was only just beginning to thin out slightly at the front.

He is still an attractive man, I thought, and then, good God, wondered if I was regarding my father homosexually.

"I see you and Randy have introduced yourselves. Allow us a couple of hours for lunch," he said to Randy.

"Take care, Henry," Randy said to my father. "I'll hold down the fort. Good to meet you Steven." We shook hands once again.

In the elevator, my father said, "Randy's eleven years younger than you, Steven. You realize that if he were a girl of the same age you would have had no choice but to think me an old fool. It occurs to me, though, that an old fool might be preferable to what you might actually think of me." So he knew that I knew about his homosexuality, and there would be no need for a nervous announcement. Good.

"Let's wait for lunch to talk about all that, Dad," I said.

My father chose a Chinese restaurant on Broadway called Mei Shung. Rather a drab place, with ten or eleven tables, only one other of which was currently occupied, by a bald, heavyset man reading the sports section from the *Trib* while tucking into a large plate of fried rice.

After we ordered—kung-pao for my father, Mongolian beef for me—we talked about beside-the-point things. I asked what he had done with the furniture from the old Hyde Park house. He asked how I found my sister. I asked if he was making any progress with his book. He told me it was going slowly but going. He asked how the shaky economy was affecting my business. I asked about his health. He asked about his grandchildren, in whom he had never taken all that keen an interest.

Finally, more than halfway through the lunch, my father said, "You know, Steven, there's an old Arab proverb that runs, 'When your son becomes a man, make him your brother.' You have long been a man, but I suspect that you may have some doubts just now about whether you want me for a brother. Were you surprised to learn about my—how to put this?—my latent, now manifest, proclivities?"

"Stunned is more like it. How long has this been going on?"

"'How long has this been going on?' You're too young to know it, but that happens to be the title of a June Christie torch song from the 1950s. But to answer your question: it has been going on just about all my conscious life."

51

"You always knew you were gay?"

"Small correction: at my age I always knew I was not gay but queer, and I wasn't at all pleased about it. I thought it a bad card dealt from a stacked deck, though who did the actual stacking I cannot say even now."

"What did you do about it?"

"What could I do? Two possibilities: give into it or fight it. I chose the latter. Marrying your mother was of course part of the fight. You have to remember, Steven, that in my day, before victimhood was a happy state, being homosexual was thought a major affliction—a thing that could, and if it got out usually did, crush a man, also a boy, in every way. I chose to avoid being crushed."

"Did mother know?"

"No. At least I don't think so. We certainly never discussed it."

"Are you bisexual?"

"I don't happen to believe there are any bisexuals, at any rate not of a pure kind. Maybe some men are able to make love to men and women with equal passion, but I've never met one. I think among homosexual men and women there are some who can tolerate, and with imaginative resources sometimes enjoy, making love with people of the opposite sex. I suppose I was one of these."

"Forgive my interrogating you like this."

"No need for apology. You have a right."

"Did you see other men when you were married to mother?"

"I never did. I don't know whether because I was afraid of getting caught or because I thought I would be doing her a double injustice. The initial injustice, of course, was marrying her in the first place."

"Why did you stay with her after Ellie and I were out of the house?"

"Because—and I hope you will believe this—I loved your mother. And because I thought she needed a man's protection, mine specifically, someone who knew all her weaknesses and could stand between her and the world. My sexual predilection doesn't eliminate my manly instincts, Steven, please believe that."

"So you waited until mother died to live an openly homosexual life?"

"That's right. I felt that at this point I owed it to myself, that I deserved it, if one can be said to deserve anything in this life. I also needed to get out of Hyde Park and away from the professoriat and their gossip, to live the way I had long wanted and was, apparently, intended to live."

"Are you happy now, Dad?"

"Happy? The older I get the more I think happiness is a concept for morons. The best one can aim for is a mild and always fragile contentment."

"Are you content with Randy?"

"Reasonably so. He's an earnest and serious young man. He looks up to me. But I won't be shocked if one day I come home to find a note explaining that he has found someone else and cleared out. It's in the nature of the life. People are always finding someone more suitable. I've decided I can live with that."

The waitress inquired if we wanted anything else. My father shook his head, and asked for the check.

"Since this seems to be confession day, Steven," said my father, "I need to confess that I realize I wasn't the best of fathers, at least by contemporary standards. I was, as you now know, under a fair amount of pressure, not only from the quiet but persistent tyranny of hiding my true sexual nature but because I didn't much like my work, flacking for a great university. I was under, please understand, a double whammy."

"Why have children in the first place?" I asked.

"Because your mother wanted them. And because in our day it was expected of married couples under a certain age that they have kids. My own upbringing wasn't all that easy; my parents didn't much care for each other. I don't know if you know this or not, but people who themselves have had unhappy childhoods tend to be nervous about having kids of their own. We don't look upon bringing kids into the world as an unambiguous blessing, and we certainly don't look upon childhood as a blessed state. But how could I deny your mother? She was a sweet and shockingly normal, if slightly *meshuganah*, woman."

"Having kids also provided pretty good camouflage for your homosexuality," I couldn't resist inserting.

"I suppose it did," he said. "But you'll have to believe that it wasn't my main motive."

"You stuck by mom through her terrible last years with Parkinson's."

"Of course I did. I'd have been a real son of a bitch if I had deserted her. I'll say this much for marriage: nothing transient about it. And in it you don't die alone, or at least one of the partners in a marriage doesn't. Alone is the way I expect to die."

"Did you ever attempt to see a psychotherapist about all this?"

"At different times in my life I saw four of them, but without much luck. Therapy isn't always easy for troubled people who also happen to be intelligent. You have to find a therapist who is brighter than you are—and that's not always so simple either. I think it was one of the Algonquin Round Table characters who said that he dropped psychotherapy because his therapist asked too many goddamn personal questions. The therapists I went to also asked lots of personal questions, which I didn't mind, except they all seemed to me the wrong questions."

"So where does that leave you, Dad?"

"It leaves me most days staring out at the lake and contemplating my own insignificance. I sit in a chair and contemplate my life, and think that, if there is a God, he surely must love a joke."

He paused, and removed his wallet from his jacket pocket.

"Let's get the hell out of here," he said, and dropped a twenty and a ten on the table and pushed back his chair.

We drove the six or seven blocks back to my father's apartment in silence. When I pulled into the driveway before his building, he turned to me, his hand on the door handle.

"I'm not sure I had much to do with it," he said, "but you've become an impressive man, Steven."

And with this, he leaned over and kissed me on the cheek, something I have no recollection of his ever having done when I was a boy. He left the car before I had a chance to reply, though I'm still not sure what I would have said. I watched him walk into his large anonymous-looking building to return to his new life.

I backed out of the driveway. Turning left onto Sheridan Road, heading south to downtown Chicago, I had to remove my handkerchief from my jacket pocket to blot my eyes, which had filled.

Out of Action

EDDIE ROTHMAN FELT IT A PRETTY GOOD NIGHT AT GAMBLERS ANONYMOUS. Rothman had been coming to these meetings, held in the basement of the Methodist Church on Lawrence Avenue every Tuesday night, except for holidays, for more than three years now. Most of the meetings were balls-achingly boring, but Rothman kept coming to them for the simple reason that his doing so seemed to work. He had been out of action, as the gamblers say, for the full time, and so he had to conclude that GA worked—at least for him, at least thus far.

Rothman had told his own story over the first month or so that he had begun attending GA meetings. His problem was sports betting, especially college football, but all other sports, too. After his father's death, Rothman had taken over the family business, the manufacture and importing of novelties: We're-Number-One gloves, miniature cameras, dream catchers, fuzzy dice, cellphone cases, junk jewelry. He was thirty-seven and had two kids. He'd been a gambler what seemed like all his life, beginning with betting parley cards in high school at the age of fifteen: pick three teams on the point spread and win six dollars on a dollar bet. He and his pals played lots of poker after school and on weekends; also blackjack and games called in-between and potluck and gin rummy, Hollywood Oklahoma, spades double, for half-a-cent a point.

Rothman, who had good card sense, more than held his own in these games. Once, though, at the age of sixteen he remembered losing $130 in an after-school potluck game, which took the edge off his appetite for dinner that evening. His friend Bobby Leckachman's older brother Ted had a bookie, and he could place a $25 bet on a ball game through him. He won more of these bets than he lost. After dropping out of Roosevelt

College in his second year and going to work for his father, Rothman acquired a bookie of his own, a guy named Lou Rappaport, and began to up his bets on ball games to $100 a shot. He came out ahead, though not by much.

He liked to have a bet going at all times. Life in action was better. The action made him feel, somehow, more alive. He probably gave more thought to the sports pages than to the novelty business. There were lots of what his father used to call "green deals" in Rothman's business, deals made for cash and off the books. When his father died and Rothman took over the business, he used a fair amount of this extra "green" to step up his bets, to $200 and sometimes $500 a game. He started betting basketball and baseball games; in baseball, he bet pitchers, of course, but also the streak system, betting on the teams that won the day before, against those who lost the day before. His craving for action grew stronger, and he was beginning to lose a lot more than winning. This was probably because he needed the action, couldn't lay off, no longer betting only on those games about which he felt confident.

Winston Churchill, Rothman somewhere read, claimed that he got a lot more out of alcohol than it got out of him. Rothman used to think the same of his own gambling, but it didn't take long for him to recognize that this wasn't so. He knew he was in trouble the weekend he bet two grand on a Friday night PAC Ten game in Arizona, lost, doubled down on Saturday taking Ohio State over Indiana giving 14 points and lost again, and doubled down yet again on Sunday on the Bears-Lions game, where the point spread beat him, making for a twelve-grand trouncing for the weekend. He did the same thing the following weekend, only at twice the stakes. He lost $4,000 on Arizona versus Oregon State, lost $8,000 on Notre Dame over Pittsburgh on Saturday, and then $16,000 on the 49ers over the Rams, putting him down $28,000, which called for just about all the money from green deals that he had stowed away in his vault at Midcity Bank.

Rothman knew he was in trouble. He knew he had to slow things down. He went two weeks in the middle of football season without placing a bet. Naturally, every bet he would have made but didn't during this drying-out period turned out to have been a winner. The third week he went back into action and won on Michigan State over Purdue, but lost twice the sum he'd won on the Packers-Colts game, putting him five grand down.

Fortunately, Debbie, Rothman's wife, was not a woman at all interested in business, or in where Rothman's money came from. So at least he didn't have to worry about hiding his losses from her—not yet anyway. He tried not going cold turkey on gambling, but on tamping things down; betting hundreds instead of thousands. But the same thrill wasn't there for hundreds, and he felt especially foolish when a slew of hundred dollar bets came in for him and he thought how much money it would have been if they had been bets in the thousands.

The weekend of the college bowl games Rothman lost $45,000, and he didn't have it to pay his bookie, a cheerful man in his late sixties named Ike Goldstein. When he told Ike he would need some time to get the money, Ike, over the phone, in a voice in which Rothman heard menace, said, "If I were you, I wouldn't take too long to get it."

Rothman had to tell Debbie as well as his older brother Mel, an orthodontist with a successful practice, about the trouble he was in. A family meeting was called. Everyone agreed it was best to keep it from Rothman's mother, who was suffering from early signs of dementia. Mel's wife Laurie was also present. Rothman felt as if he had been called down to the principal's office for writing obscenities on the walls. His brother lent him the $45,000, and a schedule for repayment was set up. The loan was given on condition of Rothman's pledge to attend Gambler's Anonymous meetings, which Rothman promised to do.

He put himself on a strict mental diet. He stopped watching ball games on television, ceased reading the sports pages. Immediately he realized how large a part of his life these things had taken up. He often found himself with nothing to say when customers and other men brought up the Bears or the Cubs, or asked him how he enjoyed the Series or the Super Bowl. He had to find other interests, subjects for conversation, damn well nearly had to revise his personality. Out of action, with no bets going, his life at first seemed flat, stale. The withdrawal, he assumed, wasn't near so rough as that from drugs or alcohol, because the addiction didn't have a physiological basis. But it was rough enough. Was gambling, he wondered, the alcoholism of Jews?

So every Tuesday night Rothman dragged himself off to Lawrence Avenue for the 7:00 p.m. meeting of Gamblers Anonymous. He worked until six on Tuesdays, stopped along the way at Wendy's for a spicy chicken sandwich and small order of fries and a large Coke, which he ate in his Audi. He took the Coke into the meetings with him.

Tonight's meeting had four new members. One, a guy in his late twenties, his hair in a ponytail, tattoos on his forearms, got up to announce that we were looking at the man who personally stopped the Miami Heat's twenty-seven-game winning streak. "I did it of course," he said, "by betting on them against the Bulls. That's all I want to say right now, but you'll hear more about my past adventures in the future."

Another of the new members, a man in his middle fifties, dressed in a velour Fila running suit, said that he woke up a week ago after his wife had gone to work, and, while having his coffee in the living room, thought how shabby the furniture in their apartment had become. So he called in a used-furniture dealer, sold the living-room furniture and the dining room set, and took the money—$1,200—to the track at Arlington. His thought was that when he returned home he would surprise his wife by telling her that the next day they would go off with his winnings and buy all new furniture. "Surprise, surprise," he said. "Didn't happen. I lost the twelve hundred. We've been eating in the kitchen ever since." After a pause, he added, "I'm here among other reasons to save my marriage."

The third new member announced that his name was Les Erhlich. He had a layered haircut, hair combed over his ears, an expensive suit. He told how he had blown his family's roofing business and two marriages through gambling. He was now selling household improvements, and on his third marriage. Unless he was in action, he said, he failed to see the point of life. He had had a number of bad weeks in a row, and instead of explaining to his wife how he had really lost his money, he began putting bits of lipstick on his shirt collars, so that she would think he was having a love affair and spending the money on a woman rather than gambling it away. "Sick stuff, I realized," he said, "and that's why I'm here tonight."

The fourth new guy stood up to say that his name was Lenny Adler and that if it was all right he'd prefer not to speak this evening, or until he had the lay of the land on how things worked. He added that his gambling had put him on the edge of suicide and that he was grateful for the existence of a place like GA where he could meet and talk with people who knew something about what he had been through.

This Lenny Adler was short, on the pudgy side, with thin sandy-colored hair, much receded, with a touch of mousse added, giving it a wet look. He wore a gray suit, a light-blue shirt, no necktie. He had an almost too-clean look about him, as if he just stepped out of the shower. He appeared to be in his early forties, around Rothman's age. He had a manicure, a blue-sapphire ring on the little finger of his right hand. He looked prosperous, or at least as if he might once have had some serious money.

At coffee after the meeting, Adler approached Rothman. "Did you by any chance go to Von Steuben High School?" he asked.

"I did," Rothman replied.

"I thought so. You looked familiar."

They discovered that they had been there at the same time, though Adler was two years older than Rothman. Would he, Adler wanted to know, be interested in ducking out for a drink to talk about old times. Maybe Rothman could fill him in on how things worked at GA.

Driving in Adler's white Porsche, a Boxter, they found an Irish pub on Ashland Avenue called Burke's. The place wasn't crowded, though seven or eight thin-screen television sets were silently playing, all on ball games, around the room. They took a booth.

Adler told Rothman that the car wasn't his. He was a salesman at Loeber Porsche in Lincolnwood. He was currently separated from his second wife, who lived with his fifteen-year-old daughter Jennifer in Morton Grove. He was living in a furnished apartment in the Somerset Hotel, on Sheridan at Argyle.

"A beautiful girl, my daughter, but a handful," Adler said. "Someday she'll made some unlucky man completely miserable, I'm sure."

"What's your weakness, your gambling jones?" Rothman asked. "Mine was sports betting."

"Casinos," said Adler. "Craps and blackjack. Fifteen or so years ago, I had to travel out to Vegas or Atlantic City to get into action. Now the goddamn things are everywhere. What's that line about the lottery—it's the tax the state charges people who don't understand basic arithmetic.

There oughta be something similar said about casinos—the tax the state charges guys dumb enough to think they can beat the house."

"What makes you think Gamblers Anonymous is going to do you any good?"

"I'm counting—I guess I better not say betting—on it, though who knows? At least the stories are better than I imagine those at Alcoholics Anonymous must be."

"Some are pretty wild," Rothman said.

"The guy who got up tonight and talked about putting lipstick on his shirt collars to put his wife off scent about his gambling problem. I think I can top that one, though I'm only going to tell it to you. Toward the end of my second marriage, I used to put a dab of lipstick on the fly of my boxer shorts to try to establish the same thing. Who knows, I figured it might even encourage my wife to outdo her rival."

"Did it work?"

"No. But I figured it was worth a try. No matter, though. One of the nice things about gambling is that it takes your mind off sex, as you may have noticed."

"Sex and everything else," Rothman said.

"It can be a problem, that everything else, no doubt about it," Adler said. "But when it's going well gambling gives a high like no other I've known."

"No argument."

"How long you been out of action?" Adler asked.

"It'll be three years four months in May," said Rothman, "but who's counting."

"Impressive. You ever feel the ache, the need to get back in action?"

"Less and less," Rothman said. "But it can still creep up on me."

"Is that why you keep going to these GA meetings?"

"I go," said Rothman, "because I'm nervous about not going. Besides, I used to be a streak system bettor, and I don't want to break my own streak. Might change my luck."

"Luck," Adler said. "I remember using that word a lot before it had the adjective 'shitty' before it."

They stayed at Burke's until nearly midnight. Rothman called Debbie at ten to let her know he would be home late, lest she thought he had fallen off the wagon and was in a poker game. They talked about their boyhoods in Albany Park, which Adler referred to as the Old Country. They talked about their similar boredom with school, about there being nothing in the classroom—any classroom—for either of them. They talked about marriage and how gambling didn't go with marriage. Rothman said he once heard someone say that a married philosopher was a joke, but a married gambler was even more ridiculous.

But mostly they talked about their adventures in the life: the big scores each had made gambling, and the even bigger losses they had taken. They discovered that they were a lot alike. The major difference between them, at least for now, is that Rothman had money, was "holding," in the term they used at the track, and Adler was tapped out, and with his alimony and child-support payments figured to be for the foreseeable future.

The following Tuesday night—it had been raining all day—attendance at Gamblers Anonymous was skimpy. Rothman counted nine people at the meeting, where usually there were twenty or so. Two of the four new guys of the previous week failed to show up, and never would again. Soon after the meeting opened, Lenny Adler, who sat across the large conference table from Rothman, stood up to speak.

"I'm pleased to be here among people who know all the pleasures and horrors of the gambling life," Adler began. "Yet for all we have in common, each of us has his own story, I'm sure. Mine is fear of being a loser, which is of course what, thanks to gambling, I've become, a big-time loser.

"But to start at the beginning, I was, or at least felt myself, a loser right out of the gate. My father came out of World War II and drove a cab. Veteran's Cab was the name of the company. He planned for it to be a temporary thing, but he did it for the rest of his life. He played the ponies, my old man, nothing serious, a two-buck bettor. Gambling didn't bring him down. The ambition gene, I guess, was missing from his make-up. My mother, who was a kind and good-hearted lady, was early afflicted with macular degeneration, which made her practically blind by the time she was thirty. I had two sisters, both older than me, each full of temperament and unhappiness. We lived above a drugstore on Wilson near St. Louis Avenue. I grew up in a home that, from the time I was maybe seven or eight years old, I knew I wanted to get the hell away from, pronto.

"And I did, even as a little kid. I found my refuge on the streets. I hung out in the schoolyard at Peterson Grammar School at Kedzie and Kimball. My first gambling took place there—marbles, mibs, we called them. I practiced very hard at mibs, because for me they were more than a game. I needed to win. I needed to think about myself as a winner because I knew that, in my family, I had drawn a loser's hand.

"My next gambling was lagging pennies, then nickels, and quarters, the kid's game of trying to pitch coins as close as possible to a line in the sidewalk. I worked hard to be good at this, too. As I grew older, I used to sucker guys into games of Horse on the half-court basket set up in the schoolyard. I wasn't a great basketball player—I was too small to go out for the team at Von Steuben—but I trained myself to shoot left-handed, which was usually all I needed to win at Horse. Other kids may have found fun at the playground, but for me a lot more than fun was involved. It was where I went to work.

"In high school I hung around with a bunch that modeled themselves on Syndicate guys. From the age of fourteen we smoked, shot craps, played nickel-dime-and-quarter poker, went to the harness races at night at Maywood, drove out to the cathouses in Braidwood and Kankakee. Gambling was at the center of everything.

"I sat in classrooms bored out of my gourd. Nowadays they would no doubt test me for dyslexia or Attention Disorder Deficit or some other learning disability. I had the greatest learning disability of all—powerful boredom about anything that didn't have a gambling element in it. The only way I could have been a good student would have been if someone bet me I couldn't get A's. I graduated somewhere in the lower quarter of my class at Von Steuben, and then lasted a single semester at Wright Junior College. Can't go wrong with Wright, they used to say. Not true of me.

"I began selling cars at the age of nineteen. I had an Uncle Earle, my mother's brother, who had a used-car lot on Western, near Thorndale. Lots of down time on a car lot. I used mine to study the sports pages and call in bets. By now the need to stay in action was second among my priorities only behind the need to breathe. Baseball, football, college, and pro basketball, I had a bet going every day.

"Las Vegas killed me. I went out there when I was twenty-three with two other guys I was working with at the time at Z. Frank Chevrolet. I thought I'd died and gone to heaven. The glitz, the glamour, the show biz bullshit, it all blew me away. These were still in the days when the Mafia ran the town. I went away from that first trip eight-grand-and-change winners, most of it from the black-jack tables. A bad omen, my good luck my first time in Vegas. I was hooked.

"I started making trips to Las Vegas every eight weeks or so. The time when I wasn't there I didn't quite feel alive. Soon I was down as a high-roller, which meant they comped my room at the Riviera, to which, after a night at the tables I would return to find a no-charge hooker waiting.

"In those days, when people asked me what I did for a living, I used to say that I was working for the Mafia. Which, in effect, I was. I might as well have had Zolly Frank send my commission checks, which were not small, directly to Mr. Samuel 'Lefty' Abrams, Board of Directors, Riviera Hotel, for the Riviera, my casino of choice, wound up with all my dough anyway.

"Was I a sucker, a chump, a loser? Of course I was, but I scarcely noticed. The question I would ask myself during those days was not how much did I lose but when would I have enough to go back. This was action to the highest power, around the clock, every day. I loved it.

"Of course when the local casinos started up, I was done for. I used to stop off at them the way another guy might have stopped at a 7/11 to pick up a quart of milk. It didn't take me long to rack up debts of more than two hundred grand. They just built a casino in Des Plaines, the Rivers it's called, a fifteen-minute drive from where I lived with my ex-wife.

"I neglected to mention that I was married and have a fifteen-year-old daughter. You want to talk about rotten luck, my wife's first husband was an alcoholic, then she marries me, a guy hooked on gambling. The night she discovered that I had put a second mortgage on our house and had loans out on both our cars, she said, in a voice so calm that it spooked me, she said, 'You know, Lenny, the nice thing about alcoholics is that at least they pass out.'

"I've probably already gone on too long to say make a long story short, but the fact is that I'm up that famous creek without a paddle, and the bottom of the boat is starting to leak pretty badly. I've got to find a way to get out of action and stay out. The last thing I wanted to be in life was a loser, and I realize that this is what I've become. That's why I've come here for help. I'll shut up now. Apologies for going on so long."

Rothman couldn't recall a better talk in his three years of coming to GA meetings. He sensed everyone else at the table was impressed. Rothman got up to say that if Adler ever needed any help, ever felt himself slipping, he hoped he'd call him. Lenny Adler smiled and said he appreciated the offer, and would no doubt one day take him up on it. The meeting was a fairly brief one. After it was over, Rothman came up to Lenny Adler to tell him that he meant his offer in all seriousness. He gave him his cell and business and home phone numbers.

"The first few months are the toughest," he said.

"I'll hang in there," Adler said.

At next Tuesday's meeting a new member named Arnie Berman got up to say that he thought he might be unusual in this company for he thought of himself as an unusual breed, a conservative, a cautious gambler.

"I've been cautious all my life," he said. "I suppose I got this from my parents. My father was in his middle fifties when I was born, and he'd lived through the Depression. He was full of advice about saving and being careful generally about money. Maybe it was in reaction to him that I took up gambling.

"But the odd part is that I took it up, as I say, conservatively. I bet only favorites. I like ponies, and I found myself betting favorites to place and sometimes even to show. A friend of mine, guy named Art Rosen, also big for the ponies, used to joke that instead of going to the track I should have bought Israeli Bonds—the return was about the same.

"Of course, it wasn't the same. You can bet conservatively and still lose your ass. Which over the years I have done. I might get down big on a heavy favorite—the Patriots against the Jaguars, say—and when I lost, usually owing to the spread, I felt the need to make it back quick. I found myself doubling down a lot. Not so conservative anymore. Anyhow

I figure that over the past decade I'm down maybe a quarter of a million dollars. I'm single. I'm not out on the street. But I'd like to learn how to quit, which is why I'm here tonight."

After the meeting, Lenny came up to Rothman. "Takes all kinds, I guess," he said, nodding his head in the direction of Arnie Berman. "But this guy ain't my idea of a good time. Betting on a horse to show! I'd as soon bet on the Hancock Building to be still standing tomorrow morning. I'm more of a long-shot man myself. In fact, Eddie, I think of my entire life as a longshot."

Lenny Adler missed the next GA meeting, but in the middle of the following week, at 6:30 p.m., in his car on his way home to Northbrook, Rothman got a call from him on his cell.

"Eddie," he said. "I'm in my car and on the way to the Rivers Casino. Please tell me I'm a schmuck and to turn back."

"Easy to do," Rothman said. "You're a schmuck, now turn back. Where are you anyhow?"

"I'm just about to get on the Kennedy at Foster."

"Get off it," Rothman said, "and meet me twenty minutes from now for dinner at an old Chinese restaurant called Kow-Kow on Cicero and Pratt. Got that?"

"Got it," Adler said. "And thanks. You're a friend."

Kow-Kow was an old Cantonese restaurant, at a time when Cantonese was all that was known of Chinese food in Chicago. Rothman remembered it when it was on Devon Avenue. The patrons in the place tonight, most in their eighties, seemed to date from that time. He took a table in the center of the room and ordered a Tsingtoa beer. He studied the menu, which still had Chop Suey and Chow Mein on it. Half an hour later, Adler hadn't yet arrived.

Nor would he. Rothman waited a full hour for him, then called his wife to say he would be home for dinner after all. He thought about calling Adler back. On second thought, he said to himself, screw him.

Lenny Adler did show up for the next GA meeting. He came in ten or so minutes late, and did not greet Rothman. When his turn came to speak he got to his feet and said:

"I missed the last meeting, for the disgraceful reason that I fell off the wagon. Last week I lost twelve hundred bucks, mostly at blackjack, at Rivers Casino. On my way out there I called my new friend Eddie Rothman, who is here with us tonight. Eddie told me to turn back and meet him for dinner at a Chinese restaurant. I was going to do so, then the thought hit me that the problem with Chinese food is that an hour later, you're hungry to be back in action again. A bad joke, OK. But what I do want to say is that after my Rivers Casino adventure I not only felt like a loser, but a guilty loser. Is this progress? I'm not sure. What I am sure about is that it's a mistake for me to miss GA meetings, and I'll try my best not to miss another."

Listening to this, Rothman had his doubts. Lenny Adler was maybe a little too glib. When he suggested a drink to Rothman after the meeting, Rothman took a pass, saying that he had to be up early the next day.

"Another time?" Adler said.

"Right," Rothman said. "Take care."

Driving home, Rothman thought about Lenny Adler's sincerity. Was he serious about coming to Gamblers Anonymous. Or was he just killing time. During his three plus years there, lots of guys, after telling their stories of defeat and heartache, never returned. Maybe the GA arrangement just wasn't for them; they weren't comfortable in it, with its confessional mode. Maybe they were able to straighten themselves out on their own. But most, Rothman thought, went back into action, with predictably disastrous results.

He recalled a young lawyer, guy named Jerry Feingold, a big guy, handsome, played basketball for New Trier, afterwards for Iowa. Went to law school, had a practice in the Loop. He broke down in tears his first night at GA. His father had twice bailed him out of heavy gambling debts, the second time for forty-odd grand. He never came back. A month or so later, Rothman read about his jumping from a window in his 17th floor LaSalle Street office. He'd heard from Marty Handler, the man who ran the Lawrence Avenue GA chapter, that Jerry Feingold had got back into the Mob for more than fifty grand, and felt he couldn't return to his father to ask for more help. He left a wife and two little kids, ten and eight.

When Rothman got home, Debbie told him he had a call from a man named Leonard Adler. She had written down the number.

"Are you ticked off at me for any reason, Eddie?" Adler wanted to know when Rothman called him back. "Did I do something to piss you off?"

"Don't know why you'd think that. You call me for help, I offer it, and you don't show up. Keep me waiting in a Chinese restaurant for an hour. Not so good."

"I owe you an apology. I thought I already made it in public earlier tonight at the meeting."

"What I wonder is whether you're really serious about breaking your gambling fix. Fell off the wagon kinda early, I'd say. I mean, you'll do what you want. But if you aren't serious about this then I would ask you not to come to me for help you don't really want."

"I am serious, Eddie, never been more serious about anything in my goddamn life. Give me another chance, another shot."

"Sure," said Rothman. He thought his voice sounded unconvincing. "Of course. Why not?"

"Thanks, pal. You won't be sorry, I promise."

"I hope not," Rothman said, hoping that in his voice he had buried the doubt he strongly felt.

Lenny Adler showed up for the next four GA meetings. At each of them he sat next to Rothman. At each he spoke briefly, announcing that he had gone without action the week before and felt terrific about it but knew he still had a long ways to go.

After the last of these meetings, he invited Rothman for a drink. Rothman wasn't eager to go, but felt it would be unkind to say no, so they agreed to meet at Burke's. The bar was more crowded tonight than on their previous meeting there. The soundless television sets showed tennis matches, soccer games, night baseball. To Rothman, even after all this time, these games were little more than porno by other means, and he kept himself from looking at the screens.

They found a booth, ordered drinks—a martini for Adler, a vodka and tonic for Rothman.

"Any interest in going to the Bears season's opener on Sunday?" Adler asked. "I've got seats on the forty."

"None whatsoever." Rothman said. "Watching a ball game, any ball game, without having a bet on it would be a torture. It would be like a big-game hunter going on safari with a water pistol. I do better to stay away."

"You really are a disciplinarian, Eddie."

"I may not have many strengths," Rothman said, "but at least I know my weaknesses."

"You're a philosopher."

"Sure," Rothman said, "right. Someone said the unexamined life isn't worth living. The problem is that the examined life isn't much fun."

"Maybe you need a vice," Adler said.

"What'd you have in mind? Drugs? Adultery? Child molestation?"

"I'll need time to come up with the right vice for you. I'm sure it's out there."

"How about you? Was another week out of action tough on you?"

"Truth is, it was. They all are. I'm not as good at admitting to my weaknesses as you are."

"Nothing to do but tough it out."

"Sometimes I think a booze or drug problem might be easier."

"More likely it would only be sloppier."

"When did you know you had the gambling jones beat?"

"I still don't know it. I don't think of having beat it. I think of holding it off. I'm playing for a tie, a draw."

"Not very glorious," Adler said.

"It is if you consider the other possibility. My goal is to avoid humiliation, because, given my style as a gambler, that's the only place gambling can end up for me. Probably a good idea to have a goal here yourself."

"I'll have to think about that," Adler said. "Just now my only goal is not to give away all my money to strangers."

"Not good enough, is my guess," said Rothman. "Something a little more specific is needed."

"I'll think about it. Maybe you'll help me on this one."

"Anything you need," said Rothman, "say the word."

Adler came in late for the following week's GA meeting, toward its close, looking harried. He barely greeted Rothman, then took off after the meeting. The following week he didn't show up at all; nor the two weeks after that. Rothman assumed that he fell off the wagon, and was back in action, with the usual disastrous results.

Then, on a Saturday night, at 2:13 a.m., according to the digital clock beside Rothman's bed, the phone rang and it was Lenny Adler.

"Eddie," he said. "Lenny Adler. This is an outrageous time to call, I know, but I'm in deepest of deep shit, and need your help."

"I'm in my bedroom," Rothman said. "Let me take this downstairs."

Rothman picked up the kitchen phone. He opened and stared into the refrigerator as Lenny Adler continued.

"Here's the thing, Eddie. I'm into the Baretta family for sixty grand. You know about the Barettas?"

"No," said Rothman, taking a pint of Häagen-Dazs peach sorbet out of the freezer. "Who are the Barettas?"

"They're the Mob in Oak Forest, and they're real brutes, killers."

"So," said Rothman, taking a spoon out of the silverware drawer.

"So they showed me a photograph of another guy who owed them roughly the same amount I do. Actually, they showed me a photograph of his hands. They'd cut off his thumbs."

"Why are you telling me this?" Rothman asked, though he already knew the answer.

"Because if I don't have twenty grand, a third of what I owe them, by Tuesday, I'm going to be in the same condition, fuckin' thumbless. I need to borrow the twenty from you, Eddie. There's no one else I can turn to."

"Any guarantee that I would get it back?" Rothman asked. "You haven't exactly proved yourself the most reliable guy in the world, Lenny." Rothman tried to penetrate the peach sorbet holding the spoon without using his thumbs. It couldn't be done.

"If I wasn't scared shit, Eddie, I'd never have made this call. I've never been so terrified in my life."

"Look, Lenny, it's past two in the morning. I'll call you when I get into work tomorrow."

"Thanks, Eddie, thanks. I'll wait to hear from you."

When Rothman arrived at his place on Washington, a block west of Halsted, he saw Lenny Adler's Porsche out front. He had already decided to lend him the twenty grand. Not because he thought he would get it back; he doubted he would. He was stuck, Rothman was, with a conscience. He couldn't allow another human being to be brutalized if he could help it. Rothman recalled the threat in his old bookie Ike Goldstein's voice, and the fear it put into him. Besides, in the more than three years out of action, he had accumulated more than eighty grand in green deals that sat doing nothing in his Midcity Bank vault.

Lenny Adler emerged from his car when Rothman appeared. They walked up the flight of stairs to the door marked Rothman Enterprises. Rothman changed nothing in his father's simple office after his father died; there was still the metal desk, the small chair on wheels, the four metal file cabinets, the plastic *chaise longue* in which his father, in his last years, used to take twenty-minute naps.

"All right, Lenny, I've decided to loan you the money. How about your car as collateral?"

"The car isn't mine," Adler said. "It belongs to the dealership. But I'm not going to let you down, Eddie. How could I? You're saving my life. I'm never going to forget it."

"I'm going to make out an IOU for you to sign. I'd also like to know how you plan to schedule your repayments on the twenty grand."

"First I'll have to repay the Barettas back the other forty I owe them. Then I'll pay you, how about at the rate of two grand a month, beginning six months from now? Does that sound reasonable?"

"It does if it's also realistic."

Adler signed the IOU. Rothman wrote out a personal check for the twenty grand, walked around his desk, and handed it to Adler, who glimpsed it, folded it, and put it in his shirt pocket. Rothman held out his hand. Adler took it, but drew Rothman to him and hugged him.

"You're the real thing," Adler said, "a true *mensch*. I'm more grateful than I can say."

When Lenny Adler didn't show up for the next night's Gambler's Anonymous meeting, Rothman was disappointed but not shocked. Adler also missed the next two GA meetings. Rothman began checking the papers and watching local television news for any word about a man having been the victim of a Mob murder, but there was nothing. He tried calling Adler on his cellphone, but the number was out of service.

After Adler missed the next, his fourth, GA meeting, Rothman called him at Loeber Porsche. He was told that there was no Lenny Adler working as a salesman there, nor had there ever been. They never heard of Leonard Adler at the Somerset Hotel either. He asked his friend Stan Margolis, who fancied himself an amateur expert in local mafia matters, what he knew about the Baretta family. Stan said he never heard of them. When his cancelled check was returned from the bank, it was signed Leonard Adler and then signed below that with the name Ira Lerner.

Rothman realized that he had been conned, and took not the smallest pleasure in the fact that it had been done by a real artist. He had unconsciously slipped back into action and had backed a long shot—what choice had he?—and lost. This was not a story, he decided, that he would ever stand up to tell at Gamblers Anonymous.

Wild About Harry

ONE OF MY FIRST MEMORIES OF MY UNCLE HARRY IS OF HIM SITTING ON THE edge of my bed, just discharged from the Navy after World War II, emptying his duffel bag, extracting gifts for me, his only nephew: one of his white duty hats, a Japanese flag, a canteen, a duty belt, a couple of loose insignia, his dog tags. I was eleven and hadn't seen him for the past four years, during which time he had served on an aircraft carrier in the Pacific. I remember at that moment thinking when I grew older I wanted to be just like him.

Harry could have gone to college on the GI Bill, but after four years in the Navy, he wanted to get back into the world without further delay. His first job out of service was selling men's clothes at a place in the Loop called Syd Jerome. Harry himself looked great in everything he wore. He was six feet tall, broad shouldered, with thick black hair, blue eyes, and a smile that got your attention. Women, my mother said, were crazy about him, always.

Harry was my mother's brother, younger by eight years. Their mother died in my mother's adolescence, so she and her older sister Lillian had a larger part than usual in helping to raise their brother Harold, or Heshie as they called him, then Harry as everyone later referred to him. They spoiled him terribly, according to my mother, but who wouldn't have? He was such an attractive kid, and he became more attractive as he grew older. Nobody, my mother said, could refuse Harry anything.

Harry lived with us in our two-bedroom apartment on Sheridan Road for his first few months after his discharge from the Navy. He shared my room, which had twin beds; he called me "Roomie." We had in common a love of sports. My father, born in Canada, didn't care about baseball or football, because he hadn't grown up playing them as did my Uncle Harry. Before the war Harry, my mother told me, was a star on the Marshall High School basketball team.

The summer of 1945, the year of Harry's return from the war, the Chicago Cubs, with a record of 98 wins and 56 losses, edged out the Cards for the pennant. Harry took me to nine games that summer. We always sat in the centerfield bleachers, where the small-time gamblers sat, betting on nearly every pitch. Harry would begin the afternoon laying down a twenty on the outcome of the game. "Always bet pitchers, never teams, Bobby," he instructed me. During the game, he favored a bet called "two-bucks-no-reach," which meant a bet that the team at bat would or wouldn't have a runner reach second base during their raps. Occasionally, he would take a flyer on a 13–1 home run bet. "A real sucker bet, kid," he told me, "but what the hell, everyone ought to try a long shot now and then."

Everyone in the centerfield bleachers knew Harry. He was a sport, buying beers for people and filling his nephew with hot dogs, Cracker Jacks, peanuts, pop. A guy named Lou Markowitz, also known as the Junk Man, who had a scrap-iron yard on Western, would arrive at the beginning of the sixth inning, always unshaven, wearing a fatigue jacket, and take layoff bets. Down on the field, Phil Cavarretta, Andy Pafko, Swish Nicholson, Stan Hack, and the other Cubs were crushing the ball, on their way to a World Series, where they met their defeat, as per Harry's theory, at the hands of a great Detroit Tigers pitcher named Hal "Prince" Newhouse. It was the best summer of my boyhood.

After one of the games—Claude Passeau had pitched a three-hitter against the Reds—Harry took me with him to a crap game held in a storage shed in the Fulton Market. Six or seven fairly tough-looking working-class guys and three young blacks were in the game. Even at the age of eleven, I felt an atmosphere of menace. Harry didn't feel it at all. He walked away more than four hundred dollars winner, and on the way home dropped two twenty-dollar bills on my lap. "That's for being my lucky charm, Bobby," he said. I hid the money in my sock drawer and never mentioned it to my parents.

Harry also took me to Windy City league softball games. He played for Midland Motors, one of the more prominent teams. He looked terrific in his gray uniform, with red and blue letters, outlined in white, a thick red stripe on the outer seam of the pants. Harry played first base, and was a left-handed power hitter. He had acquired a cream-colored Plymouth convertible, and I used to carry his bats and spikes from the trunk of the car into the dugout. Harry arranged to get me a Midland Motors shirt, which I wore around the neighborhood and would have slept in had my father not frowned on it. The shirt was the only item of my clothes of which my father disapproved.

"What do you want to wear a shirt advertising someone else's business?" he said. "I can get you sandwich boards advertising my own business, if that's the kind of thing you go in for."

I loved my father, though he didn't always make it easy. I didn't see all that much of him, for one thing. He worked a seventy-hour week, including Saturdays. He was in the appliance-parts business, had a warehouse on West Irving Park, and, as I was later to discover when I saw him in action there, came most alive when at his "place," as he called it. He had no hobbies, no recreations, no interests, really, outside his business, which he mastered through long hours of study and hard work.

My father was short (maybe 5'6"), stocky (about 180), with a heavy beard—he had to shave twice a day, if he and my mother went out in the evening—and his prematurely gray hair began receding early. He never cared much about clothes, or food, or material things generally. After we had gone to dinner one night at a restaurant called Grassfield's, one of the car parkers asked him the kind and color of his car. "Oldsmobile," he answered, but had to check with my mother for the car's color (maroon).

My father saw it as his job to remind me how a man ought to act. When I went up to kiss him for buying me a Rawlings baseball glove for my ninth birthday, he said, "Men don't kiss, Bobby. They shake hands." When I shook my father's hand, he said: "You call that a handshake? I call that a dead fish you've put in my hand. Always give a man a firm handshake, Bobby." He squeezed mine.

You didn't have to be a genius to notice that my father wasn't crazy about his brother-in-law. He never said anything against him, not in my presence anyhow. But I felt it, and it made sense, or so I told myself at the time. Here was this handsome guy, my Uncle Harry, to whom everything seemed to come easily, whereas my father scratched and struggled and planned for all that he had. I doubt my father ever mentioned his feeling about Harry even to my mother, whose admiring love for her younger brother was unwavering. If Harry sensed my father's antipathy toward him, he never showed it. Had he known about it, I'm not sure he would have cared. Harry was accustomed to the world's affection. What did he know about antipathy?

After he moved out of our apartment and into a place of his own on State Parkway, Harry continued to come over for Jewish holiday dinners, usually with a different knockout lady friend in tow. He had left Syd Jerome, was now selling Chryslers for Midland Motors, and apparently doing very well at it, or so I judged from the slight swagger of prosperity about him.

I naturally saw a lot less of him. He had asked that I drop the Uncle bit and just call him Harry—he was, he reminded me, only thirteen years older than I. From time to time, he would call to inquire if I wanted to go to a fight or a Blackhawks game at Chicago Stadium or a Bears game at Wrigley Field. The answer was invariably yes, of course I wanted to. Harry always had the best seats. He wore a suit and tie to Bears games, under a camel hair coat, with a white silk scarf, soft black kid gloves, a gleaming shine on his black loafers.

When I was sixteen, my friend Arnie Ginsburg reported to me that he saw my Uncle Harry driving slowly through heavy traffic on Rush Street early one evening in a red Chrysler Imperial convertible, top down, with Patti Page at his side. "It was like Cleopatra floating down the Nile in her barge with Mark Antony," Arnie said. Miss Patti Page, the Singin' Rage! Nothing was beyond Harry.

My father had to have known about my infatuation with his brother-in-law. He must have sensed my excitement on those nights when Harry was taking me to some sporting event or other. I don't suppose he looked on Harry as a rival, exactly, but maybe, now that I look back on it, he wouldn't have been wrong to do so.

I never bothered to formulate it at the time, but my father and his brother-in-law had two distinct and very different ideas about how the world worked. My father operated on the assumption that the world was a fairly orderly place and for the most part amenable to reason, control over which was found in the wisdom encapsulated in a small number of maxims, which he repeated from time to time as part of his continuing instruction to me on how to be a man: Nobody gives anything away. Work for someone else and your fate won't be your own. You always want to put something aside; stay liquid. Pay your debts on time, if not ahead of time. A man's word is his bond. People know more about you than you think.

I'm not sure Harry, presented with these maxims, would've known what the hell my father was talking about. If Harry had to write down his own notions about how the world worked—an unimaginable proposition to begin with—they might have included the following: Let Paris be gay, and the world is composed of winners and losers, your choice. I favored my Uncle Harry's catechism over my father's.

On my seventeenth birthday, Harry took me out for ribs at Singapore, on Rush Street. The bartender in the place didn't have to ask but already knew what he drank: a Gibson, very dry. Harry and I talked sports, as usual, and he filled me in on the latest gossip about likely trades in the works for Chicago teams. He was always in possession of inside information in these matters. After dinner, Harry said there was someone he wanted me to meet.

We walked across the street to the Maryland Hotel and took an elevator to the ninth floor. Harry knocked on the door. A young blonde woman wearing a kimono and not much else invited us in. I walked into her apartment and heard the door close behind me. I looked back, and Harry was gone.

"Hi, Bobby," she said. "I'm Jackie. Your uncle has arranged for me to be your seventeenth birthday present. Take off your jacket, sweetie, get comfortable."

One morning my mother told me that Harry had moved to California. If she knew why, she didn't say. All she said was that he had certain business opportunities in Los Angeles that he felt needed to be looked into. Now that he was living two thousand miles away, Harry's was not a name much spoken of in our household. Whether my mother or his sister, Lillian, were in regular touch, I didn't know. I only knew that I missed him.

I was twenty, about to finish my second year at the University of Illinois at Navy Pier, and bored out of my gourd. If there was anything going on for me in those gray classrooms, I missed it. My father, who had himself never gone to college, and who I sometimes felt thought that a college education tended to reduce a person's perceptions of reality, had more than once told me that, when I was ready, there was a place for me in his expanding business. I had only to say the word. My father was a fair man, but I had seen him at his place and had a strong sense that he used up almost all the oxygen in the joint, and that there was likely to be little left over for his son or anyone else.

So, after not being in touch with him for more than two years, I called Harry in Los Angeles.

"Hey! Great to hear from you, Bobby," he said, sounding very much his old self.

"You, too," I said, and I never meant anything more in my life.

"What's doing, kid?"

"That's the problem, Harry, not much is doing. My life's a kind of two-buck-no-reach bet, and I haven't had anyone on first the whole game, if you know what I mean."

"Look, why don't you come out to the Coast? I'll send you an airplane ticket. L.A. is a pretty amazing place. We'll find something out here for you."

This was exactly what I was hoping Harry would say. I thought it would be best to come on a bit cautious, though, so I told him that the idea seemed fine, but I needed a few days to think about it and would call him back.

When I told my father I was contemplating moving to Los Angeles to live with Harry for a while, he showed no uneasiness, but asked me what, precisely, I had in mind.

"I thought I'd hang around with Uncle Harry for a while and see what turns up."

"You relying on Harry to find work for you?" he asked.

"I suppose I will be, yes."

"Do you have any notion of why your uncle moved to California in the first place?"

When I told my father that I didn't, he explained to me that one morning Harry had decided to bet twenty grand, spread around with five different bookies, on a baseball game—and lost. He didn't have the money to pay up. Not a good position to be in with the Chicago mob; an unpaid debt of twenty thousand dollars figured to result in two shattered kneecaps, at a minimum. Harry, my father told me, borrowed the twenty grand from his sister, my Aunt Lillian, who had never married and wasn't all that well off. My father told me that when he found out about it, he had given the money back to his sister-in-law with the understanding that when Harry had paid her, she would return it to him.

"Your Uncle Harry's a man who has to grab the whole world," my father said. "He's not big on patience."

"People are different, Dad," I said. "It takes all kinds."

"I suppose it does," my father said, "but I wonder if a person shouldn't be extra careful in choosing which kind in particular he wants to stake his future on."

Off I went to Los Angeles, with six hundred dollars my father gave me to tide me over until I found work. Harry picked me up at the airport. He was driving a small black Mercedes convertible, with white leather seats. On the way to his apartment in Westwood, he told me that I was likely to find L.A. wildly different than Chicago.

"It's not just a different place, Bobby," Harry said, "it's more like a different planet. Everyone here is some crazy combination of malcontent and dreamer. Everyone has a complaint and also a scheme. They were unhappy where they were, and so they came out here, lured by the weather, the glamour of Hollywood, who knows what else, to find what they didn't find back home. The other day, the cops picked up a serial killer. The newspapers reported they discovered in the trunk of his car two screenplays the guy had written. Everyone here, but everyone, is on the hustle."

I neglected to ask Harry what his own hustle was. He was working for the William Morris talent agency. He described his job as analogous to what an account executive does in an advertising agency. He looked after clients, amusing them, supplying their needs, massaging their egos. His current main client was a black singer-dancer who did impressions. I had seen him more than once on *Ed Sullivan*. I asked Harry what he did for him?

"You're not going to believe this, but every afternoon, between two and four, I go over to his place and we strap on holsters with cap guns and practice fast-drawing. He's obsessed with having a fast draw, please don't ask me why. I also let him beat me at golf, a game I've had to learn since I came out here. And sometimes we go out on double dates together. I'm kinda his friend, except of course I'm not, and we both know it. As long as our firm is collecting large commissions on his television appearances, Vegas dates, and occasional movie roles, he retains the right to be a spoiled child. That's the way it works."

As Harry was telling me about the work he was doing, I was reminded of the joke my father liked to tell about the kid who runs away to join the circus. Some twenty years later, the circus returns to his hometown, and his family comes out to see him. At the end of the circus parade, as the elephants pass, the guy, no longer a kid, is sweeping up the elephant droppings with a wide broom. When, after the show, his older brother tells him that his work is degrading, not even up to undignified, and that he must find something else to do with his life, the guy, shocked, answers, "What! And leave show business?"

"What I really want to get into is movie production," Harry said. "Big dough there, over-the-top dough, you wouldn't believe the numbers. I need to find the angle. It could take some time." I remembered what my father had said about his brother-in-law's lack of patience and wondered if he would be able to ride out the wait.

Harry's Mercedes, which turned out to be leased for him by the William Morris Agency, led me to think he would be living in a much grander place than his one-bedroom apartment in Westwood, which was small and dark. He said I could stay with him for a few days but fairly soon would need to find a place of my own, since he often had visitors there, by which I took him to mean women. He had inquired about the possibility of my working in the mailroom at William Morris, but the agency had nothing to offer at that moment. He wasn't sure what else was out there for me but felt certain that there had to be something that would turn up soon. He would keep his eye peeled. If I needed him, needed him for anything at all, I was to call on him.

I bought an old car, a two-door 1947 Chevy, and rented the extra bedroom in the bungalow of an elderly widow named Susan Singer on Overland Street. (Whenever I saw her, I used to wonder if she, too, had a few screenplays of her own locked away somewhere.) The *Los Angeles Times* Help Wanted section had nothing in the way of work for me, and so I spent my days driving around, wasting gas and money, looking for help-wanted signs, and beginning to feel that maybe this move wasn't such a hot idea. I had left my phone number for Harry at William Morris when I moved into Mrs. Singer's bungalow but hadn't heard a word from him in more than a week.

I cobbled together a resume of sorts—it was pretty pathetic, working for Sanders Drug Store in my teens and for my father's business on Saturdays—and sent out copies of it to the various movie studios and large corporations I found in the Yellow Pages, with extreme doubt about why they would want to hire me to do what, in my introductory letter, I wasn't very specific about wanting to do for them. Finally, I took a job at a subway-sandwich joint called Monty's, just off the UCLA campus. I wore a paper hat and thin rubber gloves and, behind a high counter, chopped lettuce and sliced tomatoes and assembled sandwiches all day.

I can't remember any days that seemed so long. My fellow workers at Monty's were chiefly Mexicans, most without much English. I made no connection with the students at UCLA who came into the restaurant. As for girls, I figured luscious California co-eds were unlikely to find much to interest them in a guy wearing a paper hat.

At the end of another week, I still hadn't heard from Harry. I went over to his apartment on three different occasions, rang the bell, but no answer. Nights I kept pretty much to my room, occasionally taking in a movie. Days went by when I barely spoke to anyone. This was my first encounter with extended loneliness, and I found it was not at all to my taste. I had no gift for solitude. Where the hell, I wondered, was Harry?

After the third week in L.A., I called again at William Morris and learned that Harry had left the agency and gone to Europe. The woman

I spoke with said that she didn't know why he had left and was sorry but she had no further information.

I didn't want to return to Chicago, at least not too soon, if only because to do so would confirm my father in his judgment of Harry and of my foolishness in expecting anything of him. But what, exactly, had I expected? That he would help me find interesting work? That I would share his apartment and we should once again become roomies? That we would go to Dodgers games and win small bets? That he would pop girls from some L.A. equivalent of the Maryland Hotel into my bed? Harry was in his mid-thirties and intent on a career. A nephew around his neck was probably a drag he didn't need, though why I didn't think of that before I came out here I don't know. Still, to leave for Europe without a word, that seemed to be, I don't know, not quite right.

I continued at Monty's, making subs during the day, and at night I read detective stories in my room. My landlady invited me to watch television with her, but I took a pass on the offer. On my days off I drove down to Laguna Beach, where I sat on the beach and stared at pretty girls. The days creaked slowly by, and still nothing from Harry. I was hoping he might call or send me a letter from Europe explaining why he had left Los Angeles without a word. The man who gave me the best summer of my boyhood was now giving me the worst summer of my life.

Toward the end of August, I couldn't take it anymore, and I called my parents to announce that I was returning home. Over the phone my mother sounded pleased; my father didn't say anything. The Chevy, which held up nearly the entire way back to Chicago, broke down just outside Hammond, Indiana. I had to call from a gas station to have my father wire me $140 to have something called a throw-out bearing replaced. Not exactly a triumphal return.

My father never said a word about my failed California adventure, which was a relief. When we were alone, my mother asked about her brother, and after I explained his disappearance, she allowed that Harry could sometimes act impulsively and said no more about it.

That fall I enrolled at Roosevelt University, where I declared myself a political science major. My interest in school was no greater than before, but I was determined to finish, and I did. After being drafted and spending two years in the Army, all of it in Missouri, Texas, and Arkansas, I went into my father's business.

I was wrong about my father's using up all the oxygen in the joint, for he trained me carefully about the various aspects of his business and told me he hoped I would take it over someday, which I have now done. I have two sons of my own, and neither, I regret to report, is the least interested in going into what has proved a very profitable business, so what my father built and I carried on will probably die.

As for Harry, I learned from my Aunt Lillian, who kept in close touch with him, that when he had gone off to Europe, he did so with a client, a starlet thought promising at the time whose marriage was breaking up. Harry became her exclusive agent, and through her—I don't know any of the intricate details—somehow worked his way into producing movies.

Watching late-night or Turner Classic Movies I sometimes note, under the title of associate or executive producer, and more rarely producer, the name Harold Abrams; you doubtless have seen and not noticed the name yourself, one of scores of such Jewish-sounding names that show up in movie credits. So far as I know, Harry worked exclusively on B or below films, nothing memorable, but he apparently made a very good living.

In his forties, Harry married a woman, a widow six years older than he, whose husband had been an important figure during the Hollywood studio days. Lillian flew out to the wedding and brought back a photograph that showed Harry in a cutaway wearing a mustache. Among the guests was Frank Sinatra. His wife had children from her first marriage, and they had no children together. They lived in her large house in Beverly Hills. When Lillian died, Harry sent flowers but didn't come to Chicago for the funeral.

Harry died six years later, of pancreatic cancer. He was sixty-eight. My mother went, by herself, to his funeral. When I asked her what the funeral was like, she reported that her brother had twenty-seven ultra-suede sport jackets in his bedroom closet; she had counted. "Every color imaginable," she said.

"Oh, and one thing more," my mother said, "a lady friend of Harry's, a woman who looked to be in her forties, apparently his mistress for several years, showed up at the funeral, which outraged his wife. Back at the house, after the burial, she stomped around and called him a son of a bitch, a bastard, and everything else she could think of. Who can blame her? But, you know, that's Harry."

When my mother left the room, my father took me aside to inform me that his brother-in-law had never repaid the twenty grand he had borrowed from his sister Lillian. "That's Harry, too," my father said, and walked out of the room.

Widow's Pique

LARRY HAS BEEN DEAD IT WILL BE A MONTH PRECISELY THIS THURSDAY, AND until now Deborah Siskin hasn't had the courage—or is it the energy?—to go through the house and remove his things. Energy can't be the problem, for she is, within her small circle of friends and colleagues, known for her tirelessness. Deborah is head of the department of orthodontics at the University of Illinois School of Dentistry; she raised three children, two now successful physicians, the other a lawyer. Until her husband's death, she continued to cook dinner five or six nights a week after a full day's work—Saturdays, she and Larry went out for Chinese food and a movie—and even found time to iron his shirts. No, not energy but courage is the problem, courage of a peculiar kind—the courage needed to face the meaning of her marriage of nearly forty-three years. In Larry's closet, Deborah finds one suit, which she bought him to wear to accompany her to official dental school functions or to the occasional Jewish charity dinners to which she dragged him. He owned two blue blazers, one for teaching, one for travelling. She also took him to buy these. He had little sense of clothes, and with the passing years even less interest. His twelve or so shirts and nine ties (at least the unstained ones) she will take, along with the suit and blazers and odd trousers and his raincoat and down-filled winter coat, to donate to the ORT charity shop. His socks and underwear and handkerchiefs and three pairs of shoes and slippers and tired terry-cloth bathrobe she'll toss out.

The problem is Larry's various collections. Over the years, he had bought the jerseys for all the National Football League teams, both past and present. He collected model cars from the Franklin Mint, about fifty of these. He also bought antique model-train cars, sometimes spending three or four hundred dollars for them. Then there are his first editions; he was always claiming that his first edition of some now-forgotten novelist—Stanley Elkin, Vance Bourjaily, George P. Elliott—was selling for $145 or some such price, though Deborah scarcely listened when he told her such things and anyhow she has no notion where to sell these books for the sums he mentioned, if such sums are really available. The largest collection of all was his classical music CDs, not to speak of the old vinyl recordings that he kept in boxes in the basement. Maybe the university, Northeastern Illinois, where Larry taught political science for the last thirty years, would want all this stuff, though Deborah knows that the big problem nowadays in universities is finding space even for its own things.

Forty-two years ago in December, Deborah had married an attractive young man, full of promise, who, as they grew older, she watched slowly lose all that promise. She never confronted him with it; in the early years, she pretended it wasn't happening. She didn't want to admit the loss to herself. Life meanwhile rushed by. She finished dental school, then went into private practice; they had a daughter and then two sons. The question of divorce never occurred to her; she was not a divorcing woman. Instead, Larry somehow became her fourth child, one who drove a car and brought in some income, though nowhere near as much as she.

Larry didn't keep a checkbook; when they went out to dinner, Deborah, at the end of the meal, used her credit card to pay. She paid all their bills, was in charge of investing their savings, had the first and last word on raising their children, dealt with car salesmen when it came time to buy new cars. Charlie Malkin, her colleague at the dental school, was astonished when she told him about the last. "Really, Deborah," he said, "you mean Larry lets you go in there, a woman, alone, to dance with those wolves? Amazing!"

Her older sister Sharon didn't much care for Larry, and didn't mind saying so. Sharon once told Deborah that, in marrying Larry Siskin, it was as if, in the old shtetl culture of Eastern Europe, she had married a brilliant yeshiva student whom her father had agreed to support for five or six years so that he could continue his studies. "Except," Sharon added, cruelly, "Larry turns out to be not all that brilliant, and the five or six years has turned into a lifetime, with you doing the supporting."

Larry came from a wealthy family, much wealthier than the Pollocks, Deborah's own family. The Siskins lived in a vast apartment at 3400 N. Lake Shore Drive. His father and mother were both lawyers, and his older brother Mel had recently graduated from Yale Law School. He had a younger sister, Roberta, who had intended to—and eventually did—go to law school, Harvard, in fact. Larry joked that the family dog, a cocker spaniel named Rusty, had just been accepted for law school at Fordham. He never quite said that he thought himself too good for law school, but managed to convey that going into law was a pedestrian choice, a touch demeaning, something rather *declassé*.

As a young man, Larry was handsome, with dark hair combed in an ambitious pompadour, on the model of the pop singers of the day (Frankie Avalon, Ricky Nelson, Fabian); his flared nostrils gave his youthful face a dramatic look, suggesting, Deborah used to think, reserves of passion. His walk had a swagger, which later turned into something like a sashay; when he entered a room, his presence seemed to announce, All right, I'm here, things can now officially begin; it still did, but nobody any longer cared.

Deborah used to remind herself of the Larry she married through looking at old photographs. But whenever she took out old family photograph albums, that young man her husband seemed to her a stranger. Larry began to lose his hair in his early thirties, the one physical element in his makeup about which he was touchy. He had put on weight. He had grown sallow, for he had been discovered to have diabetes of a kind serious enough to cause him to take insulin and which slowed him down in various ways, not least in the bedroom. But saddest of all, though you had to look carefully to notice, a look of disappointment insinuated itself in his face, especially when he was tired, which seemed to be much of the time.

As a graduate student in political philosophy at the University of Chicago, Larry had come under the influence of a teacher named Hans Morgenthau. A German émigré, Jewish, of the school of *Realpolitick*, Morgenthau, a conservative thinker who had nonetheless opposed the Vietnam War, put Larry in touch with an important undersecretary at the State Department named George Ball, who also opposed the war. Morgenthau suggested Larry drop out of graduate school and become George Ball's protégé, and from there work his way up through the ranks of the State Department and into a life of high-level diplomacy. But Larry and Ball found too many things to disagree about, or so Larry claimed. He talked about being let down, betrayed, hinting that anti-Semitism held him back at State. After three years living in Washington, it became clear that a diplomatic career wasn't going to work out. They returned to Chicago, where Larry re-enrolled in graduate school, but now with much diminished, even shrivelled expectations.

As a graduate student, he took his time, a little more than six years, finishing his course work and writing a dissertation on Machiavelli for his PhD. Deborah was by then in private practice. They had some help from Larry's father when they bought a small house in Lincolnwood. Larry was kept on for six more years as a teacher in the political science department at Chicago, but he wrote almost nothing during this time. He complained a lot about the ignorance of his students, and even more about the wretchedness of his colleagues. When his six years were up, Chicago—no surprise here—did not offer him tenure.

Larry was lucky, or so everyone but he thought, to land a job at Northeastern, teaching political philosophy, but he didn't look at it this way. A city school, tucked away in the residential Albany Park neighborhood, most of Northeastern's students worked full-time at other jobs and were aiming for degrees they hoped would give them a leg up in the job market. Despite his not having written anything since his dissertation, Larry's PhD from Chicago carried some cachet at Northeastern. Still, it was a great comedown from his dreams of an important job at the State Department to be teaching Hispanics, Palestinians, and middle-aged Jewish housewives about the subtleties of Rousseau, John Locke, and Montesquieu. But Larry was by then in his middle-thirties with nowhere else to go.

Deborah wonders if she should have said something to him, told him to get off his duff, he had a good mind and was still young, what could possibly be the point of his settling for a life of indolence and complaint? But she never did. She had just established her academic connection at the University of Illinois, her children were growing up—her own life was full, so full that not even an unhappy husband could drag it down.

Soon Deborah began to wonder if her Larry's early promise was real. She can scarcely remember. Marrying in one's early twenties, as she had done, is of course an act of foolishness, though in her generation everyone seemed to do it. She had married a man she then thought of as attractive, not unkind, with prospects of doing serious work. Did she love him? Or did she instead feel a touch sorry for him, as she might for a relative with a serious handicap?

The rapture had long ago departed from the marriage. Larry's diabetes, which worsened over the years, put him all but out of business in the rapture department. She, Deborah, had lots of chances for love affairs—she travelled four or five times a year to academic dental conventions and conferences around the country—but chose not to venture into that land-mined field. Larry, meanwhile, seemed more interested in sex from the voyeuristic angle. She was always catching him staring at bosomy young women; when they went to movies with what she thought of as painfully slow-motion fornication scenes, she didn't know where to put her eyes, but noticed her husband staring at the screen with great concentration.

One night, at a fund-raising dinner for the dental school, one of the guests at their table, a man named Jim Breakstone, a successful personal injury lawyer, asked Larry what he did for a living. When Larry told him that he taught political philosophy, Breakstone replied: "A sweet racket. I envy you."

"What do you mean, racket?" Larry asked.

"I mean you've got the dream deal. You work six, maybe seven, months a year, no pressures, no responsibilities, just talking all day to young people who can't even tell you you're full of crap. Pretty nice, if you ask me."

Larry didn't answer, but merely shot Breakstone a look of contempt, and didn't speak to him again through the remainder of the evening. On the drive home, he castigated him to Deborah, non-stop, all the way from the Loop to their house in Evanston.

"That uncouth bastard, a fucking personal injury lawyer, thinks I have a racket. He should only know how hard I work at perfecting my lectures! Or the amount of time I put into grading my students' papers. I'd like to see him try to write my book on Hobbes!" And on and on, for fifteen miles. This was the first Deborah had heard that her husband was writing a book on Hobbes. At Larry's death, no trace of the manuscript was found.

Larry's last years of teaching were his worst. He chose not to learn how to use a computer. He loathed the new regime in universities—the rise of feminism, multi-culturalism, affirmative action—and he couldn't stop himself from making sly remarks in the classroom about how these changes were lowering the standards of higher education. One of his re-marks—he claimed John Locke was not "what one might call a strong gy-nocentric thinker, he didn't even know where the gynocentre was"—was reported to the department chairman, a Latina named Mary Rodriguez, who took it to the dean. The result was a letter of reprimand from the president of the university, an African-American. Larry responded to this letter by turning in his resignation, at the age of sixty-two.

Not that retirement changed his life all that much, at least not out-wardly. But Larry had begun to turn more and more in on himself. He be-gan watching daytime television and would report to Deborah when she returned from work who had been on Oprah that morning. The backseat of his car was piled up with books and CDs. He would sit in the room he called his study and listen to Glenn Gould play *The Goldberg Variations* over and over. At night, he watched baseball or basketball games. He and Deborah had long ceased going to bed at the same time. He was always a restless sleeper, and had in recent years begun to snore. Deborah wanted to suggest that they sleep in different rooms—every day was a full day for her, and she needed her sleep—but she hadn't the heart to do so, thinking it would only mean another rejection for him. She began to pity this man she had once loved.

Now that Larry is dead, Deborah tries to remember why she let things drift. Could she have roused her husband to shed his bitterness, resent-ments, trivial envy? Would the threat of divorce have stirred and reig-nited his lost ambition? Although she had never allowed herself to think about divorce, there were countless times when she wished she had no connection with Larry. Going out with other couples, which they did less and less, was always worrisome. He would get going on one of his obsessions—the dopiness of feminism, the emptiness of African-American Studies programs, the awfulness of rock 'n' roll, the ignorance of the young—and invariably take things a step too far, coming across as a crank. Deborah waited at such moments to find a place to barge into her husband's tirades to change the subject as smoothly as possible, which wasn't always easy.

She worried about him. She worried that he would embarrass himself, that others would see through him, that his act fooled no one. The act, of course, was that he was a superior person forced to live in a cheapened culture, where—the unspoken part—his own talents went unappreciated. She hated the notion that people would think him petty in his complaints, neurotic in his behavior, a fool and, yes, a loser. She didn't take it well when her sister Sharon noted how remarkable it was that so lazy a man as Larry held such high standards. She could live with a husband who had turned out to be a flop. What she minded—more for him more than for herself—was that other people saw through him.

The one thing in which Larry didn't let her down was in his love for their children, which was unfaltering. He was proud of them, of their accomplishments, of how well they turned out. When their daughter Lisa told Deborah that she had caught Kenny, her husband, cheating on her, Deborah was surprised at Larry's cool sense of command in taking the matter in hand. She heard him, over the phone with his daughter in Denver, ask all the right questions in an authoritative and yet calming voice: Did Lisa want him back? And if so, under what terms? Would she be willing to allow him, her father, to speak to Kenny, letting him know what was at stake and whether he understood what it was going to cost him to enjoy his little entertainments? How far did she want him, her father, to go? The next day he called Kenny and, as he told Deborah he would do, laid the lumber to him. He let him know that he was going to turn the case over to a tiger divorce specialist in his father's old firm. When it was over, he told him, he would be lucky to have his Bronco season tickets left. As Deborah sat listening to him, he seemed masterly. This, she couldn't help thinking, was more like the man she thought she had married. Her son-in-law returned to Lisa, all contrition, backed, no doubt, by the fear instilled in him by his father-in-law.

But then Larry soon enough reverted to the griper and small-advantage man he had become. When he sprained his ankle, for example, he acquired a handicap parking sign that he continued to use long after the ankle was better. He would take in old clothes to the Salvation Army and ask large tax write-offs for them. While still teaching, he began secreting Jiffy book bags from the department at school, bags for which he had no real use. What, as the kids say, was that about?

Deborah had never said a word about these things. She had felt the need to correct him, gently, only when she felt he was in danger of humiliating himself, which, with the passing years, became more and more frequent. When he would complain to her alone about the dismalness of his colleagues, the dehumanization of computers, the atmosphere of victimhood that dominated the country, she would let him, pretending to but not really listening; she had heard it all so many times before.

And now Larry was dead, beyond hope, beyond correction. His death had been sudden, a stroke, brought on by his diabetes, suffered at a traffic light, in Chicago, on his way home from buying more CDs at a used-record shop he had found on Clark Street. Had Larry's death been a slow one—a cancer death, say, or a disease of the nerves—they might have had time to talk about all this, about what had happened to all his brilliant plans, about whether she should have pushed him more than she did, and so much more.

Years ago, at a dinner party, Deborah listened with interest when at table one of the guests, a divorced woman with a leathery suntan, claimed that love was never entirely equal. In every love affair or marriage, one party was more deeply invested in the relationship than the other, and that, this woman claimed, it was probably better to be the less deeply invested party. When she and Larry were first married, as she thought about it now, she probably loved him more than he had loved her—no probably about it, she was certain of it. Larry seemed the one more at ease in the world, a young man used to getting his way, the person who at a party had only to stand off in a corner for other people to come up to him. He had his brilliant future, and she felt herself lucky—privileged even—to be along for the ride.

Slowly over the years, the balance changed. Deborah couldn't say for certain that Larry loved her more than she loved him, but he grew more dependent on her, at first for small things, later for decisive ones. Although Larry outwardly showed a superiority to his colleagues, he had inwardly begun to lose his confidence, and he would come to Deborah to ask if he had behaved correctly in one or another of his many confrontations with deans and his department chairman. Often he hadn't, or so she thought, and she felt that she had to let him know that his behavior was out of line. At first, she did so in the gentlest manner she could devise, but later she told him when he was wrong in the way a parent might correct a ten-year-old child.

Deborah couldn't help wonder if she had had a hand in Larry's slow downfall. He had his flaws, God knows, serious ones, but was she too naturally competent, too impatient with dithering, too good at carrying out all her tasks, so that her husband left everything to her but his petty disputes and idiosyncratic interests? She was perfectly content to leave him in his room listening to his music, looking at catalogues from the Franklin Mint, reading (the better to mock) the published work of contemporaries whose success he despised, collecting his model cars, and cultivating his many grievances.

There were times when she wished that Larry had had love affairs, one even strong enough to encourage him to leave her. What a relief it would have been! But his death, somehow, wasn't a relief at all. She remembered the last line of a Noel Coward song called *The Widow*, which ran, "I'm wearing beautiful mourning, oh what a beautiful day." But she felt none of that. What she chiefly felt was waste—and what a miserable mistake it had all been.

Years ago, she had read a short story—she couldn't remember who wrote it—about a man who goes into a cinema and discovers that the movie is about the courtship of his parents. As his father, in the movie, finally asks his mother to marry him, the man shouts out something like, "No. Don't do it! Don't do it!" Standing there, before her dead husband's closet, she imagines herself in the part of the man's mother in the movie; like her, she had made the mistake of doing it, of saying yes to the wrong man, Larry Siskin. She couldn't have known he was the wrong man at the time, but so he turned out to be.

Deborah tries to remember when she had emotionally if not actually disengaged from her marriage to Larry. He probably wasn't even aware of it; she herself may not have been. But disengage she did, once she began to sense that he wasn't going to come through in any serious way, but would instead give his days over to playing with his toys and grousing and brooding on his stunted career. She had her professional life; she had her children. She has long ago achieved independence—financially and in every other way.

Standing in front of her dead husband's closet, Deborah tries to imagine the kind of husband she might once have wished to have had. That perfect man, kind, gentle, modest, thoughtful, successful, a patient and proficient lover, Deborah realizes that he probably doesn't exist. Except for the modesty part, she supposes that, when she first married him, she held out hopes that Larry might turn out to be such a husband. A serious error, she decides, looking at the tired clothes in her Larry's closet. Yet she also decides that in some sick way Larry was the perfect husband for her. She would probably not, with a less neurotically self-absorbed man, have been allowed to live her own life as independently as she has.

Folding up Larry's shirts for the ORT bag, Deborah wondered why her thoughts about her marriage seem to press so insistently on her just now. Surely, it was better, as the common wisdom had it, to forget all the negative things about the dead and remember only what was best about them. The fact is that, all the while she and Larry lived together, in a busy life she never stopped to analyze their relationship, at least not in a concentrated way. She could live easily enough with letting things drift. Why was it important she make a final, a definite, judgment now? Was she seeking—what was that dopey word?—closure? Whenever she heard anyone talk about "coming to closure," she used to think of "closure" as an expensive spa in southern California. Welcome to Closure.

Deborah has now folded up the rest of Larry's clothes. She has decided to call in her son Steven, the cardiologist and the only one of her children living in Chicago, to deal with the Franklin Mint and railroad cars and football jerseys, baseball hats, the old records, the CDs, and the rest. She has also decided not to bother with the first edition novels; she'll just give them to the Evanston Library for its next book sale.

Larry's clothes fit into four shopping bags, and Deborah loads them into the trunk of her Volvo. She feels a sudden urgency to get them out of the house. Driving from her house on Isabella, in northwest Evanston, she takes Sheridan Road, which leads into Chicago Avenue, where, near Main, ORT is. But then, at Church Street, she finds herself taking a left, and driving down to the lake. She parks, illegally, near a pier that divides a small boat launch and a dog beach. No one is at the dog beach at the moment; it is October and too late for small boats to be in the waters of Lake Michigan.

Deborah removes the four shopping bags containing Larry's clothes from the trunk of her car, and, carrying two in each hand, she walks out to the end of the L-shaped pier. She empties one bag after another into the choppy water. The clothes do not sink but follow the current heading southward, toward downtown, a clear view of whose skyscrapers is available from the end of the pier. Her dead husband's dark blue down-filled coat, spread out in the water, looks, in the middle-distance, like a raft. She takes one last look at the clothes bobbing and floating away, gathers up the four empty shopping bags, and heads back to the Volvo. In the car, she turns on the ignition, looks into the rear-view mirror to check what the wind out on the pier has done to her hair, and discovers she is smiling. Not her usual, deanly, official, welcoming smile, but a smile with a slight smirk, and a touch, maybe just a touch, of the vindictive to it.

Second Family

A SENIOR PARTNER IN THE FIRM OF STONE, VINER, FUTTERMAN AND WALLER, employing thirty-seven lawyers, partners, and associates, David Futterman has stayed late at the office this evening to go over the briefs for three different cases on which Stacy Shanahan, one of the firm's paralegals, has been assigned to work with him. Ms. Shanahan is capable, quick, efficient. They finish at 6:45 p.m., and Futterman asks the young woman if she is free for dinner.

"Just let me get a few things at my desk," Ms. Shanahan says, "and I'll meet you in the lobby."

Ruth, Futterman's wife, died four years ago, at sixty-one, of a heart attack while shopping at Crate & Barrel on a Saturday morning in the kitchenware section of the crowded Michigan Avenue store. He and Ruth had been married thirty-seven years. They married the year that Futterman graduated from Northwestern Law School. Futterman always thought of his and Ruth's as a happy enough marriage; certainly it was a solid one.

Careful, prudent, Futterman does not usually fraternize after hours with the help. Especially not with attractive young paralegals or secretaries, lest gossip result. He has nothing especially in mind in inviting Stacy Shanahan to dinner, except a break in his own boring widower's routine—dinner alone on a tray in front of the television set—and to reward her for working overtime. To ensure that no sexual interpretation can be put on his invitation, he decides to take Ms. Shanahan to Harry Caray's, on LaSalle Street, a far from romantic restaurant, noisy and masculine, a sort of sports bar with steaks and chops and heavy pasta dishes added.

At dinner, Futterman learns that Ms. Shanahan's father is a retired Chicago fireman. She is one of six children, two girls, four boys, brought up in Marquette Park, the neighborhood that gave Martin Luther King Jr. a rough awakening when he brought his Southern Christian Leadership Conference movement to Chicago back in the 1960s. Two of Ms. Shanahan's brothers are now themselves firemen, one is a cop, and the other has a job at City Hall—a real Chicago Irish family. She had gone to Mother McAuley High School, and at one point, she tells Futterman, she considered becoming a nun. At Triton Community College she picked up what she needed to get a job as a paralegal.

Stacy Shanahan is remarkably relaxed through dinner, or so Futterman thinks. Although she asks that he call her Stacy, she never refers to him as anything other than Mr. Futterman. She orders and dispatches a full slab of ribs, a baked potato, a large side order of coleslaw, washed down with a beer, food that suggests that she is not trying to beguile him with her feminine refinement.

Futterman finds himself impressed with this young woman—with her independence, her taking control of her own life with, as far as he can tell, not much help from her parents. He is an old double-standards man, Futterman, at least insofar as he believes that life is harder for women than it is for men, that more traps and pitfalls await them. His own two daughters, by marrying young—one to a physician, the other to a man who has gone into his father's lucrative dress business—avoided those horrors, and he is grateful that they have.

Stacy Shanahan tells Futterman that she lives on Sheridan Road, 6300 north, and when dinner is over, he puts her in a taxi and slips two twenties in her hand, more than enough to pay the fare. She thanks him and thanks him, too, for a good dinner. Futterman makes a mental note to charge off both the cab fare and Ms. Shanahan's meal for her working overtime.

"We'll do it again some time," Futterman hears himself saying before closing the door of the cab, though of course he doesn't mean a word of it.

Roughly three months later, at the law firm's Christmas party, Ms. Shanahan approaches Futterman. Holding a bottle of champagne, he has been walking around the large office conference room, a kind of peripatetic bartender, pouring champagne for anyone he notices with an empty glass.

"Hi Mr. Futterman," Ms. Shanahan says. "How go things?"

"Things go well, Stacy," Futterman says. "The firm had a pretty good year. Hope you aren't disappointed with your bonus . . ."

"Not in the least," she says. She has a good smile, he notes.

Futterman senses that she is slightly tipsy, but fails to realize that so is he, having already drunk four glasses of champagne.

"I've got some news," Ms. Shanahan says.

"What is it?" he asks.

"These are going to be my last two weeks at Stone, Viner, Futterman and Waller. I have a new job as an assistant office manager at Sidley Austin."

"A good firm, Sidley, an old firm. Also a huge one. I hope you'll be happy there," Futterman says. "We'll miss you," he adds, hoping he didn't sound perfunctory saying it. Paralegals come and go, their departure no big deal.

"I guess I'm an ambitious person," Stacy says. "Sidley's offering me more money. I also hope one day to be an office manager for a large firm."

"I think you're doing the right thing," Futterman says. "You're right to go for it."

"I'm glad, Mr. Futterman, really glad you feel that way."

He pours her another glass of champagne, and one more for himself.

"The coyote maneuver"—Futterman remembered Barry Spackman, a young lawyer at his firm using the term talking to a contemporary in the locker room of the gym at the East Bank Club. He asked what it meant. Spackman told him that a "real coyote" is what you call a terrible woman you have slept with the night before. When you wake up the next morning in bed with your arm under her head, you look at her and want to bite off your own arm, as coyotes are said to chew off a leg caught in a trap, to make your escape.

Futterman, whose arm is now under Stacy Shanahan's head, in his bedroom in his apartment on Schiller, in the bed he and his wife had shared for decades, the sun slanting into the room, does not feel in the least like making the coyote maneuver. Before he had quite come awake, he felt rather pleased, the warm body of a young woman next to his. Then he thinks, "Christ! What have I done!" Through bleary eyes he notes the digital alarm clock on his night table: 11:27 a.m.

Futterman hasn't a clear notion how this had come about. He remembers leaving his firm's offices with Ms. Shanahan, putting her in a cab, getting in beside her. He remembers having a full, just-opened bottle of champagne in one hand and another unopened bottle under his arm, and Ms. Shanahan holding two plastic fluted glasses. After that, things get blurry: there was much laughter, he struggled with the keys to his apartment while trying to hold on to the champagne bottles. The last thing he can remember is deciding, the hell with it, not to put the shoe trees in his shoes . . .

Futterman is naked, and he looks over to his wife's antique vanity and sees the two champagne bottles, now empty, and the two plastic glasses. He hears himself groan lightly. This is not like him, David Futterman, a man who writes the wills and plans the estates for wealthy clients, solid, square prudential David Futterman, a grandfather of three, in bed with a young woman he barely knows and with far from less than complete knowledge of how he got here.

Although it would not be easy to prove at the moment, Futterman was not a player. He had never cheated on his wife during all the years of their marriage, and his experience with women before his marriage wasn't extensive. Since Ruth's death, he had gone out with four different women, but never more than twice with any one of them, and with none did he wind up in bed. Futterman did not consider sex a trivial act. Nor was he a drinking man. Last night, for some reason, everything broke loose, and here he is, hung over, naked, with a woman more than thirty years younger than he in his bed.

Futterman slips quietly out of the bed, puts on pajamas, robe, and slippers, and goes into the kitchen to make coffee. When he returns to the bedroom, Ms. Shanahan is awake, sitting up in bed, the top sheet and blanket tucked under her chin.

"What's that old Laurel and Hardy line?" she says, looking down. "'A fine mess you've gotten us into this time, Stanley.' Except I'm not even sure which one of us is Stanley."

"I must be Stanley," Futterman says, surprised at her old-fashioned movie reference. "You are much too good-looking to be taken for Ollie."

"Excuse me for a few moments, please," she says, "while I get dressed."

"I've got some coffee going," Futterman says, and leaves the room.

In the kitchen, setting out breakfast things, Futterman thinks with relief that Stacy Shanahan would no longer be working at his law firm, thank God for small blessings. He isn't sure how he will get out of this, but at least he won't have to face this girl—though in her thirties, she seemed a girl to him—every day in the office. He used to wonder how men who slept with lots of women handled the getaway part. All he wants right now is to have this girl out of his apartment, so that he can work through his hangover and get back to the calm routine of his life.

When Stacy Shanahan enters the kitchen, Futterman hands her an already poured cup of coffee. She takes her coffee black. She turns down his offer of toast.

"I don't know what to say about last night," she says. "I hope you will believe that I am not someone who ordinarily wakes up in the bed of a man without quite knowing how she got there. And I'm certainly not someone who wakes up in the bed of a man she hardly knows. It's not my way, really it's not, please believe me."

"I believe you," Futterman says. "I'm probably more to blame than you. I guess I've been lonelier than I thought since my wife died. I didn't mean to take advantage of you."

"I'm more than thirty years old, Mr. Futterman, and ought to be able to take care of myself. Advantage doesn't enter into it. I don't think anyone taking advantage of anyone else is the issue here."

"Can I get you something to eat?"

"No," she says, "I really have to get home. I've a thousand things to do today, and it's already noon."

Stacy Shanahan finds and puts on her coat. At the door, Futterman asks if he can get her a cab, but she says she prefers to take the El, which at this time of day is quicker.

"Good luck in the new job," he says at the door, sounding silly to himself saying it.

"Take care," she says, and is gone. Futterman feels a gust of tremendous relief. He takes his coffee into the living room, flops into the chair in which he watches television, where he falls asleep until four that afternoon.

Early in March, Futterman's secretary informs him that he has a telephone call from a Ms. Shanahan.

"Hello," he says, apprehensive, "how are things?"

"Not so great, Mr. Futterman," she answers. "Seems I'm pregnant."

Futterman gulps. Calm is needed here, he thinks, great cool calm. Steady, he tells himself.

"I see," is all he says, returning the ball weakly to her side of the court.

"I'm afraid this is our office Christmas party child," she says, in a slightly quavering voice.

"You're certain?" says Futterman, in his authoritative, lawyerly voice.

"Yes. I hadn't slept with anyone for months before, nor have I slept with anyone since. There's no other possibility."

"Look," Futterman says, "maybe we shouldn't be talking about this over the phone. Are you free for dinner?"

They agree to meet at a restaurant in her neighborhood, a hamburger joint on Broadway called Moody's. The place turns out to be dark, with formica tables and paper napkins. Stacy Shanahan, arrived before Futterman, is seated in a booth along the wall.

She appears—no surprise—tired, under strain. She is a striking young woman, black Irish, with long brunette hair pulled back in a ponytail, luminous blue eyes. Those eyes are now ringed with a slight shadow, the beginning of bags forming beneath them. She's wearing jeans and a red T-shirt under a white sweater.

"How go things at Sidley?" Futterman begins, thinking it best to start with small talk. "Hope the new job is all you expected of it."

"Everything there is fine," she says. "I only wish I could enjoy it, but my mind is of course elsewhere."

Futterman has had nearly a full day to think things through. Was Stacy Shanahan a con woman, playing him for money? He decided not. Ought he to demand a DNA test? Here, too, he determined to believe her when she said that the child was his. A pity, he thought, that he couldn't remember a thing about how he had helped conceive it. What Futterman decided was to decide nothing at all, but hear out her story.

"I'm sure you have thought about an abortion," he says.

"I have and I have had to reject it," she says. "Even though I no longer go to church regularly, I am still enough of a Catholic not to be able to take abortion lightly. It's a mortal sin, you know, one of the big ones. Abortion, I'm afraid, is a solution unavailable to me." Her voice breaks and Futterman notes her eyes beginning to water.

"Are you able to afford raising a child?" Futterman asks, waiting to hear of any financial demands she is going to make of him.

"I could," she says. "I've got some savings, though it wouldn't be easy. Money, though, isn't the problem, at least not the main one."

"What is?" he asked.

"My family is the problem. They aren't going to take to my being an unwed mother, no, not a bit, not in the least. They're very traditional, very old Chicago Irish Catholic."

"What'll you do?"

"What I am about to do right now," she says, "which is to ask you, Mr. Futterman, to please marry me."

"You're joking, right?" Futterman says.

"Afraid not. You're unmarried. I don't know if you're in any serious relationship at present, but I hope not. And you are the father of my child."

"I'm also more than thirty years older than you, and we don't, if I may say so, know very much about each other. Besides, how is your family likely to take to your bringing home a Jewish husband who for all I know is older than your father?"

"Actually," she says, "he's two years older than you. And my best guess is they'll say how clever of Stacy to have landed a rich lawyer husband."

"I have daughters, grandchildren," Futterman says, not quite certain of the relevance of bringing this up.

"I don't ask that we stay married for very long," she says. "Just long enough to give our child—who is to be a boy, by the way—a name and maybe stay under the same roof a year or so, after which time I promise to clear out of your life, no questions or money asked. We can even write up a pre-nup to that effect, if you like."

"I've never been proposed to before," he says, "especially by the name 'Mr. Futterman.' And I certainly didn't wake up this morning thinking I was going to be the father of, what's the current stupid term, 'a second family'."

"Forgive me, I meant to say 'David'."

"Look," says Futterman, "why don't we change the subject, finish our hamburgers, and take a few days out for me to think further about it."

"Thank you, David," Stacy says.

"For what?" Futterman asks.

"For not calling me an idiot, getting up from the table and walking away."

They eat their hamburgers, talk—he asks her more about life at Sidley Austin, she him about some of the people she liked at Stone, Viner, Futterman and Waller—and afterward he drives her the few blocks to her apartment on Sheridan Road. From the lobby of her building an Indian family emerges through the revolving door, a mother and father and three adolescent children. He thinks about leaning over to kiss Ms. Shanahan on the forehead in a fatherly way before she steps out of his BMW, but instead tells her to sleep well and reminds her that he will be in touch two days from now, a Friday.

As he drives away, Futterman thinks how preposterous all this is. Here he is, at sixty-six, suddenly to be the father of a new child, a son no less, whose mother is a young woman he scarcely knows. Too crazy, the whole thing makes no sense whatsoever. Futterman's first thought is to make a straight cash payment to Ms. Shanahan. Twenty-five grand is the figure that comes to his mind.

The next morning Futterman feels that Ms. Shanahan, as he continues even now to think of her, really doesn't want his money. He needs to take her at her word. She wants, just as she says, a father for her child, at least officially. Does this, he wonders, mean that she expects him also to live with her? Wasn't the phrase "same roof" mentioned last night? He does have a large extra bedroom in his Schiller Street apartment, and he supposes that she and the baby could have it. His mind fleetingly feels a strange stab of pride at still being able to produce a child, and a boy, too. Then he thinks, God, the vanity of men. We're all fucking nuts.

If the young woman and his infant were to live in his apartment, Futterman's bachelor routine, now firmly established after his wife's death, would be completely disrupted. He missed Ruth but, truth to tell, he also liked being free of the social obligations that marriage to her brought with it: charity dinners, theatre tickets to plays he usually found either stupid or incomprehensible, meetings with her friends and their husbands. While his wife was alive, Futterman found himself going out three or four nights a week. Now, after leaving the office at roughly six each night, he ate dinner usually alone in his apartment. He discovered he could cook a few basic things, omelettes, steaks and hamburgers, baked potatoes, spaghetti over which he poured a spicy store-bought sauce called Luchini. After dinner, he read, watched a ball game or an old movie, and usually went to bed after the ten o'clock news.

With a newborn baby in the apartment, there would be crying in the middle of the night, diapers and toys all over the place, formulas being made in the kitchen, a pram in the foyer. Impossible, hopeless, can't be done. Futterman decides he will call Ms. Shanahan in the morning and work out some kind of financial arrangement, a child-support payment, in effect, one that provided for the child's upbringing and even his education. He'd have to think through the numbers. He is a modestly wealthy man, and is prepared to pay reasonably for his single unremembered roll in the hay.

That night Futterman dreams that his son, now nine or ten years old, small, wearing glasses, braces on his teeth, fragile, obviously no athlete— looking, that is, rather like Futterman did as young boy, is seated in a large auditorium next to Stacy Shanahan. So, too, are hundreds of other boys seated next to their mothers. Futterman is viewing all this from his seat on a dais on the auditorium stage. He realizes suddenly that he is being introduced, in lavishly fulsome terms, by a man named Lester Kravitz, whose bankruptcy he had handled some years ago and from whom he had a difficult time collecting his fee. Seated next to Futterman is Miss Mary Ann Burke, his music teacher at Senn High School, a large women with buck teeth who wore gray sharkskin suits and white silk blouses open at the neck as, seated at a grand piano, she played "Smoke Gets in Your Eyes" with many florid arpeggios.

"Excuse me, Miss Burke," Futterman asks, "but why is this man Kravitz introducing me?"

"You're the featured speaker of the evening, David," she answers, and lightly pats his knee.

"What's my subject?" he asks, feeling a needle of panic in his heart.

"Why, David," Miss Burke says, gazing down at him, a surprised look on her large face, "the subject is of course fatherless children. It's the charity for which we're all here tonight."

"And without further ado," says Kravitz, "I give you a man who can be counted on always to know whereof he speaks, my good friend, that great humanitarian, the honorable David Futterman."

Futterman makes his way hesitantly to the lectern, where Kravitz, grinning, with his hand held out, awaits him. "What would you know about honorable, you creep?" Futterman whispers to Kravitz, who deserts him at the lectern without answering. The applause is thunderous.

Faltering at first, Futterman suddenly begins to speak in a flood of platitudes. Babies were not to be thrown out with bath water, apples never fell far from trees and, speaking of trees, great oaks from little acorns grow, which, Futterman allowed, might be construed as a case of apples and oranges, with the twain never meeting. Chickens should certainly not be counted before they hatched, nor bridges crossed before one comes to them, he rambled on, because one good turn deserves another. A bird in the hand is still worth two in the bush, no matter what anyone says, the piper must be paid, which makes it possible to separate the wheat from the chaff, for as ye sow so shall ye reap, and, all this being so, therefore the time was at hand to reach out and find the much-needed role model father-figures without whom, divided, we fall.

Futterman senses a rumbling in the audience. Mothers and sons are walking out. Soon the only people left are Stacy Shanahan and her—their—son and the boy is weeping. At what Futterman isn't sure. At his father's embarrassing him with this disgraceful speech? At his abandoning him years before? Does he even know that Futterman is his father? Futterman is determined to find out and steps down into the auditorium seating, when a powerful need to urinate takes hold of him, and he wakes and walks quickly into the bathroom.

When Futterman was finishing his last year at the University of Illinois, he had had a religious phase, briefly attempted to keep kosher, observe the sabbath, read a Bible portion each morning, and he told the rabbi at Hillel at the university that he was torn between becoming a rabbi or a lawyer. "Become a lawyer," the rabbi had said, "it's morally much more challenging." At the time, Futterman wasn't sure what the rabbi meant, but it didn't take him long in the practice of law to understand completely.

To be a lawyer, the Lord and the rabbi at Hillel knew, offered many temptations. One saw people in *extremis*, many of them terrified or confused or with revenge or greed in their hearts. One had people, if one wished so to have them, where one wanted them. At his firm Futterman knew about lawyers who were screwing their clients, literally in the case of vulnerable women undergoing divorce or widowhood, and financially by expensive overbilling in the case of nearly everyone else. Futterman did neither. He acted with probity, counselled his clients with all the prudence at his command. He liked to think that it paid off; a large part of his clientele was composed of referrals, and over the years he had made a handsome living. Above all Futterman needed to think of himself as a decent man, no angel but not a son of a bitch either.

The right thing, Futterman knew, was not to abandon this child of his accidental making. The cost would be exorbitant—not so much the financial cost, but the cost in disruption and embarrassment. His entire life would be disheveled, upended, blown apart. All that Stacy Shanahan asked was a year or so of marriage, to legitimize her child and please her family. For her it would, in effect, be a marriage of convenience; for Futterman, a marriage of the utmost inconvenience. Ms. Shanahan, though, wasn't the issue. The unborn child was. Was Futterman a man who could allow a child to walk around the world without knowing who his father was; or if he did know, to know that he didn't give a damn about him?

David Maurice Futterman and Stacy Katherine Shanahan are married at City Hall by a judge named John McHugh. Stacy's sister Mary Beth and her brother Tom are there as witnesses; no one from Futterman's family appears. The following day Stacy moves into the spare bedroom in Futterman's apartment. They take their meals together. Ruth's friends wonder why Futterman has made this marriage. Men at his law firm don't wonder but merely wink, and tell jokes out of Futterman's hearing about May and

December couples ("Danger, schmanger. Of course I'm going to have sex with her. If she dies, she dies.") Rachel, Futterman's oldest daughter, when asked about her father, invariably says, "Dad has a second family on the way," never without rolling her eyes up in her head.

In public with Stacy Shanahan, thirty-four years younger than he and showing her pregnancy from the fifth month on, Futterman feels a touch—sometimes more than a touch—awkward. What is this man, at sixty-six with thinning gray hair, a slight slouch, a small but distinct pot belly, doing with this beautiful—and Stacy is one of those women who become even more beautiful when pregnant—young woman. He is her father, Futterman imagines people seeing them together conclude, maybe even, who knows, her grandfather.

Futterman is much relieved to discover that his son, who is given the name Daniel, is born without any of the defects that children born of older fathers sometimes have. The child, as even Stacy's family acknowledge, looks more like a Futterman than a Shanahan. The boy's mother goes along with Futterman's wish to have a *bris* performed.

Futterman's Schiller Street apartment is redecorated and largely refurnished. They decide to turn the extra bedroom into a nursery for Daniel. When the painters are done, Stacy moves into the same bedroom as her husband. On their first wedding anniversary, at a dinner for just the two of them at Charlie Trotter's, Futterman tears up their pre-nup, an act that he would have strongly advised any of his clients against doing.

Out walking his son in the child's Swedish pram along Astor Street or State Parkway, Futterman is identifiably the very model of the second-family man. Whenever anyone uses the phrase second family to him, he smiles and says that he prefers to think of himself instead as a second-story man. The second story is his current life with a young wife and infant son, and he hasn't the least notion of how the plot of this second story is going to play out. For reasons not entirely clear to him, Futterman doesn't spend much time worrying about it.

Remittance Man

By his younger son Lenny's rough count, Samuel Greenspan's funeral service, at Piser Funeral Home off Skokie Boulevard, is attended by no fewer than 400 people. Sam was a successful man, in the cardboard-box business, the manufacturer and supplier in his day to most of the major appliance stores in Chicago. He was a heavy donor to all the Jewish charities, president for many years of the men's club at Ner Tamid Synagogue. He lived to age eighty-three, the last seven of them as a widower. Lenny's mother died of liver cancer at age seventy-six. At his father's funeral, Lenny sits in the front row, next to his older brother Gordon, who now runs Greenspan Box, Gordon's wife Arlene, and their two daughters, Lindsay and Maya.

People walk past the family to pay their respects, most of whom Lenny does not know: old customers, recent neighbors, his brother's friends. Lenny left Chicago in his early twenties, and has spent nearly all his adult life in New York. Now fifty-three, he considers himself a naturalized New Yorker. He is a writer, Lenny, a magazine journalist and author of narrative nonfiction. He hasn't published a book in the past five years. Just before his first article was published in GQ, he dropped the *span* from the name Greenspan. The world, an ever smaller and smaller part of it, knows him as Leonard Greene. An attorney charged him $600 to accompany him to court to have his name legally changed.

Lenny pasted on that final *e* with Graham Greene in mind. Not that he wrote like, or even aspired to write like, Graham Greene. Instead of guilt-ridden and God-haunted Catholics, Lenny writes about businessmen, celebrities, the well-heeled who must come to terms with their affluence, their complicated domestic arrangements, their family sagas. He began publishing at the tail end of the New Journalism boom, and a few of his books—one about the designers of a new computer, another about a murder-suicide in the Hamptons—were well-reviewed and even sold to the movies. The Hamptons book was optioned and re-optioned by producers for several years, and every now and then there would be an announcement that Tom Hanks or George Clooney or Brad Pitt had expressed interest in starring in it. But nothing ever came of it.

A slow writer and a nervous reporter, Lenny takes far too long to finish an article or complete a book and as a result has made far too little from his publications to live off them. He once tried his hand at editing, at a magazine called *Avenue*, but found he had no gift for restructuring the work of others; he could barely structure his own. He takes occasional teaching jobs, when offered, and has taught journalism courses at the New School, at NYU, at Hunter, at Boston University, and once spent a year teaching creative nonfiction at the University of Missouri.

From the age of twenty-four, when he left Chicago for New York, Lenny has been sent a monthly check for $2,500 by his father. Nobody but Sam Greenspan and Lenny knew about it, not even Lenny's brother Gordon or their mother. "Keep it under your hat, kid," said Sam Greenspan, who, Lenny always enjoyed noting, had no fear of clichés. "Let this be strictly between you, me, and the lamp post." The twenty-five-hundred a month, while it does not allow Lenny to live grandly, certainly not in Manhattan, is what keeps him afloat. The checks arrived on the first of every month, written out in his father's hand, like clockwork, religiously, as Sam, who also didn't mind mixing a metaphor, might have put it. Was it in an Anthony Powell novel or a Simon Raven novel that Lenny first came across the term "remittance man"? He can't recall. The concept, though, sticks in his mind. A remittance man was someone who for one reason or another was considered a family disgrace, and sent money to stay away from home. Lenny was pleased to have his father's monthly checks, couldn't have continued to live in New York without them, but from time to time he couldn't help wondering if he himself didn't qualify as a remittance man of sorts—though it was unclear to him what, if anything, might have constituted his disgrace.

In a purely—when younger he used to think it a grimly—commercial family, Lenny is the son with talent, specifically literary talent. His teachers recognized it early: in his love of reading, his facility with language, his ability to make up stories that charmed his grade- and high-school classmates. His parents and older brother did not so much disdain this talent as fail to notice it. Lenny's mother took the commercial course at Marshall High School. His father read only the Chicago newspapers. His brother Gordon was a business major at the University of Illinois. Apart from a *World Book Encyclopedia* and the weekly issue of *Time*, there weren't any books or magazines in the Greenspan house.

Lenny sent home copies of the magazines with his articles in them to his parents and his brother as they were published. He inscribed copies of his four books, and dedicated one of them to his parents. "Keep up the good work" is the most in the way of a response he ever got out of the old man, on Greenspan Box, Inc. stationery in notes dictated to and typed by his secretary, Estelle Fishman. He was certain that neither of his parents ever read his books. Gordon once wrote to say that Arlene "enjoyed" his Hamptons tale.

The Greenspans weren't a family that went around telling one another how much they loved one another. Yet Lenny, in the Greenspan way, loved his father. He was a fair and honorable man, Sam Greenspan. And, of course, generous. More than once Lenny told his father how much he appreciated his financial support, but Sam shook him off by saying that if he couldn't afford it he wouldn't do it. Lenny was always planning to write him a careful letter setting out just how appreciative he was, but, somehow, he never got around to it. Lenny has come to understand that he is one of life's spectators, with a seat on the sidelines watching other people do their dance. He lives, as he has always lived, in his mind, in his imagination. He's had his lady friends; lived for a couple of months, at different times, with two of them—one a poet, the other a photographer who, swept away by feminism, moved out when she turned to lesbianism. But he has never come close to marrying. Nor has he felt the least desire to have children. His books, he tells himself, are his children.

Lenny lives to write, but in recent years he now finds himself increasingly challenged by it. His ideas do not resonate with his editors; four book proposals were rejected on the grounds that there were other works under contract that dealt with the same subject matter. He turns out the occasional piece, usually reviews of novels, and appears on this or that panel on the future of magazines. He is always on the lookout for a teaching gig. He has a rent-stabilized studio apartment, a fourth-floor walk-up in Hell's Kitchen, where he has lived for nearly thirty years without a new appliance or a new paint job. The apartment allows him, if he is careful, to make do on his income and his father's monthly stipend.

Henry James, Lenny read somewhere, thought the two most beautiful words in the English language were "summer afternoon." For Lenny in recent years the two worst words in the English language are "writer's block," from which, little as he likes to believe it, even now, he suffers acutely. He forces himself to be at his computer by 9:00 a.m. He writes and writes, but nothing pleases him. Over the past seven years he has begun no fewer than fourteen novels. (He keeps the manuscripts of his aborted efforts in a suitcase in his front hall closet.) On one he got as far as page 216 before realizing that it was hollow, dead in the water, a corpse lying there on the page. He takes long walks uptown along Madison Avenue, glimpsing the high-maintenance women, straining to imagine stories into which to place them, waiting for useful ideas to arrive. But the ideas that show up turn out to be frauds.

Five years ago Lenny had a short story in the *New Yorker*. He followed this up four months later with a second story—striking while the iron was hot, his father would have said—but the editor who had accepted his first story had left, and a different editor greeted his second story with a cold note of rejection, making plain that what Lenny writes isn't really his sort of thing. He sent the story to the *Sewanee Review*, which accepted it and paid him $150 for it; no one he knew ever saw it there.

On Lenny's visits to Chicago—he comes in every year for a week at Passover—neither his parents nor his brother questioned him about the progress of his work or the fact that he hasn't for some while sent them copies of a new book. The few old Chicago friends he sees on these visits are sufficiently impressed with him as "a published author," as one of them once put it while introducing him to his wife's divorced sister, not to question the absence of a continuing flow of books from him. His father used sometimes to ask, "So how's business, kid?" and then accept Lenny's vague answers—"Going along," "Not bad," "Could be worse"—without further questioning.

Lenny knows he has been lucky to have been born the son of a generous father, and understands that it was Sam who made it possible for him to work, as he thought of it, with a net under him. When the notion sometimes came to him that, upon his father's death, he figured to inherit a respectable sum of money, which might put him out of the financial wars for good, he did his best to put it out of mind. He prefers to think he is better than that; he is a writer, the novelist Leonard Greene, not some over-age spoiled rich kid, a trust-fund baby. Yet the possibility of a serious inheritance coming his way never quite disappears from the back of his mind: It is his unwritten 401(k), his insurance policy against the future.

Sometimes Lenny drifts into thoughts of what he would do if he had a million, or even three-quarters of a million dollars, or whatever his share of the inheritance from his father will turn out to be. Without money worries, he might live a year in Europe, in Italy, specifically in Tuscany, which he'd long ago visited with his poet lady friend and much liked. Such a year, a complete change of scene, might, he thinks, reinvigorate him, break up his writer's block. A substantial sum in the bank would in itself be a natural confidence-builder.

Even when he knew he hadn't long to live, Sam Greenspan never made any mention of his will to Lenny. Nor did Lenny have any but the crudest idea of how wealthy his father might be. When Lenny was a boy, he once asked his mother if they were rich. "We're not rich," she told him, "we're comfortable." Unthinkable, he knew, to ask his father the same question. The Greenspans always lived modestly, without pretension, well below their means.

In what novel did Lenny read that a person "is wealthy when he can meet the demands of his imagination"? It certainly applied to Sam Greenspan. His father, Lenny felt, was good at making money but did not have much imagination when it came to spending it. He was pleased to help his sons, to buck up a poor relative in a time of crisis with a check for a couple of grand, to make generous donations to his Jewish charities. He didn't need to fly the Concorde or sail the QE2 or drive a Mercedes or do anything flashy.

Before his parents moved from their three-flat on Talman Avenue into their two-bedroom apartment on the 15th floor in Winston Towers, Lenny, then a junior at the University of Wisconsin, asked his father why he didn't buy an apartment in one of the elegant buildings on Lake Shore Drive. Living on the Drive he would be closer to his place of business on west Adams, cutting down on his drive to and from work and giving him the comfort of doormen and building staff and the pleasure of a view of Lake Michigan.

"What do I need it for?" Sam answered. "Every time I want to use my car I have to call down and have some flunky bring it up and tip him a buck. That's not the way I care to live." Case closed.

When Lenny's mother wanted her husband to buy a condo in Boca Raton, where some of her friends now wintered, Sam said: "An elephant graveyard! Nothing down there but hospitals, Walmarts, and old Jews walking around in pastel-colored pants carrying home the remains from their lunches in Styrofoam boxes. If I want to see old people, I don't have to go to Florida. All I have to do is look in the mirror." Case closed on Florida.

Sam Greenspan had had two heart attacks, the first of which caused sufficient damage to make bypass surgery too risky to attempt. He had been living with congestive heart failure for more than four years. Toward the end he was in a wheelchair and had a Bulgarian woman preparing his meals, doling out his pills, and cooking (badly) for him. Lenny began visiting his father every other month, staying in the guest room in the Winston Towers apartment for a week at a time, but the truth was, however genuine the love between them, he and his father hadn't all that much to say to each other. They talked about the news, about the more colorful of Sam's old customers, about how much Sam hated losing his independence now that he was ill. Money never came up for discussion.

When Sam could no longer come down to Greenspan Box, Gordon would call the old man every afternoon to report on what was in the mail, what new orders had come in, what the competition was up to. Gordon still asked his father's advice, though he didn't really need it.

Lenny assumed that his father was much more open with his older son, a businessman like himself after all, than he was with his younger. Lenny also assumed that Gordon had a precise idea of their father's wealth, though, like their father, he isn't saying much.

The day after the funeral Lenny and his brother drive down to the office on south Michigan Avenue of Irv Kornfeld, their father's attorney. Taking the Kennedy Expressway into the Loop, the brothers haven't all that much to say to each other. The six-year difference in their ages has always kept them from ever establishing anything like intimacy, even though for a good stretch they shared a bedroom in the apartment on Talman. Yet their interests have always been so far apart that there has never been the least rivalry between them. As kids, Gordon was an athlete and a joiner, president of the Sammy house his last year at Illinois, and Lenny was a reader who wasn't unhappy spending a lot of time by himself and steered clear of fraternities at Wisconsin.

A book on the importance of birth order Lenny once read made the general point that firstborn children tended to be more conservative, later children more radical. Gordon seems to qualify here. Lenny views his brother—slightly contemptuously, if truth be known—as a man who has always played it safe. He married his high-school girlfriend, he went into his father's business, his current passion for Christ's sake is golf. Except for the golf—Sam Greenspan viewed it, Lenny knew, as a game strictly for morons—Gordie did everything his father approved. Lenny never looked to his father for approval. How could the old man approve things he didn't know the first thing about? He felt that he aimed higher in life than his brother. He was aiming for the world's approval.

Halfway down to the Loop, speeding along in Gordon's white Audi, after a bit of small talk about the weather and who was notably absent from their father's funeral, Lenny asks his brother if he knows anything about the arrangements in their father's will. "Not a thing," Gordon says. "Dad played his cards close to his vest, especially when it came to money."

"How much do you suppose he left?"

"Nowhere near as much as he might have done four years ago. He took a terrific hit in the stock market. That much I do know."

"Did Dad ever talk to you about me?" Lenny asked.

"Not really," Gordon said. "But don't take it personally. I'm not sure that he talked all that much about me, either. I remember, though, he once told me that he thought you were a dreamer. Another time, as if out of nowhere, he said, 'You know, your kid brother, when he bet that his talent is up to his ambition, has made a bigger bet than maybe he knows.'"

"I don't think we ever had a real conversation," Lenny says. "When I was a kid, he mostly lectured me. You know, on all the standard things: Save for a rainy day, people know more about you than you think, that kind of thing. When I grew older and had something to contribute to the conversation, he didn't show much interest in what I had to say."

"Lots of successful men are like that. They do the talking, you do the listening. But he gave us the down payment on our first house. He picked up the dental bills for the girls' braces. He offered to pay their college tuition, though I told him that I didn't need him to do that. Some people express love through money. There are worse ways, I suppose."

Irv Kornfeld played fullback in the same Austin High School backfield in which Sam Greenspan played halfback. He specializes in wills and estates. Now a fat man with a ridiculous combover, Kornfeld exudes a false intimacy that, Lenny now recalls, put him off on the few previous occasions when he had met him. In his early eighties, he is still going down to the office five days a week. His unctuousness, Lenny discovers, hasn't slackened over the years.

"Your father and I go back more than sixty years," Kornfeld begins by saying. "I could tell you stories about him and me you wouldn't believe. He was a fine man, a wonderful man, your dad. He gave something on the order of a hundred grand annually to Israel and to Jewish charities, and, as you will presently learn, he planned to continue to do so from beyond the grave."

It doesn't take Lenny long to feel that he has heard enough from this old bullshitter. He wants to hear the details of the will.

Kornfeld passes out copies of the will and testament and trust of Samuel I. Greenspan. The document runs to some forty pages.

"I could read through this will with you boys page by page, but maybe I do better to summarize and then take any questions you have after you've had a chance to peruse the document at your leisure." Kornfeld paused. "Either of you care for a cup of coffee or a soft drink before we begin? No. Allow me, then, to proceed.

"The general arrangements are pretty straightforward," Kornfeld says. "Gordon, you are to get the business, Greenspan Box, Inc. From the proceeds of your late father's stock holdings and the sale of his apartment, small trusts have been set up for your two daughters, paying them, roughly, a thousand dollars a month, to begin when each of them turns thirty. Your father left twenty-five thousand dollars to Ruth Greenspan, his brother Henry's widow in Los Angeles. The rest, a little more than four hundred thousand dollars, will go to the various Jewish charities he denoted on page 29 of the document in your hands to which Dad made pledges before he died. And that, boys, is pretty much it."

Lenny wants to hold back, but isn't able to do so. "What about me?" he asks. "What did my father leave me?"

"Sorry, son, but you aren't mentioned in the will, except on page 34, under division of chattels."

Lenny feels a stab of rage at this fat man and his preposterous hairdo referring to him as "son" and his father as "Dad." He knows he has to take control of himself.

"I was of course with your father when he made his will in this very office. I asked him at the time, 'Sam, what about your son Leonard?' 'Don't worry about Lenny,' your father said, 'Lenny's already had his inheritance.' When I asked him what he meant, he chose not to explain."

Gordon looked over to Lenny, who looked away. Kornfeld cleared his throat, then added, "You and your brother will share in your father's chattels, so-called—the furniture in his apartment, his clothes, watch, and other personal effects. The division of these items is something your father left for you boys to work out on your own."

The brothers were in the Audi, barely back on the Kennedy Expressway, returning to Highland Park, when Gordon asks Lenny, "What do you suppose Dad meant when he told Kornfeld you already had your inheritance?"

Lenny hesitates slightly, then says, "Now that he's dead, you may as well know that Dad had been sending me a monthly check for twenty-five hundred for nearly the past thirty years."

"He never said a word about it to me."

"He asked me to keep it to myself, told me not to tell you or anyone else."

"I'm sure the money came in handy when you were starting out, but do you still need it?"

"Need it?" Lenny says. "Last year from my combined magazine writing and lecturing and my peasantries, as I call the pathetic royalties from my books, I earned a grand total of $8,745. And I believe that was a slight increase over the year before. So, yes, I still need the money."

"Why do you suppose he cut you off? He must have had some sense that you could still use it."

"I wish I knew," Lenny says. "I haven't yet absorbed it. I'm not angry. I'm disappointed. Mostly I guess I'm shocked."

"I could let you have fifty grand or so till you work things out," Gordon says. "And if you're interested, you could work for Greenspan Box."

Lenny looks over at his brother, behind the wheel of his Audi, and his heart fills with gratitude. Would he, he wonders, have made so generous an offer if things had been the other way around? Has he all these years underestimated his brother? "Thanks, Gordie," he says, "I appreciate it. I have some small savings that will get me by for a bit."

That night, turning in bed in the guest room in his brother's house, Lenny tries to sort out his future now that he is no longer his father's remittance man. He has sixteen thousand dollars and change in the bank, the end of the money from the last movie option. That won't last long in New York.

"A dreamer" his father called him, Gordie told him earlier today. His father was right about his betting everything on his talent being up to his ambition. He bet it all, his whole life, he now sees, and has lost. He never thought he would be a star among American writers, but he had hoped to be a serious and productive one. That dream is now over.

Lenny realizes he will probably have to leave New York, which maybe wouldn't be such a bad thing. Earlier this year his agent, Claudia Kipnis, told him that a television production company in Los Angeles was looking for someone to help craft scripts for reality television shows—yes, they have writers, she told him, and they design plots, and they feed the non-actors lines. At the time he felt himself above such work. That was while he was still receiving his father's regular stipend. Now, though, it might be worth looking into. Or he could return to Chicago, possibly even take up Gordie on his offer to work in the family business, though what he could possibly do for Greenspan Box he hasn't a clue.

Falling off to sleep, the question playing in Lenny's mind is not the usual one of how to advance the sterile plot of the novel he is working on at the moment, but how to live out the rest of his life without his father's net under him. He should be feeling frightened, but is surprised to discover that what he feels instead is relief. He is off his father's payroll at last. His final thought before sleep overtakes him is that he will have to shell out another $600 or so to have his name changed back from Greene to Greenspan.

My Five Husbands

It's a mistake, somebody or other once said, to have three cats, for if you have three, why not five or six, or more? The same may be true of husbands and wives. If three, why not five or six? I've had three cats at various times in my life and, as it turns out, five husbands, so maybe there's something to it. Five husbands, the number boggles the mind, whatever "boggles" means.

I also have ovarian cancer, or so I've just been told, which makes this as good a time as any to try to explain my life, if only to myself. The theme of my life, as I've known for a long while now, has been freedom, or at least the hope of gaining freedom, and just as it looks as if I have it, here comes my death sentence in the form of ovarian cancer.

I've always had a man problem, the problem being how to get away from them, beginning with my father. I grew up in a small town in north-central Arkansas, Batesville by name. A handsome man, my father had a beautiful but nutty sister, my Aunt Velma, and a kindly but retarded younger brother named Roscoe. Velma flounced and fluttered around and Roscoe walked the yard of their small house, with his kindly face behind which who knew what was going on. My father worked as a stone mason, always in business for himself, for he was too independent—"too damn mean," he would have said—ever to work for anyone else.

Why my mother married him I haven't the foggiest notion. My mother was reserved and artistic. She made beautiful quilts and also the uniforms for the cheerleaders and marching band at Batesville High. My father didn't so much give her a hard time as mostly pretend she wasn't there. When he wasn't working, he was out hunting and fishing. He kept a large freezer stuffed with fish he had caught and rabbits and squirrels he had shot. The freezer was near our bathroom. For some reason my father never saw fit to put a door on our one bathroom, which was covered by a sliding drape, making for a terrible absence of privacy. I was ashamed to bring friends home from school, and rarely did.

Daddy kept his drinking to the weekends, and he was not a happy drunk. He never beat my mother, nor my older sister Dottie and me, but on his rampages he did a pretty good job on our furniture and dishes and glassware. The effect of her marriage on my mother was to make her seem defeated, old before her time, and resigned—above all, stuck with a man who had no sense of what stirred her soul. I'm not sure that I ever openly said it even to myself, but I decided never to be resigned in life, never to settle for a situation like my mother's.

I hope I'm not giving the impression that I hated my father. I didn't. He could be humorous, even affectionate. But I knew I wanted to get away from him. Dottie must have felt the same, for she left home at sixteen, to marry a man who sold potato chips and other snack foods on his truck route through the Ozarks. I made it until seventeen, when I left home four months pregnant with the first of my five children.

Van Willis was a high-school football star. The Willises were more middle class, which I guess is to say more respectable, than our family. At least they had a door on their bathroom. Ernie Willis sold insurance; he was in Kiwanis. They were members of the second Baptist Church. They lived in a modest but well-maintained white house in a better part of town than we did. Ernie and Edna Willis were disappointed to learn that I was pregnant with Van's child. They wanted something better for him and made no secret of it. Van, as they say, did the right thing, and we married while still in high school.

I should say here that I am not knock-out beautiful, but I must be sexy. I don't think of myself as flirtatious, but I guess I suggest, in some mysterious way, availability. At least I have never had trouble attracting men. My third, my Jewish, husband used to call me *zaftig*, which he defined as having lots of curves and all in the right places.

I didn't plan my pregnancy with Van. We made love on the backseat of his 1948 Plymouth and, with one exception, always used condoms. The exception, of course, proved the rule, or maybe I should say the fool.

A fool is certainly what I felt walking the halls of Batesville High my last semester there pregnant. A fool and ashamed. After we married, Van and I found an apartment in town. Not long after graduation, and six weeks before our baby is to be born, he comes home to report that he has enlisted in the Navy. I could have—I really should have—killed him.

My mother stood by me through the birth of my first son—I seem only able to produce boys—moving into my small apartment for the first month after Donald was born. My father, less than pleased by the embarrassment having a knocked-up daughter caused him among his pals, pretended the whole thing never happened, and was a no-show until his grandson was three months old. Around that time Van had finished boot camp, and was transferred to Norfolk, Virginia, from where he called to say that he had found an apartment for us, and would send money for Donald and me to meet him there in a month or so.

I took my little son on a Greyhound bus trip up to Norfolk, Virginia, to meet his father. Van was an awkward father at best. When I put Donald in his arms the expression on his face seemed to say, "Where did this come from?" I realized right then that even with the best will in the world it wasn't going to work out. I was on my own. A girl of eighteen, with an infant child, and no job training of any kind. Meanwhile, Van informs me two weeks later that he is shipping out, to just where he isn't certain.

Van is not gone two weeks and I wake at four in the morning, needing to throw up. Morning sickness. Pregnant again. I suppose I could have arranged an abortion, though in those days it would have meant a back-alley kitchen-table nightmare. So my second son, Allen, was born. He looked like his father, whom I suppose I was by now looking for some excuse to ditch. Van gave it to me by allowing me to discover that he was seeing another woman—a girl, actually—in Norfolk, the daughter of his chief petty officer.

So there I was, with two small kids, no work, and a husband—soon-to-be ex-husband—on enlisted man's Navy pay. My only choice was to return home to Batesville, which I did. But life there soon became impossible. I left the children with my mother and returned to Norfolk, hoping to find work. The work I found was bartending. The bar was a large place called Jimmy's that used women bartenders to attract sailors. The pay wasn't great, but the tips from drunken customers helped a lot: tips from the tipsy, I used to call them.

One of the rules at Jimmy's was the help was not allowed to go out with the customers. But I broke it one night when a sailor named Mitchell Hendrix, a regular, finally prevailed on me to let him take me out to dinner. He was tall, slender, with a wide mouth and lips that had a slightly collagen look, long before anyone had ever heard of collagen. He had a mischievous sense of humor, Mitch did.

Mitch was from Bozeman, Montana, where, he told me, his father had been a state senator. His family had a ranch there and lots of land. Mitch was in the Navy because, at the age of twenty, after being caught stealing a car and holding up a garage, a judge in Bozeman gave him the choice of three years in jail or three years in the Navy. "Not much of a choice, really," is the way he explained it to me that first night at dinner.

He was fun to be around. He liked to be in action, to have scams going. By this time my divorce from Van had come through. Mitch did not exactly move in with me, but he kept some civvies in my apartment and we were, outside of Jimmy's, a couple. One of his games was to pretend to be my pimp. He would get young sailors to give him twenty dollars for a meeting with me, and then, after I didn't show up, explain to them what an impossible bitch I was and somehow arrange to keep the money.

Mitch was also sexually adventurous. He taught me a trick or two—actually five or six—that I hadn't known. I was myself never squeamish about sex; I enjoyed it. I suppose here I was a little ahead of my time. Anyhow it was after a marathon night of sex that he asked me to marry him and I, foolishly, agreed. I say foolishly because it should have been clear that Mitchell Hendrix, at twenty-two, was incapable of the least loyalty to anyone.

Not long after my marriage to Mitch I learned, from a long-distance telephone call from my mother, that Van Willis and his parents had taken my two little sons from her, and were going to court for permanent custody of them. I was twenty-three years old, with no money, working as a bartender, and six hundred miles away from Batesville. Mitch was no help. Neither was my father. I wanted to blame my mother for giving up the boys, but she was what she was, a weak woman, and it was probably my mistake for leaving them in her care in the first place.

Van and his parents won their custody case uncontested. I was given no visitation rights, nothing. While Van was still in the Navy—he turned out to be a thirty-year career man—Donald and Allen lived with the Willises. My marriage to Mitch lasted all of eleven months, broken up by mutual consent when his three-year hitch was up, and he wanted to return to Montana without the extra baggage of a wife. I decided to return to Arkansas, not Batesville, which would have been too sad, and where I wasn't likely to find work, but to Little Rock, ninety miles away. I was hoping that Van's parents would allow me to spend some time with my kids.

I moved in with my sister Dottie and her husband Chester. I arrived at a time when Dottie was in the middle of a love affair with a married man named Lester Hoopston, who owned a laundromat in Little Rock. All my possessions were in a single suitcase, and I slept on Dottie's couch in her living room. I was able to get a job as a waitress at a restaurant and lounge in the basement of the Hotel Marion in downtown Little Rock called the Garhole—called that because a garfish swam in a tank behind the bar.

Van's parents did not make it easy to see my children. I took a bus up to Batesville every week to be with them, but the Willises would only allow me to see them in their presence, usually out in their large back yard, and then for no more than an hour or two. When it was time to leave, the children would ask me why I couldn't take them with me. I had no explanation, except to promise them that someday they would live with me, a promise I had no real hope of making good on. I never left my boys without tears in my eyes.

I worked three hours during lunch and then returned to the Garhole to work from 5:00 p.m. to 11:00 p.m. Guests of the hotel came down for drinks, and so did the men who worked at the nearby *Arkansas Gazette*. Politicians hung out there. Occasionally soldiers who worked at the recruiting office at 3rd and Main dropped in after work.

My style as a waitress was cheerful, and with men even slightly flirtatious, though I made it a policy not to go out with customers after work. This was a policy I broke when one day, at a table of soldiers—enlisted men—I found myself teasing a guy with the nametag Goldstein on his uniform about his drinking coffee when everyone else at the table was ordering beers. He had fine features, soft brown eyes and, I noticed, delicate hands. "With you nearby, what I do need alcohol for?" he said. I fluttered my eyelashes and went into my best obviously phony plantation southerner act: "I declare, sir, you do say the kindest things."

After this Goldstein left with his Army buddies. Half an hour later he returned alone, and asked if he might take me out to dinner one night. I told him that I worked nights, and didn't get off till eleven. He asked if he could meet me after work that night, and I found myself saying, "Sure, OK, why not?"

We took a cab from the Marion fifteen or so blocks to his apartment on Louisiana Street, a quiet block backing onto the governor's mansion. David Goldstein was his name. He had a large studio apartment, sparsely furnished—a couple of upholstered chairs, a small table for dining, a foldaway double bed in the closet—and uncluttered. No television set, but a stereo, lots of books, on the table and on the floor. He asked if I'd like him to open a bottle of wine, or if I would prefer a coke or something else.

We drank two bottles of wine and, seated far from each other, talked straight through until six the next morning. He had less than ten months to go on his military hitch; he had been drafted. He worked as a typist at the recruiting station on Main Street and 3rd. We talked about our backgrounds, our families. He was from Chicago, Jewish, had gone, he said, to Columbia College in New York City. He never asked me if I had gone to college. He told me that he wanted to be a writer, but was embarrassed to say this to most people because he hadn't in fact published anything. He asked me what my ambition for myself was. I mumbled something about a peaceful and worry-free life. Truth is that I hadn't had time to think about my ambition; nor had any man ever asked me about it before.

As the sun was coming up, I brought up the subject of my boys, and how I had lost custody of them. He told me that he couldn't imagine anything worse, and said it in a way that made me believe he meant it. When I began to cry, he walked across the room, gave me his clean handkerchief, then returned to his chair.

Except for the owner of Jimmy's in Norfolk, a brute called Lou Silverman, I had never known a Jew. I certainly had never met anyone like

David Goldstein. At 6:30 a.m. he said that he had better shower and get ready for work at the recruiting station, where he had to report at 8:00 a.m. If I wished to sleep in his apartment before going off to work myself, he said that would be fine. He set the alarm for me for 10:30 a.m. He made no moves on me, none whatsoever. I wondered if he might be queer.

David called me during my lunch shift at the Garhole to say that he was knocked out from no sleep and probably going to fall asleep as soon as he got off work, but if I were free one night later in the week he'd like to take me to dinner. We agreed to meet on Wednesday, my night off, at McGeary's, a BBQ restaurant on 12th and Main Street, at 6:30.

At dinner David asked me when I was next to see my kids and, if I didn't mind, he would like to join me. I said that I was planning to go up to Batesville on Sunday afternoon. He said he'd borrow a friend's car and drive me up there. I was hesitant, wasn't sure how the Willises would look upon my arriving with another man, especially someone like David, but in the end I said sure, why not? He picked me up that Sunday morning in a green Ford. We drove the ninety miles to Batesville, talking mostly about his family who, he said, were Jewish and very middle class. He asked me lots of questions about how Van had been able to take my kids away from me. He was of course no lawyer, but he said he didn't think such a thing would have been possible in Chicago courts.

I explained to Edna that I had brought a friend along to meet Donald and Allen, and to my relief she didn't give me a hard time about it. David turned out to be great with them. He called Donald Monsieur Canard explaining that *canard* was French for duck, and that of course the world's most famous Donald was Donald Duck. Allen he called "Allsy." He played tag with them. He tried to teach the six-year-old Donald to catch. They really went for him. For the first time in all my meetings with my kids since I lost custody of them I did not leave them with a heavy heart.

When David dropped me off at Dottie's, I was nervous about inviting him in. My sister's life, with her squalid love affair, her naturally unhappy husband, and her two kids, the younger of whom was a genuine brat, was a mess. The house, on the far east side of Little Rock, was ramshackle, a badly painted business with a slightly falling-in porch. I could see a look of critical disappointment as he looked at the place upon dropping me off.

"We have to find you a better place to live," he said, after I kissed him on the cheek and got out of the car.

I should tell you that until now David and I had not slept together. So he must have been more than a little surprised when I showed up at his apartment the next night, after work, at 11:00 p.m. with a suitcase containing all my clothes and cosmetics.

"You said I needed to find a better place to live," I told him, standing in his doorway. "And I think I know of one. With you."

"Welcome home," he said, and took my suitcase.

The first thing that impressed me about David was how unpossessive he was, even after we had begun sleeping together. Working at the Garhole, I kept odd hours, yet if I happened to come in at one or two in the morning—sometimes I would unwind after work at an afterhours club downtown—he never asked where I had been or with whom. Nor did he ask me to share his rent. In some ways, he was the ideal boyfriend: always there when I wanted him, but never insisting that I be there.

David seemed to have a lot going on in his life. He was always reading or tapping away on his portable typewriter. He published an article, his first, in a small New York magazine, which pleased him a lot, though, he told me, it paid him all of twenty-five dollars. He never asked me to read it. Every Sunday he drove me up to see my kids.

One day David told me that, through an acquaintance of his on the *Arkansas Gazette* named Jerry Neil, he had arranged for us to see a lawyer in Batesville to get regular visitation rights for me, so that I wouldn't be under sufferance of Van's parents. The lawyer, Herbert Samson, was able to persuade the court to give me two weekends per month visitation, and a full month in the summer. I was very happy. I don't know how much the lawyer charged. David paid the bill, and told me that I could pay him back later, which of course I never did.

Maybe I should be put up for chairwoman of the Unplanned Parenthood Association, but one morning not long after this I woke to discover myself with morning sickness, which in my mind could mean only one thing: pregnancy. I used a diaphragm, but something or other about it obviously didn't work. I faced the prospect of telling David that he was about to be a father, and without the least certainty about how he would take it.

Credit where credit is due, he took it well. He didn't do the stupid thing and ask if I were sure the baby was his, which it was. He didn't suggest my looking into getting an abortion. He only asked me if I was certain I was pregnant. I told him I knew my body and there could be no mistake. "We'll get married," he said, "as soon as possible." Then he added: "My father will of course disown me, but maybe not forever."

"What for?" I asked.

"For marrying a gentile," he said. "No one in our family has ever done so."

"Is he that religious?" I asked.

"He's an atheist," David said, "but that doesn't matter. It's complicated. I'll explain it to you some day." He never did.

We bought our two silver wedding rings from a small Jewish man named Kleiderman, who had a modest shop on Main Street and 6th. That same day we drove over to city hall and were married by a justice of the peace, a kindly man who took a few minutes out to lecture us on the sacredness of marriage. I was touched by what he said, and so I think was David. When we came out of city hall, married, he had a parking ticket. Not, some might say, a good omen. And yet my marriage to David lasted almost nine years, much longer than either of my first two marriages.

In the fourth month of my pregnancy, we drove to Fort Sill, Oklahoma, where David was formally discharged from the Army. As he predicted, his father did disown him, though David stayed in touch with his mother, who eventually convinced his father to forgive him. We moved into a furnished apartment in a dump of a building called the Sherwin Arms on the far north side of Chicago, a block or so from Sheridan Road. David got a job working on a trade magazine, and I spent my days walking the few blocks down to Lake Michigan, and drinking coffee in a little shop under the El.

David was getting up at 4:30 a.m. to write. He was having some success. Magazines, none of which I'd ever heard of, began to publish his articles and reviews of books. I didn't have much luck reading what he wrote, though whether I did or not didn't seem to bother him. He was ambitious. I had never been with, or for that matter before now even met, an ambitious man.

The Goldsteins treated me decently enough. Yet I couldn't help feel that they had something else in mind for their only son than a twice-divorced woman with two children. They never questioned me about my past, which, in modified form, David had filled them in on. Only after our son—my third son—Richard was born did we begin to see more of David's family. Despite their courtesy to me, I couldn't help feeling an outsider among them. One day I heard my mother-in-law, on the phone, tell a friend that "My *goya* comes to clean on Wednesday"—David had filled me in on twenty or so words of Yiddish—and I thought, your other *goya* is here right now in your kitchen.

Richard was born with the help of a man named David Turow, who believed in induced labor, and delivered my son and five other kids on the same Tuesday. He must have golfed on the other afternoons. David said that in the waiting room the expectant fathers had a pool going on whose child would arrive in what order.

Based on his recent publications, David had been offered a job in New York on a small political magazine. He talked with me about it, but I could sense that he had already made up his mind to take it. And so we moved to New York. Because of the expense of Manhattan, he found us an apartment in a new building in Flushing, in Queens, and soon after I became pregnant with my fourth child. We had no health insurance, and so we joined an HMO in Jamaica, Queens, where I saw a quite nutty OB-Gyno doctor, Ephraim Berlin. I heard that soon after my fourth son, Joel, was born, they had to drag Dr. Berlin off the premises of the hospital. What I'm getting at is that none of the births of my sons—and a fifth would turn up twelve years later—was an occasion for joyousness.

While we were living in New York, my first two sons, Donald and Allen, arrived for my summer visitation. Van, still in the Navy, now was living in Balston Spa in upstate New York. He had meanwhile remarried, to a woman from Louisiana, and when my boys arrived they were not in good shape. Under some questioning from David and me, we discovered that they were being badly mistreated by their stepmother, Allen especially. She locked him in closets and used to spank him with a hairbrush. The clothes she had sent with them were unpressed and barely clean. Donald's glasses were held together with Scotch tape.

"These kids aren't going back," David announced. He said that we were going to be in a custody fight for the boys. He told me that from the time he first met me he sensed a dark sad hole in my life because I did not live with my children, and that this was the perfect time to fill in that hole. My first husband's monstrous second wife had given us that chance.

At great expense—three thousand dollars, a lot of money in those days—we won. Donald and Allen came to live with us. Us included Richard and his baby brother Edward. David at this time was twenty-six, I was twenty-seven. Life with four young boys in New York was, in David's word, "crushing," and he decided that we would all do better to move back to Little Rock, where he thought he could get a job on the *Arkansas Gazette*.

I boarded a Greyhound bus with my four kids, and the plan was for David to follow a month later. He needed to give proper notice at his job and to close up our apartment in Flushing, where the lease would be up in less than thirty days. I was to find a house to rent, and there was enough money for me to hire a nanny to watch the kids.

Back in Little Rock, I found myself stepping out on David. I would go down to the Garhole, as a customer now, and, along with an old friend, Linda Ferguson who went to high school with me, we would pick up younger men. All my cheating were one-night stands.

I can hear you asking why would you cheat on a man who had saved your children for you? Was the problem sex? Did you feel neglected? Was he cruel to you in any way? None of these things apply.

I know this is going to sound weird but I cheated on David because I didn't want to feel beholden to him for returning my older boys to me. I cheated on him because I needed to prove to myself that I was bound to no one. I cheated on him for his fucking saintliness. David thought he was rescuing me, but he was wrong. He never really understood how important my freedom is to me, and until then neither did I.

We lived in Little Rock for two years. David wrote editorials for the *Arkansas Gazette*. He wrote a piece on poverty in America for *The Atlantic* magazine that got him the job of director of the anti-poverty program in Pulaski County, which included Little Rock, North Little Rock, and the surrounding area. The year was 1964, the time of the civil rights movement.

All sorts of young people from New York, working summers for the Student Nonviolent Coordinating Committee, were popping into and out of our house. David was conspiring to try to get them money for their projects.

A year or so later we moved to Chicago, where, through a man named Harry Ashmore, David got a job at Encyclopedia Britannica. He bought a house in a suburb called Berwyn. Even though there weren't any Jews, he moved us to Berwyn because two of my cousins, Pat and Shirley, my father's brother Archy's daughters, lived there. Archy had come up to Chicago after the war, and worked for General Electric in Cicero. David thought it might be more comfortable for me to have these cousins nearby. He must have sensed that our marriage was coming apart. I don't know how much he really loved me. I do know that David hated failure, and among his hatreds a failed marriage scored high.

David was always telling me how smart I was, and at one point he suggested that I enroll in college. But where was I to find the patience at this point to sit in classrooms with kids fifteen years younger than me answering dopey questions and writing hopeless papers? I signed up for secretarial school, but lasted less than a month. My patience was growing less the older I got. Mostly I shopped, looking for antiques in second-hand furniture shops. Some days I would find myself at the Anti-Cruelty Society, from which twice I brought home dogs, one a storybook mutt named Luv, another time a large collie left by a young man who had to go off to Vietnam. We kept Luv, but David insisted I take back the collie.

I had all my sons, I had a lovely house, I had a successful husband, I had my cousins living nearby, but none of it did the trick. I began going out evenings, at first telling David I was visiting friends I had met at Anti-Cruelty. I don't think he believed me from the first, and he certainly didn't when I would return home at four in the morning. Once I told him that my mother was ill, and I needed to be with her for a week or so after she returned home from breast-cancer surgery. In fact, I used the ten days to drive down to New Orleans, and called him from there, telling him that my parents' phone was out of order.

It was the late 1960s and feminism was in the air. I can't say that I bought all the ideas bopping around about the suppression of women, the hopelessness of being a wife and mother, and the rest, but it did strengthen me in my decision to leave David. When we finally sat down to work out the details, he suggested that I take Donald and Allen and leave Richard and Joel, his own kids, with him.

"You take all four children," I said, "or it's no deal. Otherwise I'll take all four and have you pay alimony and child support." I knew how David's conscience worked. He couldn't bear the idea of living away from his sons. He agreed. I promised not to ask him for any alimony. He bought me a new yellow Volkswagen and gave me two thousand dollars. The plan was that he would get a divorce in Chicago on the grounds of desertion. Which was fine with me. I wanted only to get the hell away.

"Away" meant New Orleans, which I had enjoyed during my ten days there. New Orleans was southern but without any of the dreary Baptist unforgivingness hanging over it. I found a small apartment in the French Quarter and took a job as a chambermaid in a place on Chartres Street. I didn't mind the work and it felt good to be alone. I suppose I should say that I missed my kids, but I didn't, at least not much. I sometimes wondered if they missed me. In later years I neglected to ask.

Ziggy Watkins, my fourth husband, was a musician, a clarinet player. I say "was"; I suppose he still is. I met him one night at Pat O'Brien's, where he was playing. He was large, like I mean 280 lbs large. Also a drinker, rum and coke his specialty, though he didn't really need the coke, unless it was cocaine, for which he also had a powerful taste. Ziggy used to describe himself as a "happy cat," which he was when he wasn't drunk, which was most every evening. I see I forgot to mention that Ziggy was black. A white woman marrying a black man in those days still carried a certain shock factor. We'd been together maybe six weeks, when he said he wanted to marry me.

"Know it, sweet baby," he told me. "We good together. Let's make it deal permanent."

Ziggy was part of the inner circle of musicians in New Orleans. He taught me a lot of things, too, about music and drugs and blacks and New Orleans. He could be very seductive.

Only after we married did I learn that Ziggy, when fully tanked up, didn't mind hitting women. I also learned that faithfulness to one woman was not an idea with any interest for him. Our marriage lasted less than eight months, when we had what Ziggy called a black divorce. "You cuts out the middleman," Ziggy explained. In other words, no lawyers. A black divorce is when a husband closes the door and never returns. The only difference in my case is that the black divorce occurred when a white woman, me, closed the door and never returned. I never mentioned my marriage to Ziggy to anyone, and until now nobody knows anything about it. Of all my marriages, it was the most stupid. I can't even explain it to myself.

With the help of fifteen hundred dollars from David I left New Orleans for Las Vegas. A terrible place, but one with lots of work available. I was able to get a job first at a dry cleaner, then not long after I found a better one working the buffet at Caesar's Palace, refilling and cleaning up the food display after the attacks upon it by depressed gamblers, gluttons, and assorted freeloaders. I began playing a little blackjack myself in other casinos and found I wasn't too bad at it, some nights taking home a couple hundred bucks or so.

Las Vegas is, as someone I met at Caesar's once told me, a mecca for losers. They come from all over. Everyone seemed to have a story of nearly hitting it rich, nearly scoring big, coming this close to a swell life. But you didn't have to look too closely to see that they were all sad cases, flops, suckers. Everyone was running away from something or other. I suppose I was too, though I couldn't have told you exactly what it was.

Lloyd Blakely was a member of the hotel workers' union—a handyman of sorts. He did twenty years in the Air Force as an enlisted man, where he worked with flight simulators. He had been retired for the past ten years. He was black. Do you suppose that black men know when white women have been with black men? Since my relationship with Ziggy, I sensed black men coming on to me more than in the past. Not that Lloyd did. He was a large gentle man—one of nature's teddy bears. But whenever he was in the buffet area of Caesar's, he would stop to talk with me, until one day he asked me if I would care to have dinner with him.

At dinner I learned that Lloyd, who was in his early fifties, had never married. He had family in Houston, three sisters and a brother, a mother and father still living. He was devoted to them. He owned a small house just outside Las Vegas. He liked to cook. He wasn't church-going, but the church was important to him in his upbringing, he said. He was a square, but a sweet one. I found my heart going out to him.

How is it that some very attractive, even very smart women can't seem to close on marriage? However appealing they may seem, men don't finally ask them to marry them. Others of us attract not just men but husbands. Men want to marry us. To protect us? To save us? To have exclusive rights to us? Who knows? Getting men to want to marry somehow wasn't my problem, though maybe, now that I think of it, it was.

All I know is that, roughly a month after our first dinner together, I became Mrs. Lloyd Blakely. Life with Lloyd was calm. Calm seemed just fine. Lloyd made a decent living. I kept my job at Caesar's Palace. When we visited his family in Houston, I asked him to withhold all the information about my previous marriages. The Blakelys seemed to like me well enough. (I don't think the same could have been said if I had brought Lloyd back to Batesville to meet my father, which I never did.) My only complaint about my new husband was that, as a fix-it man, he was a pack rat, and would bring home lengths of cable, canisters, wiring, lumber, and other things that were no longer useful at the casinos at which he worked.

Lloyd never said so openly, but he wanted a child—really wanted one. I hadn't exactly proved the model mother, but maybe now, settled at last, with no pressure on me things would be different. I was forty-three, late for child bearing, yet all my pregnancies—after the initial morning sickness—and births had gone smoothly. So I became pregnant. Lloyd was hoping for a boy, and I told him not to worry—boys were all I was able to produce.

And we did have a boy, Matthew, who turned out to be badly brain-damaged. We had him at a nearby military hospital, and all I can remember is the OB-Gyno man yelling at one of the nurses and leaving the operating room. I later heard that my child's umbilical cord wound around his neck, choking off his oxygen. You apparently can't sue the US government for malpractice. What the government did offer was care for my poor baby.

The extent of the damage to Matthew, who turned out to be beautiful, as so many biracial children I've noticed are, was pretty complete.

He lost just about all powers of locomotion. He was never able to speak. We couldn't even be sure if he had sight or not. The decision arose about whether to institutionalize Matthew, or care for him at home. Lloyd wouldn't hear about institutions, where the child's life was certain to be shortened. Matthew lived to be twenty-nine, and died less than a year after Lloyd died of his third heart attack.

Much of the responsibility for taking care of our child fell to Lloyd. He wanted it that way. He rigged up special contraptions for the child to sit comfortably in. He bathed him. He cleaned him. He moved his own bed into Matthew's room, so that he could help him if he was uncomfortable during the night. I don't mean to say that I didn't do anything—I fed Matthew, I washed and changed his clothes—but Lloyd was the main guy.

I can easily imagine anyone reading this thinking that Matthew was my just deserts for being not much of a mother to my other children. The truth is that Donald, now living in Oregon, no longer wished to speak with me or any of his brothers. Allen had two marriages, and his second wife wanted nothing to do with me because I had married a black man. Richard turned out to be like his father, David, a good student type. He'd gone to college, and afterwards made a lot of money working for some stock-market company in San Francisco. He stayed in touch with me, and would occasionally help me out with a few thousand dollars, but I know he felt I had made a mess of my life. Joel, my fourth child, who had been wild as a teenager, died in a car accident in his late twenties in Chicago. I wasn't able to attend the funeral.

I've tried to be as candid as I know how here, and so I had better go on to say that, after Matthew was born, I began to drink in a way I hadn't done before. I was always what Mitchell, my second husband, called a short hitter, by which he meant that it didn't take more than two or three drinks to get me flying. But now I looked forward to the haze curtain that alcohol drew across the sadness of my life with my broken, feelingless last child.

Lloyd understood, or at least he pretended to, when I would go off for two or three days alone and get quietly snockered. I don't say that he liked it, but he put up with it. What was he going to do about it, anyhow? I had put on weight—maybe 50 or 60 lbs—and men no longer hit on me the way they once did, so at least he didn't have to be jealous. I was as little interested in men as they now were in me. Things had got beyond the stage of guilt and repentance in Lloyd's and my marriage. I would come home from one of my little benders and pick up the old routine as if nothing had happened. After a while Lloyd stopped asking where I had been.

I watched Lloyd die. He was lifting a steel beam from the back of his pickup, when he stopped, the beam dropped to the street, he clutched his heart and fell forward. I ran out to the street, but he was already gone. He was the husband I was married longest to, and he also treated me best. Ours was hardly an ideal marriage, if such a thing exists. We'd long ago stopped making love or having long conversations. What held us together was our poor sad child.

After Lloyd's death, I had to put Matthew into an institution. I visited him there, at first every day, then once a week, then less than that. When I would arrive, he made a gurgling sound. I'd put my index finger in his hand, and he grasped it tightly. There was no way that, without Lloyd's help, I could have brought Matthew home. He died three weeks before his thirtieth birthday, roughly five months after his father.

I put our house on the market and moved into a studio apartment closer to the main drag. I was, finally, free to live as I wished—for the first time since I was seventeen and had become pregnant with Donald. I luxuriated in it. I stayed up late, drinking and watching old movies on television. I woke when I pleased. I took walks, played a little blackjack, ate what I wanted when I wanted. I thought about my life, where I had been and what I had done. I'd planned on living this way—quietly, freely—for another ten years or so. Then I started noting a bloating and loss of appetite and having to go to the bathroom all the time. I'm not one for rushing off to doctors at the least jigeroo in my health. When I started bleeding vaginally, I knew something was up. What it was, as I've already told you, was ovarian cancer.

I'm told that I can buy some extra time if I'm willing to put myself through chemotherapy. I've decided against it. With Matthew gone, no one is dependent on me. I don't really have all that much to look forward to. I'll be seventy-three next month, and I don't figure to grow more beautiful or much smarter.

Was it freedom I longed for? Or was I only running away from responsibility? Maybe I had responsibility thrown on me too early in life: a stupid father, a meek mother, a baby to worry about at seventeen. When I think of having had five husbands even I am a bit amazed. Maybe I should have dug in and made the best of one of them. But I couldn't. I just couldn't settle. Was I wrong? I honestly don't know. Now, with time running out, I'm pretty sure I'm never going to know.

Irwin Isaac Meiselman

NEVER TRUST A WRITER ON THE SIZE OF HIS AUDIENCE OR THE SUM OF HIS royalty checks, and so when I say that I estimate the crowd attending my lecture on Willa Cather at Roosevelt University at seventy-five, I suppose it was probably closer to forty. Whether the lecture went over or not, I am the last person to say, for all my energies went into the delivery of it, with not much left over for judging its reception. During the question-and-answer session afterwards, no one had any questions to offer, probably not a good sign, but that was fine with me. The $2,500 fee was decent, and my love for Willa Cather's fiction—my subject—genuine, and so, all in all, I thought it wasn't a bad evening's work.

Standing at the lectern, putting my lecture notes back in my briefcase, I note a pudgy guy with a round face, rimless glasses, bald, alone, who had not left his seat in the second row.

"Excuse me, Ed, but do you have a moment?" he asks.

Ed? Do I know him? "Of course," I reply. "What can I do for you?"

He gets to his feet and comes up to the lectern. He is short, looks to be in his middle fifties, is wearing jeans and gym shoes, and a heavy blue crew-neck sweater. He, too, has a briefcase.

"Irwin Isaac Meiselman," he says, extending his hand. He says the name with authority, as if he had expected me to know it.

"I'm writing a book about immigration to America," he says, "which is why I attended your lecture on Willa Cather this evening. She is, as you mentioned in your talk, one of the great chroniclers of immigration, and she figures heavily in the chapter of my book on the Scandinavian migration. My chapter's still in draft form, but I thought you might like to read it."

Were this a world in which candor was allowed, I should have said, "Of course I don't want to read your chapter. Why the hell would I want to do that? " Instead I hear myself saying, "Sounds interesting. I'd very much like to read it."

He has already fished out of his briefcase what looks like a manuscript of fifty or so pages. I glimpse at it only long enough to note that it is typed single-spaced.

I have been sandbagged by experts in this line. People write me flattering emails. My answer occasions further flattering emails, which eventually lead to a request that I read a seven-hundred-page historical novel my correspondent has written, set in fifth-century AD Byzantium. "This correspondence," as the old *Times Literary Supplement* used to note of exchanges in its letters columns that had gone on too long, "is hereby ended."

I thought my radar for such supplicants was by now fairly well developed, but I have never been confronted so directly as by this man Meiselman. After I put his somewhat smudgy manuscript in my own briefcase, he presents me with his business card. "Irwin Isaac Meiselman, Independent Scholar," it reads, and lists his address, 6327 N. Bell Avenue, Chicago, IL, 60645, in the lower left-hand corner and his phone number, 773-262-3444, in the lower right-hand corner.

"I'll be eager to know what you think about it," he says.

"I'll get back to you," I say, eager only to slip this Meiselman's company and get home.

"Take your time," he says. "If I don't hear from you in three or four days, I'll call you." He extends a small padded hand, more like a paw, for me to shake as he takes his leave.

When I returned to my apartment, I removed the manuscript from my briefcase, and placed it in the bottom of my already overcrowded in-box. So much, I thought, for Stanley Melvin Mitzenmacher, or whatever the hell his name is.

Five days later, a Wednesday, mid-morning, my best working hours, my phone rings.

"Hi, Ed, Irwin Isaac Meiselman here."

My name is Edward Kastell, the name under which I both write and live. When I was a kid, friends called me Eddy, but no one, now or then, has ever called me Ed. My wife doesn't call me Ed. I have never for a moment thought of myself as Ed. Why, suddenly, am I cut down to Ed and this Meiselman, a stranger, gets three full slightly preposterous names? Beware, I tell myself, three-named Jews.

"Hello," I say, trying to put as much formality in my voice as possible, "this is Edward Kastell. What can I do for you, Mr. Meiselman? "

"I was just wondering, Ed, what you thought of my Scandinavian chapter."

"Haven't quite finished it, but I've found what I've read thus far full of interest." I hadn't of course read a word of it.

"Any chance for lunch today to give me your ideas about it?"

"Afraid I'm booked for today, and the next few weeks are crowded ones for me," I say.

"OK," he says, "how's Tuesday, February 11? I can come to Evanston."

February 11 turns out to be one of those Muscovite-like Chicago days, the temperature around 10 above zero, a sleety schmutz blowing in the wind. At Meiselman's suggestion we meet at a Greek restaurant called the Golden Olympic, upon whose awning is written, you'll have to believe me on this, "A Family Restaurant with Just a Touch of Greece."

Meiselman is awaiting me, sitting at a table toward the back of the restaurant, papers spread out before him. In preparation for this lunch, I had dragged my eyes across his manuscript. Not exactly what people nowadays call an easy read. The writing is serious but with an air of hopelessness about it; or maybe it is hopeless with an air of seriousness about it. I'm not sure which. When I say hopeless what I mean is that it is beyond question unpublishable. Meiselman's prose is clotted, filled with academic locutions (lots of "as it weres" and "if you wills"), its author stopping several times in his narrative to put down earlier scholars on the subject. Having said this, I have to add that it showed a great deal of hard work. Some of the footnotes reference books in Scandinavian languages, which made me wonder if its author had taught himself Swedish and Norwegian for this book.

Meiselman waves but does not get up.

"How goes it, Ed?" he says, extending his childlike hand. His finger-nails are dirty. Hair grows out of his ears.

"OK," I say. "Colder, though, than a politician's kiss out there."

"Chicago, what do you expect? I'm just getting ready another draft chapter for you. It's on the Jews, our people," he says, with an odd, slightly contemptuous, chuckle.

"I'd have thought that subject maybe has been done to death."

"Not at all," Meiselman says. "Besides, I think I have a new angle on it."

"What is that?"

"It's that in emigrating from Europe, and especially Eastern Europe, the more adventurous Jews went inland and down south. The tamer Jews, exhausted by their trip, stayed in New York, which offered less in the way of opportunity. So it turns out that in New York you had lots of proletarian Jews—factory workers, house painters, milk men—but not so many in other American cities, where Jews tended to open shops, sell goods, take more risks, be more entrepreneurial."

"Interesting," I say, and mean it. Have I underrated Irwin Isaac Meiselman?

Meiselman orders a bowl of chicken noodle soup, a turkey-bacon club sandwich, and a Coke. I have just the soup, hoping to make a fairly quick escape from this lunch.

When I ask if he is married, Meiselman tells me that he isn't, though he had come close once. "It's a long story," he says. I ask him where he works (in connection with his manuscript the old line, "Don't give up your day job" comes to mind), and he says that he doesn't have to. His mother died when he was seventeen, and father, with whom he continued to live, died nine years ago, and left him, an only child, with enough money to be able to devote the rest of his life to study.

"My father was a hustler," Meiselman says. "He came out of World War II and drove a cab. He bought a second cab. He went from there to acquire a hot dog joint on the old West Side, near the Sears mail-order center. Then he bought a second hot dog stand on Western Avenue, a joint called Beefy 19, you may remember it, near Foster. He never ran any of these places himself. He always had partners doing the actual work. He finally sold everything and acquired an appliance-parts business, which allowed him a minor monopoly on appliance parts for the whole northern and northwestern suburban sections of Chicago."

"Impressive," I say. "My own father was an accountant. Unlike yours, he was a cautious type."

"My old man," Meiselman continues, "once said to me that he thought that if he were away from his business for six months his employees could only cheat him out of eight percent of the profits. A funny thing to tell me, when you think about it, since I was one of his employees."

Meiselman slurps up the last of his soup and starts on his club sandwich. He pours lots of ketchup on his fries.

"I believe my father was dyslexic," Meiselman says. "I never saw him read anything. Whenever I'd give him anything to read, he'd say, 'You read it to me'."

"How come you didn't take over his business?" I ask.

"Because I wasn't any good at it. My father thought about business, money, the angles, full-time. My mind was always elsewhere."

"Where did you go to school?"

"Illinois here in Chicago," he says. "I was a lousy student. I daydreamed. I wasn't a conventional person and couldn't be expected to learn in the regular way, though I didn't know it at the time. A lot of geniuses didn't do well in school. You probably know that."

Modesty was not Irwin Isaac Meiselman's problem. Nor did he need the world to concur with him in his high estimate of himself. He paused to take a large bite out of his club sandwich, a quarter of the contents of which fell onto his plate.

After his father's death, Meiselman went on to recount, he sold the appliance-parts business and went off to live for two years in Israel, but he didn't find it to his liking. He moved to Los Angeles, hoping to write sitcoms, but nothing came of that. He worked for six months for Steppenwolf Theatre, in some vague capacity that he did not explain very well. He published a book of poems, privately printed, a copy of which he promised (I took it as a threat) to send to me. He thinks of himself, he tells me, as an observer, an unattached intellectual, or, as he puts it, his mouth full of french fries, "Chicago's only full-time *flâneur*."

He scoffs up the remainder of his sandwich and orders a second Coke. He has a bit of mayonnaise on the right upper corner of his lips. I decide not to tell him about it; it adds to his charm.

"To change the subject," Meiselman says, and here I thought he was going to ask me about my life or my own writing, for I had after all published five works of fiction, and a book of literary criticism, "do you by any chance have an agent?"

"I do, a woman in New York named Letitia Baumgartner."

"Think she might want to take me on as a client for my immigration book?"

I think of Letitia, tall, thin, cool in judgment, utterly professional in bearing, phlegmatic, properly pessimistic. I try to imagine the letter I might write introducing Irwin Isaac Meiselman and his hopeless single-spaced manuscript to her. Impossible.

Not a chance in the world, pal, I think, but instead say, "I know Letitia isn't taking on any new clients at the moment. But this could change."

Meiselman orders rice pudding for dessert. He tells me an off-color joke about rice pudding, so gruesome that I tell myself to block out that I'd ever heard it. His own laughter at its punchline doesn't travel up to his eyes.

When the check arrives, he asks the waitress if the restaurant takes American Express, which it turns out it doesn't. In other words, I am stuck for the bill, which isn't for a great sum—$26.17, plus tip—but, given that I had read his manuscript and that he was coming to me for advice, shouldn't have been mine to pay.

As we leave the Golden Olympic, I resolve never to allow myself to be trapped into seeing Irwin Isaac Meiselman again. And I wouldn't have, but for his reminding me, once we were out on the street, that I had forgotten his seventy-eight page (single-spaced, of course) chapter on the Jews, which we both go back into the restaurant to recover.

Two days later, 10:15 in the morning, my phone rings. I see from caller ID the name I.I. Meiselman. What does that *nudnik* want now, I wonder, but not enough to pick up the phone. After a brief interval, I check my voice mail.

"Irwin Isaac Meiselman here. Just wanted to let you know that I took the liberty of contacting your agent. I sent her an email. I told her we were friends and that you were nuts about my immigration book, at least of those parts that you've seen. I attached my chapter on the Italian immigration for her to read. Call once you've had the chance to read my Jewish chapter. Take care, Ed."

I made a mental note to call Letitia to explain that I scarcely knew this guy. But first to Irwin Isaac flamin' Meiselman.

"Hi, Ed," Meiselman says when I telephone him.

"Mr. Meiselman," I say, not in the least having to feign anger, "you were out of bounds in using my name in writing to my agent about your manuscript. Way out of bounds. I never gave you permission to call my agent or use my name. I never even said that I liked what you had written, goddamit."

"Call me Irwin, please," he says, calmly.

"I prefer to call you Mr. Meiselman, and I distinctly prefer that you call me Mr. Kastell."

"I didn't mean to give offense," he says, without any note of apology in his voice that I can discern.

"Give offense?" I say. "Mr. Meiselman, if I weren't myself Jewish, I'd consider what you've done a one-man incitement to a pogrom."

"Calm down, Ed, please," he says.

"Kastell, Mr. Kastell," I say, scream actually. "When I get off the phone, I'm going to call my agent to let her know that I am not in any way your sponsor. We're quits, Meiselman, you got that?"

"Just one thing," he says. "My chapter on the Jews—you have my only copy. May I come by to pick it up?"

"I'll mail it to you," I say.

"I don't trust the mail. Lots of work went into that chapter. How about we meet for coffee, and I take it from you then?"

"I'll FedEx it to you. It'll go out today." And I hang up.

The next day I myself receive a small package from FedEx. It contains Meiselman's slender book of privately printed poems and a letter. The letter, with its opening salutation of "Dear Mr. Kastell," offers an abject apology, of an elaborateness that resembled the chapters I had seen of his immigration book, overwritten, though without the footnotes. Its postscript, presumptuous as always, reads: "I hope we can put all this behind us, Ed, and meet again soon for lunch."

As for the book of poems, it was inscribed "With affection and admiration." *Flinches* is its title, a title much superior to the poems, every one of them spoiled by undistinguished social-science language that has no business winding up in poems. Glimpsing the poems in the book, I myself flinched at one line that read: "The hebetude of my lifestyle left her unwilling to interact." The content was something else. Each of the poems registered a defeat or disappointment in its author's life. The first disappointment is about his mother's dying before he really got to know her. Another is about his failure to live up to his father's expectations. Others are about different women, as he delicately puts it, "dumping" him. A poem called "Double-Cross" is about a boyhood friend who betrayed him, stealing his high-school girlfriend. One poem describes his disgust with his own body. Not exactly instructive or delightful, Irwin Isaac Meiselman's poems, yet in their cumulative effect sad and strangely moving. What became clear from the poems is that Meiselman considered himself a loser but without the least clue about the appalling pushiness and insensitivity to others that helped make him so.

When Meiselman's book of poems arrived I knew its author would not take long to follow. One Wednesday morning, as I felt I was breaking through on a crucial chapter early in my new novel, the phone rang, and, without the aid of caller ID I was certain it was Meiselman. He may not have had much talent for writing, but his talent for calling at precisely the wrong time was unsurpassed.

"Ed, Irwin Isaac Meiselman here."

"Yes?" I say, attempting to get as little welcome and as much disdain into my voice as possible. I decide to give up on the lost cause of telling him not to call me Ed.

"Hope you received my book of poems."

"I did," I say, and deliberately do not offer any even tepid compliments, lest they offer him an opening wedge. My intention is to treat this call as if it were from a charity rumored to be strongly anti-Semitic.

"The reason I'm calling," Meiselman says, "is that I have to ask a favor of you. A big favor, I'm afraid." ,

"What is it?"

"I'd rather ask you in person," he says. "Are you by any chance free for coffee this afternoon?"

"Not this afternoon," I hear myself saying. "Tomorrow afternoon is better." Weakling, I think to myself. Enough of this jerk already.

We agree to meet the next day at 4:00 p.m. at the Mozart Café coffee shop in Evanston. When I arrive, Meiselman is seated at an ice-cream table along the back wall. He looks up as I enter. Do I imagine it, or does he look thinner, grayer? He is unshaven; if he is going for the Don Johnson *Miami Vice* look, it's not coming off.

"Hi, Ed," he says, not getting up. He has a cup of coffee before him and a biscotti. He makes no offer to buy me a coffee, so I excuse myself to walk over to the counter and buy a coffee and biscotti for myself.

When I return to the small table, I remark that biscotti is really nothing more than a $3 piece of mandel bread with a slight Italian accent. My small joke gets no response.

"So what's your big news?" I ask.

"I have cancer," he says, looking down at his coffee. "Pancreatic. A death sentence, I'm told."

I was expecting to hear that he had found a publisher. Or that he was planning to write a novel. Or had obtained another agent. I wasn't expecting to hear cancer.

"Shitty luck," is all that I can think to say.

"Yeah," he replies. "It comes at a time when I was closing in on my chapter on Asian immigration to the West Coast. Anyhow I've agreed to undergo chemotherapy in the hope of lasting another eight or ten months, which I hope will give me time to finish my book."

"Is the chemo rough?"

"Very," he says. "That's what I wanted to talk to you about."

What's next? What's he going to ask of me? Pancreatic cancer, I think, doesn't involve bone marrow transplant, thank God, or I'm sure he'd ask me for that.

"I'm exhausted after my chemo sessions. I can get to St. Francis Hospital here in Evanston on my own. But can I ask you to take me home after? I'm too zonked to call and wait for a cab."

"How often do you go?"

"Three times a week, Mondays, Wednesdays, and Fridays, two weeks on, one off. It's a lot to ask, I know."

Meiselman had shown up at my Cather lecture unaccompanied; at our lunch he never mentioned friends. The poems in *Flinches* are as much about loneliness as they are about disappointment. Not that I have any difficulty understanding why, but he must be utterly friendless. How else explain his turning to me, whom he barely knows, to help him out in this crisis?

Better not to get involved, I tell myself. Time to jump this ship on which I never booked passage.

"What time are your chemo sessions?" I hear myself ask.

"From ten to eleven in the morning," he says.

If I pick him up outside the hospital and drive him over to his apartment on Bell, then allow another twenty minutes or so to get back, I can make this entire trip in under an hour. God knows I waste at least an hour most mornings on the phone with friends or futzing around on the internet.

I arrange to pick Meiselman up the following Monday in front of St. Francis, on the Ridge Avenue side. He is standing there, not far back from the curb, as I drive up. When he gets into my Honda, I note his color is drained, his eyes have a slight glint of terror. He pulls the seatbelt around him, sets the seat back, and closes his eyes.

"Thanks for doing this," he says. "If I had to wait for a cab, I'm not sure I could make it. Mondays are the worst, especially after a week off."

"It's poison, chemo," I say, just to make conversation, "poison meant to counteract the poison of the cancer," which exhausts my knowledge of the subject.

"That's what they say," Meiselman replies. "They also say that a person can die from the chemo." He lets his head turn toward the window.

As we climb the three flights to his apartment, Meiselman leans against me. This is the apartment in which he had grown up, the apartment he lived in with his parents and shared with his father after his mother's death. Walking into it I feel I am returning to the early 1960s. A lime-colored green shag rug, wall-to-wall, covers the floor. A white couch is against one wall, under a painting of a girl in profile with a large tear falling from her eye and holding a pet rabbit. A glass coffee table sits before the couch, a bowl filled with hard candies upon it. A large ornate lamp is on a table between two red velour chairs at the front window. On the mantle over the sealed-up fireplace is a shadow box, in whose many inserts are different kinds of tea cups and saucers, a collection doubtless of Meiselman's long-dead mother.

This living room is not so different from the one I had grown up in, though Meiselman's is, from age, shabbier. I note lots of dust everywhere. Another difference is that every flat surface in the room is covered by papers or books and magazines, a mark of the bachelor intellectual, even, as in Meiselman's case, the failed one.

Meiselman flops on the white couch, without bothering to take off his New Balance running shoes. "If my mother saw me like this on her couch," he says, "she would have three conniptions and four heart attacks."

"Mine, too," I say, "except our white couch had plastic covers. You and I are the children of the white-couch brigade."

Meiselman's eyes are closed. He doesn't hear me. He is falling asleep.

"Excuse me if I'm not more sociable," he says.

"Don't worry about it, Irwin," I say. It strikes me that I have not before now called him by his first name. "I'll pick you same time, same place, on Wednesday."

"Thanks, Ed," I hear him mutter, as I close the front door behind me.

Driving back to Evanston I think about what it was that had given Meiselman first his artistic and now his scholarly aspirations. How does it come about that a guy like Meiselman can think he is able to write poems that anyone in the world is likely to care in the least about? In his sleep right now, it occurs to me, he may well be dreaming of the acclaim his book on immigration will earn.

My own case, was it all that different? I wrote novels. A firm in New York agreed to publish five of them, though I couldn't be sure how many more they might want. The novels were respectfully reviewed, but sold in modest numbers. The small advances I got for them supplemented the income from my teaching job at Northeastern Illinois and lent me cachet as a teacher of creative writing. They also allowed me to think of myself as a writer.

We'd both swallowed the Kool-Aid, Irwin Isaac and I, both believed that writing elevated us above our backgrounds, making us more than guys hustling appliance parts like Meiselman's father or doing other people's taxes like my own. Writers were grander than that, mind-workers, artists. Meiselman, scribbling away, was of course kidding himself. What about me?

I made seven more trips to pick up Meiselman in front of St. Francis and drop him off at his apartment. In my mind they all blur into the same trip. He would get in my car; scarcely say more than hello; fall asleep on the short trip to his Bell Avenue apartment; struggle up the stairs, leaning against me; flop on the white couch in his living room, mumble a thank you as I departed his apartment. The only difference is that after my third trip he began wearing a wool pea-cap, which he didn't take off in the car or in his apartment. The hat was there to cover up the loss of what little hair he had to begin with. He was notably thinner, and the look of terror in his eyes—a premonition of death?—seemed intensified. Because at fifty-six he was relatively young, they filled him with powerful potions of chemotherapy. "With pancreatic cancer," he told me, "they figure what do I have to lose, except for my sideburns, my appetite, and my energy?"

Three weeks later, Meiselman called to say that he wouldn't need to be picked up any longer. His oncologist at St. Francis, a Dr. Mutchnik, had determined that the chemo wasn't doing any good, and he would be checking him into the hospice section of the hospital.

"Is there anything I can do?" I ask.

"Yeah," Meiselman says, "you can find a cure for cancer. But in my case you better make it quick." I feel a tinge of relief when he doesn't ask me to run any errands or visit him in the hospice at St. Francis.

Truth is I didn't think much about Irwin Isaac Meiselman after that last call. I don't read a Chicago paper, and therefore had no exact notion when he died. In such matters, what difference does exactitude make? All I knew was that I would receive no more mid-morning Meiselman calls; have no more single-spaced manuscripts thrust upon me; with luck would for the last time in my life be called Ed.

Then, one day, mid-morning, my phone rings, and my caller ID displays the names Frankel & Berman.

"Mr. Kastell, my name is Sidney Frankel, and I represent the estate of the late Irwin Isaac Meiselman. Mr. Meiselman mentions you in his will."

"Really?" was all I can think to say.

"Yes," this Frankel says, in a lubricious voice. "His will stipulates that you are to receive $30,000 in return for services to be rendered."

"What services?"

"The sum of $30,000 is to be paid out to you for editing and completing Irwin Isaac Meiselman's work in progress on the subject of immigration to America."

A joke, right? I think. Someone's pulling my chain. Yet I never told anyone but my wife about Meiselman.

"There are other stipulations," Frankel continued. "The completed book is to bear the name Irwin Isaac Meiselman alone on the title page. The book is also to be copyrighted in his name, with all royalties going to the Irwin Isaac Meiselman Estate."

"Mr. Frankel," I say, "I think you should know that I scarcely knew Mr. Meiselman. I also know nothing out of the ordinary about immigration, to America or anywhere else. Much as I'd like to have the thirty grand, I am in no position to undertake the work needed to collect it."

"Interesting," said Frankel. "In my meetings with him at the St. Francis hospice, Mr. Meiselman led me to believe that you were friends and that you have had a deep interest in his book."

"I was not a friend of Mr. Meiselman's, and it is more precise to say that I had—and continue to have—a nearly complete lack of interest in his book."

"Maybe before you make a final decision you do best to visit my office, where Mr. Meiselman's unfinished manuscript and notes reside in three large boxes. This book, as you must know Mr. Kastell, was everything to Mr. Meiselman."

"I know it very well," I say. "But I don't feel the need to give three or four years of my life to making a dead man's dream come true."

"Your call," says Frankel. "But if you change your mind, the manuscript and other items are here, 116 S. Michigan Avenue, 14th floor. If I don't hear from you within the next six months, the $30,000 will revert to the estate."

I thought a fair amount about that $30,000 during the next few weeks. I thought about it when I took our seventeen-year-old daughter Janeane on a tour of colleges in the east. I thought about it when I learned that I would have to have three back teeth removed and implants set on the lower left side of my jaw. I thought about it when my editor instructed me that the characters in the rough draft of my new novel failed to come alive, and perhaps I would do best to abandon it. I thought about it because it seemed a shame to allow Sidney Frankel and the other legal bandidos in his firm slowly to filch the money over the years in legal costs. I thought about it just because, as the man who climbed Mount Everest is supposed to have said, it was there.

And so here I sit, in the small extra bedroom in our apartment that I call my study, Meiselman's three boxes of manuscripts and notes dominating the room, heavily rewriting the book he planned to call *Huddled Masses*. Turns out I was mistaken when I told Sidney Freifeld that it would require three or four years to clean up Meiselman's book; I now think that working nights and weekends, it can be made presentable and I hope publishable in a year or so. I don't say it will be a great book; I don't think it will be a distinguished one. I've shown a few of my reworked chapters to Letitia Baumgartner, who has no interest in handling it but tells me that it is a book that might find a home at a secondary university press, Missouri, maybe, or Northwestern. God, I hope she's right. I want this book out in the world so that for the rest of my life I need never give another thought to Irwin Isaac Meiselman.

Adultery?

DOES HIS FRIEND LARRY GOODMAN KNOW THAT FELDMAN KNOWS HE SLEPT with his wife? Feldman himself knows because his wife Elaine told him. In words Feldman shall never forget this side of dementia, the day they decided on a divorce, Elaine, in their kitchen, announced: "You aren't doing me any good, either in bed or out of it. And by the way, you should know that I slept with your great pal Larry Goodman." On which triumphal words—triumphal to her, devastating to Feldman—she departed the room and drove off in her red Mazda convertible from the house on Lake Street in Wilmette.

At first Feldman wondered if Elaine made up the story about sleeping with Larry. He didn't, though, wonder too long. Not that Elaine was always truthful. She was full of little deceits; these helped to bring their marriage down. But the pleasure she took in saying she slept with Larry didn't allow much room for doubt.

For Elaine the announcement struck a double wound. Not only did it make Feldman aware that he was a cuckold, a figure of humiliation every man wishes to avoid becoming, but she had brought this about through the agency of his oldest and dearest friend. Where they had done it, how frequently, with how much pleasure were details Elaine spared him, though this only added to the torture.

Elaine was home most nights, so she and Larry must have met during the day. Since the Feldmans had children in school, with kids coming in and out of the house through the day, they must have met at his apartment at Sandburg Village, though they could have ducked into motels. Did they do the same things in bed that in better days Elaine and Feldman did? Did Larry have a few new tricks into which he initiated Elaine? Is it possible she offered Larry favors she never bestowed upon Feldman? Like a man unable to keep his tongue from probing an aching tooth, Feldman played and replayed various pornographic scenes his wife and best friend might have enacted together. This hideous, unending little home movie played in his mind for more than a year after Elaine and he divorced. Sheer mental masochism, all this, of course—but what's a cuckold to do, if Feldman was in fact a cuckold?

A man knows his love is dead when he can imagine with equanimity his wife or lover making love with another man or, as must also be considered nowadays, with another woman. This Feldman eventually could do. He awoke one day a year or so after his divorce and no longer cared with whom Elaine slept, or how much pleasure it gave her, or if he compared well or badly with Larry or with any new lovers she might since have acquired.

Apart from any effect that her fate might have had on his daughters—when they divorced Diane was eleven and Miriam nine—Elaine was no longer of any personal interest to Feldman. She was now the woman who endorsed and cashed his ample child-support checks, nothing more. Were it not for his daughters, dark truth to tell, had Feldman learned that she had died in a car accident or on an operating table, he should not have been much moved. She was dead to him already.

Feldman decided not to confront Larry with what Elaine had told him. He had no evidence beyond Elaine's word, and while he felt the truth of his wife's accusation in his own bones, this wasn't evidence that would, so to speak, hold up in court. Bringing it up could only destroy his friendship with Larry.

Feldman cared a lot more about Larry Goodman than he did about his ex-wife. He might have cared more about him even when he and Elaine were still married. They went back a long way, Feldman and Larry—to grade school, in fact. Feldman had already lost Elaine; he didn't want to lose Larry, too.

How many times had Larry and Feldman been together since he and Elaine had been lovers, if in fact they were lovers, Feldman wondered? He had no way of knowing, since he didn't know how long ago Larry and Elaine had begun their affair, if affair it truly was. An affair implied duration. For all he knew, they might have had sex together only once; it could have been a fling, a roll in the hay, a thing of the moment, wham, bam, thank you, ma'am. Elaine had said, Feldman recalled, that she "slept with," not "had been sleeping with," Larry.

Feldman replayed over and over Larry's and his meetings during the past year or so of his marriage, in the hope of registering any change in his friend's behavior in Feldman's company. Surely something would have been noticeable. Feldman felt fairly certain that he himself could not have kept his cool dining with someone with whose wife he had been having sex; but then he, Feldman, had never had sex with another man's wife.

Larry had been single for roughly fifteen years. He had had a disastrous first marriage, which he entered into at twenty-three and which lasted less than two years. No children came from the marriage, and the only effect on Larry of this marriage that Feldman could make out was a permanently low view of women. "In the end they're all in business for themselves," he remembered Larry telling him. When Feldman reported his own divorce to his old friend, Larry said that he was sorry for the girls, Diane and Miriam, but not for him. "You'll be happier on your own," he said. "Believe me."

Larry Goodman and Allan Feldman first met when they were eleven. Feldman's family had moved from Albany Park to Rogers Park, and, luck of the alphabetical draw, F coming before G, in class Allan Feldman sat in front of Larry Goodman. At that first morning's recess, Larry introduced Feldman to his friends, and the two of them walked home together after school; they lived only a block apart.

From the very beginning there was nothing the two of them couldn't talk about: sports, girls, their vague ambitions. Larry was a kid with no meanness, no malice, to him. Feldman remembered Larry once telling him that he thought he couldn't bring himself to hit another boy in the face. Feldman thought it the statement of a boy with a good heart, especially since at the time he felt he himself would have no difficulty in doing so, and often fantasized about doing it. Of course, Larry said nothing about kicking a guy in the nuts—which, in sleeping with Elaine, if he did, is what Larry had done to Feldman.

In their friendship Larry and Feldman never asked much of each other, certainly not through their boyhood years. Nor did Feldman recall their burdening each other with their troubles.

Feldman had a ping-pong table in the finished basement of his house, and he and Larry played hours and hours of ping-pong together. Feldman didn't remember those long games as competitions so much as their being in tandem, as if they were a doubles team, though each was playing on different sides of the table. Their rallies could run to sixty or seventy shots. In ping-pong as in life, they knew each other's moves, all of them, or so Feldman thought. Elaine's claim to have slept with Larry made him think otherwise.

Feldman went to the University of Wisconsin, Larry to Illinois. Spring vacation of their junior year fell on the same week, and Larry proposed they take a tour of the great cat-houses of the Middle West. And so they did: beginning in Danville, moving on to Kankakee, Terre Haute, Steubenville, and Covington, in Kentucky. They drove Feldman's mother's Chevy Bel Air. What Feldman chiefly remembers of the trip is endless laughter. Once, outside Youngstown, Ohio, they were laughing so hard the Chevy went off the road and into a ditch.

After college Larry went to work for an uncle in the cardboard box business. The uncle had no children, and the plan was that someday he, Larry, would take over the business, a lucrative one. The plan went up in flames when, a few years later, the uncle, a widower, remarried a strong-willed woman with two sons, whom his uncle brought into the business, leaving Larry odd man out. Around this time Larry's marriage, to a girl he went to high school with named Marilyn Rothman, fell apart.

Larry's life was a shambles. He was working in a dead-end job and had just departed, at some cost, a childless and hopeless marriage. After his divorce, he began putting in lots of time at Rush Street bars, dedicating himself to the woman chase. He would sometimes show up for dinner at Feldman's house in Wilmette with a stewardess or nurse in tow. He was by then in his mid-thirties, rather late for such antics. Elaine, strangely enough, used to make fun of him, at least to Feldman. His defense of his old friend was that he was going through tough times and would right himself soon enough.

Feldman had gone to law school, at DePaul, and at the time of his divorce was working for a small firm in The Loop called Horowitz, Friedman & Simon. He would eventually go out on his own, doing estate planning, real-estate, and all-purpose law for individual clients. He made a decent living, but less than a killing. So when, in their early forties, Larry came to Feldman to borrow twenty grand, it was not an insignificant sum. Feldman came up with the money, and didn't ask him what he needed it for; nor did Larry volunteer to tell him. Feldman's suspicion was gambling debts.

This was roughly twenty years ago. In some ways Larry's asking Feldman for the loan was a good sign, or so Feldman thought. Larry would never ask a favor of this magnitude of him if he had slept with his wife, or so he supposed. But then Feldman thought, if Larry had slept with Elaine, why not ask for a loan of twenty grand? In for a penny, in for a pounding was one of Feldman's favorite sayings. In any case, Larry paid back the twenty thousand when he said he would.

Feldman could not quite shake free of the awfulness of Larry's betrayal, if betrayal it in fact was. Innumerable times he thought of calling Elaine, who was now living in Los Angeles, married to a man named Levinson working for the William Morris talent agency, and asking her if she had in fact slept with Larry, or instead just said so in the heat of the moment to add to his feeling of defeat in their marriage. He tried to word the way he would bring up the matter, but every rough draft he composed in his mind sounded utterly hopeless. "Oh, hi, Elaine, Allan here. I have been meaning for years to ask you if you were really serious when you told me that you had slept with Larry Goodman." Or: "Oh, Elaine, quick question: what you said about having sex with Larry Goodman when we were married: a joke, right?" Or: "Not that it matters after all this time, Elaine, but I was wondering, did you mean it when you said, just before we broke up, you screwed my old friend Larry Goodman?"

Twenty-eight years had passed since Elaine ended their marriage. Feldman would probably not have ended it himself, being conservative—or was it long-suffering?—by nature. He has remarried twice since. The first time, on the rebound, was a sad mistake, and lasted four miserable years.

His third—and final—wife and Feldman married when they were both in their late forties, and their marriage has been satisfactory in every way. Feldman has had no other children. His daughters with Elaine survived the divorce, and both seem to have landed on their feet. Diane is a pediatrician, married to a heart surgeon, and living in Oregon, outside Portland; Miriam's husband heads a hedge fund, and they and their three kids live in Manhattan and appear to be flourishing. Elaine died of lung cancer three years ago. Feldman saw no need to trek out to Los Angeles to attend the funeral.

Larry never remarried. So far as Feldman could tell, since his first marriage he never had a real or lasting relationship with a woman, though up through his early sixties he was still in the woman hunt. Then his health began to break down. He had an early hip replacement, and not long after a triple bypass. After his surgery, instead of losing weight as he was supposed to have done, he put on forty or so pounds.

Some of Feldman's and Larry's old intimacy leached away, as is perhaps normal over the long haul of years, even with close friends. They phoned each other less. Their lunches were more infrequent. Two or three months would pass without their seeing each other. They made it a point to go to at least one Bears game and one Cubs game every year. They still saw each other five or six times a year alone. More and more they now met at the funerals of old friends and acquaintances.

When together they mostly talked about the old days. Sometimes they shifted into what Feldman called "crank," which was to compare the way people live today with the way they did when they were growing up, and finding the latter, inevitably, much better. Talking crank, they agreed, can only be done with contemporaries, lest one sound, quite literally, a crank among the young. But when alone together they gave way to it, with much pleasure.

They talked a lot about the kids they grew up with and what time and fate had done to them: the great athlete who died young of colon cancer, the nebbish who ended up a billionaire, the dazzlingly beautiful girl who turned out to be bipolar and ended her life by suicide in her early fifties.

Feldman thought less and less about the probability of Larry's sleeping with Elaine. Meetings between them would go by without his thinking of it at all. Then something would trigger it. One day, sitting in their regular seats at Wrigley Field, Larry told Feldman that the last time he took his then ninety-one-year-old father to a Cubs game, the old man asked him who this new pitcher Gotteratti was. Larry hadn't the faintest idea; then he looked up at the scoreboard and saw in neon letters the words, Gatorade Pitching Change. "That's very amusing," Feldman said, and suddenly found himself thinking about Larry sleeping with Elaine, and the rest of the afternoon was shot.

They would meet occasionally for lunch in Chinatown, at a restaurant Larry liked called Emperor's Choice. He reminded Feldman that for six weeks one summer, when they were fourteen, he worked as a busboy at Pekin House, the local Cantonese restaurant. As a busboy, he was allowed to eat anything he wanted there after work, except shrimp dishes, shrimps being too expensive to fritter away on the help. He recalled the owner, a tall Chinese gent who with the passing of years began to dress, talk, and even look Jewish. He did a great imitation of him, using Yiddish words with a Chinese accent: "What you be, some kind messugarner?" Feldman began to laugh, and then thought: this guy, whom he liked so much, banged his wife. Why, Feldman wondered, didn't he just clear the deck and ask him, "Larry, did you sleep with Elaine? More than thirty years have gone by, and please believe me I no longer care. Or at least I don't care in any of the standard ways. I'm not jealous. I'm not angry. I'm not, I swear, in any way going to resent it. But I really would like to put a longstanding suspicion to rest."

Yet Feldman couldn't bring himself to do it. He couldn't, he supposed, because behind the simple question Did you sleep with Elaine? loomed the accusation of how could you have betrayed me, your closest friend, for a quick roll—or even several slow ones—in the hay? Behind the question Did you sleep with Elaine? lurked the more serious question of What kind of a son of a bitch are you?

A dirty mind never sleeps, somebody or other once said, and now Feldman saw Larry in his current physical state—artificial hip, bypass scars on his chest and leg, pot belly—making love to the then thirty-two-year-old, quite beautiful Elaine Feldman, née Lippman. It was the old porno show, but in historical montage.

Feldman thought that if Larry and he had been drinkers, they might have got loaded one night, and Feldman could have thrown his arm around Larry and said (add your own best slurring diction here), "Nothing personal, kiddo, but do you remember the first time you schtupped my wife?" But they weren't drinkers, and sober Feldman couldn't even tell his old friend that he was worried about his having put on too much weight, that he was looking scruffy, and not taking decent care of himself. Feldman decided that living in ignorance about this matter was finally not crucial. He told himself that he had forgiven Larry, if he had really slept with his wife. Forgiving, though, was easier than forgetting, or so at least Feldman found.

Then two summers ago, sitting together in their regular Wrigley Field seats on the third-base side, at the seventh-inning stretch, Larry said, "Al, something important I've got to talk with you about. Do you have time for a drink after the game?" Feldman answered that of course he did, and to himself thought, at goddamn last, he's going to tell me that he slept with Elaine, has felt terrible about it all these years and wants my forgiveness.

After the game—the Cubs lost to the Braves 6-4—they went to a bar at the corner of Sheffield and Addison. The place was filled with people mostly in their twenties—attractive girls in cut-off jeans, guys with weightlifter arms—and noisy. Everyone seemed almost unbearably healthy. Lots of sexual vibrations in the air. As a non-contender in this game, Feldman felt even older than his age. He and Larry found two seats at the bar. They ordered beers, Heinekens.

"Something I have to tell you, Al," Larry said. "It's been on my mind for a while."

Between the seventh-inning stretch and this moment Feldman had been composing his forgiveness speech. It all happened a long time ago, it's history, no harm done really, Larry was not to give it further thought, at this point in their lives it was nothing to worry about . . .

"Three months ago," Larry said, "I was diagnosed with ALS, Lou Gehrig's Disease. I haven't told anyone else."

"Holy shit," was all Feldman could say.

"I'm terrified," he said. "Take my advice and don't Google ALS. You won't sleep that night."

"Rotten luck!"

"I may have to call on you during the months ahead," Larry said. "I haven't minded living alone all these years, but now I have to start thinking about caregivers, nursing homes, hospices, the full goddamn catastrophe. With ALS taking away my speech and every goddamn thing else, which it eventually does, I may not be in good enough shape to make some of these decisions, let alone express what I want. I'm going to need help, especially toward the end when, I learn on Google, I won't even notice that I'm crappin' in my pants, if I'm wearing pants. I'm going to need you to stand by me, Al. There's no one else I can call on."

Were Larry's eyes welling up? Feldman couldn't be sure, because his own were.

"You can count on me," was all he could think to say.

"I knew that," Larry said.

In the months ahead, Larry first lost the strength in his arms; then his legs went, forcing him into a wheelchair. This caused Feldman to hire a so-called caregiver for him: a Filipino in his fifties named Felix Phau. He charged $900 a week, and earned it. Felix's job was to spoon-feed Larry, dress and undress him, carry him to bed at night, bathe him, lift him on and off the toilet and clean him up afterwards.

Feldman's power of attorney, which Larry had arranged earlier, kicked in. Feldman wrote the weekly checks for Felix, paid Larry's utilities and condo assessment and other bills. Larry's speech grew slurred, and soon the slurry slipped into the unintelligible. His head, which he could no longer keep up, dropped to his chest.

Feldman came over two or three times a week, and spent much of Sunday with Larry, standing in for Felix whose day off it was. They sat with the television set on, tuned to baseball and football games. Feldman brought in Louis Armstrong and Ella Fitzgerald CDs to play for his old friend. Larry would grunt—more like a gurgle—and Feldman would guess from the grunts what he needed: the bathroom, water, his pureed food, the television turned off. Larry was dying the slow death by subtractions that we all fear.

His speech now entirely gone, Larry's only communication came through his blinking his eyes. Felix taught Feldman the crude system of communication he and Larry had worked out. Two blinks from Larry meant yes, three blinks no. One Sunday evening, Felix away and not expected back until ten, Feldman wheeled Larry in his chair into the bathroom, and lifted him onto the toilet. After he was done, he placed him back in his chair, and then set him on his back in bed.

"Larry," Feldman found himself saying, "Elaine, my first wife, you remember Elaine, Larry did you screw her?" Feldman hadn't meant to ask it; it just came out.

Feldman looked down at his friend's oddly serene face.

Larry blinked twice. Feldman awaited a third blink but it never arrived.

"Larry," Feldman said, "are you sure? Are you saying that you did sleep with Elaine?"

No answer. Larry's eyes were closed.

"Look," Feldman said, "even if you did, it doesn't matter. It's trivial, without consequence, doesn't matter."

Larry's eyes were closed. Was he asleep? Feldman couldn't tell for certain. He left the room feeling that he shouldn't have done what he did.

The next morning, at seven, Felix called. "Mr. Goodman die," he said. "Try to wake but no possible. Die in sleep. Quiet death. Good blessing."

Feldman thanked Felix for letting him know, and told him that Mr. Goodman wanted him to have an extra month's pay for all his good service, and that he would be over in an hour or two to relieve him of any further responsibility.

After hanging up, Feldman walked into the kitchen to make coffee, and thought he had no satisfaction whatsoever from learning that his best friend, decades ago, had slept with his wife. He wished he had never found out. The truth, Feldman felt, doesn't always set you free. Sometimes it just makes you feel lousy.

Onto a Good Thing

"Ron?" he asked. "Ronnie Rosenberg?" Rosenberg hadn't a clue who was asking, and the man who had must have sensed this, for he quickly added, "Nathan, Nathan Klein." Rosenberg still didn't remember. "Camp Ojibwa," the man said. "Eagle River, Wisconsin, 1956."

Natey Klein, of course. Skinny kid, talked with a lisp, wet his bed, the cabin goat. Everyone in the cabin was ten years old. Ojibwa was a sports camp, all Jewish, with a bit of arts and crafts added: lanyard-making, wood-carving, that sort of thing. But athletics was at the center of things—softball, basketball, tennis, boxing, ping pong, canoeing, swimming—and Natey had been a lousy athlete, uncoordinated, a slow runner, couldn't catch, terrified of the water, really awful.

With nothing to do but play games all day, eat good food, and learn about the world from the older campers and junior counselors, Rosenberg had been in heaven. Natey Klein had gotten nowhere near so much out of Ojibwa. Small, scrawny, pale, his curly-kinky hair always unruly, he had sometimes sobbed at night in his bed, Rosenberg recalled. Every so often the junior counselors had to hang out his wet sheets in the morning. Natey's parents, Rosenberg had heard, were wealthy. His father was something called a liquor distributor, which, Rosenberg later came to understand, probably meant that he or his family had been bootleggers during Prohibition. Natey was an only child and had to have been a disappointment to his old man, Morrie Klein, who in the 1960s made the Chicago papers because of his connection with the Boys, as they called the Mafia in those days. Mr. Klein must have sent Natey to Ojibwa in the hope of toughening him up. It hadn't worked.

"Of course I remember you," Rosenberg said. "You look nothing like you did when you were a kid." Natey was still short, but now portly, wore rectangular black-framed glasses, had a comb-over hairdo, with hair of a suspicious darkness, resembling a little the tint of oxblood shoe polish. When Rosenberg asked him what he did for a living, Natey replied that for much of his working life he had been a stockbroker but in recent years had been running a hedge fund. He looked prosperous.

They were at the bar mitzvah party for Lou Roth's grandson, Tyler, at a hotel called The Public that used to be the Ambassador East. Lou had gone into the family business, Roth Textiles, supplying linen to Chicago hotels and restaurants. Rosenberg and his wife, Arlene, Natie and his wife, Rochelle (very high maintenance, from the look of her), and two other couples were at the same table. Lou Roth and Rosenberg had played basketball together at Senn High School. Natey Klein mentioned that he had been Lou's stockbroker and, as he added with a confident smile, had done well for him.

For the party Lou and Sheila Roth had hired a disc jockey. "Six grand, he charges just to plug in CDs," Lou told Rosenberg, "and his schedule's so crowded we were lucky to get the son-of-a-bitch at all." The four-piece band Rosenberg's parents had hired for his bar mitzvah party had been led by a man named Phil Lind. Held at the Ridgeview, a residential hotel in Evanston, Rosenberg's bar-mitzvah dinner had been catered by a heavyset middle-aged woman calling herself the Duchess, who also served as mistress of ceremonies. The Ridgeview is today a halfway house for the mentally ill, but in those days, under the direction of the Duchess, it might to a stranger from another country have seemed a full-out madhouse. The Duchess led the room in singing "The Old Gray Mare" and forced everyone out of his and her seats to do the Mexican Hat Dance. Everyone, that is, but Rosenberg's very formal grandfather, who spoke very little English and was a leading figure in Hebrew education in Montreal.

Still, it had been a party for adults. Not this one. All the music played by the DJ at Tyler Roth's party was for kids, and noisy and obtrusive it was. No real chance for dancing, not to the music the six-grand DJ was playing, not for grown-ups, that is. Not much chance for talking either, at least not in a normal voice.

"So what've you been doing for a living, Ron?" Natey asked.

"I went into my father's business," Rosenberg said. "Office furniture. We're on Lake Street, near Wabash."

"Interesting," Klein said, though he didn't look in the least interested.

As the evening progressed, Natey revealed he was a member of Bryn Mawr Country Club, had a winter home in Palm Springs, drove a Bentley, had a son who had gone to the Wharton School of Business and was running a software company in Silicon Valley, and had a daughter who had married a cardiologist and was living in Los Angeles. He and his wife had sold their house in Glencoe five years ago and moved into a co-op at 219 E. Lake Shore Drive, a very expensive address.

"You golf, Ronnie?" Natey asked.

"No," Rosenberg said. "I assume you do from your mention earlier of Bryn Mawr." Never having taken up golf, Rosenberg felt, was one of the few completely sound decisions he had made in his life.

"Love the game," Natey said. "Not that I'm so hot at it. Rochelle, in fact, frequently beats me." Here he patted the back of his wife's bejeweled hand. "We're thinking of buying a condo on a golf course in Scottsdale."

"Sounds lovely," Arlene, Rosenberg's wife, said, looking at her watch.

"Shame you don't golf, Ron," Natey said. "I'd like to have taken you out for a round at Bryn Mawr."

"Maybe we can meet one day for lunch," Rosenberg said. Why did he say that, he thought, for the fact was that Rosenberg had heard all the bragging about his wealth from Natey Klein he needed.

Before they left, Natey and Rosenberg exchanged business cards, and Natey promised to call sometime the following week.

"What a dreary, boring little man!" Arlene said on the drive back to Wilmette.

As promised, Natey Klein called to invite Rosenberg to join him for lunch at the Standard Club the following Friday. Rosenberg said yes, sure, glad to, looked forward to it, then wondered what the hell they would find to talk about.

When Rosenberg was a kid, the Standard Club might as well have been the Union League Club in New York, or White's in England, or the

Jockey Club in Paris, so remote had it been from him and his family and most of the people he grew up with. In those days the Standard Club's membership was purely German-Jewish, and the Rosenbergs and almost everyone else who lived in West Rogers Park were Jews from Eastern Europe. In Chicago, the Jews of Rosenberg's caste had had the Covenant Club, which his father, Sam, joined in the early 1960s when his business became more profitable. In a small room off one of the dining rooms, Sid Luckman, the legendary Bears quarterback, long retired from football and by that point in the cardboard-box business, used to play high-stakes gin rummy. Later in the evening you could hear Luckman swearing in his strong New York accent.

Most unlikely that you would ever hear anyone swear at the Standard Club. Rosenberg had been there once for a fund-raising event for Soviet Jews and was impressed with the general feel of the place, its vast rooms, solid furniture, heavy draperies. He imagined its regular membership as dark-suited, solemn, solidly wealthy, humorless, not likely to be impressed by the accomplishments of Sid Luckman.

But when Rosenberg entered the Standard Club on Friday and told the young woman at the reception desk that he was a guest of Mr. Nathan Klein, he was struck by the view in the lobby of the large number of men in sport shirts, sweaters, chino pants, and even jeans. Several members were wearing those five-day growths of beard called, Rosenberg recently learned, double-stubble or perma-stubble.

When Natey entered the club lobby on the Plymouth Court side, ten minutes late, he was wearing a dark blue suit, a gray silken necktie, and highly polished black shoes with a single line across the toes. He gave off a strong whiff of men's cologne.

"Ron, good to see you," he said. "You know this joint."

"I know only that fifty years ago neither of us would have been able to meet here for lunch."

"Yeah," Natey said. "The old joke was that the only Jewish event ever celebrated at this club was Kristallnacht. The place always had a great kitchen, though. Still does."

When they were seated, Rosenberg asked Natey where he had gone to high school.

"Same place you did: Senn," he said. "I was a semester behind you, but you obviously never noticed me. You were at the center of things—on the basketball team, in the best clubs, and all that—and I was out on the periphery, a nebbish. I didn't have very happy high school years, or for that matter a very good adolescence."

"I sometimes think I peaked back then," Rosenberg said, "and it has been pretty much downhill since I was eighteen."

"You were all-city in basketball, no?"

"Actually, all-north section. I had a ride to play at Bradley, but decided I had got all I could out of basketball. I went to Illinois. What about you?"

"Michigan. Started out as pre-med. My old man's idea, my becoming a doctor. But he died my sophomore year, heart attack, so I switched to economics before organic chemistry, and boredom completely crushed me."

"Looks like it was the right move."

"I've had my share of good luck. How about you, on the money front, I mean?"

"I guess I do all right," Rosenberg said. "My daughter has an autistic child and a husband who deserted her, so I'm pretty much supporting two households, which wasn't in what is nowadays called 'retirement planning.'"

Rosenberg rarely told anyone, even friends, about the condition of his grandson, Zachary, or about his daughter Sarah's loathsome ex-husband. Why was he telling all this to Natey Klein, whom he scarcely knew?

"Sorry to hear it," Natey said. "If there's any way I can help out, don't hesitate to ask."

Rosenberg thought to say that, since you asked Natey, how about letting me have half a million or so. "Nice of you to ask," he said instead.

"I wasn't trying to be nice," Natey said. "I have something in mind. Let me ask, Ron: How liquid are you?"

"By liquid you mean . . . ?" Rosenberg was one of those men who, even though he ran a small business, could never bring himself to think for long about money outside the confines of the office-furniture business. Debentures, leveraging, buying on margin, selling short, capital appreciation—it was all Hungarian to him. Not that he thought he was too good for it. On the contrary. When Rosenberg saw some of the dopes he grew up with having made fortunes in the stock market, or through investing in real-estate development, putting them safely out of the financial wars, he felt woefully inadequate.

"I mean how much money do you have that's not otherwise tied up in long-term investments?"

"If I scrape a few things together, maybe a hundred grand or so," Rosenberg said. "Why?"

"Because I think I can put you onto a good thing. I can turn it into a lot more than that for you, and fairly quickly. That is, if you're interested."

"Really?" Rosenberg said. "Let me think about it and get back to you, Nathan."

"Natey, please, like in the old days, Natey, will do fine."

"Onto a good thing." Rosenberg remembered some years ago asking his friend Norm Brodsky about the sudden wealth of a guy they had known in the Sammy house at Illinois named Earle Pollock. He was no genius, Pollock. In fact, he flunked out his freshman year; couldn't do accounting. Norm told him that someone Pollock knew who worked in the commodities market had put him "onto a few good things," which made him a rich man.

What did Natey Klein have in mind by his "good thing"? He assumed a killing on some fast rising stock. How much of a killing? How quick a turnover was involved? When Rosenberg said that he could scrape together a hundred thousand, he was lying. The only way just now that he could get together a hundred grand was to borrow on his 401(k). And why trust Natey Klein, with his bragging and his oxblood comb-over, with the money?

Rosenberg decided not to talk it over with Arlene. She was even more cautious about money than he. Besides, he knew what she would say. "Put a hundred thousand dollars in the hands of that drip! You must be crazy!" is what she would say. So often the little decisions in life get lots of attention, and the big ones are made on impulse and instinct. It was purely on instinct that Rosenberg decided to trust Natey with his money.

When Rosenberg called Klein at his office the following Monday, Natey said that a certified check, either sent by FedEx or delivered in person, would be best. Rosenberg decided to bring the money himself, just to make sure that Natey wasn't operating out of a boiler room.

The Hawthorne Fund, Natey's firm was called, and his office at 110 N. LaSalle was impressive. The layout was similar to that of a successful law firm: comfortable reception room, long corridor, expensive-looking art all along it. In an office with large windows on three sides sat Natey, behind a large uncluttered desk, on which was a laptop and two pictures of his family in silver frames. On a credenza behind him, three large computers were flickering with lit-up numbers. His suit jacket off, his rounded shoulders, the softness of his chest and pot belly evident, Natey seemed even less impressive.

"Ronnie," he said, "good to see you." He got up to shake Rosenberg's hand and motioned him to one of two chairs in front of his desk. "I think we've found something for you that will produce a substantial profit in a fairly short time. We're going into it in a big way here at Hawthorne, and I thought maybe you could pick up a few shekels going into it in a smaller way. I have to tell you that we usually don't deal with accounts of less than five million dollars. I'm doing this for old times' sake."

"I'm grateful," Rosenberg said, though the truth was, with the certified check for $100,000 in his coat pocket, he was a lot less grateful than nervous. A hundred grand may have been petty cash for Natey Klein, but for Rosenberg it was a serious sum.

"Don't mention it," Nate said. "And speaking of old times, I was thinking about our days at Camp Ojibwa. I spent only that one horrible summer there. Did you keep going?"

"I went for three more years," Rosenberg said, "and then I went to Ray Meyer's basketball camp."

"Ray Meyer? Coach at DePaul, no? When they produced winning teams."

"The last time they did, in fact."

"Getting back to Ojibwa, that summer, 1956, I was friendless, with tormentors everywhere. I've never felt so lost and lonely."

"I hope I wasn't one of those tormentors," Rosenberg said.

"You weren't. On the other hand, you weren't a protector, either. No one was. It would have been a help to have the best athlete in the cabin on my side. But then I suppose it would have been unnatural if you had been."

"My memory is that I was having too good a time to worry about your or anyone else's troubles. Kids, I guess, are pretty thoughtless."

"I wonder at what age a child develops a moral sense," Natey said. "Eight? Ten? Twelve? I suppose it differs from kid to kid. I came to mine early because I had a tough father who didn't hesitate to show his disappointment in me. I craved justice, especially at home, where I didn't very often find it. But back to business."

With a tremulous hand, Rosenberg reached into his suit jacket and took out and handed Natey his certified check for one hundred thousand dollars. Nate picked up the phone—"Malcolm, need your help," he said—and ten seconds later a young man, very well turned out, came in to take Rosenberg's check.

"See that Mrs. Lindstrom prepares a receipt for Mr. Rosenberg to pick up on his way out," Natey said.

When the young man left the room, Natey returned to Ojibwa days. "You remember a kid named Barry Dobrin? He taunted me without letup. He used to come over every morning to check my sheets. He once nailed a blue ribbon to my bed with a sign attached to it that read, 'Congratulations to Natey for not wetting his bed six days in a row.' I begged my father to let me come home, but it was no-go. 'Be a man, Nathan,' he told me. 'Stick it out. Don't let them push you around.'"

"Do you think about this stuff a lot?" Rosenberg asked.

"When I saw you," Natey said, "it all came back to me. But I've more important things to think about, like earning a few bucks for you and my other clients."

Back on the street, Rosenberg realized that he hadn't even bothered to ask Natey Klein what, precisely, the "good thing" was that he was putting him onto. He supposed he could call Natey when he got back to his own office, but then thought doing so might reveal him for the financial idiot he was. He'd just have to wait it out.

Rosenberg gave Natey the hundred grand out of a simple enough motive: He had a strong hunch that he could make some easy money that way. The fact was that Rosenberg had never made any easy money in his life. Everything he'd earned he had to work for, to grind it out. His father had been no different. Rosenberg remembered when he was a kid his father had a fairly large chunk of AT&T stock, blue chip it was called in those days, when AT&T had the monopoly on the phone business. Then in 1969 the stock market took a serious dip, and every night his father would come home, open the *Daily News* to the stock-market pages, and note that he had lost another five or six grand. It made him almost sick with worry. After less than two weeks Sam Rosenberg sold off all his AT&T stock, put the money in CDs, and never went back into the market.

Rosenberg recalled his father explaining at the dinner table that the stock market wasn't for little guys, small-time investors. It chewed them up and spat them out. What he most disliked about having his money in stocks, his father said, was that it wasn't in his control. His inventory of desks, file cabinets, chairs, lamps, and the rest, he could change the prices on; hustle around to find outlets for them; lay them off on another supplier. He had the whip hand.

His father wouldn't have been proud of him, Rosenberg thought, turning over so large a sum to a stranger. As he walked back to his office, he wished he had the nerve to call Natey and tell him that he had had a change of mind and would like to have his money back, though he guessed that by now Natey had already put it into play in some investment or other.

Over the next weeks, Rosenberg scarcely thought about anything else. The worry became so intense that life before Natey Klein suddenly seemed wonderfully simple and placid and manageable—sad daughter, autistic grandson, and all. What the hell was I thinking? Rosenberg asked himself. Ten or twelve times he picked up the phone to call Natey to ask how the "good thing" was going, but each time he hung up. To show nervousness about his money would seem unmanly.

Rosenberg also began to wonder why Natey Klein was doing Rosenberg this big favor. What was in it for him, apart from showing what a powerful operator he was? And then a frightening idea occurred to Rosenberg. What might have been in it for Natey was, just possibly, revenge. Nathan Klein was going to take Ronald Rosenberg for a hundred grand for not coming to his aid during his summer of torment at Camp Ojibwa.

Hadn't he all but told Rosenberg that this was what he was doing— with his rehearsal of his misery of those awful days, mentioning that he didn't usually take on small-potatoes clients like him, not bothering to fill him in on the good thing he had lined up for him? A hundred grand down the crapper! God! How was Rosenberg going to explain this to Arlene?

The more Rosenberg thought about it, the more certain he became that Natey had decided to bilk him out of his money. In bed, sleepless, he imagined different scenes in which Natey told him that things hadn't worked out, that the good thing turned out to be a rotten thing. He imagined Natey, behind his desk, with a sly smile, saying, "Way it goes, Ronnie. Sorry. Better luck next time, pal."

Roughly five weeks after he had handed over his certified check to Natey, on a Tuesday morning, a little after ten o'clock, a woman's voice asked him to please hold for Mr. Nathan Klein.

"Ron," Natey said, "some disappointing news. Can you drop over later this morning? I'll explain."

Well, thought Rosenberg, the shoe had fallen; hell, make that the guillotine blade. He hailed a cab, and on the way over to Natey Klein's office he wondered just how much of his money had been blown away: a third, half, all of it?

Natey didn't get up from his desk this time when Rosenberg entered his office. He had his suit jacket on. Behind his black-frame glasses he had a dour look.

"Sit, Ron. I'll explain," he said.

"How much did I lose?" Rosenberg asked. Natey didn't answer but took an envelope from the top of his desk and handed it to Rosenberg.

"Open," he said.

The envelope contained a check. Rosenberg put on his own glasses to read the sum. The check was made out for $100,287.26. He exhaled.

"Pathetic, I know," Natey said. "I was hoping it would be a check for at least a hundred and fifty grand, maybe two hundred. The action we had figured on for the stock never turned up. It was a fizzle, a wash. Sometimes happens."

Rosenberg was trying to hide his relief. Everything ventured, at least nothing lost, he thought. After the anxiety of the past weeks, nothing lost felt like pure triumph.

"I was hoping to make a nice little score for you, Ron," Natey said. "First because I sensed you could use the dough. And second I guess because I wanted to impress you, to show you that the pisher from Cabin Three at Camp Ojibwa was now a serious player."

"Don't worry about it, Natey," Rosenberg said. "I appreciate your effort on my behalf."

"If another good thing turns up, I'll get back to you pronto. Promise."

"Sure," said Rosenberg, "that'll be great."

Natey stood up, leaned over his desk, and held out his hand. Rosenberg shook Natey's small soft hand, noting the clunky Rolex on his wrist.

Out on LaSalle Street, Rosenberg felt himself grinning. He touched the left breast of his suit jacket, the inside pocket of which held his check from the Hawthorne Fund. $287.26 profit for five of the worst weeks of his life: For all his anguish that came to a little more than fifty bucks a week. Easy money! Back at the office, he instructed his secretary that if a man named Nathan Klein should ever call, she was to tell him that Mr. Ronald Rosenberg had died.

Race Relations

"C'MON, FLOWERS, YOU REDNECK, YOU CRACKER BASTARD, THROW, LET 'ER fly, baby, if you got the balls."

I don't exactly know what had happened: whether in the boredom of a Saturday afternoon at the end of our fourth of eight weeks of basic training Bobby Flowers, late of Jonesboro, Arkansas, had called Jackson Gates, late of Detroit, Michigan, a nigger, or Gates had applied some similar magic word to Flowers. But someone had said something to someone, and it appeared as if we might have a small race war on our hands in Charley Company, Second Battalion, Third Training Regiment, Fort Leonard Wood, Missouri. Gates, along with five of his black pals, was on the porch of their barracks, while Flowers, with nine of ten of his good ol' boys, rocks in their fists, was about to charge up after them.

The scene reminded me that when I was a boy growing up in Chicago, at Riverview, the great amusement park at Western Avenue and Belmont, for a quarter you could get three lumpy baseballs with which to try to knock a black man in the water. The blacks, four of them, sat in separate cages, each upon a swinglike platform three or so feet above a shallow pool of water. A bar extended out from the left of each of these cages, at the end of which was a disc of steel perhaps a foot in diameter. Hit the disc with a ball and the bar triggered the platform, which fell away, dropping the man in the pool of water. In accomplishing this feat the lumpiness of the baseballs and the throwing-distance of some ninety or a hundred feet were really minor obstacles. The major obstacle was that the men within the cages taunted the customers, picking out some trait in them and playing it for a public laugh at their expense. "C'mon ya squinty little mothah," a black man in one of the cages might call out to a Chinese guy about to try his luck, "les' see what you got." And then, when the man missed all three throws, the black would return with, "Sorry, squints—no bowl of rice!" Men with girlfriends or wives in tow were especially vulnerable. "That the best you can do, Peewee?"—or, as the trait might have been, "Fatso," or "Four-eyes," or "Baldy." Sometimes they would turn their buttocks toward the customer, bend over, and call out from between their legs, "Pit-i-ful." I have seen men grow so enraged that they forgot the disc that triggered the platform and threw directly at the cage, hoping the ball would go through the wire and crash against the black's skull. Often a man would spend five or six dollars and damn near throw his arm out before he had the satisfaction of knocking one of those jeering blacks in the water.

"All right," Sergeant Alerton boomed, striding across the company area. "I see where I got me the chance to kick some ass before I knock off for the weekend." A tall man, ebony and elegant in fatigues, boots, and helmet liner, Sergeant Alerton adopted the style with trainees of a menacing Kingfish: he could make jokes—fine Kingfishian ones—but he was not a man you fooled with. His first announcement to us recruits after we had arrived at Charley Company, our heads freshly shaved, writhing in the itchiness of our new uniforms and nearly lame from the stiffness of our boots, was about religious services. "On Sunday mornings," he yelled, *en basso,* "every swinging dick among you will get your can out of the sack to attend church in the denomination of your choice. As for those of you of the Hebrew extraction, you will haul your cans off to Friday evening services, making arrangements to help GI the barracks for Saturday inspection later in the evening." While helping out for two days in the orderly room when the company clerk took sick, I learned that Sergeant Andrew Alerton had been awarded a Bronze Star and a Purple Heart in Korea. Eleven years ago, before joining the regular army in 1948, he had worked as a soda jerk in St. Louis.

Alerton's intervention was enough to calm things down. Gates and his gang disappeared into their barracks, Flowers and his walked off. Some of the troops went back to their touch football game in the Fort Leonard Wood dust; others returned to writing letters or to poker games or to listening to radios in the barracks. I went off to the PX with two guys from my platoon for a beer and to pick up a can of shaving cream. The

Gates-Flowers wrangle could have turned into something very ugly. Before I had thought Jackson Gates a somewhat comic figure; I now began to think him perhaps also slightly dangerous.

Whatever else I might have thought about black people, I was not accustomed to thinking of them as dangerous. Most of what feelings I did have, I suspect I must have taken over from my father. Without being a particularly political character—years later I was surprised to learn that he had twice voted for Eisenhower over Adlai Stevenson—my father had rather special feelings about black people. Ernesta Robinson, a most upright middleclass black woman, was the secretary and bookkeeper for his small but successful business at a time when blacks, men or women, were not generally allowed in office jobs. Once, when I was four or perhaps five years old, my father heard me recite the street rhyme "Eenie meenie minie mo, catch a nigger by the toe, if he hollers let him go," and upbraided me for it so severely that, not knowing why he was angry or where his anger was coming from, I collapsed into tears. "Of all people," my father said, "we as Jews must never use such words."

Then at home, not living with us but coming in two days a week to clean and iron, was Dell, a short and very dark woman who was "with us," as my mother used to put it, for as long as I could remember, but whose last name I never knew. Dell did not say much, but I remember her being especially kind to me, the oldest child, perhaps because she knew me longer than she knew my sister. "How Dell's baby?" she used to say to me when she had changed into her work clothes. When I was seven or eight, she would occasionally slip me a nickel. My mother told me I must find a polite way not to take these nickels; Dell worked hard for her money and had better things to do with it than give it to me to spend on candy or gum. My mother used to give Dell those of her dresses she was no longer interested in, or make up for her a bag of fruit—some of it bruised, which neither my sister nor I, being finicky about such things, would eat—to take home for her family. One day in my eleventh year I came home from school to learn that Dell had had a heart attack while washing our dining-room windows and, before an ambulance arrived, had died on our living-room couch. She was forty-seven years old. Could she have borne a son like Jackson Gates?

Although Gates was in the third platoon and I was in the second, I recalled noticing him on our first full day in Charley Company. Sergeant Roscoe Mullins, our field sergeant, a white man with a devoted beer-drinker's stomach—"Ah," he used to exclaim, as we headed back to the company after one of our long marches, "I can taste that Falstaff now"—asked if anyone among the trainees had any ROTC experience. Gates sprang forward to announce that he had had three-and-a-half years of ROTC at Morgan State College. That three-and-a-half years sounded fishy to me—with four years, after all, he would have qualified as an officer—but apparently it did not sound so to Sergeant Mullins, who appointed Gates trainee sergeant of the third platoon. With exaggerated posture, Gates saluted and screamed out, "Thank you, sir!"

"Goddamn it," Mullins returned, "what the hell they teach you in ROTC, Gates? You don't, damn you, salute and you don't say 'sir' to a noncommissioned officer!"

My father used to write an annual check of $1,000 for the NAACP, but as he wrote out those checks I doubt that he had in mind someone who looked like Jackson Gates. In appearance, Gates was a liberal's nightmare of a black person, a middle-class black's nightmare of a black person, but a Ku Klux Klan cartoonist's delight. He was not merely very dark but about four or five different colors; his skin rather resembled the leather of an old boot that had been shined first with black polish, then with cordovan-colored polish, then with oxblood, then brown, then black again. His large lips protruded, the bottom one pendulously; two of his bottom teeth in the front were capped in gold. His nose was flat, the nostril holes the size of quarters. His skull had an odd shape to it, as if it had once been bashed in on one side. His hair was shaved, as was everyone else's in basic training, but in civilian life I imagine it must have been straightened and heavily pomaded in the style known as processed. He wore glasses with thick lenses and wide black frames, which, when he took them off, left him squinting with the look of someone who had just come up from a lengthy underwater swim. He was about five-foot-nine and muscular, but his muscularity had no athletic gracefulness about it—a point worth mentioning if only because, at a later time, he told me that in college he played second-string behind the Chicago Bears' great running back

Willie Gallimore. Certainly it seemed unlikely that Gates played behind Gallimore, yet who knew for sure in those days how deep in talent black colleges like Morgan State were? He probably didn't, but then again he just may have. The same went for those three-and-a-half years of ROTC. Why three-and-a-half years? Nothing in Gates's way of speaking or general manner hinted at his having gone to college at all.

None of these need have been pressing questions but for the fact that, when basic training was completed, I was sent to clerk-typist school at Fort Chaffee, in Arkansas, and so, too, was Jackson Gates. I was sitting on my bunk, unpacking and laying out my gear the morning we arrived, when Gates threw his duffel bag atop the bunk next to mine.

"What's happenin', baby?"

"Not a hell of a lot," I said.

"Arkansas! Daddy, this ain't exactly my idea of a sweet place for a man with my suntan. Dig?"

I replied that, since we apparently were not to be allowed to leave the base anyhow, it didn't matter too much where we were. My own situation, I said, was really not so different from his.

"Let's face it, Gates, the army shows no favoritism. It treats everyone as if he were black."

"Hey, daddy," he said, "you ain't too bad, you know that?"

As it turned out, Chaffee was a great improvement over Fort Leonard Wood. It wasn't so cold; one wasn't always biting down on coal dust. Clerk-typist school entailed less spit and polish, less overall harassment, than basic training. After morning chow we would line up in fatigues, boots, helmet liners, and field jackets, but instead of rifles on our shoulders we would tote typing manuals under our arms. ("Titless WACs" was the old army joke.) We would be marched off to spend the morning learning to type to music, usually to very upbeat stuff such as the theme from *Bridge over the River Kwai* or John Philip Sousa marches; return for lunch; then march back to afternoon sessions about how to fill out morning reports. Although we could not go into the nearby town of Fort Smith (not yet, at any rate), or even keep civilian clothes, our evenings were pretty much our own. Our regular army platoon sergeants not only didn't mind poker games in the barracks but generally took a hand. Lights went out at nine, yet no one minded if you sat in the latrine and read. After not being allowed any books or magazines through all of basic training, I now went on a reading binge, gorging myself after lights-out on nineteenth-century Russian and English novels.

One night around eleven o'clock I was sitting propped against the wall in the latrine, using my folded-up field jacket as a pillow, reading a Chekhov story entitled "An Anna Round His Neck," when Jackson Gates walked in.

"Hey, man," he said from one of the urinals, his back to me, "you got it made, you know that?"

I didn't respond because I wasn't quite sure exactly what he meant. Was he commenting on what must have been my evident pleasure in my book? Or was he, more significantly, talking about the fact that this was Arkansas, the South in the year 1959, and that I was white and he black, and that made all the difference in the world? Whichever it might have been, Gates was evidently not going to elaborate upon the point.

"Sacktime," he announced, zipping himself up as he walked out of the latrine.

Odd: it was a Wednesday night and Gates was wearing not his fatigue but his dress green uniform. He appeared, moreover, to be coming in from off the post, something strictly forbidden. But if he hadn't gone off the post, then why was he wearing his dress greens?

The last man who told me that I had it made was also a black man, LeRoy Fortess, who worked for something like eleven years for my father as his shipping clerk, porter, mail clerk, and odd-jobs man. LeRoy was in his early forties, natty even in work clothes, and never without his hat, usually a fairly expensive gray fedora. LeRoy had an eye for the ladies; once, when I was sixteen and working on Saturday for my father, LeRoy asked me to fetch him some cigarettes out of the drawer of his workbench. The cigarettes were there, all right, but so were two decks of playing cards with porno pictures on them and a half-dozen or so of an item that used to be known as a French tickler. Because of this discovery of LeRoy's penchant for the illicit, I one day asked him if he could arrange to get false identification for a friend and me, so that, though under age, we could be served in bars. Not a problem, said LeRoy, and one Sunday my friend and I traveled out to the West Side to pick up LeRoy. LeRoy wore a pearl-gray hat with a midnight-blue band and my father's hand-me-down double-breasted camel's hair overcoat, and, in this getup, looked oddly Jewish. He had us drive over to a black undertaker's on Lake Street. In the basement, where the undertaker worked, corpses were strewn about on tables, the blood and other body fluid still being drained from one. LeRoy explained to the undertaker what it was that we wanted. The undertaker, a muscular man in an undershirt and wearing a stocking cap, took out two affidavits, filled in our names and false ages, and then signed and notarized them. We each paid him $5. Unfolded, the affidavits measured roughly three feet long and were, of course, absolutely useless; any bartender presented with a document of this kind would double over with raucous laughter. But we said nothing, lest we offend LeRoy, who had done the best he could. "You got it made now," he said when we dropped him off at his apartment. A few years later, when I was at college, my father discovered that LeRoy, who for more than a decade had been taking off Tuesday afternoons (with pay) to get treatment for an advanced case of diabetes, never had diabetes at all. Although my father regretted doing so, there was nothing for it but to fire him.

However he may have intended it, there was a sense in which Gates was correct about my having it made. While I was committed to the draftee's bleak view of army life, the truth was—though I should not have admitted it—that I rather liked my time at Fort Chaffee. The duty was light, except for pulling an occasional KP or guard duty. I played poker in the early part of most evenings and won fairly steadily at it, and I read myself nearly to sleep afterward in the latrine. I was even learning to type and taking a certain pleasure in becoming good at it. Of course, my situation was different from that of others. I had not had to leave a good job when I was drafted but instead dropped out of graduate school, which I had intended to do anyway. Nor did I leave a wife or even a regular girlfriend in Chicago. After the indolence of graduate school, the routine of the army was something of a relief. Things could have been a lot worse, especially if I had been married.

I didn't know that Jackson Gates had a wife in Detroit. Even though his bunk was next to mine, he never mentioned being married. Nor could I remember, at mail call, his named being yelled out for regular letters, as was the case with most married men among the trainees. I only first learned about Gates's marriage when Otis Cook, a light-skinned and rather heavyset black man in our barracks, with whom Gates usually ate in the mess hall, told me that Gates had just received a Dear John letter from his wife and was getting emergency leave to return to Detroit to try to patch things up. The reason that Cook was telling me this was that he was collecting from everyone in the barracks to get up some money for Jackson to get home on. I gave him twenty bucks, out of my poker winnings. Gates was to leave for Detroit the next day, a Saturday, after inspection. He seemed defeated before he left—as who in his place would not have been—and not very optimistic about being able to hold his marriage together. Dressed in his greens and bulky army overcoat, he left amid our calls of good luck. If I thought it at all strange that he had bothered to take along on so dour a mission a recent PX acquisition, his portable hi-fi, I didn't, in my sympathy for the poor guy, choose to dwell on it. As my mother's Aunt Sophie used to say, "Go understand the *shvartzers!*"

While Gates was in Detroit, I spent the worst day of my two years in the army. It was a day of KP, which started out like all such days, except that I did not get the job I had come to prefer on KP, that of scrubbing pots and pans. I preferred it because, while it involved the most drudgery, it also involved, so unrelievedly dreary was it recognized to be, the least harassment. Instead I had to take the job of dining-room orderly, which involved setting and cleaning off tables, mopping floors, filling salt and pepper shakers, cleaning the milk machines, replacing condiments. Under a tough mess sergeant it meant a number of additional chores. And our mess hall, a large one shared by four different companies, had a tough mess sergeant: a short black man from New York of compact build and yellowish color with the misleadingly soft name of Larry Winslow.

It looked to be the normal grueling fifteen-hour day on KP, but Sergeant Winslow had added a new twist to the usual torture. After our dining-room chores following lunch were finished, instead of allowing us a short break, he put the eight dining-room orderlies to the tedious and knuckle-busting job of rubbing down his huge black ovens with steel wool. To what purpose we did this was unclear, yet the job, because you could not determine if you were making any progress on it—you just kept rubbing those frigging ovens, which didn't get any shinier or any duller—was impossible to concentrate on for long. Winslow caught us joking about the endlessness of the job. In an accentless voice, without a tremor of passion in it, he warned that if he caught us again we could expect to spend the entire night working in his kitchen. I doubt that there was anyone among us who did not believe in his ability to make good on the threat, but the tedium of the task simply proved too much. Half-an-hour later we were joking again. None of us noticed Sergeant Winslow approach from behind. "More grab-assin', I see," he said in that terrifyingly calm voice. "All right. You will all spend the night taking off the old wax from these floors and rewaxing them." And so we did. We worked till 5:30 the next morning, a full twenty-four-hour shift, knocking off only when the next day's KPs came on, leaving us bleary-eyed and with time enough only to shave and change into fresh fatigues for the day's classes.

Everyone who has put in his time in the army has run into a man of quiet but quite earnest cruelty like Sergeant Winslow, and the only reason I bring him up here is because, two weeks after our twenty-four-hour KP shift, when we were given our first pass into the town of Fort Smith, I saw the fearsome Sergeant Winslow. He was driving through town in a current year's white Buick convertible. The top was down and he was laughing and sharing a feeling of comfortable cordiality with a companion who turned out to be my old bunkmate, Private Jackson Gates.

This glimpse of him on obviously chummy terms with Sergeant Winslow altered my opinion of Gates. But then, my opinion of Gates regularly underwent alterations. While we were at Chaffee, a Liston-Patterson title bout was scheduled, and near the day of the fight I stood a few men down from Gates in the chow line at lunch. He talked about the fight with great authority. Doing a bit of fancy footwork, feigning and snorting in a shadowboxing dance, he allowed as how, back in Detroit, he had had five professional fights as a middleweight. Bull, I said to myself. Then I heard him say that he had lost four of these fights, two by knockout, and after the last knew it was time to get out before he had his brains permanently scrambled. Artful bull, I thought, but still bull. Yet not long after Gates returned from his trip home to save his marriage—a trip whose outcome, along with my twenty bucks, was never mentioned—he began wearing a T-shirt across the front of which was printed "Detroit Golden Gloves 1957." Could he have had those pro fights? Who, with Gates, knew?

What was known was an extraordinary performance that Gates had put on in the company commander's office. I myself learned about it from Marv Gradman, the company clerk, who had been a ZBT at the University of Illinois, as I had been at the University of Michigan. Gates, as Gradman told the story, had requested permission to speak with the "old man." I put quotes around "old man" because he, our company commander, was a first lieutenant who had gone through the ROTC program at Auburn University in Alabama and who could not have been more than twenty-five, or two years older than most of us in clerk-typist school. He was blond, the old man, with perfect teeth and well turned-out in his tailored and starched fatigues. He had, as Gradman explained, less than ninety days to serve before returning to Mobile, Alabama, a fiancée, and a profitable family construction business. Never very wide-ranging in his interests to begin with, the old man, according to Marv Gradman, at this time had only one thing on his mind: getting the hell out of the army and back to Mobile with as little complication as possible.

Since the old man had not a ghost of a clue who Jackson Gates was, one has to imagine his surprise when Gates, this strange-looking creature in thick black-framed glasses, shows up before his desk, pops him a salute that would have been overdone if offered to Benito Mussolini, and, after his salute was limply returned, began:

"Sir, Private Jackson Gates reporting, sir! The reason I am here is to report acts of racial discrimination against myself in this company, sir! I do not want at this time to go into any detail about these acts, sir! I have considered reporting them to my uncle, Mr. Samuel Gates, attorney-at-law and executive secretary of the Greater Detroit Chapter of the National Association for the Advancement of Colored People, sir! But I do not wish to be a snitcher, sir! No, sir! Instead, sir, knowing that you are a white man from Alabama and I am a black man from Detroit, sir, I thought I would show you some of the best damn soldiering you ever seen out of any draftee, white or black, sir!"

And with this, Gates, still at rigor mortis attention, clicked his heels, popped another extravagant salute, executed an about-face of furious agility, and marched out of the old man's office. The old man's mouth had not yet closed when Gradman, having been rung on the intercom, appeared in his office.

"Specialist Gradman," the old man drawled, "what in the cotton-pickin' hell was that all about?"

Whatever it was, it was decidedly not something that was going to keep the old man from getting back to Mobile in eighty-odd days. Suddenly, at morning lineups and elsewhere, Private Jackson Gates emerged from obscurity.

"Okay, Gates," the first sergeant announced, "march the men off to class."

"Gates," the sergeant in charge of Saturday morning P.E. called out, "help me demonstrate to these young troopers how a push-up ought to be done. Watch Gates, men."

"All right, Gates, you take over as sergeant of the guard. Assign the shifts. But you're not to walk any guard yourself."

To pick up an extra $20 or $25 Gates would every so often contract to do guard duty for someone else in the barracks. Easy money for him, since he never actually had to walk shifts himself—he could count on being picked as sergeant of the guard—but merely had to dress for it. One weekend, when he had taken on someone else's guard duty under these terms, he found he had no clean dress shirt and asked if he could borrow one of mine, which he promised to have laundered and back to me before the week was out.

I handed him a shirt from out of my footlocker.

"Thanks, baby," he said. "I won't forget it."

Although our bunks were next to each other, Gates and I could scarcely be said to be friends. He for the most part hung around with the seven or eight black men in the company—and, on weekends, or so I gathered, with Sergeant Winslow. What conversation we had was the usual common grousing, complaints about the food, or the weather, or army life in general. When he came in late—where from, I still had no idea—he would greet me in the latrine with a perfunctory "How ya makin' it?" or "What's happenin'?" That, though, was about the extent of it. But with my loaning Gates a shirt for guard duty, I sensed a slight change in him toward me; if not precisely a new friendliness, then a recognition that I wasn't just another white face. One Saturday morning, when I was running late for inspection, I was hurriedly straightening out my footlocker and looked up to find that Gates, without being asked, was making my bed. I was touched.

Not that any real friendship between us was likely to develop. Less than four of our sixteen weeks of clerk-typist school remained, at which time we would all be shipped out of Fort Chaffee to work as company clerks or in headquarters companies on other posts. In 1959 there was no war, and no serious threat of war. The only question was where each of us would be assigned: some dreary hole like Fort Bliss, Texas, or Fort Polk, Louisiana, or Fort Benning, Georgia; or Korea, which sounded grim but at least offered the prospect of some leave-time in Japan; or, plum of plums, Europe, anywhere in Europe.

Early one Saturday afternoon Gates and I were alone in the barracks. An Erroll Garner record was playing on his hi-fi. I was writing a letter home and Gates was sitting on the edge of his bunk shining a pair of boots when he asked me where I hoped to be transferred to after clerk-typist school.

"Anywhere in Europe would be great," I said. "What about you?"

"I'm heading back home to Detroit," he said. He said this with absolute confidence.

"How can you be sure?"

"Cause it already been taken care of." Gates admired the shined boot, put it down, picked up its mate. "No sweat, daddy."

When I pressed him, Gates told me that through his friend Larry Winslow he had got to know another sergeant at G-1, personnel, where all the transfer orders were cut. "He a good cat," said Gates, "my man at G-1."

"Jackson, do you think your man could find a way to get me to Europe? If he can swing it, tell him there's three hundred in it for him. And, by the way, there's another two hundred in it for you."

I had blurted it out, said it without thinking about it, almost as if by instinct. But now that I had said it, I did not wish to withdraw what I had said. The quality of the next eighteen months of my life hinged on where I would be sent. Would they be lively or dead months? Eighteen months in Germany or France as opposed to eighteen months in Texas or Missouri made all the difference in the world. As for the money I had promised Gates, well, I had poker winnings stowed away of more than $250; and the remainder I could get from friends in Chicago, or if need be from my parents. Of course, Gates could be lying, in which case it would come to nothing anyway. But then again he might not be, in which case I would have been foolish to have said nothing. As long as no money passed hands, it was worth a try.

"No harm my asking the cat," Gates said. "We'll get back to you on it, hear?"

Gates was apparently in no great hurry. A week went by without my hearing anything further from him. My mind, meanwhile, feasted on fantasies of weekends in Paris, London, Rome: myself seated before a small glass filled with amber liquid at twilight at the Brasserie Lipp; being fitted for an elegant and indestructible English suit on Jermyn Street, Savile Row; dashing about on a Vespa in the neighborhood of Vatican City. The contrast with the likely alternatives—beery weekends in Rollins, Missouri, tattoo shops in Killeen, Texas—was more than demoralizing. My patience ran out.

"Jackson," I asked one morning as we walked back from chow, "hear anything from your man in G-1 about getting me to Europe?"

"I told him about you, baby. Told him you ofay but okay. He say he gonna look into it. He supposed to let me know tonight."

I awaited Gates that night in the latrine. I tried to read Turgenev, but it was no-go. My mind drifted to tableaux of myself squirting wine into my mouth from a leather pouch in Andalusia, strolling leisurely among the tables at Blackwell's in Oxford, skiing in Austria. Around 11:30 Gates walked in.

"What's happenin', daddy?"

"My question to you exactly, Jackson."

"How do Brussels, Belgium, sound, daddy?"

"Really? Brussels? It sounds beautiful. Tell me more."

"They need typists at something called NATO headquarters there—eight of them. My man says, why shouldn't you be one of them typists? Trouble is, there ain't no American base in Brussels, so you'll got to live in an apartment. Just like a civilian, pops." Knowing this made it all the sweeter, Gates flashed a gold-toothed smile.

"What about the money? Does your man want it now?"

Much as I ached for Brussels, I was still wary of being conned. Important to keep my head here.

"Not yet," Gates said. "He says wait till the final orders is cut—that'll be time enough to pay him."

"Jackson, I'm very grateful to you for this. I want you to know that."

"No big deal, baby. I say, if you can help a cat, why not help a cat?"

"What about your two hundred? Do you need it now?"

"Keep it, man, you'll be needing it in Europe. One day maybe you'll find a way to return the favor."

My condition was one of edgy ecstasy. Brussels! Wonderful! I pictured the map of Europe and placed Brussels at its center. Yet so many things could go wrong. We had seventeen days left at Chaffee. Orders, we were told, would be issued in fifteen days. In fifteen days, then, I would know for certain. As the days dragged on, I found myself wanting to ask Gates if things were proceeding as planned. But I hesitated to do so, lest I seem a pest, or, as bad, somehow uncool. Instead I asked him about his own plans to return to Detroit.

"The cat has it fixed up for me to work in a recruiting office about a mile from where I live. It gonna be sweet, baby, real sweet. You can have Europe, daddy. Detroit is Paris enough for me."

I could have Europe. I read hope in that line. Oh, I would take it. Yes. Yes. Yes. Give me Europe. But my hope was mixed with dread that it wouldn't come off; dread of scandal; dread of some illness that would keep me at Chaffee. I stopped playing poker, for fear I would lose back my winnings and not have the money to pay off Gates's man at G-1. I could no longer concentrate on my reading, and so went to bed at lights-out, where I alternated thoughts of European delight (a Belgian mistress) with U.S. disaster (venereal disease in Oklahoma). The days crept on. With six to go I asked Gates if he had heard anything about orders having been cut, on the thin pretext of wondering if his man wanted his money yet.

"Stay cool, daddy, stay cool. He'll let me know when he need the bread."

With three days to go, Gates told me he wanted a word with me outside the barracks.

"Orders is cut," he said. "Like the man promised, yours is for NATO headquarters, Brussels, Belgium. Mine is for Detroit, Michigan, U.S. of A."

"What about the money?"

"He says he don't need it till after you got them golden little orders in your hands. But I think maybe it's a good idea to give him half now, the other half after the orders is posted. Anyways, that's what I going to do—to show the man appreciation for the trouble he gone through."

This was the first indication I had that Gates, like me, was coming up with money. Somehow, foolishly, I thought that his being black, as I assumed the sergeant in G-1 was, would get him the transfer to Detroit for nothing. We were, then, Gates and I, in the same boat. It made his not taking the $200 from me for setting this up all the more impressive. I went back into the barracks and took my poker winnings from where I had them hidden, in the pages of the Penguin edition of *Felix Holt,* counted out seven twenties and a ten, and brought it back out to Gates.

"Thanks, Jackson," I said, "for everything."

We shook hands. "Hey, daddy," he said, "no sweat."

Orders were to be posted on the bulletin board outside the orderly room on Saturday afternoon after chow. Sunday and Monday we would draw travel vouchers and ship out to our new assignments. I rather hoped that I might have a day between flights in New York to spend with college friends. If not, all right; but still, a day in Manhattan would be nice.

I was on my way to the bulletin board outside the orderly room, trying to control myself from breaking into a run, when I passed Walt Doherty, who was in my platoon in basic at Leonard Wood. He was angry.

"Something wrong, Walt?"

"Fuckin' A, something's wrong. I'm being sent to fuckin' Fort Hood right in the middle of fuckin' Texas."

"That's really lousy luck," I said.

"Save your sympathy for yourself," he said. "You're going there, too."

"What? Are you sure?"

"Unless I misread the list, you are."

I ran the rest of the way over to the orderly room. A crowd had gathered in front of the bulletin board. Names were listed in alphabetical order with destinations for each man marked on the right-hand side of the page alongside his name. Easily the majority of our company was being sent off to Fort Hood. When I found my own name, so, damn it, was I. What about Gates? I looked down the list; I looked down it again. Gates, Jackson, was not on it.

I walked back to the barracks in a daze. No Europe—Texas! Gates better have some explanation. At a minimum, I would get my money back, or goddamn know the reason why. Eighteen months of Texas loomed unrelievedly ahead. I walked faster, then broke into a sprint.

Gates's bunk was stripped, the blankets and sheets gone, the mattress turned back against the foot of the bed. The door of his locker was open, the inside emptied out of all but a few hangers. Six or seven guys were in the barracks. Over in the far corner I saw Otis Cook, who had collected money for Gates's return to Detroit after receiving his Dear John letter. Otis was packing his gear and looked up as I approached.

"Where they sending you?"

"Fort Hood," I said, becoming by now half accustomed to the dismal idea.

"Me too. Supposed to be a place loaded with snakes. Ain't my idea of much of a place to be."

"Otis, have you seen Jackson Gates? I need to talk with him."

"Too late, man. Jackson went home early this morning, back to Detroit."

"I didn't see his name on the orders sheet."

"That's 'cause he got him a Section 8. Jackson done psyched himself out."

"Gates psyched out of the army?"

"He been taking tests the whole of the last two weeks. Trying to convince a headshrinker that what with his marriage bust-up and all he's having a nervous breakdown or something and going crazy. Jackson's about as crazy as a fox, for my money. But I guess he convinced them. He's gone. The crazy fox is a gone goose."

Otis stuffed a boot into his duffel bag, then began to stuff a second boot in. "See ya in Texas, man."

"Yeah," I said, "in Texas." I thought to add, "No sweat, daddy," but I realized that during the next eighteen months, under the scorching Texas sun, sweating and little else was precisely what I figured to be doing.

The Casanova of LaSalle Street

I AM SITTING HERE AT THE BAR IN THE RESTAURANT CALLED KIKI, ON FRANK-lin, not far from the East Bank Club. I'm awaiting Cindy Olsen, a personal trainer who works out of the East Bank. She's not my trainer, I don't have one, but I have had my eye on Cindy for several months now, and last week, after an earlier meeting in the club over coffee, I asked her out to lunch. My sense is that women are much more likely to accept a lunch over a dinner invitation. Lunch suggests a briefer meeting, fewer strings attached, no trips to apartments afterward, "the victim ate a hearty meal" and all that. I hope to wind up in bed with Cindy, who is a knockout, Scandinavian division: blond, deeply blue eyes, in her late twenties, maybe early thirties, the body you would expect of a woman who exercises all day long.

I'm thirty-eight, a personal injury lawyer, a partner at Dubinsky, Kotler, and Levy at 101 North LaSalle Street, and have been married for twelve years, having cheated on Carol, my wife, for roughly the last nine of them. I'm fairly sure Carol has to know about my extracurricular ac-tivities, though she has never said anything about them. Perhaps because she hates a confrontation, which she does, perhaps because she is afraid to be out on her own if she forced a divorce, she lets it ride, doesn't say a word. We have a son (Zack) and a daughter (Melissa), both in middle school. How do I justify cheating on my wife? Truth is, I don't. But I have no desire to be separated from her either. She and my kids need me, and having a family gives ballast to my life.

I sometimes think that being married also adds to such allure as I might have, at least with certain women. Having a family makes me safe. I've never once suggested to any of my lady friends that I planned to leave my wife for them, and none has ever suggested I do so. They all seem to have understood that another marriage is not what I'm looking for, and it turns out that neither were they. We are all after something else.

I don't pursue married women. The few times I've done so I've found the complications outweigh the pleasure. For one thing, I have no interest in breaking up homes. For another, married women ready for love affairs usually have too long stories, and I have no taste for hearing elaborate bills of complaint about negligent husbands. Nor do I want to be chased down by these same husbands looking to punch me out or worse.

Neither am I one of those guys I think of as actuarial seducers, playing the long odds, hitting on every woman they meet, figuring they're eventually bound to get lucky. The humiliation factor seems not to trouble them. The line of reasoning here seems to be that the first ninety-nine women may kick you in a tender place, but the hundredth will make it all well. Herb Margolis, a lawyer in our firm a couple of years older than I, operates on this assumption, or so I've noticed. He tries them all. He also doesn't mind telling women anything that will get them in the sack. Herb is maybe sixty pounds overweight, untidy to the point of scruffiness, sweats a lot. That he actually finds women who will take him up on his propositions does not speak well for womanhood. A year or so ago he told me that he arrived home to discover one of his recent lady friends, a paralegal in the Friedman & Levine firm, in his living room in Lincolnwood. "Come on in, Herbie," his wife said. "Kimberley here tells me that you are planning to leave me to marry her. Is there anything to it?" I asked him what he did. "What the hell could I do?" he said. "I got the girl out of the house as quickly as possible, and promised Franny I'd go back into therapy."

Philandering is expensive, and while I make a decent living—it fluctuates, but averages somewhere around three hundred grand a year—I can't afford to court my extramural lady friends in the grand style: no Bvlgari watches, apartments on the Gold Coast, open credit cards. No romance without finance, I've heard men much older than I say. But I'm not ready to consider myself a variant of a sugar daddy, someone women make love with because of his money. I have too much vanity for any such arrangement.

I notice the term "sex addiction" is getting a pretty good workout these days. I've never counted, but I suppose I must have slept with maybe a hundred and fifty, a hundred and seventy or so women over the years; that is, from my earlier bachelor days and now since my marriage. With luck, I hope to sleep with maybe thirty or forty more before I hang it up. Does this make me a sex addict, or instead, as I prefer to think of myself, merely someone who likes women? I do like them, I like talking with them, I like all the steps in the elaborate dance of seduction, I like to make them like me, I like the deep intimacy with them that only sex makes possible. If things don't work out, I don't take it personally. I move on.

Unlike the Herb Margolises of this world, I have to be really attracted to a woman. The reasons for the attraction aren't always obvious. I need to see a mystery in her that I want revealed, if only to myself. Shyness in a woman can sometimes do it for me, but then so, sometimes, can an apparent hardness. The central thing for me in a love affair is the revelation it brings with it. I've never looked on seduction as any sort of triumph. Conquest's not what's in it for me. When I pursue a woman, I leave my ego at the door. Strange though it may seem to say this, in some sense it isn't really about me. To win over the confidence in a woman to the point where the outer shell she shows to the world slips off is for me the pleasure and the thrill of the game. I'm not saying I don't enjoy the sex, I do, a lot, only that sex isn't the only, or even the main thing, at least not for me it isn't.

Take Cindy Olson. Never married, I learned from my earlier coffee meeting with her. Brought up in the western suburbs, went to La Grange High School, did two years at the University of Illinois in Chicago. Her father died when she was fourteen. He worked for Allstate. She has very few pretensions, cultural or otherwise. Not all that much humor, either, at least not that I can thus far make out. Yet I sense something beneath this blandness; a grand passion, maybe. I could be wrong. I hope fairly soon to find out.

What, you might around now be wondering, would Cindy Olson see in me? I'm not a lavish spender. I'm not impressively good looking or well set-up physically. But then women are better, more tolerant about physical deficiencies than are men, who tend to be interested only in the obvious: face, boobs, bottom, legs, over and out. I like to think my general agreeableness first attracted Ms. Olson, at least enough to accept my invitation to coffee at the East Bank, and now to this lunch at Kiki. Maybe she thinks I'm someone she can talk to, complain to about her clients or the various jokers who must regularly hit on her in the club. My greatest weapon is the art of patient listening. I can usually tell after half an hour or so with a woman whether I have a chance. With Cindy Olson, the vibes have been good. We'll see.

Here she is now. The man holding open the door for her is—Jesus!—the man is my father. With him is a striking redhead, deeply tanned, obviously high maintenance, and distinctly not my mother. I don't wave, for Cindy sees me and begins walking over to the bar. My father, though he obviously also sees me, shows no sign of recognizing me. I stand up to greet Cindy. My father and his redheaded friend are given a table toward the back of the room. We order drinks: a vodka and tonic for me, a margarita for her. Before the drinks arrive, I excuse myself to use the men's room. I need a moment to think.

Standing at one of the urinals, I hear the door to the men's room open, and my father, without looking at me, takes his place at the adjoining urinal.

"You know, kiddo," he says, staring straight into the wall, "this is damn awkward. I think one of us ought to leave, and I'm going to claim seniority here and ask you to be the one to do so. Hope you don't mind."

"Of course not," I say. "I understand completely."

"Thanks," he says. "Much appreciated."

I zip up and walk out. We, my father and I, never make eye contact.

I've long suspected, until now without actual proof, that my father, like me, is a player. He kept odd hours, even when I was a kid, and I gather does so still. Women were always drawn to him. He's tall, with dark good looks. (I more closely resemble my mother.) At sixty-two his hair is still without a touch of gray, and he seems to have lost none of it. He'd been a high-school athlete—football and basketball at Roosevelt in Albany Park—and he moves with a jock's easy grace. Clothes look good on him. He's kept himself well groomed, always closely shaven, shoes shined.

He was in Vietnam, my Dad, though he rarely talked about it. He sells cars, Nissans, at a dealership in Schamburg. He does reasonably well, though my sense is that his heart has never been in it. His marriage hasn't been an easy one. My mother can be a tough customer. She's one of those maniacs of common sense, *her* version of common sense that is, which means that one does things her way or it's the highway. My mother can't imagine how anyone of any intelligence can think other than the way she does. "What do you want to do that for?" I remember her saying to me as a kid whenever I suggested doing anything with which she didn't agree. "Are you crazy?" was another of her favorite expressions. She hauled it out when I told her I was planning to marry Carol. I could escape her, and when I married finally did, but his marriage can't have been a smooth ride for my father, who, for reasons unknown to me, has chosen to stick it out with her.

I've never felt especially close to either my mother or my father, even though I was their only child. They married young; my father was twenty-four when I was born. Why they married, why they bothered to have a child, was never clear to me. They must once have loved each other, and the love soon died out, maybe under the tyranny of her common sense. The three of us went through the paces of being a family: had family dinners with cousins, celebrated Jewish holidays, even went on a few not especially joyful vacations together. True good feeling, though, was never there, or if it was I never felt it. As I grew older I began to feel sorry for both of them.

When I return to the bar, I tell Cindy that, while waiting for her, I'd looked over the lunch menu and couldn't find anything that really interested me. I was in the mood for a steak. Would she mind, after we finished our drinks, if we left Kiki and went on to Gene & Georgetti's, four blocks south on Franklin Street? She looks at me questioningly, but doesn't argue.

The lunch at Gene & Georgetti's goes well. We talk—or rather I encourage Cindy to talk—about what turns out to be her thwarted ambitions. She had wanted to be a nurse, but couldn't get by the killer course called organic chemistry. She had briefly been engaged to a man, twenty-three years older than she, who, she discovered, was a serious depressive.

She has a dog, a Yorkie-Poo named Edwin. She lives alone, in an apartment in Andersonville. She loves to cook. She wonders if I would be interested in coming over one night for dinner.

"I would like that a lot," I say. We decide the following Wednesday would be good. I put her in a cab back to the East Bank Club, feeling that in laying the groundwork here I have accomplished a good day's work.

Jules Feingold, for whose law firm I signed on as an associate right out of law school, a man of wide experience with a taste for philosophizing about human nature, once told me that in his time he knew quite a few skirt-chasing men. "Funny thing," he said, "none seemed ever to regret it." Jules himself, married to a woman still beautiful well into her late sixties, was, far as I could tell, not himself a player. Was he right about the absence of regret on the part of men devoted to the chase?

So far it is true for me. Has it, I wonder, been so for my father? I don't of course know the extent of my father's philandering. Whatever its extent, it doesn't appear to have brought him much happiness. Certainly he doesn't carry himself as a happy man. He fought in a war nobody appreciated, he married an unobliging woman, he works at a job that gives him a living but little pleasure. I hope his love affairs enliven his days.

Mine do. Everyone needs something that does. My love affairs are for me what litigating was for Jules Feingold, who came most alive in the courtroom. My wife seems most alive in her role as mother, driving our kids around to their various tennis, ballet, and piano lessons, exulting in their achievements in school. My mother is most alive expressing disapproval.

What we don't know about even the people supposedly closest to us! That I knew absolutely nothing about the side of my father who is the charmer, the lady-killer, the seducer, is just one example of what I mean. And while I'm at it I have to wonder if my father's playing around turned my mother into the chronic complainer she is or did her complaining turn him into a player. I'm unlikely ever to know.

"Can you talk?" my father says over the phone.

"Yes, sure," I say. "Carol's out. What's up?"

"I wanted to thank you for accommodating me earlier today at Kiki's. It made things a lot more comfortable."

"For me, too," I say.

"The thought of the two of us in one room with women not our wives seemed not such a hot bad idea?"

"No argument," I said.

"A beautiful young woman you were with, by the way."

"Her name's Cindy Olson. She's a personal trainer at the East Bank."

"You seeing her regularly?"

"Not really. This is the first time I took her to lunch." I thought about asking him about the redhead he brought in to Kiki, but decided that might be pushing it.

"Well," my father says, "I mainly called to say thanks. Take care, kid."

"Take care," I say, and we hang up.

Wednesday night I arrive a bit before six at Cindy's apartment on Rascher off Ashland Avenue. (I told Carol I had an appointment with a client in Valparaiso, a guy with lung problems suing a construction company that used asbestos in its buildings, and that I might be home late.) I have an expensive bottle of Merlot in hand as I ring Cindy's bell. Her apartment is small and doesn't get very good light. The night is warm, and she is in shorts and a tank top, over which she is wearing an apron with dogs on it. From the front, it looks as if she has no other clothes on but the apron. Very sexy. Her own dog, Edwin, is asleep on the carpet, and doesn't move when I enter the living room.

"Not the greatest of watchdogs, my Edwin," she says, with a smile.

She says she hopes I like French food. She's cooking a *cassoulet* for dinner, made from a Julia Child recipe, very complicated. She's not done it before, and hopes it will turn out.

"I'm betting it will be great," I say.

She says she has a bottle of white wine, a Reisling, open, and asks if I'd like a glass. I sit on a red velour covered couch in front of the windows and look down at the sleeping Edwin. Dejected people say that it's a dog's life, but his looks pretty good to me. Cindy returns from the kitchen, hands me a glass of the Reisling, and sits in an armchair facing the couch.

"I'm glad you could come," she says.

"My pleasure. I like the smells coming from the kitchen. Very promising."

"Is your wife a good cook?" she asks. A trick question, or so at least I sense it to be, a way of feeling me out about my feelings toward my wife. "A good but not an ambitious cook," I say, "everything wholesome and tasty, but nothing fancy. She has to feed two kids and a moderately gluttonous husband."

"Does she know you're here tonight?"

"I told her I was with a client in Indiana," I say.

"Would she be angry if she knew where you really were?"

"If she knew how good-looking you are, I don't see how she couldn't be."

"Flattery will get you everywhere," she says.

"I was hoping so," I say. "This Reisling is excellent, by the way."

I ask her how long she's lived in Andersonville. Did she know that the neighborhood was also called Mandersonville, because so many older, now settled-in gay couples lived here? Mandersonville opposed to Boys Town, around Belmont and Broadway, where younger gays had clubs and baths and leather shops, and the rest of it.

"The neighborhood feels wonderfully safe," she says. "I can walk Edwin as late as midnight and not have to look over my shoulder."

The *cassoulet* is good. I sop mine up with a sourdough bread Cindy bought from the Swedish Bakery on Clark. During dinner I tell her I admire her being able to live alone, that I think her brave, being on her own, and that not everyone could do it.

"My therapist thinks my being alone so much is pure avoidance mechanism on my part," she says, "and therefore unhealthy."

"Been in therapy long?"

"Nearly seven years," she says. "Have you ever been? In therapy, that is."

"Not thus far, though a few of my angrier clients have suggested I could use it."

"My therapist tells me that I have a fixation on my father, who died at a crucial time in my life, when I was just fourteen."

"What's his evidence?"

"Hers, not his. My therapist's name is Brenda Spivak. She claims I have a thing for older men."

"Really?" I say. "I wonder if I qualify."

"Very funny," she says, "but by older she means twenty and thirty years older. I'm afraid I've got entangled with a few such men, each time with unhappy endings. She's also suspicious of my having no desire to marry."

"Marriage isn't a good fit for everyone," I say.

"I grew up with parents who didn't have a very good marriage. They didn't yell at each other, or argue much. But there wasn't much feeling there. You didn't have to be a genius to tell there wasn't much love lost. My sister Maggie, she's four years older than me, she lives in L.A., works as a masseuse there, is also unmarried. Our parents made the whole proposition of marriage pretty unattractive."

We both had parents with unhappy marriages in common, I think, but decided not to bring it up.

"I don't want children," she says. "I hate the thought of being completely dependent on a man. Solitude doesn't bother me. I'm fine the way I am. I don't really have anything against marriage, it's just not for me."

After we finish the *cassoulet* and the bottle of Merlot, she brings out coffee and sorbet. I am less than certain where this is going, but still hopeful.

"May I help with the dishes?" I say, after we finish.

"No need. I'll get them after you leave."

I take that to mean I won't be staying.

"A great dinner," I say.

"Thanks," she said, "but I ought to think about getting to bed. It's been a long day, and I have a client, an overweight cardiologist named Rosenbloom, scheduled for a 6:30 a.m. appointment."

We get up from the table. She walks me to the door, leans in, and lightly kisses me on the mouth.

"It's been sweet," she says. "Thanks for the wine. See you at the club."

"I enjoyed it a lot," I say, playing at being the good sport.

No point in pushing it, I tell myself, walking to my car. Give it time. The next day I send a dozen yellow roses to her Rascher Street apartment with a note: "Thanks for a lovely evening. Hope we can do it again soon. Next time on me."

I stay away from the East Bank Club the whole of the following week. My plan is to give her room to breathe, not to feel in any way pressured, time to let her think about linking up with me.

"How go things?" I say, when the following week I see her in the workout room.

"You've been away," she says.

"I was out of town," I lie.

"Someplace pleasing, I hope."

"Boston, trying a case. Are you up for dinner sometime this week?"

"I don't think so," she says.

"The following week maybe?"

"Think I'll pass."

"Anything wrong?"

"No, nothing," she says. "I just think things between us aren't going to work out. No hard feelings, I hope."

"Of course not," I say. "Everything's cool here. Good to see you."

"I'm glad," she says, and, touching my elbow, walks off.

Were the roses a mistake? Make me look too earnest, too insistent? How did I misjudge Cindy Olson? She invited me to her apartment for dinner, after all. Should I have pressed my case more firmly that evening in her apartment? Some women prefer a stronger lead than others; some don't in the least mind sexual aggression. Maybe I shouldn't have stayed away from the club for a full week. I did something wrong, but what exactly?

Over the next few weeks, I thought a good deal about how I blew it with Cindy Olson. My judgment in these matters, while far from perfect, is usually pretty good. This time I went off the tracks, but how, and at what point exactly? Normally I don't like to dwell on these things. I do, though, like to get them right, to learn from experience. Who knows, maybe someday I'll write my memoirs. *The Casanova of LaSalle Street* is the title I have in mind.

I have a new client, a young woman, an assistant professor at Northwestern who is suing the anthropology department there for not giving her tenure. She's been giving me proceed-with-caution signals since our first interview. I'm hesitant. She's a bit nuttier than I like. Far from concealing some deeper inner personality, everything about her is too much out in the open. Still, if I can arrange it, I like to have something going, at least simmering on the back burner, at all times.

It's five weeks or so after Cindy Olson put the kibosh on what I hoped would be our pleasing relationship, and I am sitting in Gibson's on Rush Street with a client, a man named Ernie Ross, who wants to sue for negligence the nursing home where he stowed his ninety-two-year-old mother. She fell, fractured her pelvis, and died a week later. He wants me to sue for $10 million. Where he got that number, I don't know. I tell him to think more in the neighborhood of $25,000, if we can get that, and to think hard about it while I excuse myself to use the men's room. As I'm heading toward the men's, I spot the crowded bar twenty or so yards away, and who is standing there, margarita in hand, but Cindy Olson. In the men's I decide to go up to her, just to say hello, to show her that I'm a man who holds no bad feelings of any sort. On my way toward the bar, I note her standing there still, when the man standing next to her turns around, and goddamn if he isn't my father.

You may be way ahead of me here, but let me nevertheless try to connect the dots, if only for myself. When my father first saw me with Cindy in Kiki's, he must have been attracted to her; she is, after all, a beautiful woman. Over the phone that same night, he asked me who she was and if I'd been seeing her for long. I both gave him her name and told him she worked at the East Bank. He must have called her, using what line to get her to see him, I don't know, but it must have been very impressive. At her apartment, Cindy mentioned her problem of being attracted too much to older men, and there aren't many older men more attractive than my father. Had he called her and met with her before I had dinner at Cindy's? Can't know for certain, but I suspect so. I, standing there with my $85 bottle of Merlot in hand at her door, was probably already out of the picture. What a schmuck!

I suppose I should be angry, feel betrayed, and by my own father, of all men. Somehow, though, I can't work up much anger nor feel betrayed. If anything, I rather admire my father's prowess. A joke is buried here somewhere in all this, but I haven't quite got it.

I return to my table and Mr. Ross, my client.

"I've been thinking over what you said," he tells me, "and maybe you're right. Let's ask for $5 million, and see where things go from there."

You live, I guess, and you yearn.

Kizerman and Feigenbaum

SOME PEOPLE, INCLUDING MAYBE EVEN MY KIDS, PROBABLY CONSIDER ME A
flop. I lasted less than a year in college, at Drake in Iowa, and went into
the family business, the only member of the third generation in our family to do so. My older brother Arnie is a successful dentist, specializing in
root canals. Carol, my younger sister, is a partner in the family-law firm of
Levin, Feldman, and Engel. After working fourteen years at Rappaport's,
our family's delicatessen, some say the last authentic one in Chicago, on
Broadway two blocks north of Belmont, I took over the business after
my dad died, and I have been running it ever since, a total of thirty-two
years in all.

Started by our grandfather and featuring my grandmother's soup
and fish recipes, Rappaport's was originally on Kedzie, just off Lawrence.
Following the migration of the Jews northward across Chicago, the deli
moved under my dad's management to West Rogers Park, at the corner
of California and Devon. When the Jews in West Rogers Park moved
again, this time mostly to the northern suburbs, and Indians and Pakistanis
moved in along with a community of ultra-Orthodox, who consider most
of the food I serve *treyf*, I moved the restaurant to its present location.
We're not setting the world on fire, but we do a steady business. Steady
enough to have sent my two girls to college—Naomi to Miami of Ohio,
Sheryl to Dennison, also in Ohio—and to keep a condo in Boca Raton,
where Bobby, my late wife, who died of cervical cancer three years ago,
used to stay through most of the winter. I've been thinking about unload-
ing the Boca place, since I myself can't get away for more than a week or
so at a time. You run a restaurant, you need to be on the premises: greeting
people, kicking ass, worrying. Believe me, I know.

I've never regretted going into the family business. My brother stands there all day, jabbing away at dead nerves in people's mouths, my sister further inflames angry women to get the most out of men they once loved. In running a good deli I'm providing a service. People come into my place with clear and specific wants, and I'm able to satisfy them. We won't include here those occasional *mumsers* who dedicate themselves to giving my waitresses and me a hard time.

To accommodate diet-conscious women customers, I've had to add "The Liter Side" to my menu, which is mostly salads and egg-white omelettes. My dad used to say that the only green thing allowed in a Jewish deli should be a dill pickle. Cholesterol is another big worry. The other day a woman asks me if there is any cholesterol in our pastrami. It was all I could do not to tell her she shouldn't worry, we've managed to trap all the cholesterol between the fat and the grease. She ordered a Caesar salad. Chiefly, though, people come in for the old Jewish staples: the soups (mushroom-barley, chicken matzoball and kreplach, cold borscht, lentil, split pea), the brisket and corned-beef and salami, the white fish and flounder, the cheese cake and strudels and rugelach.

The people left who enjoy these things, who grew up on them, are no longer kids. Some days I look around at my customers and feel I'm not running a restaurant but a nursing home. I've had to keep the aisles wide to allow for customers on walkers. I've got a number of elderly men and women, regulars, coming in with Filipina caregivers. Also men who eat wearing caps that show they fought in World War II. Occasionally they'll bring in their grandchildren, or, more accurately, their grandchildren will bring them in.

I got a customer, Mrs. Rose Kleiderman, she comes in every Monday, Wednesday, and Friday at noon, she must be ninety-five. Her skin looks like parchment. She lives somewhere in the neighborhood. She comes alone. She can't weigh more than eighty pounds; maybe she's four foot six, eight tops. She orders the same things every time: a bowl of chicken matzoball soup, a salami omelette with hashbrown potatoes, drinks maybe four cups of coffee, finishes it off with a piece of rugelach, leaves a ten percent tip, reminds me that she knew my parents, and shuffles out onto Broadway.

I got a customer, Morton Grolnik, he comes in every day except Sunday for a breakfast of coffee, orange juice, oatmeal, and whole-wheat toast. He tells me that he likes to start his day among Jews. He lives in a nearby assisted-living joint on Sheridan Road called The Wrenwood. He brings a *Sun-Times* in with him and every morning makes a number of hypothetical bets on baseball, football, and basketball games. "Can you believe it, Jerry," he'll say to me, "the Bears are six-point dogs," or "I'm taking the Eagles and the points." Every morning, on leaving, he tells me how much he is ahead or behind for the year.

I've lots of other regulars, but maybe the strangest are two guys, Harold Kizerman and Morrie Feigenbaum. They meet here every Tuesday and Thursday for lunch. They both sport beards, white and not very well trimmed, and they eat with their caps on. Feigenbaum, a large man, must weigh somewhere around 300, maybe more, rides in on a motorized chair. Kizerman is slender, tall, with a permanently somewhat pissed-off look. They take one of the center tables—in his chair, Feigenbaum can't fit in a booth—and usually stay at least two hours.

One day a year or so ago, Kizerman left a large black spiral notebook behind. I couldn't resist looking inside. In a scrawling handwriting he had written what I guess are a number of poems. One, with the title "Climate Change," ended with these words:

Tsunami and fire, earthquake, tornado, and storm,
Disaster's man's lot, misery henceforth the norm.

Not very cheery stuff, if you ask me, but then no one's asking, certainly not Kizerman, and what he does is his business.

One day, heading back to the kitchen, passing their table, I noted they were reading aloud to each other, each holding a bunch of typewritten pages in his hand. I couldn't make out what it was, and later, after they had gone, I asked Gladys, their waitress, who has been at Rappaport's since my father's day, if she knew what the reading aloud was about.

"They're writing a play," she said, "leastwise that's what they told me."

Gladys, who has waited on them for years, had earlier filled me in on what she knew about Feigenbaum and Kizerman. They're both in their mid-eighties. Feigenbaum was formerly an accountant, Kizerman in mail order. Both are longtime-widowers. During their married days, they lived in Skokie, and met through their wives, who played mah-jong together. They bowled on the same B'nai Br'ith bowling team.

Feigenbaum is confined to his motorized chair because of his weight and varicose veins; he also suffers from gout, which hasn't slowed down his appetite. He lives in an apartment at The Wrenwood. Not long after his wife died, Kizerman moved in with his plastic-surgeon son Gary and his family, who have a four-bedroom condo at The Barry Apartments on Sheridan Road.

Gladys's story is she married an Irishman, who worked at Bethlehem Steel and who deserted her maybe thirty years ago, leaving her with two young kids. She brought up the kids by herself, waitressing full time. Her son Tony is now a cop, her daughter Beverly teaches kids with disabilities in Lawndale. I wish I had ten Gladyses working at Rappaport's. She's always on time, completely reliable, no crap about her. She's Polish—maiden name Rostenkowski—but she's been around Jews so long by now she's practically Jewish herself. She probably knows as many Yiddish words as I do. She smokes, but only in the alley behind the restaurant. If she ever needed me for anything, I'd be there to help without hesitation. I think she knows it.

I don't hire college kids or people in their twenties as waiters. Their minds aren't really on the job. Where their minds are I don't pretend to know, but a customer the other day told that me in L.A, if some young person tells you he or she's an actress, you reply, "Oh, yeah, at what restaurant?" I hire older women, the occasional gay man, to wait tables. They stick around, are pleased to have the job, aren't dreamy. My busboys, mostly Puerto Ricans and some Mexican Americans, come and go. I've had good luck with my two short-order cooks, Juan Diaz and José Esposa, who have been with me for two-and-a-half and four years respectively. Impossible to run a deli these days without knowing a little Spanish. I've learned just enough myself to get by.

Five weeks ago, a rainy Tuesday, Feigenbaum and Kizerman fail to show for lunch. They're not there again on Thursday. The next week they don't show either. I asked Gladys what's the story? She doesn't know. Maybe one or the other is in the hospital. Guys in their mid-eighties, they could crap out at any time. I started checking the obits in the *Trib*. Nothing. One day I called The Wrenwood to see if Mr. Morris Feigenbaum was still a resident. He was. I hung up before they asked if I wanted to be connected to his apartment. Maybe it was Kizerman who was ill. I wasn't about to call his son's apartment. I mean, what's it my business?

Then the third week, a Wednesday, Kizerman walks into the restaurant alone. He takes a booth. The booth isn't in Gladys's station, but I arrange for her to wait on him anyway. He orders a corned-beef on an onion roll, coffee, nothing more. Half an hour and he walks out. I'm at the register, and when I ask him how're things going, he mumbles, "They've been better."

I call Gladys over. "Where's Feigenbaum? What's with these guys?"

"I'm going on my smoke break," Gladys says. "Meet me outside and I'll fill you in." Gladys takes a ten-minute break for a cigarette every hour. Anyone else, I wouldn't allow it.

In the alley behind the restaurant, Gladys lights up a Marlboro, exhales, through her nose and mouth, a terrific cloud of smoke.

"I asked Mr. Kizerman how Mr. Feigenbaum was," she said, "and he replied that he wouldn't know. He was reading the paper with his lunch and didn't even bother to look up.

"'Nothing wrong, I hope,' I said. 'Hope to see you and Mr. F back here soon.'

"'Not likely,' he said, still not looking up from his paper. He then told me that Feigenbaum insulted him. I didn't think it was my place to ask him how.

"'Sorry to hear it,' I said. 'You two go back a ways.'

"'Nearly 60 years,' he said. 'Can I get some more coffee?'"

The following Friday Feigenbaum shows up, alone. His motorized chair is so large he needs help with the door. Usually Kizerman holds it open for him. Today I do. He motors in and drives to his usual table. I follow him.

"Expecting Mr. Kizerman to join you?" I say.

"Not for a long while," he says.

"Nothing wrong with his health?" I ask, pretending not to know there's been a serious falling out.

"No. Just with his brain," Feigenbaum answers.

"Meaning?"

"It's a long story. Got a minute? Sit down." Before Kizerman begins, Gladys comes up to take his order: a large bowl of kreplach soup, a brisket sandwich on rye with a side of fries, a Dr. Brown's Cream Soda, coffee and cheesecake for dessert. Not one for "The Liter Side" of our menu, Morrie Feigenbaum.

"Anyhow," he begins, "my old friend Hal Kizerman comes to me six, maybe seven weeks ago, to announce he's thinking about remarrying. He'd not mentioned any woman before, you understand, and Hal and I are pretty close. I held back. Offered no opinion. Where'd he meet this lucky lady? I ask him. At a benefit dinner for Rush Memorial Hospital, he tells me, where his boy Gary is on staff. What does she do? I ask. Some hospital volunteer work, he says. How old? I ask. Sixty-two, he says, which would make her twenty-three years younger than Kizerman. Married before? Three times actually, he tells me, no children. Is currently living at Imperial Towers, on Marine Drive. Will I get to meet her? Soon, he says.

"So maybe a week or so later, I get an invitation to dinner at Kizerman's son's apartment, where I'm to meet this broad who's caused my old pal to lose his normal good sense."

Gladys arrives, sets a bowl of kreplach soup before Kizerman and brings a cup of coffee for me. Kizerman plunges into his soup. He's one of those guys who can talk and eat without losing the rhythm of either. He'd already done a pretty good job on the bread basket. But I guess that's how you get to be 300 pounds or whatever he is.

"Anyhow," says Feigenbaum, "at Kizerman's son's place I get to meet my old friend's new heartthrob. Her name is Deborah Shapiro. She's good-looking, expensively dressed, goes a little heavy on the warpaint, is obviously a woman still on the attack. The only other people there are Dr. Gary Kaiser (Kizerman's plastic-surgeon son, who did a bit of rhinoplasty on his own name), his wife Robin, and me. Kizerman is wearing a suit I haven't seen before, very Italian. He and Ms. Shapiro stick close together. I get the strong impression that, jacked up on Viagra or something more powerful, he's canoodling her, if you take my meaning.

"At dinner she tells me that Harold has told her about our collaborating on a play together. I tell her we have been working on it for more than a year now and hope to have it performed at the retirement home where I live, and that it's a play about growing up in the Depression and its effects on two young boys with artistic instincts, sending them into the business world.

"'I'm a big fan of Hal's poems,' she says.

"I ask her about her own life. She says that her father was a liquor distributor. Her maiden name was Weiss. The family lived in West Rogers Park. She went to Mather High School. Shapiro, her third husband, did something with fire insurance that wasn't clear to me, but didn't sound quite strictly on the up and up. Her second husband died of congestive heart failure, four years ago, at seventy-eight. Which suggests that maybe she has a thing for older men, a father complex maybe, who knows? About her first husband she didn't speak."

Feigenbaum has by now finished off his soup with their two large kreplach. ("They're Brobdingnagian, Daddy," Sheryl, my youngest daughter, the English major, used to call our kreplach.) Gladys arrives, and sets before him his brisket sandwich and fries and Dr. Brown's.

"But I sensed," Feigenbaum says, "something out of kilter. I looked at her and thought, this is a woman whose life hasn't worked out. This is not a happy woman. Something has gone profoundly wrong for her. She's in choppy waters, adrift, and looking for something to cling onto to get to shore. My friend Hal maybe."

"What made you think that?" I asked.

Kizerman reached for another slice of pickle.

"Instincts," he says. "Disappointment is written in her eyes. Of course I said nothing about it. I kept my own counsel. The dinner went on. Pretty dull talk, I thought, but not for my old friend Kizerman. You could tell he was delighted to have been taken up by a still good-looking woman more than twenty years younger than himself. You reach a certain age, you no longer think of yourself as in the hunt, if you know what I mean.

"My first suspicion is that she is a gold-digger and has taken Kizerman for loaded. As someone who has done his taxes for the last forty or so years I can tell you he isn't. He gets by, not much more. You know the line about older men seeking out rich widows, how's it go, they're looking for 'a nurse with a purse,' that's it. We need something similar for women going after older men, 'An old babe who forgot to save,' maybe. In any case, if Ms. Shapiro is a gold-digger, in Harold Kizerman she's working the wrong claim."

Kizerman's cheesecake arrives. Gladys sets it down along with a cup of coffee, which he drinks black with three heaped spoons of sugar.

"My problem was what to do about it. Should I warn my old friend that he is making a big mistake? Or should I let it go, let things play out, as they figured inevitably to do? I decided on the latter.

"Then less than a week later, Kizerman calls to inform me that he is going to propose marriage to this broad, Ms. Shapiro. Does a good friend stand by, despite his own forebodings, say congratulations and wait for the disaster that is sure to follow? Or does he say what he thinks?

"'Hal,' I say, 'I think you may be making a grievous error here.'

"'Grievous?' he asks. 'How so, grievous?'

"'I think it's a dumb idea to marry at our age, and even if it wasn't I don't think this is the woman to do it with. This is an unhappy woman, Hal. See her, screw her, do anything you like, but don't marry her is my advice. This is a woman likely to ruin your last years. Don't do it. Big mistake,' I say.

"'Who're you, Ann Landers?' he says. 'Deborah is a beautiful and dear woman, and she needs my protection.'

"'Protection from what?' I ask.

"'From the world,' he says. 'It's a damn cold and cruel place, especially for a woman alone. If you'd get your fat ass out of that chair every so often, maybe you'd notice.'

"So, there it was. We got to the insult stage that fast. I stopped it before it got to the shouting stage."

"'Look, Hal,' I say to him, 'You'll do what you want. I wish you nothing but the best.'

"'Like hell you do,' he says. 'You obviously take me for an idiot.'

"'Look,' I say, 'if I've done anything to hurt your feelings, if I've gone too far, I apologize.'

"'I know envy when I see it,' he says. 'You're envious of my having a good life with an attractive woman. I'm not a goddamn moron.'

"'Envious'?" Feigenbaum says to me. "I swear it hadn't occurred to me to be envious. I saw a dear friend in danger of going down the tubes with the wrong woman, nothing more."

I notice his cheesecake's gone.

"Anyhow, I say to Hal. 'See you on Tuesday, at Rappaport's.'

"'I don't think so,' he says. 'Nor Thursday or any other day. I wish you well, Morrie, but, as the Jews used to say about the Tsar, not too close to me.' And he hangs up. And that's where things stand. A nearly sixty-year friendship, down the crapper."

I hadn't said a word while Feigenbaum recounted all this, but the fact was that I knew Deborah Shapiro, or at least I knew her when she was Deborah—called in those days by everyone Dinky—Weiss. She was one of the most popular girls at Mather, went out with the star of the basketball team, a guy named Teddy Levinson, who went on to play for Ohio State, though he spent most of his career there warming the bench. A looker, too, Dinky Weiss, at least in those days, tall, slender, dark, well-built. The Weiss family lived in a sprawling ranchhouse on Francisco and Coyle. Liquor distributor, which Feigenbaum mentioned her father was, was one of those occupations that had its origins decades before in bootlegging, and you didn't have to search too far to find those who practiced it usually loosely connected with the Mob. A clutch of successful bookies and other men in the jukebox, slot-machine, and other illicit businesses lived on those blocks off Francisco between Morse and Touhy. In those days Dinky Weiss, rich, popular, good-looking, was out of my league, certainly not someone I would ever have had the nerve to call for a date. I couldn't help thinking, though, that as the ladyfriend of Hal Kizerman she had come down in the world—way down, with a thump.

Please don't ask why, but I decided to call Deborah Shapiro. I'm not sure exactly why. Curiosity mostly. Was she still good-looking? What had time done to her to put her in the position of needing Hal Kizerman's protection, if she really did need it? She was in the phone book under D. Shapiro on Marine Drive, and when she answered the phone I mentioned my name, but—no big shock here—she didn't remember it, or know who I was. I lied and said that I was chairman of a planning committee for our class's 45th Mather High School reunion, and was calling to ask if she would be willing to serve on the committee. She said that she wasn't in the least interested. I told her I understood, and suggested if she had an hour or so free to talk about the old days at Mather someday I would love to meet her for coffee. I was surprised when she said "Sure, why not?" We agreed to meet two days later, at three in the afternoon at a coffee and pastry joint called Jules Minhl, on Southport, off Addison.

I arrived ten minutes early. The scattering of customers in the place were mostly women. The lunch menu was all salads and quiches and female sandwiches. The pastry on display was also for less than hardy eaters: croissants, muffins, small cookies. In this joint any of my regular customers would have seemed like they came from another planet.

I recognized Dinky the moment she hit the door. She was still tall, lean, her hair dark, probably now with the help of a beautician. She was wearing designer jeans, moderately high heels, a long red sweater. She had one of those deep poolside tans that Bobby, my wife, used to call "extra crispy." The look was high maintenance, a touch on the hard side.

I thought about ducking out, but she must have noticed me staring at her, because she came over to my table.

"You must be Jerry Rappaport," she said. "Hi, I'm Deborah Shapiro, formerly Weiss."

"You're still recognizably the girl I knew in high school," I said, "and that's a compliment."

"I'll take it as such," she said. "And please forgive me for not recognizing you, on the phone or here, though you do look vaguely familiar."

"I spent a lot of my free time at Mather working in our family restaurant," I said.

"Then you're a Rappaport from Rappaport's on Devon and California. My Dad used to take me and my brother Donny there for Sunday morning breakfast."

"Are you still in touch with any of the kids we went to school with?" I asked.

"I was when I lived in Glencoe with my first husband. But during my second and third marriages, living in the city, I fell out of touch. You married?"

"A widower," I said.

"If it doesn't sound too cruel, I wish I were a widow, at least where my third husband is concerned, but I guess you can't have everything."

We ordered coffee, and she walked over to the pastry display and brought back a croissant, which she nibbled at.

"Are you seeing anyone at present?" she asked.

"Not at the moment. The restaurant—we're now on Broadway near Addison—keeps me busy. How about you?"

"I was. A much older man," she said. I didn't say I knew that older man.

"Funny but I happened last to be seeing a much younger woman. She was in her early thirties, but it didn't work out. We didn't know the same songs, if you get my drift. I also felt uncomfortable going with her to her clubs with people younger than my two daughters."

"You have two daughters," she said. "I have no kids myself, but if I had I would have wanted girls. I think I would have understood them better than boys."

"Ever hear from Ted Levinson?"

"He died in his forties, I heard, from cancer. He was living in Milwaukee. But tell me about this 45th reunion."

"It's all very tentative," I lied. "I don't know why I even offered to serve on the planning committee. I don't see why we can't wait until the 50th year reunion."

"This reminds me," she said, "of a friend of my last husband. He was nuts about a little college he went to in upstate New York. Hamilton or Madison maybe was its name. I don't remember exactly. He was a wealthy man, and he gave the school lots of money. He showed me a letter announcing his 60th year class reunion. As I began to read it, he said look at the bottom. 'Walkers and wheelchairs will be provided.' 'Screw it,' he said. 'I'm not going.'" She laughed.

She had a good laugh, Dinky Weiss, lots of nice teeth. Expensive dental work? Hard to say. I searched her face to see if she had had work done. Maybe an eye-job, I decided. She was an appealing woman.

"Do you still go by the name Dinky?" I asked.

"Only with old girlfriends. It's a name my parents gave me, and comes from my infant attempt at saying daddy."

"It has a nice ring to it."

"I never minded it. Maybe it's not so fitting for a woman of a certain age, but call me it if you like."

We began talking about the old days in West Rogers Park, about some of our teachers at Mather, about the kids we grew up with. Lots of laughter. Looking across the table at her, I saw the attractive girl I knew from high school. It was as if the forty-odd years since that time had never happened. I, Jerry Rappaport, was on a date with Dinky Weiss, and enjoying the hell out of it.

I looked at my watch. It was 5:30 p.m. I should have been back at the restaurant for the dinner hour. We'd been together two-and-a-half hours, schmoozing away. I walked her to her car—a three-series white BMW. At her car door, she offered her cheek for me to kiss. She asked me not to wait too long to call so that we could meet again. When I got to my car, parked on Southport, I found a $60 parking ticket, but didn't mind, so much did I enjoy myself with Dinky Weiss.

She was good company, with a sense of humor, and an interesting outlook. She'd been around the block a few times, but she didn't come back from the trips empty-handed. She was no dope. As for Kizerman's telling Feigenbaum she needed protection, about that I wasn't so sure. I was fairly sure that if she really did need it, Hal Kizerman, in his middle eighties without much dough, wasn't in any position to provide it.

Kizerman came into the restaurant the following Friday. He greeted me as always, curtly, and took a booth, ate his lunch alone reading the *Sun-Times*. I was awaiting some sign that he knew I had met with Deborah Shapiro, but he gave none. My best guess is that she never bothered to tell him. No reason for her to do so, really. Maybe she was no longer seeing him. She said she "was" seeing an older man, past tense.

I waited a full week to call Dinky Shapiro. She was free for dinner on Friday, and I took her to a dark and rather noisy Italian joint on Clark Street in Andersonville called Calo. She ordered salmon. I thought of ordering the barbeque ribs, but decided I didn't want the mess that ribs bring. I ordered the white fish, tail portion.

"Why the tail portion?" Dinky wanted to know when the waitress left.

"Fewer bones in the tail portion," I said, "Old Jewish wives' wisdom. I learned it from my grandmother."

The restaurant was darker and noisier than I remembered. I don't know what I hoped for from the evening, except getting to know Dinky Weiss-Shapiro, as I started to think of her, better. Nothing that Feigenbaum said about her checked out, at least in my reading.

She told me she never went to college, and resented it. Lack of money wasn't involved. Her father, an old-fashioned tough guy, didn't believe in college for women.

"He never said so directly," she said, "but he believed women functioned best in the kitchen and on their backs. In not getting to go to college I've always felt I missed out on something major. Not that I was such a hot student, because I wasn't, but I felt a hole in my life that I could never fill in."

"I went for a year, to Drake in Des Moines. I found nothing there, at least for me. I would sit in a class in biology or political science and ask myself what am I doing here anyway? I decided I'd rather spend a week at the Drake Hotel than four years at Drake University. At the end of my first year I never went back. I've never regretted it."

"At least you had a shot at it," Dinky said. "That's something."

"True enough," I said.

"What not going to college did to me was to turn me into a professional wife. I went to work for my father at eighteen, and at nineteen married a man, also in the liquor business, twenty years older than me. The marriage lasted twelve years, which was eleven years and ten months longer than it should have lasted, but I didn't want to admit failure and so rode out all those years of misery."

She didn't mention her other two marriages, which was fine by me. The conversation jumped around. We had a bottle of wine with our dinner, a Cabernet Sauvignon.

"I don't know anything about wine," I said, after ordering it.

"I prefer that you don't," she said. "My last husband was a great wine connoisseur. He didn't mind dropping 200 dollars for a bottle of wine, and making goo-goo eyes at the bottle as he drank it. Someone once told me that there are three kinds of people: highly educated people who talk about ideas, normal people who talk about other people, and trivial people who talk about wine."

We were out of the restaurant by 8:45 p.m. I asked her if she'd care to catch a movie.

"I'm not very comfortable in the new Cineplexes," she said. "I also find myself disappointed with lots of movies. Why don't we go back to my place? Maybe there's something we can watch on television."

I am in Dinky Weiss-Shapiro's bed, in my boxer shorts, waiting for her to emerge from her bathroom. I've been in this position before with other women, awaiting them, listening to jars opening and closing, atomizers spraying, and whenever I am I have the same slight feeling of doubt whether I am the successful hunter or instead the prey subdued, the seducer or the seduced. I feel some of this at this moment. But I also feel strangely elated. A high-school fantasy of mine is about to come true forty-odd years later.

During my high-school days guys practiced what was then called kiss-and-tell. My own suspicion then was that there was a lot more telling going on than there was kissing. I'm not going to attempt to describe what Dinky and I did in her bed. I'm not that great at description. I'll only say that at the conclusion I didn't want my money back and leave it at that.

"It's times like these," she said as we were lying in bed afterward, "that I most miss smoking. Were you a smoker?"

"Practically a professional," I said. "Two packs a day. Kools."

"Why did you quit?"

"Little thing called fear of death."

"Me, too."

"May I ask you a question?" I said.

"Of course."

"You know a man named Harold Kizerman?"

"I know him very well. He proposed marriage to me three or four weeks or so ago. I must have given him the wrong signals," she said, "either that or he misinterpreted my kindness to him. I told him that I was honored to be asked but I've already had all the marriage I can handle. Three marriages is a lot—four practically makes you a sociopath, or something."

"You're serious about never remarrying?" I asked.

"Absolutely," she said. "I have come to the conclusion that I am not a good judge of men, present company excepted, at least so far as I know. I also receive a decent alimony payment from my last husband that is an additional inducement not to marry again. If I remarry, he's off the hook, where, if I may say so, he richly belongs."

Listening to this, naked, under a sheet, I thought of Kizerman. Did being turned down leave him heartbroken? Defeated? Feeling that life now really was at an end for him? I also thought of Morrie Feigenbaum, who got the woman lying next to me so wrong, Feigenbaum who sacrificed a friendship of so many years through the need to give unnecessary advice. What a stupid muddle the whole thing was!

Four days later Feigenbaum drove his chair into Rappaport's. He took his usual table. I had greeted him at the door, but now walked over to his usual table.

"How goes it, Jerry?" he said.

"Not so bad, Mr. Feigenbaum," I said, "not bad at all. But I wanted to ask you if the situation with you and Mr. Kizerman has changed."

"Why should it have changed?" he asked.

"Because I heard that your friend isn't going to marry this woman you told me about a few weeks ago."

"Where'd you hear that?" he asked.

"From her, actually," I said. "She told me she never had the least intention of marrying him."

"Really?" He looked up at me, his right eyebrow raised. "Where do you come to know her?"

"Turns out we went to high school together," I said, "and I had dinner with her the other night. I found out that she doesn't need your friend Kizerman's money, doesn't require his protection, and never had any intention of marrying him. Oh, and there was no canoodling going on, either."

"Ex-friend, you mean," Feigenbaum inserted. "I miss the son of a bitch."

"I wonder if you shouldn't call Mr. Kizerman," I said, "and confess you had everything all wrong about Deborah Shapiro and apologize? Not, you understand, that this is any of my goddamn business."

"It isn't," said Feigenbaum, "but in this instance you happen to be right. To be out of line is one thing, but be both out of line and completely wrong is worse. I'll have to get up my nerve, but I'll make the call. At least I'll think about it."

"Lunch today is on the house," I said, and left his table.

The following Tuesday Hal Kizerman walks into the restaurant, and holds the door open for Morrie Feigenbaum and his motorized chair. I am at the register. Kizerman doesn't bother to nod to me, Feigenbaum winks as he drives past. After lunch, Gladys reported they were reading aloud to each other, back to working on their play, I guess.

As for Dinky and me, I almost wish I could say that I was still seeing her and we were going strong. Wasn't in the cards. We went out together another five or six times, and found ourselves running out of things to say to each other, both before and after sex. Can't live in the past, I guess. A damn nice place to visit, though, at least for a while.

The Man on Whom Everything Was Lost

VIA EMAIL I RECEIVED AN INVITATION TO CONTRIBUTE TO A MEMORIAL TRIB-
ute to Jeremy Jacobson, of whom I'm fairly certain you've never heard,
unless you happen to be deeply addicted to the internet. Jeremy was a
college teacher of English, and a blogger and twitterer of relentless energy.
He died in his late fifties, and in his lifetime wrote a single book: a published version of his doctoral thesis on the incursion of literary critics into
American English departments beginning in the 1950s and through the
1980s. Jeremy Jacobson was also, briefly, my student. I didn't take long to
decide that I would not be contributing to his online memorial.

He came in ten or so minutes late, took a seat in the front row, and,
looking up eagerly at me, spread out his notebook and made himself at
home. The course was on Henry James, with forty or so students, which
I taught from 10:30 a.m. to noon, on Tuesdays and Thursdays. First day
of class, I hadn't planned to keep everyone the full ninety minutes. I gave
a twenty or so minute talk outlining James's life and career, passed out
copies of the syllabus, wrote my office hours on the board, and ended by
remarking that Henry James was a leading figure in my small pantheon of
gods. Before dismissing the students, I warned that I planned to do all in
my power to convert them to the cult known as Jamesianism. As everyone
was beginning to leave, Jeremy raised his hand.

"How, exactly, do you expect us to read these novels?" he asked.

"I'm sorry," I said. "I'm not sure I understand."

"I mean," he said, "from a Marxist or feminist or Derridean perspective, or what?"

"I hope I don't disappoint you," I said, "but we'll read them to discover what is in them and what Henry James might have had in mind in

writing them. I'm fairly sure this will be enough to keep us busy through the term."

After everyone had left the room, and as I was gathering up my notes, he came up to introduce himself.

"Jeremy Jacobson," he said, putting out a hand. "I'm a graduate student, but very passionate about Henry James. With your permission I was hoping to audit this course, even though it's for undergraduates."

A small man, on the plump side, wearing rimless glasses, brown hair parted near the middle of his head, he looked Jewish, though as I later learned, he wasn't. He was twenty-six, older than most beginning graduate students, having worked for a while on a small-town newspaper in Oregon. He had gone to school at the University of Washington.

"I'm especially interested," he said, "in the influence of Henry James Senior's Swedenborgianism on the development of William but especially on that of Henry James."

"I know next to nothing about it," I answered. "You may be wasting your time sitting in this class."

"I don't think so," he answered. "I've read your novels and really love them. If you don't mind, I'd like to continue auditing."

"I'll be pleased to have you," I said, as we walked out of the classroom together.

Turned out I wasn't in the least pleased to have Jeremy sit in on my class. As Henry James would never have said, he was, not to put too fine a point on it, a royal pain in the ass. He spoke three times more than anyone else. He offered many opinions, most of which went contrary to my own views. He regularly compared James to Philip Roth, for example, to the favor of the latter. One day he asserted that the greatest novel of the past century was *Lolita*. I suppose I could have argued him out of these views—they were opinions, really, little more—but I didn't wish to interrupt the flow of the class's discussion of James's novels, so I just let them pass.

Truth is, I didn't want to seem to be putting Jeremy Jacobson down. When he spoke his younger classmates would often roll their eyes or make faces at what they took to be his outrageous pretentiousness. Pretty pretentious he could be. Once in class he carried on for a full five minutes—it seemed to last a full academic quarter—about his possession of a first edition of James's early novel *Roderick Hudson*. He often dragged in nearly incomprehensible disquisitions about the views of R. P. Blackmur and F. R. Leavis and other critics on James. The other students in the class hadn't a notion of what he was talking about. They must have wondered why I didn't cut him off.

The reason I didn't was that I grasped that Jeremy Jacobson was one of those unfortunate people who, so enraptured are they by their own performance, haven't the least notion of the effect they have on other people. I thought about talking to him in my office about his misguided behavior in class. I thought I might tell him that he was giving the mistaken notion that we were team-teaching this course, making plain to him that if he wished to continue auditing the class, he would do well to remember that the root meaning of the word audit was to hear, to listen. Somehow, though, I couldn't bring myself to do it. I regretted that he was the unknown (to him) target of my other students' probably appropriate yet still philistine disdain and felt sorry for him because of my foreknowledge that his life, with his crippling imperception, couldn't possibly be an easy one. Henry James it was who invoked his readers to try to be young men and women on whom nothing was lost. Jeremy Jacobson was a young man on whom nearly everything was lost.

One day we bumped into each other off campus, and he suggested a cup of coffee at a nearby Starbucks. Over coffee he told me that he planned to write a dissertation about how practicing critics would slowly replace philological scholars in English departments across America.

"A rich subject," I said.

"And one still relatively untouched," he said. "I was wondering if I could get you to serve on my dissertation committee."

When I asked him if he had approached anyone else, he mentioned two men for whom I had very little regard, one a dogmatic older professor, the other a refugee from the country known as the Sixties, a man who taught in jeans and unlaced Air Jordans and insisted his students call him by his first name in class. Jeremy Jacobson's taste in people, I concluded, was not of the best, and that he had chosen me to join these other two teachers was no compliment.

"A lot of the critics I have in mind were of course Jewish," he said. "I'm thinking of men like Lionel Trilling and Irving Howe and Alfred Kazin and Philip Rahv and William Phillips. I'm not Jewish myself, though with my last name I'm often taken for a Jew. My parents were born-again Christians. They came to it late in life, too late to bring me along with them."

When he pressed me about when he might have my decision on being on his dissertation committee, I told him that, not having a PhD myself, I didn't think it would be quite *de rigueur* for me to serve on his committee.

"That's a shame," he said. "I know you lived in New York and you've had dealings with some of my key figures—Howe and Kazin, for example—and your input and feedback would have been helpful. Hope you don't mind if I pick your brain, even though you won't be on my committee."

I thought to tell him that if he one day planned to teach English he would do well to knock off phrases like "input" and "feedback" and "pick your brain," but decided not to do so. His speech and anything else about him was none of my business, and, frankly, I wished to keep it that way. I didn't want any responsibility for him.

Instead I asked him how he was finding life in the midwest. A little dull, he allowed, but otherwise OK. He tried to get me to gossip about my colleagues, but I resisted, telling him that, as a writer and man without tenure, I wasn't at the center of English Department affairs, but was only here—though I had been at the university now for more than a decade—on sufferance, signing a new contract each year.

I could feel his loneliness, his wanting my friendship, even though I was nearly twenty years older than he and married with children of high school age. I'm not usually so guarded, but something told me to keep Jeremy Jacobson at a safe distance without being outwardly or obviously cold to him. He asked if it would be all right to call me by my first name, Ted, and I said sure, that would be fine, except of course not in class.

In the following weeks I would see Jeremy from time to time in the English Department office. As usual, he made himself at home, and took mistaken liberties. One afternoon, while getting my mail, I noticed him ask the department secretary, a Southerner in her early sixties and of stern dignity named Clarisse Hansen, if she would make copies for him of five scholarly magazine articles, and winced while she instructed him that she didn't extend such services to graduate students. He should have figured this out on his own, but, typically, didn't. He called two of the older professors by their first names, until one of them, a Chaucerian named Vandermeer, said that some of his oldest friends and acquaintances always called him Professor Vandermeer and he would be pleased if he, Jeremy, would do likewise?

Jeremy Jacobson vastly overestimated his charm. Lots of people do, of course, and any of us who think ourselves winning have seriously to consider that, God forfend, maybe we're not. I don't believe Jeremy ever considered the possibility. From what I could tell he didn't have many friends among his fellow graduate students. The younger faculty, some of them, tolerated him, barely. His power for turning people off was nearly pitch perfect.

I say nearly because one day downtown, off campus, I saw Jeremy holding hands with an attractive young woman. He stopped to introduce me to her.

"Tiffany Carlson," he said, "have you met Professor Ted Ross? Ted's one of the leading novelists of our time. Tiff's an undergraduate, Ted, majoring in communications."

"Ted?" I thought. I suddenly realized it had been a mistake to let him call me Ted.

Tiffany was small, blonde, very well set-up physically, wearing a sorority sweatshirt, Kappa Alpha Theta across the front. She was obviously taken with Jeremy.

"Pleased to meet you, Professor," she said. "Jeremy has told me all about you."

What could "all" be, I wondered? I wondered even more what this rather standard female undergraduate saw in Jeremy Jacobson, with his various pretensions, not the least of which was his rather preposterous sense of self-importance. He was five or six years older than she, at a stage of life when that separation could make him seem impressive. Perhaps she took him for a true intellectual, though I wasn't sure she had the word "intellectual" in her vocabulary; more likely she would have called him, or at any rate thought of him, as, "a real brain." E. M. Forster somewhere says that there are women who are stimulated by worthlessness. I suppose, as in the case with this attractive girl and Jeremy, others are stimulated by neediness.

I saw Jeremy off and on over the next few years. He told me that his doctoral dissertation was almost finished and asked if I could find the time to read it. I had no choice but to say yes, and, with a slightly sinking feeling, said of course I should be pleased to do so. Later that afternoon I found a copy of his manuscript in my mailbox at the English office.

The dissertation was well enough written. Jeremy led off by recounting the historical anti-Semitism in American English departments, and got that right, or so I felt. His larger point, that the scholarly had given way to the critical in the study of literature in universities, was also well handled. Where he went off the rails, I thought, was in overrating—blowing up might be the better term—those figures among the critics who had been at the forefront of his subject. He compared Irving Howe favorably to Samuel Johnson, Alfred Kazin to Matthew Arnold. I recalled how, when I lived in New York and used to see them fairly regularly, I always thought that Irving's shirt was out of his pants, even when it wasn't; and I remembered Alfred Kazin, at a cocktail party, fawning over Hannah Arendt and being frozen out by Mary McCarthy. Hard to imagine Matthew Arnold in similar case. I thought I might tell Jeremy about this, but in the end decided not to do so. His dissertation revealed Jeremy Jacobson as smart enough but wanting—no surprise here—a sense of proportion, or measure. He had two modes, exaggerated praise and, as I was later to discover, vicious attack. His dissertation got through, and he was now, officially, Dr. Jacobson.

I meanwhile published my fifth novel, a 587-page doorstopper called *Lost Departures,* about which I had grave doubts when I not so much finished as abandoned it and sent it off to my agent. These doubts were confirmed when the book won the Pulitzer Prize for Fiction the year of its publication. So many wretched novels and plays and books of poems have won Pulitzers that I was a little sad to find my book among them. In the end a Pulitzer Prize is good for pleasing one's aging parents, impressing lots of people who don't know any better, and earning the empty esteem of universities and other institutions. The year I won my Pulitzer I received a raise from the university a little more than double that I had ever received before. As Pulitzer Prize winner, I was suddenly in demand for university publicity events. Not my idea of a good time, any of this, but I went along with most of it.

The Pulitzer Prize was probably one of the main reasons that Jeremy Jacobson asked me to write a recommendation for him for a job at the University of New Mexico. A morally complicated business, the writing of recommendations, especially when it came to people you don't think all that highly of yet at the same time don't wish to sink. Which was my position with Jeremy.

I wrote, in a much more extended and slightly florid way, that Mr. Jacobson was passionate in his love of literature, that he was well and widely read, that he was penetrating in analysis, and possessed a lively mind. None of this was exactly a lie, but it was of course far distant from the whole truth. I wrote the recommendation because I was tired of feeling sorry for Jeremy, of watching him overstep his bounds with people, and of many of these same people not really caring enough about him even to bother disliking him. I wished him well, in other words, but not near me.

Jeremy got the job at New Mexico. He stayed there for twenty-three years. I learned that he was offered tenure after a very close vote, for he became a figure of contention in the English Department. A friend of mine named George Bankoff, a geologist, was to spend a year as a visiting professor at New Mexico, and when he asked me if I knew anyone there on the humanities side he might look up, I mentioned, with some hesitation, Jeremy Jacobson. When he returned, I asked George if he had met Jeremy. He had indeed, though he said he didn't spend much time with him. Met him once for a drink, another time for lunch. "Strange guy," George said, "not much to my taste, if you don't mind my saying so."

"He's a bit controversial, I discovered," George added. "He's a libertarian, very extreme in his views. So extreme, someone there told me, that the joke is he would prefer to deliver his own mail. I was also told he doesn't mind mocking lots of his colleagues for those of their views opposed to his own. He's not very well liked, apparently."

I also learned from George that Jeremy had married a successful divorce lawyer in Albuquerque. He had become Catholic, and was very serious about his religion. As a convert, he was, as George, fearless about clichés, put it, more Catholic than the Pope. He complained about the loss of the Latin mass, wouldn't eat meat on Fridays, never missed confession, denounced liberal-leaning clergymen. I would later learn that Jeremy named his three children, two boys and a girl, Evelyn, Graham, and Flannery, after the three leading Catholic writers of the twentieth century.

The way I learned this was that momentous event, the arrival of internet, had happened and taken hold, and Jeremy Jacobson became an early blogger, using his blog to discuss his personal as well as his professional life. Earlier he had sent me—and who knows how many other people—offprints of reviews he had published, usually of contemporary novels, in the quarterlies: *Sewanee, Georgia Review, New England Review, Virginia Quarterly*. He did two fiction chronicles for *Hudson Review*. Two pieces in the same place was unusual for Jeremy, for he seemed able to find ways of falling out with editors, I gathered, and wasn't invited back. I'm an occasional contributor to *Hudson Review* myself, and I asked a sub-editor there about his experience with Jeremy.

"He comes on sweet and enthusiastic," he said, "but soon the complaining starts. Why do we wait to print before we pay contributors? He doesn't like the placement of his pieces in the magazine. He tells us we ought to fire our dance critic, whom we all adore and whom he called an ignoramus. The guy's a walking alienator."

As for the reviews, they tended to be very, even wildly, enthusiastic. Jeremy was regularly finding some great—the word "great" came to him readily—new novel that took the question of "man's relation to faith head on." He was not my notion of an ideal critic. But, then, I was born in another era, a time when a fundamental part of the job of the serious critic was to serve as gatekeeper of culture. The gatekeeper was there to keep all but the best of art outside the holy citadel of culture. Jeremy preferred to fling the gates wide open, declaring a new literary genius every three or four weeks.

The internet was Jeremy Jacobson's salvation. On his blog—which he signed as J. J. Jacobson, his middle name being Jonah—he could write what he pleased, and not have to deal with fussy editors, eliminating the whole question of human relations that had always been so troublesome for him. I must confess that I became addicted to his blog. He had a way of exposing himself like no one else I had hitherto encountered; he was master of the art of telling one a little more than one wanted to know. One morning he might write about his relations with his wife, who in his account seemed to consider him slightly nuts and out of it; the next morning recount his youthful sexual escapades. He wrote a fair amount about his religion, naming saint's days, quoting Ronald Knox, explaining the pleasures of confession.

Then one morning I tapped onto his blog and discovered he had written about me in a post called "My Great Teacher." In the post he suggested an intimacy between us that of course was never there. We weren't so much teacher and student as buddies, men who deep down knew what was important in life. What my "great" teaching consisted of was never made clear, never actually touched on, really. He hinted at my flaws. I could be touchy, I could be doctrinaire, even dogmatic, but never with him. By the time the blog ended he seemed to be the teacher and I the student, mildly but genuinely in need of guidance, maybe even psychotherapy. Did he really think he was writing in a complimentary way about me? I felt the strong inclination to fire off an email to him asking him where he got this stuff, in his imagination, I assumed, and if he had ever considered writing fiction. But I held back, as I always seemed to be doing with Jeremy.

Not long after this Jeremy announced on his blog that he had been diagnosed with multiple sclerosis, and of a virulent strain. He wrote that he was given three, maybe four years to live. He wrote that he trusted his religious faith would hold him in good stead during these last years. He added that he would be reporting on his illness and the state of his soul in the months ahead.

I suppose Jeremy was reassured in this dubious venture by the several specialists in literary grief who had opened shop in recent years. Two female novelists wrote books about the loss of their husbands, one of which—the books, not the husbands—became a bestseller. A provocative English journalist had offered an account of his slow death by cancer, much of it published, in, of all places, the celebrity magazine *Vanity Fair.* An American historian arranged to record his death by Lou Gehrig's disease. An Australian critic was currently chronicling his forthcoming death by emphysema and other illnesses in poems. Why, Jeremy must have figured, shouldn't he give us a blow-by-blow account of the nightmare of multiple sclerosis?

And a blow-by-blow account he provided. He began recounting the loss of strength and eventually the use of his left arm. He wrote a lengthy blog on what it was like to adapt to life on a walker, the awkwardness and inconvenience of it, especially of getting into public toilet stalls. He mentioned that his handwriting was shot, for the strength was now also departing his right arm. His wife had to cut his meat for him. His eyesight was going, and he thanked God for his Kindle and iPad, which allowed him to enlarge the print of his reading. He was now showering in a chair, he reported, for he no longer had the leg strength to stand up for the duration of a shower, his wife always in the room in case he needed help. Why he neglected to fill us in on how he got on and off the toilet I cannot say.

Despite all his physical problems, Jeremy continued plugging what I assume were negligible contemporary novels. He was sending off thirty or forty tweets a day. In his tweets and on his blog he wrote about his time with his children. He recounted his sessions with his parish priest, who fortified him in his desire to get the most out of the life that remained to him. He never, let me add, complained, but seemed comfortable in the role of victim and martyr.

I'm a touch embarrassed to say that I continued to be addicted to Jeremy's blog and tweets—the unnecessary self-revelation, the self-importance, the sheer disproportion of the entire enterprise—and checked them every morning on my computer along with the *New York Times* and the *Daily Beast.* I checked Google in the attempt to learn what, if any, reaction Jeremy was getting to his chronicle of his own dying. Not all that much, it turned out, but while doing so I discovered that he gave a podcast to a fellow blogger which began with his talking about his book on critics invading English departments. He mentioned that it was more influential than he thought, and the way he knew this was that a lot of important writers had plagiarized from it. Among them he named three contemporary critics and me, or as he referred to me, "my old mentor, the Pulitzer Prize winner, Ted Ross." He didn't go into details about just what I or anyone else had plagiarized from him.

Doubtless it was a mistake, but I straightaway sent Jeremy an email, informing him that I had listened to his podcast, and was curious to know just what it was he thought I had plagiarized from him.

"Hi Ted," he wrote back, "great to be back in touch. It's been too long. Sorry to learn that you are offended by my citing you for plagiarism, but it's really true you know. I was referring to your saying, in a talk you gave at Michigan State that a man I tweet with told me about, that the great critics did best to steer clear of academic settings, which is one of the points I made in my dissertation, which you read and approved. But feel no need to apologize. Truth is, I'm honored to have you steal from me."

I felt a vein throb on my forehead. I did give a talk roughly three years ago at Michigan State, but if it touched on critics it could only have been in the most oblique, the most grazing, way. My talk was on whether universities were inimical to novelists by taking them out of the world.

"Jeremy," I emailed back, "thank you for relieving me of the duty of apologizing to you, but, since I never said what you claim I said, I think the need for apology is on your side. I'll await further word from you."

"Here's the further word," he shot back. "You're wrong and lying to cover your tracks. But then you've always been a small man, insecure in your literary fame. And as long as I'm on the subject, I might add that I don't think you're much of a novelist, which is one of the reasons I've never reviewed you. I'm probably the most accomplished student ever to have passed through your classes and you've never said a kind word about me in public, which I also resent. I don't know if you know this or not, but I happen to be dying, and I don't need to put up with your petty-minded cruelty in the little time left to me. Please don't ever contact me again."

I wrote back: "I shall accede to your wish." And I never did contact him again.

I did, though, continue to tap in his blog and to read his tweets. You won't be surprised to discover that I was now doing so chiefly to discover if he were attacking me on the internet. He never did. A year or so later, he stopped writing his blog, and then, not long after that, he ceased to tweet messages. Two weeks later, on the website for his blog, his wife wrote that Jeremy died, peacefully, in his sleep, she, a priest, and his children at his bedside.

He left the earth despising me, who had joined the long list of his enemies, or so I have to conclude. Any lingering bad feelings I felt toward him fell away with his death. Ought I, I wondered, have been a better teacher to him, a teacher not of literature but of life, taken him aside and attempted, gently, obliquely, to show him the mistakes he was making with people? Could I have made a difference, helped make the way smoother for him, by counseling him in some way to play around his social tone deafness? Whether or not I could have done, the cold, the now irrefutable fact is that I didn't.

Through her law practice Jeremy's wife would, I gathered, have the money to raise their three children, all of them still under twelve years old. They, I hope, would have only sweet memories of their father. May they never know that their father was always embattled, felt himself surrounded by enemies, most imaginary, some real, roused by the absence in him of any knowledge of how he came across to other people.

The handful of online tributes to Jeremy began to dribble in. I read various novelists, whose names were all unknown to me, thanking him for his support of their work, and a few readers expressing appreciation for what he had taught them. Jeremy Jacobson was gone, and would soon enough be forgotten by the infinitesimal segment of the world who knew of him and would now carry on its business well enough without him. I wish I could be among those who could easily forget him, but I find, damn it, I cannot.

The Bernie Klepner Show

NOT EASY HAVING A *MESHUGENER* FOR A FATHER. HAVING HAD ONE, I DON'T recommend it. At what point in life does one notice that one's father is unlike other fathers, and not necessarily in a beneficial way? In my case, though I can't date it exactly, it must have been around the age of four or five. Our mother, for whom I thank God, used to warn me, my brother Howard, and my sister Melissa when our father was in a bad mood, which was fairly often. "Leave Daddy by himself for a while," she'd say. "He's tired from working all day." Or: "Don't bother Daddy just now, sweetie, he didn't sleep very well last night." Or: "Daddy's not feeling very good. Let's give him some time to feel better." And, most frequently: "Daddy's just back from the doctor. You know how he's sometimes a little on edge when he gets back from the doctor."

The doctor, I soon learned, was Louis Slotnik, my father's psychoanalyst, then head of the Chicago Institute for Psychoanalysis. I don't know how long my father was in psychoanalysis, but it must have been at least beyond a decade, probably a lot more; it wasn't a subject he was eager to talk about. If his analysis was successful, you couldn't tell by me, since his behavior in all the years I knew him—he died at eighty-three, when I was myself fifty-five—never changed a jot. In all that time he did and said what it pleased him to do or say.

Culture was one of the bees in my father's bonnet. He wanted me to play violin—the Jewish instrument, he called it, *"par excellence."* The problem here was that I hadn't the least scintilla of musical talent. After six years of lessons and practice, he finally allowed me, at the age of fourteen, to quit. When I told my mother, her eyes teared up. When I asked if my quitting the violin made her sad, she said no, quite the contrary, she was crying with delight at no longer having to listen to me scratching away at my instrument seven days a week.

I am the oldest of my father's three children. As the oldest, I took the brunt of his nuttiness. Not that he was all that consistent in his demands. He would often change them without notice. "Just because the kid is Jewish," I heard him tell my mother, "doesn't mean he has to play the goddamn violin." Febrile, showing lots of agitated energy, is probably the word that best describes my father. He displayed every emotion in the book except calm.

My father—Bernard Kepner is his name—has for years had a late-night radio interview show on WMAQ in Chicago. Before that he taught political science at Roosevelt University. His father, who was in the furniture business and with whom he didn't speak for more than a decade before my grandfather's death, died intestate, and so his not inconsiderable fortune—something just over a million dollars, a lot of money in those days—went to my father, his only surviving relative. (My father had an older brother, Samuel, who died, of cancer, in his fifties.) I never knew my grandfather. When I asked my mother about him, she said that he was a man who seemed to be angry full time.

I never found out the cause of their falling out, but with my father any of a thousand causes was possible. My grandfather would have been outraged to know that his money went to his disputatious son. His money freed my father from teaching, which he never really enjoyed. "Time to set the pearls before swine," he used to say when he went off to Roosevelt. "Sorry, swine," he said in a self-toast at a small retirement dinner given him by the three colleagues who still spoke to him, "no more pearls."

My father had a thousand opinions, all of them strongly held, but even as a kid I never found it easy to make out exactly his point of view. On only two items was this unmistakable: he was certain that we were living in a time of momentous debasement of culture, and he felt the world was out to get the Jews. "The barbarians are no longer outside the gates," he once told me, "they've had the gatekeeper on their payroll for decades." He also instructed me never to forget that everyone keeps a cold place in his heart for the Jews.

I remember the time I was ten years old and my father took me to buy a parka for the rough Chicago winters. The salesman at Marshall Fields took a hooded, khaki-colored coat off the rack and said, "Here's a coat that's been very popular this year." To which my father answered, "In that case we don't want to see it. Show us something that isn't so goddam popular."

I had a slump my sophomore year in high school. For reasons too boring to go into here, I just stopped turning in homework. My father was called into the office of the guidance counselor, a Mrs. Miriam Ginsberg, to decide on a course of action. I sat there next to my father when Mrs. Ginsberg, after explaining my conduct, said, "Maybe the boy is more role than goal oriented." I saw my father's jaw set. "More role than goal oriented?" he said. "In that case, if I continue to let him get away with this outrageous behavior, my role would be that of a schmuck, wouldn't it?" I wanted to jump out the window behind Mrs. Ginsberg, but the point got across, and I promptly returned to doing homework.

When the time came for me to go to college, my father made plain that he would only allow me to go to one school, the school he had gone to, the University of Chicago.

"Let's get this straight, kiddo," he told me, "you apparently have a good brain, and I'm not sending you off to Brown or Tufts or Williams or Amherst, or any other of these dumb designer colleges, and that includes Harvard, Yale, and Princeton."

"But, Dad," I remember saying, "I was hoping to get out of town for college." Naturally I didn't add that I was also hoping to get away from him, at least for a while.

"It's the University of Chicago, or I don't pay," he said. "The school may have lots of flaws, and it's probably not as good as when I went there, but it's still the only serious joint the country. The place was the making of me, and if it was good enough for me it'll be good enough for my son. Case closed."

Thank God I was able to get into Chicago, so I never had to test him on the firmness of his promise never to pay for my education anywhere else. The University of Chicago turned out to be far from my idea of a good time. My father was right about its seriousness, and maybe the problem is that I wasn't myself serious enough, at least not at age eighteen, for it. I also fairly quickly sensed that there was a not-so-hidden agenda at the University of Chicago, and it was that there were four things, and four things only, worth being in life: an artist of some kind, a scientist, a statesman, and (the loophole) a teacher of artists, scientists, or statesmen. I had neither the talent nor temperament nor even mild interest in becoming any of those things, which meant that, by the standard of the University of Chicago, I would be just another peasant, no matter how much wealth I might acquire, raking gravel under the sun. That I didn't take to the University of Chicago, though I managed to graduate from the place, was, I suppose, another reason for my father's disappointment in me.

On my father's interview show he sometimes spoke with local politicians, or mildly famous actors passing through Chicago, but chiefly his guests were authors flogging their books. "An interesting word, 'flogging,'" I remember him saying, "suggesting as it does a dead horse." He was on radio five nights a week, from 9:00 to 11:00 p.m., with the second hour devoted to calls from listeners. On a given week he might interview an athlete, a nuclear scientist, a stand-up comedian, a civil-rights leader, and a ballerina. Some of these people, innocently hoping for a little publicity, didn't know what they were in for when they encountered Bernie Klepner.

A sports fan as a kid, I stayed up one night to hear him interview Kareem Abdul Jabbar, recently retired from the Los Angeles Lakers. "Mr. Jabbar," my father said, "what does it say about our country that a man like you can become famous and a multi-millionaire because he is inordinately tall and has acquired the knack of throwing a rubbery ball through a metal hoop?" I remember a long silence followed, then a sudden break for a commercial; and when my father returned he announced that Mr. Jabbar was called away by an emergency, and he would now replay an old interview he had done with Nelson Algren, who had died three weeks before.

On the air my father once asked Mayor Daley—the son not the father—if corruption was absolutely necessary to run a big city, or, as in the case of Chicago, was the rampant corruption instead only an Irish thing? In later years, I heard him begin an interview with Bill Clinton, then promoting his memoir, by asking if he had any interests in life apart from sex, money, and power. He had the editor of *Poetry Magazine* on and asked him how he felt about his job now that poetry had become a mere intramural sport, read only by the people who were writing it. He asked Jesse Jackson how he had the gall to mount his own pulpit after it was revealed that he had a child out of wedlock. Why people put themselves through my father's buzz-saw by appearing on his show I never understood, but they did, five nights a week, for decades.

On air or off, my father said whatever it occurred to him to say. What was on his lung, as the old Yiddish expression had it, was on his tongue. Was he candid, or fearless, or merely nuts? My mother once told me that it was through his years of psychoanalysis that my father had learned never to hold back. Circumspection, like repression, was, he held, for idiots. His listener ratings in Chicago were high. As many, maybe more, people listened to "The Bernie Klepner Show," I'm told, because they hated him as because they liked him. But either way he had a steady following.

I once asked my mother what drove my father into psychoanalysis.

"Your father's mother favored his older brother," she said, "and made no bones about it. The unfairness made it very hard for your father as he was growing up. This was made worse by the fact that he could never get along with his father. Talking about it with Dr. Slotnik relieves some of the pressure he still feels from being unwanted as a child."

My father was short, muscular, with heavy forearms, and dark wavy hair that he brushed straight back. He had to shave twice a day: once in the morning, and then again before going off to do his show downtown. There was something of the scrapper about him, not just mentally but also physically. Once, when I was nine years old, he took me to a White-Sox–Cleveland Indians game. At the game, two rows behind us, two drunks began taunting Al Rosen, the Indians' third baseman, yelling anti-Semitic remarks at him.

"Excuse me a moment, kiddo," my father said. I watched him make his way to the drunks, bulky working-class guys, and, moving in close to the one sitting on the aisle, I heard my father say: "Shut the fuck up, or I'll see you jagoffs are thrown out of the park." I thought sure they would punch him out there and then. Something in the intensity of the way he said it must have cowed them, and they stayed quiet for the rest of the game. My father had made himself into a man not to be trifled, or otherwise fooled, with, not even by brutes.

I was at the end of my first year at the University of Chicago when my mother died. Ovarian cancer took her in just less than a year after she was diagnosed with it. My father was solicitous through his wife's illness, but he didn't seem thrown by her death. "Life goes on," he said more than once. He gave the main eulogy at my mother's funeral, and it was quite as much about him as about her, about his not being able to have attained what he had in life without her, about how extraordinarily generous she was to him, about how sorely he and his children would miss her.

Less than a year later, he remarried. I met his second wife two weeks before he married her. He knew her from the Chicago Symphony, where they both had Friday afternoon tickets. Clarisse Froehlich was her name. She was a German-Jew, more German than Jewish, from Alsace-Lorraine. She was also roughly six inches taller than my father. Her pretensions were extreme. The first time I met her, when she discovered that I was a university student, she said that she hadn't herself gone to university, adding there was really no need to, for her *gymnasium* education was quite complete.

"We studied Goethe, Schiller, Rilke in *gymnasium*," she said. "Very serious. Not like here."

What my father saw in her, I cannot say. Her influence on him, though, was immediate, and first showed up in his wardrobe. Married to my mother, he showed no special interest in clothes, went around in slightly rumpled sport-jackets, baggy gray trousers, and loafers. Now he began wearing Armani suits and Charvet bowties and Ferragamo shoes. When I asked him what was going on, he replied, with a smile: "I'm under new management."

During this, my father's Armani phase, he attempted a late-night television talk show on Saturday nights on the local PBS channel. His producers brought him such guests as Carol Channing, Sammy Davis, Jr., and Rodney Dangerfield. All wrong. He had nothing to say to them. On television his boredom was visible. He was too highbrow, too polemical, too (his word) rebarative for the medium. Television of that day called for an agreeable placidity. Two things my father wasn't, nor could ever hope to fake being, was agreeable or placid. His television show lasted less than three months.

At twenty-one I was pretty much out of the house, and so suffered my father's second wife's regime only glancingly. Things were tougher for my brother and my sister. Howard called her—behind her and my father's back, of course—the Krautessa.

One sometimes comes across a couple and wonders what one saw in the other that caused him or her to marry the other. In the case of my father and the Krautessa, it worked both ways: what he saw in her, or she in him, was a mystery. She didn't need his money; she was a widow, and her first husband had had a contract with Nike, for whom he made athletic socks, and left her well off. Maybe her Europeanness attracted him. My father, for all his brusqueness, not to say neurosis, seemed to attract women who wished to look after him. My mother did so in a quiet, the Krautessa in a more aggressive, way. Neither could finally change him.

My father sold our house in Highland Park after his second marriage, and moved into the Krautessa's large apartment, on East Lake Shore Drive, two buildings down from the Drake Hotel. Howard, two years younger than I, was about to go off to Northern Illinois University (an uninterested student, he couldn't get into Chicago) and Melissa, with two years to go in high school, was transferred to the Latin School. Howard and I shared a room at the Krautessa's, and Melissa had her own room. But I continued to live mostly in Hyde Park and was already making plans to get out of my father's life soon after graduation.

As it turned out, my father's marriage to the Krautessa lasted a little less than two years. An old story: an unmovable force met an irresistible object, and the marriage caved in. The Klepners moved out of the East Lake Shore Drive apartment, and into a two-bedroom apartment in a much, less grand building on Pearson Street. My father dropped the Armani, Charvet, and Ferragamo and returned to his sport-jackets, gray trousers, and loafers.

I never moved into the Pearson Street apartment, for my father and I had a falling out that blasted our relationship. At twenty-one, my last year in college, I found I needed to marry. (I'll explain that "needed" in a moment.) I told my father in the hope that he would offer to help me financially to bring it off.

"Let me get this straight," he said. "You don't have any money, your education isn't finished, you don't have a job or any prospects for one. And now you want to marry some lucky girl. Sounds to me like a splendidly well-thought-out move."

"I was hoping you might help me out," I said.

"Forget about it," he said, "I would only be helping you to destroy your life. Your marrying at twenty-one is preposterous."

This didn't seem like the best time to tell him that I myself didn't think my marrying was such a hot idea either, but that I had no choice, having made pregnant Jessica McNeil, the girl in question, a serious Catholic and hence implacably opposed to abortion.

"You were only five years older than I when you married Mom. You were twenty-six, right?"

"But I'd finished school. I was employed. I knew what I was doing."

"Dad," I said, "it's complicated."

"Not as far as I'm concerned it isn't. Marry this girl and we're finished. Done. *Kaput*. Expect no help of any kind. Not now, not ever."

"I see," I said, and walked out of the room.

Two weeks later, Jessica miscarried; a blessing, I realized even then. But I had already made my decision to cut things off with my father. I felt I couldn't put up with any more of his bullying. My tuition was paid through the end of the term, my final quarter at the university. I had friends I could move in with, at least temporarily. I could go it on my own, and decided to do so.

I rousted about for a year or two, working at various jobs, then I found real estate, for which it turned out I had a knack. I began by selling homes on the Northshore, then went into commercial real estate in the Loop. With two partners, I bought an eight-story apartment building on Sheridan Road. That led to my acquiring, this time on my own, three greystones on the Gold Coast, which I was able to renovate and flip fairly quickly. I could tell you more about my adventures in Chicago real estate, but suffice to say that, against all I was taught at the University of Chicago, I've made a lot of money, and, peasant raking gravel in the sun though my old professors and classmates might think me, I don't have any regrets. I may not be able to create either a poem or make a scientific discovery, but I enjoy putting together and making a deal, and I hope to continue doing so for years to come.

Twelve years after my non-marriage to Jessica McNeil, I married Susan Levinson, a pediatrician in private practice on the near north side. My brother Howard was my best man, Melissa was one of Susan's maids of honor; my father wasn't invited to the wedding. We hadn't spoken in all this time. I thought about inviting him, felt maybe this was the right occasion to make things up between us, but then I decided it was his, not my, place to make the first move toward a reconciliation, and in all this time he never made such a move. From time to time I asked my brother if my father ever mentioned me. The answer was always negative. I wasn't upset by this; it let me off the hook. He was too preoccupied to be much of a father anyway.

I listened to "The Bernie Klepner Show," not every night, but at odd times: driving home from a movie or play or dinner with friends, in the bathroom while brushing my teeth before going to bed, up at night paying bills. He was as wild as ever, my old man. One night I heard him ask Edward Albee how he had come to hate the American family so much. Another night he asked the president of Northwestern University, a Jew at a school that once had strict anti-Jewish quotas, how it has come about that the Jewish presidents of so many American universities were just as mediocre as their gentile predecessors. He told an advocate of gay marriage that he was for gay marriage because he didn't see why, as a divorced man himself, gay men and lesbians should be spared the legal complications and nightmares of formal legal divorce. He had an environmentalist on one night I had tuned in, and promptly asked him what the hell the environment ever did for humanity, apart from floods, landslides, earthquakes, tornados, monsoons, droughts, and raging fires. A famous rapper came on and the host asked him when he first realized there was a good buck to be made composing songs hating white people. Wild, like I say.

My brother Howard, who studied accounting at Illinois, eventually came to work for me. When he told our father he was planning to become an accountant, our father said, "Howard, dope, you don't become an accountant. You hire an accountant." Howard kept me up to date on my father's doings, not the least notable of which was, at age sixty-six, a third marriage, this time to a personal injury lawyer, Teri Rabin was her name, who specialized in spousal abuse cases. She was in her mid-fifties.

"Her aggressiveness," Howard reported, "makes Dad look like Peter Pan. Her name's Rabin but it could more accurately be Rabid. Our dad doesn't seem to mind. He finds it amusing."

"Sounds like a woman dangerous to divorce from," I said.

"Maybe we better set up a trust fund for our father," Howard said, "just in case."

The marriage lasted four years, when Teri Rabin acquired early onset Alzheimer's, and had to be put into a nursing home. I never met her. My brother told me that our father attended to her well past the time when she could no longer remember his name, continuing to visit her in the dementia floor at the Northwest Home on California and Rosemont. She lived on, in a cloud of obliviousness, for nine more years. Give my father his due. He could be rough, verbally brutal, tyrannical, but he wasn't a skunk.

Susan and I had two kids together, sons, and on more than one occasion, when still young, they asked me how come they never got to see their Klepner grandfather. I remember as a kid asking my father the same question about not seeing his father. He told me his father was working abroad. When I asked him where "abroad" was, he said "Sudan." When I asked what he did there, he said he owned and ran a drugstore. I wasn't as imaginative in lying to my children. I told them that their grandfather was nervous around young children, and would love to see them once they were older. After a while they stopped asking.

Looking back on it, my father hadn't had an easy run. He had three marriages, none of which gave him enduring satisfaction. One of his sons turned out to be an accountant, which, by the standards set by the University of Chicago, fell on the prestige scale somewhere between a garbageman and a child molester. His other son, me, with whom he hadn't spoken in more than thirty years, he had long ago written off as a coarse money man, nothing more. He had, in effect, sat *shiva* over me, or I over him, I'm not sure which, long ago.

Saddest of all was his daughter Melissa—Mel as we used to call her when she was a kid—who never really got over our mother's death. Mel was sixteen when our mother died, which as everyone knows can be a tough time for girls; I know it was for her. (The only tenderness I saw my father expend when I was growing up was to Mel, his beautiful but clearly fragile daughter.) She went into therapy soon after our mother's death and never really emerged from it. She had two kids from her first marriage, to a man she had to chase for child support after their divorce. After having a child with a second husband, she was, in her early thirties, diagnosed as bipolar. She drank when depressed, and hung around with all the wrong people when manic. Her second husband, a decent guy, left her, remarking that not many marriages with one person being bipolar make it to their fiftieth wedding anniversary. He agreed to raise all three of her children, whom he promptly took off to live in Oregon. My father felt he had no choice but to take Mel in to live with him, which couldn't have been all that easy for either of them.

Through all this sadness and chaos, "The Bernie Klepner Show" kept going, five nights a week. So he plugged away, night after night, talking with experts on climate change, authors of books on reducing crime, politicians on the make, with women who wrote about the child abuse they had undergone, with poets, pacifists, people who wanted to legalize pot, end gun control, save the planet, leaders of one liberation movement or another, with anyone looking for a bit of free publicity. How he kept it up, I have no notion, except that he needed his show, he needed a forum, a place to perform. "The Bernie Klepner Show" was the one inviolate part of his life.

Then the people at his station decided that my father's show was to be cut down from two to a single hour. "They're dumbing down the whole damn station," he told my brother, "goddamn *goyim*."

Then our sister died in a motorcycle accident, killed on the Eisenhower Expressway, when the motorcycle of the guy she was riding behind jumped the median and ran head on into a truck headed east. If you're wondering what a Jewish woman of forty-four was doing riding on a motorcycle driven by a guy named Steve Woszjewhawski, I would send you to consult the Wikipedia entry on Bipolarity, with special attention to the manic phase.

The funeral for Melissa was at Weinstein-Piser on Skokie Boulevard and Church Street. I sat with Howard and his family and my wife and our two sons and my father in the front row. Melissa's coffin was closed. My father decided it made no sense to have Mel's children flown in for this horrendously sad occasion. This was the first time I had seen my father in roughly thirty-two years. He still had all his hair, but it had turned white; he wore glasses; his stockiness was gone; he walked with a slight limp. He was near eighty.

"Not the prodigal but, I'm told, the plutocrat returns," he said at greeting me.

"How are you?" I asked.

"Apart from being broken-hearted," he said, "I'm going along. I loved that poor girl. I hope you know that."

"Of course I do. It was good of you to take her in after her divorce."

"And now she's gone, and I'm a member of that saddest of all fraternities, parents who have buried a child. I don't like it, not a damn bit."

Somehow we got through the funeral: the platitudes of the rabbi about the early death of a woman who had been plagued by mental illnesses from a man who never knew her, the long ride out to Westlawn Cemetery, the sad lowering of my sister's casket into the grave that was next to our mother's. As the rabbi recited the *kaddish*, I looked across the grave to see if my father was crying. He wasn't. But he seemed a bent old man, and for the first time I could remember, vulnerable.

As my father and Howard and his wife and daughter got into the limousine to return to town, my father rolled down the window.

"Next time you come out here will be to bury me," he said. "Try to remember to be respectful."

Before I could answer, the window closed and the limousine pulled away.

The next piece of bad news visited upon my father was the cancellation of "The Bernie Klepner Show." The station replaced him with a sports talk show, which somehow made it seem all the more degrading to him.

"Chewing up stale items about preposterous athletic salaries and trades and last night's game," he said. "If that's what the morons want, fuck 'em, let 'em have it."

He attempted to shop "The Bernie Klepner Show" to other stations around town, but there was no interest. Without a show to go to every night, my father, it was obvious, felt lost. Now that we were back in touch, I offered to take him to lunch. Our first lunch together, at the old Tavern Club, at 333 N. Michigan, where I was on the board, was awkward. At first he hadn't much to say. He did remark, though, he thought it interesting that he had fallen out with his father just as I had fallen out with him.

"Maybe we have more in common than either of us thought," I said.

"I doubt it," he replied. "Your brother tells me you're a wealthy man."

"I suppose I am," I said.

"I gather you sit around all day conjuring up deals. I'll bet you drift off to sleep thinking up how you can make still more money?"

"Actually I don't," I said. "But I sometimes wake up with terrific ideas about how to do so.

"Fact is," I continued, "I do spend a lot of time thinking about money—about how to make it, about how to keep it safe, about how to make more out of what I already have. You find that objectionable?"

"No," he said, "I find it unimaginable. I can't concentrate on money long enough to balance my checkbook, let alone read financial reports."

"Are you saying your mind is on higher things?"

"Yep," he said, "that's what I'm saying."

"I'm pleased you are able to feel so good about yourself."

"We can't all be *luftmenschen*, I understand that. I might envy you your dough, but I don't admire you."

"I on the other hand might admire you your freedom, but I don't envy you at all, so I guess we're even, or pretty close to it." I felt as if I were a guest trapped on "The Bernie Klepner Show."

"You're not as dumb as you look," he said with a smile. "Maybe you're a Klepner after all."

At other lunches—we met every six weeks or so—we talked about the great world. Or rather he talked about it, and I listened. He felt everything good in life was slipping away, all politicians were crooks, academics hopeless, current novelists unreadable, poets non-existent, plays not worth paying the outlandish sums asked to see them, social scientists mostly full of crap, journalists whores. These were rants, pure rants, but fairly impressive ones, I thought.

"You've probably never heard of a writer named Umberto Eco," he said at our last lunch together. "Eco somewhere writes that as a sapient man grows older he gradually develops contempt for whole segments of contemporary society: physicians, lawyers, professors, businessmen, civil servants, diplomats, and so on, until there is no one left for whom he doesn't feel contempt but himself. Soon after he dies. I think I'm about there."

As we were leaving the Tavern Club, on the elevator down from the 25th floor, my father said: "I apologize. I regret the years we missed out on."

"I'm equally to blame," I said. "No apology needed."

Had we been different men, we might have hugged. Instead we both kept our eyes on the floor until the elevator arrived at the lobby. Out on Michigan Avenue, before departing, we shook hands.

"There's an old Arab proverb," he said, "I wish it were a Jewish proverb but I guess you can't have everything, an Arab proverb that goes, 'When your son becomes a man, make him your brother.' I think maybe it's time I did that for you."

"Sounds good to me, Dad," I said. "I would like that a lot."

Three weeks later my father had a stroke.

I visited him at Rush Medical Center. His left side was completely paralyzed. His face seemed frozen, his speech greatly slurred. I approached his bed, grasped his hand.

"I," he said, very slowly, with long pauses between the words. "Loved. Your. Mother."

My father died that night. There was a brief obituary in *The New York Times*. His death made the front page, below the fold, of the *Chicago Tribune*. "Iconoclast Bernard Klepner Dead at 83" read the headline.

"The Bernie Klepner Show" was over.

The Viagra Triangle

BILL DOLAN'S THE NAME, AND I'VE BEEN DOORMAN HERE AT THE CONdorcet Condominiums at 146 E. Cedar for twenty-six years, it'll be twenty-seven in August. Before this I was a fireman. I played football at Lane Tech High School. I was a linebacker, third team all-city in 1972, to which I owe the fact that my knees gave out at the age of thirty-six and I had to retire on disability from the Chicago Fire Department. With my small pension from the city and my salary from The Condorcet, I make out all right. My wife Marlene and I live in a bungalow in Jefferson Park on the northwest side, and our two kids are grown and long gone.

I sit behind my reception desk at The Condorcet much of the day, receiving packages, making sure no one gets in who isn't supposed to, meeting a few requests to run errands for our wealthy owners, watching, you might say, how the other half lives. The Condorcet is located between Rush Street and Lake Shore Drive, with Oak Street beach just to the east. The neighborhood is what used to be known as the Gold Coast, but Cedar, along with Bellevue and Elm Streets, are what lots of people have begun to call The Viagra Triangle, so named because there's lots of older, financially well-off men with wives or in some cases girlfriends thirty and more years younger than themselves.

Over the years I've seen guys with funny, hobbling walks, or even on walkers accompanied by knock-out young women who are definitely not their caregivers, unless you put a very loose interpretation on the word "care." On Oak Street, site of Jimmy Choo, Prada, Barney's of New York, retired guys in Ralph Lauren suits hit on older girls from Walter Payton High School in the hope, who knows, of getting lucky. In The Condorcet there is a man named Lou Pearlman, must be in his mid-eighties, been in a wheelchair for some years, who is never seen without his wife Candace, who once gave the weather on the local NBC station under the name Candy Phillips, better known in those days for her rack than for the accuracy of her forecasts, and who must be forty years younger than he.

On the twenty-sixth floor, in one of the building's two duplexes—they go for over three million—lives Sheldon Fishman with what I believe is his twenty-five years younger mistress. Three weeks ago, a very high maintenance blond, she's maybe thirty-five, approaches the reception desk, and asks for the floor of Mr. Fishman's apartment. I ask her name, and she tells me Brittany Connors. Fishman asks to have her put on the phone. She calls him Shelly, and laughs loudly at something he's told her. Before hanging up, she says into the phone, winking at me, "I'll be right up. Don't start without me." When a few hours later the two of them passed my desk on their way out, Fishman, smiling, in a low voice, says to me, "Chemistry is our most important product." I'm not sure what the right attitude is to take to a man who cheats on his mistress.

The Condorcet has more than its share of widows and widowers, people in their seventies and early eighties. I'm sixty-two myself, a kid to most of them. I've been around the building long enough to watch some of the owners grow into old age. The stages are sadly familiar. Often it begins with the funny walk. Next comes the walker. This is usually followed by the wheelchair and the Filipino caregiver. The fall and the broken hip spells the beginning of the end.

The widows do better. Some, in their early eighties, continue dressing provocatively, in designer jeans, dyed hair, heavy makeup, still on the attack, I guess you might say. Many are still looking for new husbands, though they tend to be very critical. Over by the mailboxes, which are near the reception desk, this past Tuesday I overheard Mrs. Faye Schwartz, on the ninth floor, say to Elaine Spivak, 12B, "He's looking for a nurse with a purse. Count me out."

The widowers do less well. Three or four months after their wives die, most of them start to look kind of rumpled: clothes not pressed, spots on their shirts and jackets, letting hair grow out of their noses and ears. Maybe they go a couple days without a shave. Who's noticing, they must figure.

What's clear is that it was their wives who kept them in respectable order, and with them no longer on the scene things start to cave in pretty fast.

Sometimes, though, there will be a startling change back to orderliness, or even more than orderliness. Mr. Arthur Handler, from the seventh floor, fell into this kind of widower's scruffiness in a fairly extreme way a month or two after his wife Sarah died from liver cancer. Then one day he shows up in the lobby in a double-breasted suit, an expensive-looking tie, black tassel loafers with a high shine. Later that evening, just before I go off duty, he returns to The Condorcet with a woman, a redhead, maybe thirty or so years younger than him, which explains everything.

I was pleased to see this didn't happen to Philip Sherman, who owns the other penthouse duplex at The Condorcet. I don't befriend the owners in the building, or maybe it's more exact to say that they don't befriend me, but I can't help liking some more than others. Philip Sherman and his wife Anne were a couple I liked a lot. They seemed to be not just man and wife, but also each other's best friend. I like to think the same is true of Marlene and me. Without any attempt at fake intimacy or anything like that, they always treated me graciously, as if I were something more than hired help. They were very dignified people, and they acted under the assumption that everyone else had dignity, too. Every Christmas I would get a handwritten note from Anne Sherman wishing me happy holidays and thanking me for my help during the past year, with a crisp one-hundred-dollar bill enclosed. When Anne Sherman was diagnosed with Alzheimer's, her husband wouldn't let her be sent off to a nursing home, but hired a full-time nurse to watch over her. I don't think I'll ever forget the two of them walking through the lobby, her holding tightly onto his arm, a look of frightening emptiness in her eyes. For two years she staggered on, until, I'm told, she didn't remember her husband's name. She died not long after.

I was working in the building the day of Mrs. Sherman's funeral, but I learned from the building manager, Eddie Slaughton, who did go to the funeral, that the Shermans had no children. Mr. Sherman, in other words, was alone in the world, living on the thirty-fourth floor in his 4,000-odd square foot apartment. He was long retired. I'm not sure what he did for a living; something in finance, I think, commodities market, hedge funds,

I don't know for sure. Money, though, definitely wasn't his problem. On the few occasions I was in the apartment I noted lots of art on the walls. He and his wife went to the Symphony most Friday afternoons. Once Mrs. Sherman offered me opera tickets they weren't able to use. My wife and I sat in their box in the mezzanine. Once at the opera was enough for me. The story, something Italian, was preposterous. At one point a fat guy stabs himself and starts singing, loud. Not my idea of a good time. Marlene, though, was pleased to be there.

Philip Sherman is a small man, but with good posture. He's kept most of his hair, which hasn't yet all turned gray. He's slender, always well dressed, even in casual clothes. He must be eighty-three, eighty-four. He drives a two-year-old black Audi, nice but nothing pretentious, unlike Saul Pollock on the fifth floor with his white Bentley, his mottled bald head, and his thirty-or-so-years-younger-than-he Chinese wife Jessica. Or Harry Feitlson, from the twenty-first floor, who twists his old bones into his red Porsche Carrera Cabriolet.

Mr. Sherman was better than that. He was a gent. So you can imagine my amazement when, a week or so later, a young woman approaches me at the reception desk to say that she is here to visit Mr. Philip Sherman. This woman is, I would say, maybe twenty-five, she's wearing low-slung jeans, showing her midriff, and wearing a rhinestone in her belly button. She's maybe 5'10", and her hair is blond with pink in her ponytail. Her right ear has maybe six piercings. When I ask her name, she answers Vanessa Ross. Mr. Sherman, when I reach him, tells me to send her right up.

This young woman showed up four more times in the next few weeks. And then one night she turns up with a small suitcase.

"Mr. Sherman," I say, when I get him on the phone, "your lady friend is here. May I ring her up?"

He laughs. "Lady friend?" he says. "Thanks for the compliment, Bill, but the lady in question is my grandniece. She's beginning Northwestern Law School next month. Send her up."

I'm not sure why, but I was relieved. But maybe I do know why. Philip Sherman is a serious person, and I guess I don't like the idea of him making a fool of himself owing to too-late-in-life-arriving sexual fantasies and urges.

Eight or nine days after this, I'm standing waiting for the bus on Foster, just west of Sheridan Road—normally I drive to work, but that day my wife needed the Camry—when a black Audi pulls up to the curb.

"Need a lift, soldier?" the driver, Mr. Sherman, says.

When I get in he explains that he is headed out to O'Hare, to pick up an old high-school friend he hasn't seen in more than forty years.

"Hope this doesn't happen to you," he says, "but two years ago, when I reached eighty, I became nervous about driving freeways. I've become one of those old guys who hugs the right lane and probably drives too slow. I don't mind taking city streets. I've lived in Chicago all my life, and I like to drive through it from time to time, noting all the changes." He adds that he has time to take me home.

"I was amused the other day that you thought my grandniece Vanessa was my lady friend. Given all that's going on these days, the assumption wasn't crazy."

"Hope I didn't embarrass you," I say.

"Not at all. Who knows, maybe I should have been honored at your assumption that I could—I want to put this delicately—accommodate such a young woman."

I'm a bit nervous here about talking about anyone else in the building, not sure how Mr. Sherman will take it. But I take a chance. "I don't think your neighbor Mr. Pollock would worry too much about it."

"You're right there," he says. "Nor Harry Feitlson or a few others among my distinguished contemporaries I could mention."

"There's a lot of it going around in the neighborhood, you may have noticed."

"Hard to miss it," he said. "I feel sorry for these young women. Someone once said that when you marry for money the pay's good but the hours tend to be long. Can't be such an easy row to hoe for young women married to these *alte kockers*. You know that phrase, *alte kocker*, it's Yiddish."

"I think I can figure it out," I said.

"You know, Bill, older men like me run the risk of falling into bemoaning the way the world has changed, claiming it was so much better when we were young. Maybe it was, maybe not. I make a strong effort to avoid going on these rants. But since we're on this subject, I'm going to break my rule and say that one of the main things that has changed during my lifetime is the loss of embarrassment. People do things casually today that, forty or so years ago, they would have been embarrassed to do. Once embarrassment goes, there goes shame. Do you suppose some historian will one day look back on our time and call it the Age of Shamelessness? A distinct possibility, I'd say."

He turned off Foster at Milwaukee.

"I had a friend, Alexis Poulous, a Greek, he was with me on the original board of the Museum of Contemporary Art. An amusing fellow, Alexis. He married a woman thirty or so years younger than himself and also had a mistress roughly his own age, around fifty-five at that time, I'd guess. I asked him, 'Alexis, what is this about? Don't things usually work the other way around? Older wife, younger mistress.' 'I know,' he said, 'but married as I am to a woman who is twenty-five, I need someone to talk to.'"

As Mr. Sherman turned up Bryn Mawr, where we have our bungalow, he continued: "Sometimes these older men also want to have children with their new young wives, even though they know they won't be around to watch them grow up. Who knows, sometimes maybe the woman wants the child, something to remember the old guy by. I'm told it's dangerous. A very high proportion of the children from fathers past seventy have serious birth defects. A Chicago painter I knew named Vincent Orticelli, in his mid-eighties, no doubt jacked up on Viagra, or some such drug, had a child with a forty-two-year-old wife and the poor kid turned out deeply autistic."

When he said this I couldn't help but think of his and his wife's own childlessness. Long-married childless couples always leave you wondering if they feel a hole in their lives. And they make you wonder which of them, husband or wife, made it impossible to have children.

"Life has stages," he continued, "morning, noon, and night. Not a good idea to violate these. Lots of nonsense talked about how you're only as old as you feel. Seventy is the new fifty, eighty the new sixty. Don't believe it. Eighty is the old eighty, it'll always be eighty. Anyone who gets there ought to consider himself lucky and not push it."

Pulling up in front of my house, Mr. Sherman said: "I'd say it's been nice talking with you, but I seem to have done all the talking. I guess this is a subject much on my mind. Apologies."

Before getting out of the car, I told him no apologies were needed, I said that I found what he had to say full of interest, which I really did.

At home, at dinner that evening, I told Marlene how impressive I thought Mr. Sherman. Unlike most of the rich ninnies at The Condorcet, he had perspective, saw things as they really were, had his head on straight. I didn't of course tell her my own thoughts about what I would do if I were a weathly widower in his position. I wasn't sure myself. Would I go out on the skirt-chase? Nothing to stop my doing so. Young female flesh is always pretty exciting. I love my wife. I've never for a moment thought my marrying her a mistake. Marlene has a good heart, was a fine mother, a good wife. I still find her attractive. Yet at the age of sixty-two, I find I'm still checking out pretty women, imagining myself with them in intimate situations that I'm not ready to confess. My guess is that things won't change much here when I'm seventy- or eighty- or even ninety-two, if I get there. We men, I sometimes think, are baboons. We're filled with desire long after we ourselves are in the least desirable. Unless their money makes some of them desirable, which I guess it must, or how else explain all the young women married to or living with geezers at The Condorcet and in other buildings on the Viagra Triangle.

Seven or eight months after Mr. Sherman drove me home, one evening, close to 5:00 p.m., just before I'm to go off duty, a woman enters the lobby of The Condorcet, mentions her name is Andrea Simon, and asks to be announced to Philip Sherman. She's slender, well-dressed, brunette, fifty or so, I'd say.

"Tell her I'll be right down," Mr. Sherman says.

When he arrives in the lobby, she puts out both hands in greeting him. He takes her hands, draws her to him a bit, and kisses her on the cheek.

"Wonderful to see you, Phil," she says.

"Same here, Andrea," he answers.

Is she a niece? Maybe a cousin? Who knows? I do know he is pleased to see her, no doubt about that. As they pass through the front door of The Condorcet, I think again about what a good man he is.

Another day this Andrea Simon—she's not wearing a wedding ring— shows up with a small suitcase. I don't see her again until noon of the following day, when she approaches the reception desk to ask if I could call her a cab. I next learn, from himself, that Mr. Sherman is going to be away in Paris for a week; I am to keep all packages for him, but if a FedEx arrives from the Sidley Austin law firm, I am to forward it to the George V Hotel there, whose address he has written out for me. He ends his note by thanking me.

Eddie Slaughton tells me that he believes "my friend" Mr. Sherman has a "girlfriend." Funny thing to say about a man in his early eighties—he has a "girlfriend." Eddie keeps up on all the gossip at The Condorcet. He knows who is heartbroken because his only grandson has declared himself gay. Whose daughter has lost her medical license because of having been caught with cocaine in her possession. Who did time years ago for tax evasion. Whose family money was made by a bootlegger grandfather. Eddie pretty much has the lowdown on everyone in the building.

What's his evidence that Philip Sherman has a girlfriend? Turns out he saw Mr. Sherman holding hands with a woman coming out of the elevator on his way to the building's garage. The woman was in her fifties, and when he described her his description matched Andrea Simon.

"She could be a cousin, or a niece?" I said.

"Suppose we bet ten bucks that you're wrong?" Eddie said.

I took the bet. Why did I so strongly prefer that Mr. Sherman not be an old fool, another lost wanderer in the Viagra Triangle? What was it my business, anyhow? If he wanted to chase a women twenty-five or thirty or even forty years younger than himself, if that is what gave him pleasure, then let him do it. Still, something in me wanted Mr. Sherman to steer clear of this craziness?

Another day this Miss Simon turns up and asks to be connected to Mr. Sherman's apartment. When I make the connection, he asks to speak with her. I hear of course only her end of the conversation. She calls him "sweety," she says she has a surprise for him. "Yes, dear," she says, before hanging up and walking over to the elevator.

So it turns out Philip Sherman, despite his convincing lecture to me on our ride to my house, has a lady friend. There can't be much doubt about it. His wife had been dead a little bit more than a year, and his last few years with her Alzheimer's can't have been so easy. He has no children.

I could see where he might be lonely for female company. Why not; it was perfectly normal. Who was I to judge? I wished him well.

Eddie Slaughton it was who told me that Mr. Sherman was planning to marry Andrea Simon. How did he come by this knowledge?

"Because Mr. Sherman called me to ask if I knew of a notary public in the neighborhood," Eddie said. "He wanted to transfer some property. I called my cousin Fred, who works at the nearby Chase Bank. The property he wanted to transfer was a court building on Damen on the northside, twenty-six apartments, he wanted to make one Andrea Simon a joint-owner of it with him."

"Serious stuff, sounds like," I said.

"I'd say," said Eddie. "The old boy isn't just screwing around here."

"I hope it works out for him. I hope he gets what he wants. He's a decent guy."

A week later, Mr. Sherman called again for Eddie's cousin's notary services. This time it was some commercial real estate he owned in Wicker Park that he wanted to have her own jointly with him.

"I'll take the ten bucks now, please," Eddie said, holding out his hand.

I don't mind saying I was disappointed. Not so much at losing the ten bucks but at the thought that Mr. Sherman, for all his sensible talk, in going for a woman thirty or more years younger than himself made him seem just another rich dope from The Viagra Triangle. Would I have been less disappointed if Mr. Sherman had joined up with one of the widows in the building? I probably would have been. I hoped this Andrea Simon was worthy of him. I couldn't help liking him.

Next I heard—again from Eddie—that Andrea Simon was under arrest. Mr. Sherman's lawyer, a guy named Sidney Feig, suspicious about his longtime client turning joint ownership of costly real estate over to her, put a detective on Miss Simon. The detective discovered that she had a boyfriend, a guy named Carlo Grandison, who had done time for forgery, burglary, assault and battery and had, as Eddie said, "a rap sheet longer than a pro basketball player's wingspan." The police were called in and, under grilling, were able to discover that the plan was for Andrea to marry Mr. Sherman and not long after for her friend Carlo to step in and murder him. Murder him how was never revealed. When his lawyer explained this to Mr. Sherman, he thanked him, said nothing else, and walked away.

The next time I saw Philip Sherman after this, maybe ten days later, he was returning to the building with a bag of groceries in his arm. He had, I swear, developed a stoop. He walked past the reception desk, eyes looking down, not greeting me. He had become elderly.

A month later, as he passed in the lobby of The Condorcet, again without a word to me, he was on one of those metal three-pronged canes. His hair, which was none too clean, was whiter than I remembered. Previously always impressively dapper, he now looked as if he were dressing out of the dirty-laundry basket. He moved very slowly, tentatively, on his cane.

Months went by without my seeing Mr. Sherman in the lobby. Kenny Cooper, the guy who does the doorman shift after mine—from 5:00 p.m. till 1:00 a.m.—said that he hadn't seen him pass through the lobby either. Eddie had no word of him. Then, May 21, spring window-washing day at the building, one of the window washers, from his perch outside the Sherman apartment, saw Mr. Sherman face down on the living-room floor. He reported it to Eddie, who went into the apartment and discovered Mr. Sherman dead. How long he was dead wasn't clear. The man from Piser-Weinstein who picked up the body said it couldn't have been less than a week.

"Poor bastard," Eddie said, as they took Mr. Sherman's body outside the backway, through the servants' entrance, "I don't know whether he died of a heart attack or stroke or what, but the real cause of death was depression."

I didn't say anything, but to myself I thought, No, Eddie, he didn't die from depression, he died from embarrassment.

Less than two months later the Sherman apartment was sold. The place went for $3.6 million. The new owner is a retired personal injury lawyer named Mort Feldstein. He lives with a wife, Tiffy he calls her, thirty-eight years younger and six inches taller than him. He walks her two Yorkies three times a day. Within the Viagra Triangle the beat, as the disc jockeys from my high-school days used to say, goes on.

JDate

"Schlubs and losers," Laurie Cohen's friend Maddy Levine said, "that's what you'll find on JDate, schlubs and losers. Believe me, I've been there, I know." Maddy recounted meeting on the Jewish online dating service a man named Larry Plotnik, a real-estate man in Flossmore. He was fifty-six, divorced, with three kids, two of them out of the house, the youngest finishing college. After a number of phone calls, they went to see a play at the Goodman Theatre, Arthur Miller's *The Crucible*. The play was a drag. Plotnik was maybe forty pounds overweight, wore a comb-over, but was affable. That was the word Maddy used, *affable*, so when he asked her out again, she figured why not?

Their second date he took her to Gibson's, a steakhouse on Rush Street, very expensive. The bill came to just under three hundred dollars, and they'd just had one drink each. Plotnik talked mostly about himself, his children; he mentioned his psychotherapist twice. He felt he was an inadequate father. Over Macadamia Turtle Pie, he teared up. Maddy was touched. The third date ended up in her bed. "Suffice to say," said Maddy, looking away, "the heavens did not open up, the earth did not move."

Still, when Plotnik invited her on a week-long cruise in the Caribbean, Maddy figured why not? At a minimum, it was a chance to get out of a gray February in Chicago. First day out, at one of the shops on the ship, Plotnik bought her a Coach bag, four hundred bucks. But it was downhill from there. He didn't dance, complained about the food, was untidy in all sorts of small but infuriating ways, talked endlessly about his problems with his children. "A schlub, a loser," said Maddy, "but at least I got a winter holiday and a Coach bag out of the deal."

Laurie knew she was less tough than Maddy Levine, more vulnerable. They were both fifty-three, had gone to Highland Park High School together. Maddy had been through a rough divorce and brought up her two daughters mostly on her own. Sleeping with men was no big thing for Maddy, while Laurie could never think of sex as an insignificant act. Maddy saw the world as a place to do business, to acquire what advantages for herself she could; Laurie felt there was something important in life that she had missed out on and for which she was still searching.

What Laurie Cohen had missed out on, specifically, was what Maddy called a "relationship." She had never lived with a man, nor had any man ever asked her to marry him. She was, she knew, not unattractive. Small, slender, a brunette, she dressed carefully, her skin had held up, she felt herself still in the game—if not, like Maddy, on the attack. Friends fixed her up, men still occasionally asked her out. But at fifty-three she was now up to going out mainly with divorced men and widowers. Months went by when she didn't go out with a man at all. Which was why she was thinking about JDate. Why not, she thought, give it a try?

Laurie went online. She set out her date of birth (2-9-60), height (5'3"), weight (115), hair color, marital status, synagogue attendance (conservative, infrequent), interests (reading, jogging, design), and the rest of it; she included a picture of herself that was only six years old.

Soon enough men sent emails making their case. One claimed to be the last master Jewish plumber in the midwest. Two siding salesmen wrote, one to tell her that her photograph reminded him of his mother, whom he had lost earlier this year; the other to ask if she had any interest in extraterrestrial life. Three different dentists replied, one of whom loved folk singing, another still played in a rock band on weekends, as did a guy who had recently quit his job as a CPA to return, at sixty-four, to do graduate work in communications. A man named Harry Rubin wrote to report that he had made his "pile" in the mail-order business and, though now eighty-three and long retired—he included a photograph of himself in aviator glasses and a tank top—assured her he was still "sexually very active."

Laurie had been teaching grammar school, fifth grade, at the Dr. Bessie Rhodes School in Skokie since graduating from National Louis

University in the Loop. She enjoyed the kids, though in truth she had tired of the regular interference of their parents, many of them Russian émigrés and east Indians. Having been told that education is the key to success in America, parents regularly called or came in when their kids didn't get all A's.

A good job for a spinster, teaching, Laurie had begun to think. Hateful word, *spinster*, but this might be her fate, to live and die alone. She knew that her father, a successful urologist, had been disappointed she never married. Henry Cohen hadn't any social or even financial ambitions for his only child, to whom he expected to leave several million dollars, but, as he once told her, he wished she would find the right man, a companion in life and someone who would watch out for her. He wished to live to see her sail into safe harbor. That was the phrase he used, "safe harbor." Well, the truth was, Laurie, in her fifties, hadn't yet come close even to sighting land.

The one mildly interesting response to her JDate enrollment arrived two or so weeks later. A man in Milwaukee, fifty-eight years old, a pharmacist at a Walgreen's there, wanted to be in contact with her. He was a bachelor and lived in a condo along Lake Michigan near the Milwaukee Art Museum. He would be willing to drive to Chicago, a less than two-hour trip, if she were interested in meeting him. His name was Howard Klein.

He signed his emails "Howie," and seemed cordial enough generally. He told her he was a big sports fan, and joked that his being a Green Bay Packers fan and her coming from Chicago, home of the Bears, might make any relationship between them a little like that between Romeo and Juliet, though he hoped with a happier ending. He told her that he thought of himself as a serious reader, though he rarely read fiction, mostly biographies of scientists and books about World War II. He mentioned that he was a terrible cook and ate most of his meals out, or else brought food in, and loved Chinese, which he called "the food of our people, meaning of course the Jews."

In Laurie's emails to him she brought up the joys and frustrations of teaching. She mentioned that her father was a Bears fan but not so rabid a one as to think her exchanging emails with Howie would constitute a betrayal. She brought up her addiction to running and said that unlike him she read fiction almost exclusively, favoring nineteenth-century novels. She, too, was mad about Chinese food, and should he ever come to Chicago, she would be pleased to take him to Emperor's Choice, her favorite restaurant in Chinatown.

Sex never came up in these emails. Nor was it even hinted at, which Laurie found a relief. Laurie had slept with three men—make that two men and a boy. The boy was Nathan Engel, with whom she went out her senior year at Highland Park High. When she thought about it later, she had sex with Nathan almost out of boredom. They had been a couple for five months, and there was nothing else for them to do, nowhere else to go. They had sex in the backseat of Nathan's father's Mercedes, and it was awkward, quick, and, as Laurie thought back on it, vaguely gross.

As an adult, she had had two affairs, if they could be called that. One was with a fellow teacher, when she was in her late twenties, and lasted roughly four months, when he came to announce to her that he was returning to Seattle where he was planning to marry a woman he knew in college. The second was with a man she met at a dinner party given by Maddy and Ben Levine. He turned out to be married, the pure type of the narcissist, or so she thought, less interested in pleasing her than in demonstrating that his power of seducing women was still intact. She saw him five, maybe six times. The sex in both cases had been less than thrilling. No beams of light, no earthquakes.

Laurie sometimes wondered if she was someone low in libido, or possibly even frigid. She even considered that she might be a lesbian, though not for long, for she often found herself looking at attractive men and fantasizing going off to bed with them. She preferred to think that her problem was that she hadn't met the right man and that, if she kept up her standard and was patient, he would eventually turn up.

When Howie Klein came to take her out to dinner in Chicago, Laurie, on meeting him in the lobby of her Sheridan Road apartment building, was disappointed. He had a slight paunch. His light brown hair was thin and substantially receded, and he was dressed in a blue blazer and khaki trousers and scuffed loafers. He drove a light blue Prius. He talked about the good mileage he was getting in it nearly halfway to Chinatown. He was still explaining how hybrid engines worked as they pulled into the parking lot on Wentworth Avenue off Cermak Road. Laurie thought her mascara might be running with boredom. JDate, she thought, schlubs and losers.

The Emperor's Choice wasn't crowded; people occupied only five of its fifteen or so tables. On the walls were elegant imperial robes in large glass frames. At a small bar near the entrance the owner, who recognized Laurie with a nod, was watching a White Sox game on an old television set.

"The dismalness of this place bodes good food," Howie said.

He let Laurie order for both of them: hot-and-sour soup, Mongolian beef, Singapore noodles, Kung-pao chicken. He suggested Tsingtao beers.

"Forgive my going on so long about my car," he said. "I know I talked too much. Truth is, I'm nervous. I've had a few JDate exchanges online, but this is the first actual meeting I've had."

"Mine, too," said Laurie.

Laurie told him that her father was a physician, that she was an only child. She told him that she had never been engaged, and regretted being too old to have children, but had by now learned to live with it. She told him that she loved Chicago, had lived here all her life, and had no longing to end her days in Florida, Arizona, or any of the other, as she said her father called them, "elephant graveyards." She told him that she lived a fairly quiet social life, meeting a few women friends for dinners and a movie afterward and that she hadn't been in a "relationship" with a man for a long while, without specifying how long. She said nothing about how comfortably off her father had left her.

Howie told her that his father, an immigrant from Romania, had a small grocery store in Milwaukee. His mother died when he was sixteen. He had two sisters, Evelyn and Judy, both married, one with two children, the other with three. He had gone to the University of Wisconsin at Milwaukee. He said nothing about women or his social life. He did tell her that he had the world's simplest resume; he had worked only at Walgreen's since finishing college.

"There's something else I should tell you," Howie said, "and this is that as I approach sixty I have the haunting feeling that I blew it. I'm starting to feel I missed out on life, or at least on its two most important things."

"Which are?" Laurie asked.

"Family and interesting work. I wish I'd had the nerve to aim for something higher in life than I did. Becoming a pharmacist was a step up for a grocer's son. But I could've done better. I was good at school. I should have gone to med school, maybe become a surgeon. When I see the jerks who have become physicians, and as a pharmacist I deal with these guys every day, I could kick myself. I should've had more guts."

"And family?"

"I wish I'd had kids. They'd've given me a stake in the future that's missing from my life. But you can't have kids without a wife, as I'm sure you've noticed. Doofus that I was in my twenties and thirties I decided that I preferred my freedom to marriage. Thing is, I didn't do all that much with that freedom. Didn't have lots of love affairs, didn't travel to Africa or the Orient, didn't live in Paris or in Tuscany. All I did, I see now, was fail to commit myself."

"It's not too late," Laurie said. "A younger woman could give you children."

"I suppose she could," he said, "but I doubt she could also give me conversation. The other thing is, why would a younger woman be interested in me. Besides, I don't want to be one of those guys playing with his kids in the sandbox at sixty-three, or yelling at little league umps at seventy-two. No, the time for kids for me is over."

"Which leaves you where?"

"Which leaves me kind of baffled? But I didn't mean to start whining. Forgive me."

"You weren't whining," Laurie said. "I'd call it a realistic appraisal of your situation. Nothing wrong with that."

"Your situation is better, I hope," Howie said.

"Well, it's different," she said.

Fortunately she was spared going into details on the subject, for the hot-and-sour soup arrived.

They walked around Chinatown after dinner. Howie offered to buy her an exotic plant, a guzmania, with a red stalk, a souvenir of the evening, he said. But she said that her apartment was a place where plants went to die; she had a black instead of a green thumb, thanks anyway.

On the way back to her apartment, Howie remarked on the Chicago skyline. She told him that she had thought of moving downtown, in effect moving into that wonderful skyline, but that it would put her too far away from her school. She didn't go to the theater much, but she loved the ballet and modern dance. He said that he knew nothing about ballet, adding that maybe someday she could introduce him to it. She didn't respond.

When they arrived at Laurie's building at Sheridan and Thorndale, she kissed his cheek in a grazing way and said she enjoyed their time together. She didn't invite him up to her apartment.

"I enjoyed it, too," Howie said, as she closed the door of the Prius and turned to go into her building.

Later that evening, Laurie thought she had been wrong not to have invited Howie Klein up. He had driven all the way from Milwaukee. Not that she had the least intention of any intimacy between them after a single meeting. Perish the thought. But simple courtesy called for it.

In bed that night, Laurie couldn't help thinking of Howie Klein's telling her that he "blew it." Had she, too, she wondered, blown it? Had she let life slip by, missing out on the central things? She used to tell herself that her young students were her children, but that of course was nonsense; they were just passing through her classroom. Many of them at term's end were probably glad to be done with her, for she was known as a fairly strict disciplinarian, insisting on careful spelling and trying to teach grammar to eleven-year-olds.

Laurie was critical, maybe hypercritical, about men, but she couldn't help that. She recalled how earlier that evening she had rejected Howie Klein at first sight. No flair—that had been her first judgment. She might like to think she had high standards, but wasn't such behavior really rather shallow? Was she superficial? A snob? In any case, her critical sense, her high standard, or whatever it was, wasn't working; it hadn't improved her chances of finding a man she could love and trust and could live with in intimacy.

While not exactly rude, Laurie's treatment of Howie Klein was *brusque*, a word her mother often used to criticize her behavior as a girl. She regretted it, but didn't see that there was much at this point to be done about it.

When she woke the next morning, an email from Howie Klein was on her smart phone:

> *hi Laurie, sorry things didn't work out last night. hope I didn't bore you too much with my car talk and, even worse, my self-pity. I'm usually better than that, or at least I think I am. anyhow apologies. it was nice meeting you, and I'm glad to know about emperor's choice, which I hope to return to someday. meanwhile, best of luck in finding someone worthy of you. best wishes, howie*

Laurie felt herself moved by this, even though she had a thing about people who didn't bother to use capital letters in their emails. She could of course ignore it, not answer and just forget about it. That, though, didn't feel right. She felt she had already been cold enough to Howie Klein.

She tapped out the following answer:

> *Dear Howie,*
>
> *No apologies necessary. I suspect we were both a little nervous last night. Why not? Online dating, after all, is more than a touch artificial. But I do want you to know that I enjoyed myself in your company, and if you wish to meet again, I'm up for it. Weekends are best for me. Cordially, Laurie.*

A mistake? She wasn't sure as she clicked the send button.

They arranged to meet on a Sunday, for brunch. Laurie thought a daytime meeting best, less entangling, less complicated somehow. This time when Howie rang from the desk in Laurie's lobby, she invited him up.

"Spectacular view," he said, as he looked out the large windows of the living room of her sixteenth-floor apartment that faced the lake and downtown Chicago to the south. "And you've furnished the place elegantly."

"Thank you, Howie," she said, suddenly aware that this was the first time she had called him by his name. Howie, a boy's name, she thought, but not yet unseemly for a man his age. He looked like a Howie. In his seventies, he may have to start calling himself Howard, but for now Howie still worked.

"I thought we'd go to a place called The Bagel for brunch. Lots of older Jews there, but good food of the kind we both grew up on. If you like, you can leave your car with the doorman, and I'll drive."

As soon as they arrived at The Bagel, Laurie felt that it had been a bad choice. She expected an older clientele, but not so many older women on walkers. Sad old men in running suits sat before enormous salami omelets. At one point an overweight elderly woman rolled in on a complicated motorized chair; tubes in her nose were connected to a small oxygen tank.

"I didn't expect so dilapidated a crowd," Laurie said once they were seated in a booth toward the rear of the restaurant.

"Not many sprung chickens, as an immigrant friend of my mother's used to say. Don't worry about it. These people make me feel young."

Laurie ordered orange juice, an egg-white omelet with mushrooms and tomatoes, whole-wheat unbuttered toast. Howie ordered a bowl of kreplach soup and a corned-beef sandwich on an onion roll.

"I take it you don't go in for healthy eating," Laurie said.

"I have no interest in getting to the age of ninety-five," Howie said, "so that someone can bring me to lunch here on a stretcher. As a pharmacist I see so many people hungry for longer life. Where long life is concerned, truth to tell, I'm not all that hungry."

"How do you suppose that is?" Laurie asked.

"I could tell you that Isaac Newton's only sensuous pleasure in life was in roasted meats, and that if they were good enough for Newton they are certainly good enough for me. I could also tell you that I believe in living for the moment, but you wouldn't believe it, and neither do I. What I do believe is that it is probably a mistake to deny yourself small pleasures in a life that is fairly perilous to begin with. I mean I could go for my next annual physical and learn that I have three cancers, the beginning of Alzheimer's, and all the signs of forthcoming ALS. If I did, after my initial disappointment, one of my first thoughts would be, damn, I should have had the kreplach and the corned-beef sandwich on an onion roll that morning I went to brunch with Laurie Cohen."

Laurie, laughing, said, "I suppose that is an original if not exactly healthy point of view."

"I might feel differently if I knew people were depending on me," Howie said. "Since no one is, hey, bring on the rich food. But why do you eat so carefully? Why do you jog every day? What are you staying in shape for? I'm sure you've asked yourself these questions."

In fact, Laurie hadn't, apart from thinking that they might extend her life. "I feel good after my late afternoon jog," she said. "I feel better for eating carefully."

"When was the last time you had a corned-beef sandwich?"

"I don't know. Maybe twenty years ago."

"If I were to offer to donate a thousand dollars to your favorite charity, would you cancel that egg-white omelet and eat another one now?"

"I don't think I could get it down," Laurie said, with a smile. "The idea is too upsetting."

"And what do you deduce from this?"

"What should I deduce from it?"

"Maybe that you don't have to be so tough on yourself. Worrying all the time about what you eat or missing your daily run. On the subject of running I have always been impressed by the claim that running lengthens a person's life but only by the exact amount of time he or she has spent running. It's a wash, in other words."

The waiter appeared with their food. Howie's soup had two enormous kreplach. Laurie's omelet, with a few red grapes, a large sad strawberry, and a slice of cantaloupe on the side, seemed rather pale.

"I have a friend named Eliot Rosen, seven years older than me, who still competes in triathlons," Howie said. "I told him that I thought he was in training for Alzheimer's. Stay in such great shape you're sure to live long enough to make it to dementia, I told him. I'm afraid I ticked him off."

"I think it does me, too," said Laurie, dabbing at her egg-white omelet.

"In which case I take it all back," Howie said. "But if you saw the pills I purvey every day to pluck up people's health, you might not feel so differently. You know, Jews always say, 'Just so long as you've got your health.' 'The main thing is you should be healthy.' 'What good is money if you haven't got your health?' True, all of it. But it seems to me one thing to have your health and another to be thinking about the damn thing nearly full-time."

Laurie found herself giggling, which she ordinarily never did.

"Look, the main reason I went into this diatribe is that, with the size of these kreplach being what they are, I'm going to need your help in eating half my corned-beef sandwich. Can I count on you, kid? Whaddya say?"

"Maybe I'll try a half of a half," she said. "But if word of this gets out, I'll know who told."

"What happens at The Bagel stays at The Bagel," Howie said.

When the sandwich arrived, it was enormous, the corned beef piled four inches high. Laurie ate not a quarter but a full half of Howie's sandwich. He gave her the slice of pickle as "a reward for her courage."

"The awful thing is," she said, "I really enjoyed it. God, it was good."

"If you'd care to belch emphatically," Howie said, "I'll be glad to give you privacy and leave the table."

After lunch they left Laurie's BMW convertible in The Bagel parking lot and walked east and then over to the Lincoln Park Zoo. They discovered a common affection for giraffes, for what Howie called "their goofy serenity," and lingered for perhaps half an hour watching two giraffes and their baby cavort behind the fence in the open air. When they got back to Laurie's car, it was nearly four o'clock.

"I better get back," Howie said. "I have tickets to the Milwaukee Symphony. I have to change clothes and pick up a friend."

Somehow or other Laurie thought he might stay on and they would have dinner together. And this "friend" he mentioned going to the Symphony with. A man? A woman? Am I jealous? she wondered.

Laurie didn't hear from Howie on Monday or Tuesday. She had expected one of his all lower-case emails, but nothing arrived. She checked her phone for emails first thing in the morning and just before going to bed, and twenty-odd times during the day. Nothing. Had she said or done something to offend him? Or had he had enough of her after two meetings?

And why was she worried in the first place? Howie Klein was not in any way the sort of man she was hoping to meet when she joined JDate.

What she hoped for was a tallish man, dark, a lawyer, an artist, maybe a physician like her father. She had in mind someone serious, authoritative, in command of the world. When her father spoke of wishing to see her in safe harbor, he meant, surely, that she would find a man who would look out for her, protect her from the sharks, wolves, and other beasts out there who might prey on a woman alone. The man would probably be a widower or divorced, or so she assumed. Howie Klein, as the old song had it, was not the type at all.

Laurie remembered reading an article that argued that the least suitable mate, the worse possible catch, was a man who had got to the age of 50 or beyond without ever having married. By that age, the article argued, they had locked in habits unlikely to be changed; they also figured to be too fault-finding, too critical, finicky in the extreme. No woman could possibly be good enough for them. A great mistake on the part of any woman to pursue such a man, or so the author of the article claimed.

On Wednesday, an email from Howie arrived. In it he explained that the wi-fi service in his building had gone out. He didn't carry a smart phone and the only computer he had was a desktop klunker, so he had no way of getting back to tell her how much he enjoyed their lunch at The Bagel and their walk in Lincoln Park Zoo on Sunday. He hoped she enjoyed it, too, and wanted her to know he was ready for what he called "a rematch" whenever she was. The email, all in lowercase letters, was signed "best wishes, howie."

The ball, Laurie knew, was in her court. She decided to return it with a heavy topspin forehand by suggesting that, if he was free, she wouldn't in the least mind driving up to Milwaukee this coming Sunday, when he could, if he didn't mind, show her the city. This would be their third meeting. Perhaps by the end of it, she felt, she could sort out her thoughts on Howie Klein. An email came zinging back:

> *Laurie, great idea. meet me at my apartment at 11:00 am. instructions on how to get here along with map attached below. fondly, howie*

Well, thought Laurie, we've gone fairly quickly from "best wishes" to "fondly." That was progress, or so she thought. She assumed progress was what she wanted made.

Howie's apartment was on the eleventh floor of a white brick building. Lovely light from Lake Michigan lit up the rooms. He kept the place simple and orderly. The furniture was mostly of black leather and metal, the tables of glass. A large television hung on a wall over a screened-in fireplace. Howie didn't offer a tour of the place, but instead they went directly to the Milwaukee Art Museum, with its dramatic Calatrava annex in the shape of a whale's tail.

Once in the museum, Howie took Laurie over to a painting by a nineteenth-century Pole named Jan Matejko of *Stanczyk, The King's Jester*. The jester is seated in a chair placed at the end of a bed in a darkened room. He is a small man in a red costume, with cap and bells, and in repose, the fingers of both hands entwined, looking as all jesters not on the job should, thoughtfully sad.

"I love this painting," Howie said. "It's nearly a perfect likeness of my dearest friend Marty Selzer, who may have been a genius if he hadn't been so screwed up. Marty died at forty-two, of prostate cancer."

In another room he stopped at a painting called *Feast of the Trumpets* showing Hasidim praying alongside a creek, the background darkly late autumnal, the sky overcast, small fishing boats in the background.

"These could have been my ancestors, or so I always think when I see it. I'm afraid I'm a pretty sentimental Jew. Not sentimental enough to belong to a synagogue, you understand. But sentimental enough to be unable ever to imagine myself as anything other than Jewish. I even like being a member of a minority. On my one trip to Israel, I was sitting in the Jerusalem Music Centre, listening to Shlomo Mintz, when I had the thought that everyone in the room might be Jewish. It made me oddly uncomfortable. I prefer not to be of the majority, no matter where I am. You figure that one out."

This man, Laurie felt, was more interesting than she had at first thought.

Later Howie drove her past the neighborhood in which he had grown up. He showed her the location of his father's grocery store, whose lot was now the location of a Taco Bell, which he joked was a good name for a Mexican telephone company. They walked the River Walk. He told her about the anti-Semitism his father endured in his early days in Milwaukee from the city's then heavily German working-class population. He said that she didn't know how lucky she was that he was sparing her a tour of the breweries.

He took her to an earlyish dinner at a restaurant called The Rouge in the old Hotel Pfister, where they sat next to each other on a banquette facing out toward the center of the room. They had an easy flow of conversation going, much of it about the snobberies of what he called fancy feeding. He ordered a cabernet sauvignon to go with their dinner. He waited until the sommelier disappeared after the smelling and tasting nonsense were done with to raise his glass to touch hers and say: "I think you'll find this a promiscuous but ultimately responsible little wine, with ever so faint a hint of a Snickers bar in its aftertaste." She giggled. Again.

After dinner they walked from the Pfister back to Howie's apartment. In the lobby he asked her if it were possible for her to spend the night. Laurie looked at him, and heard herself say, "Thank you but I have to be up early for school tomorrow. And I didn't bring a change of clothes."

"I understand," he said. "Don't give it another thought."

He walked her to her car in the garage of his building. After she got in behind the wheel, he leaned in, and they kissed, lightly, on the mouth.

"Thank you for a perfectly lovely day," Laurie said. "I really mean it."

"I'm glad," said Howie. "I enjoyed it, too."

As Laurie got back on the freeway, US 41, back to Chicago, she wondered if she had lost her nerve in telling Howie that she couldn't spend the night at his apartment. In fact, she had packed an overnight bag that was in the trunk of her BMW. Did she think it too soon for them to fall into bed with each other? Why was she nervous about it? And what, precisely, was she nervous about? She was coming to like this man, who met none of her expectations. Did she fear that sex with him would be a disappointment and kill everything? What was she saving herself for? The Senior Prom, which was already thirty-five years ago? These questions occupied her during the ninety-five-mile drive back to Chicago.

When Laurie was back in her apartment, it was 10:38 p.m. She called Howie in Milwaukee.

"Glad you got home safe," he said.

"The reason I'm calling," Laurie said, "is to tell you that I regret not spending the night with you in Milwaukee. It was a mistake on my part, and I wanted you to know that."

"I don't know when I've ever had a nicer phone call," Howie said, "and that's no kidding."

"I'm glad," Laurie said. "We'll be in touch soon, OK?"

"Sleep tight," he said.

"Don't let the bedbugs bite," she returned and clicked off her phone.

The next day, at 4:15 p.m. coming out of school, Laurie saw a light blue Prius with Wisconsin plates at the curb. Before she was able to walk up to it, she felt a tap on her shoulder.

"Excuse me, lady, but you know anywhere I can get an egg-white omelet with half a corned-beef sandwich on the side?"

Laurie turned and hugged him. His lips grazed her cheek. Her heart jumped. Lots of details to be worked out, but land, she felt, was in sight, and she thought she glimpsed, off in the distance, a safe harbor at last.

About the Author

JOSEPH EPSTEIN IS AN ESSAYIST, SHORT STORY WRITER, AND, FROM 1974 TO 1998, the editor of the Phi Beta Kappa Society's *The American Scholar* magazine. He was also a lecturer at Northwestern University from 1974 to 2002. He is a contributing editor at *The Weekly Standard* and a longtime contributor of essays and short stories to *Commentary*, *The Atlantic*, *The New Yorker*, and the *Wall Street Journal*.

.